Trapped

Witchlight flared, blindingly bright. I leaped back, but hands seized my arms and jerked me inside. The door slammed shut behind me. I blinked in the dazzling light, staring into the rigid face of the man who had grabbed my arms. He wore the uniform of the Circle Guard. Beyond him, I could see four more men in the same uniform, seated on the beds, crossbows leveled.

At the very end of my bed sat an older man in a scarlet robe, with chill yellow eyes. He rose, his lips tight. "It's the roommate," he said. "Bring her here." He indicated the floor directly in front of him.

"Sit," the guard said, shoving me toward the man in scarlet. "And be silent."

My knees shaking, I sank to the floor. I could hear my heart pounding. With a flick, the man in scarlet dispelled the witchlight and sat back down. We waited in silence, staring at the door in the fading daylight.

They had to be here for Mira. *But why?*

I could hear the man in scarlet behind me, his breathing calm and even—like this was something he did every day. I had looked at him only for an instant, but his yellow eyes were burned into my mind. I shuddered, and felt his hand close over my shoulder like a claw.

We heard footsteps approaching the door. I felt a

gloved hand cup my throat. My stomach lurched with the desire to escape, but I bit my lip and remained still. I could hear the soldiers tense, then rise. The door started to swing open.

"Run!" I screamed to Mira. "Run!"

Fires of the
Faithful

Naomi Kritzer

BANTAM BOOKS

FIRES OF THE FAITHFUL

A Bantam Spectra Book/October 2002

ISBN 0-553-58517-7

Published simultaneously in the United States and Canada

Bantam Books are published by Bantam Books, a division of Random
House, Inc. Its trademark, consisting of the words "Bantam Books" and
the portrayal of a rooster, is Registered in U.S. Patent and Trademark
Office and in other countries. Marca Registrada. Bantam Books, 1540
Broadway, New York, New York 10036.

PRINTED IN THE UNITED STATES OF AMERICA
OPM   10   9   8   7   6   5   4   3   2   1

To Ed Burke, with love and gratitude
for all your support.

Acknowledgments

First I'd like to thank my editor, Anne Groell, my agent, James Frenkel, and his assistant, Tracy Berg, for their help, support, and enthusiasm.

I'd like to thank the members of the Wyrdsmiths, past and present, for critique, encouragement, and friendship: Bill Henry, Doug Hulick, Ralph A. N. Krantz, Harry LeBlanc, Kate Leith, Kelly McCullough, Lyda Morehouse, and Rosalind Nelson. Very special thanks to Lyda, who, when I told her that I wanted to write a novel but was afraid that I'd write myself into a corner, simply said, "You won't." Two days later, I started writing *Fires of the Faithful*.

Quite a few people answered questions, helped me with research, or let me borrow ideas. Thanks to all of them, but special thanks to Michelle Herder, for historical information; Curtis Mitchell, for letting me borrow some ideas on marriage customs; Geriann Brower for Italian language consultation; and Sharon Albert and Louis Newman for Aramaic language consultation. Of course, any linguistic mistakes or historical anachronisms should be blamed on me, and not my consultants.

Thank you to all of my beta readers, who read and commented on earlier versions of this book: Ed Burke, Jason Goodman, Rick Gore, Michelle Herder, Jennifer Horn, Curtis Mitchell, Rudy Moore, Rebecca Murray, and John Savage.

My most heartfelt thanks go to several people. To my parents, Bert and Amy Kritzer, who encouraged my writing and creativity, and my love of reading, pretty much from birth onward; my sister, Abi, and brother, Nate, for being my very first fans; and my wonderful husband, Ed Burke, who has an unerring sense for when I need to be nagged, when I need to be reassured, and when I need two pints of premium ice cream.

Finally, when I was a very young novice writer, my neighbor Nancy Vedder-Shults offered to critique one of my first completed stories. Her comments were both incisive and supportive, and gave me the tools I needed to begin to edit my writing; her encouragement since then has been unfailing. Every young writer should have a mentor as insightful and kind as Nancy.

PART ONE

The Poisoned Honey

CHAPTER ONE

For God so loved Her only son,
She redeemed the world.
—*The Journey of Gèsu, chapter 4, verse 19.*

*M*ira arrived at the Verdiano Rural Conservatory for the Study of Music the same week that the song did. In retrospect, if either Mira or the song had appeared alone, I might have understood things sooner. But I was distracted from the song by my new roommate, and distracted from Mira by the puzzle of the song, and I didn't learn the truth about either one until it was too late to do anything but try to contain the damage.

When I heard that the conservatory had taken on a new student—a sixteen-year-old girl—I knew she'd be placed with me. My old roommate, Lia, had left Verdia with her family months ago, tired of famine and war. I'd gotten rather accustomed to the extra space, and the Dean would be pleased to remind me that it wasn't really mine. Sure enough, I returned after ensemble practice to find the stranger in my room, her meager possessions strewn over the bed I'd reluctantly cleared for her. She had her back to me, and as I paused in the doorway before saying hello, I realized that she was trying to light a candle with flint and steel by striking them over the wick.

"You're never going to get it lit that way," I said. I startled her more than I meant to; the flint and steel skittered across the stone floor and she whirled around to face me. I held out my hands, one empty, the other holding my violin case. "I assume you're my new roommate," I said. "My name is Eliana."

Her eyes flicked past my shoulder, just for an instant, looking to see if there was anyone behind me. Then she looked me over—her gray eyes taking in my short hair, square jaw, shapeless gray robe. I'm very tall for a woman—almost as tall as most men. I'd heard that the boys called me stuck-up; I knew that many people at the conservatory found me a little intimidating. As my new roommate sized me up, I had the eerie sense that she . . . approved.

"My name is Mira," she said, and gave me brief flash of a smile. "I'm pleased to meet you." She ducked to pick up the flint and steel.

I hung up my cloak and put away my violin. There was a violin case on Mira's bed as well, tightly buckled and dusty from the road. "You play violin?" I asked.

"Yes," she said.

I hoped she was decent with her instrument; sharing a room at a conservatory with a bad musician could be almost unbearable.

Having retrieved the flint and steel, Mira held them out to me. "Please, would you show me how to use these?"

I took the flint and steel out of her hands and set them on her bed, then scraped some lint off my robes. "You need something that lights easily to catch the spark. These robes they make us wear must be good for something, right?" I glanced up and she smiled cooperatively. I put the lint in the cupped edge of the candle holder and lit it with a spark from the flint and steel, then lit the candle from the burning lint. "There you go."

"Thank you," Mira said, and set the candle in the windowsill. It would blow out in a minute or two. She really had *no* idea how to deal with a candle.

I studied Mira in the flickering light. She had some of the palest skin I'd ever seen—she couldn't have come here from a farm. But she was well fed—given the famine, she couldn't have come from any town in Verdia. She was clearly my age, too old to be just starting at a conservatory, but her hair was freshly cut—she couldn't have transferred from a conservatory in another province. But it was the candle that really had me puzzled.

I was always reasonably adept at magery, probably because playing the violin had honed my ability to concentrate. I couldn't draw magefire down from the sky to melt stone, of course—I wasn't Circle material—but I could light a hearth fire from damp wood with a moment's effort, which impressed most people well enough. Still, even a child could kindle witchlight to light a dim room—or, if she didn't want the distraction of keeping the witchlight glowing, she could light a candle with her cupped hand. Even my half-wit friend Giula could do that much. There were people who *couldn't* use magery, but very few—and they would have already known how to light a candle the hard way. The only real reason I could think of that Mira might avoid using magery would be if she were trying to conceive a child. Using magic decreased fertility; that's why my mother had taught me how to use flint and steel, even though childbearing was the farthest thing from my mind at the conservatory. I wondered why Mira's mother hadn't taught her the same thing; maybe Mira's mother was one of those women who had children whether she used magery or not.

The wind blew out the candle and I watched as Mira fumbled for a moment before she managed to get it lit again. I set it down on the table beside her bed.

"Where are you from?" I asked.

"Cuore," Mira said. Then she hesitated for a moment and added, "Most recently."

"Cuore?" Whatever answer I'd imagined, that wasn't it. I tried to hide my surprise. "How are things up there? They say the famine is affecting everyone . . ."

"Not Cuore." A sardonic smile flashed across Mira's face. "The home of the Circle, the Fedeli, and the Emperor will always stay well supplied." She turned away to hang up her cloak on a peg by the foot of her bed. "How are things here?"

"Not too bad, not at the conservatory. This part of Verdia didn't see any fighting during the war; my friend Bella and I used to go up to the top of the bell tower to look at the countryside beyond Bascio, and we never saw so much as smoke, let alone magefire. Food was a little short during the war, but at least it grows here now. The famine areas are closer to the Vesuviano border, where the fighting was—we don't waste much, but we don't go hungry, either."

Mira picked up her violin and moved it to her desk. "Is it true what I've heard?" she asked, her back to me. "About the seeds?"

"That the seeds die in the ground without even sprouting?" I sat down on my own bed, staring at Mira's back. "Yes. At least in the worst areas."

"Where are you from?" Mira asked.

"Doratura," I said. "It's west of here, but nowhere near the famine areas. Don't worry, my family is fine."

"That's good," Mira said, turning toward me again and sitting down on her stool.

"There are others here who aren't as fortunate," I said. "My friend Bella, her family's farm isn't in the truly devastated area, but everything they plant grows stunted, and withers in a strong sun."

Mira was silent, rubbing the edge of one sleeve with her fingers.

"If you are from Cuore 'most recently,' where were you from originally?" I asked.

"Tafano," Mira said. "It's a very small village south and west of here. I wouldn't expect you to have heard of it."

I blinked. "How did you end up in Cuore? And what are you doing back in Verdia?"

"I thought I had a calling." Mira studied her hands. "My order was pretty obscure, and I had to go to Cuore to go to seminary."

"You're a *priestess*?" I said.

"No," she said. "I was only ever an initiate. I didn't get as far as the ordination, and now, obviously, I'm never going to." She looked up to give me a rueful smile. "I decided I wanted to pursue my first love—music. I came here because, well, I was born in Verdia. I felt like I belonged here."

I shook my head. Starting at a conservatory so late, she couldn't possibly have been sponsored by the Circle with a scholarship—she had to be a paying student. I was curious to know where she'd gotten the money, but it would have been too rude to ask. I wondered if she'd stolen it from her order; the Dean was unlikely to inquire too carefully regarding the source of any silver crossing his desk.

"Eliana!" There was a sharp rap at my door. "Are you in there?"

"Come in," I called.

Giula flung the door open. "You *were* going to come meet me, weren't you? To practice? Remember?"

"I'm sorry," I said. I hadn't forgotten; I'd just decided that Giula could wait. "Giula, this is my new roommate, Mira. Mira, this is Giula, one of the other violinists."

"Oh!" Giula's indignation melted; a newcomer was certainly excuse enough to be late to a practice session. "How nice to meet you." She smiled at Mira, showing her dimples. "Where are you from?"

"Tafano," Mira said.

"Tafano!" Giula actually seemed to recognize the name of the village. "Where *ever* did you get lovely pale skin like that in Tafano?"

"Well, most recently I lived in Cuore," Mira said.

Giula's eyes bugged out.

I grabbed Giula's arm. "Did you want to practice, or not?" I asked. Giula shot me a venomous glare, but let me drag her off. "It's not like she's going anywhere," I said once the door was closed. "You can interrogate her later."

Giula was cheerful again by the time we'd reached the practice hall. "So that's your new roommate! Not quite so bad as you made it sound at lunch, is it?"

"I still say there are enough empty rooms that I shouldn't have to have a roommate if I don't want one," I said. Giula shrugged unsympathetically. In the practice room, Giula and I set our music on the stand. We would play a duet in the autumn recital the following week; I was a better violinist than Giula, but we shared a teacher, Domenico, and he had instructed us to play together. She would take the easier part.

"Did she tell you why she came here from *Cuore*?" Giula asked, still incredulous.

"She was in Cuore preparing for ordination," I said.

"She was going to be a *priestess*? But why would she ever come back *here*?"

"You can ask her later, can't you?" I flipped open the music to the duet. "Are we going to practice or not?"

Giula tightened her bow and started tuning her violin, still talking. "And why would she be starting at this time of year? Auditions were in the spring. Though she couldn't have auditioned anyway—she's our age, or maybe even older. She *has* to be a paying student. But why would you pay to come *here*?"

I rolled my eyes and tucked my violin under my chin.

"Maybe her family lives near here," Giula said.

"Maybe." Students who left the conservatory, even for a day, lost their scholarships and could not return. We assumed it was to discourage all but the most dedicated from pursuing a life as a musician. But our families could come and visit us, which was a possibility if they lived close by. Lia's family had visited once. "We need to work on this duet," I said. At least Giula needed to work on it, because if she didn't sound at least decent at the recital, nobody would notice my playing at all.

Giula reluctantly tucked her violin under her chin. "Why do you suppose she's so pale?"

"Presumably she spent most of her time indoors at her seminary," I said. Giula started to lower her violin again, and I tapped the music pointedly. "Let's take it from the top."

I counted out a beat and started to play. Giula picked up her part in the third measure, and stumbled almost immediately.

"Again," I said. "Start here."

"Wait," Giula said.

For a moment, I thought Giula was going to start gossiping again, but her head was tilted to the side, and after a beat I realized that she was listening to the musician in the next practice room. The musician was Celia, one of the sopranos; I recognized her voice. But she wasn't practicing anything I'd heard before, and since Celia was at least nominally a friend of mine, I was familiar with most of her repertoire.

> I've come to wed your father but I want to make you mine.
> If you'll take me as your mother, you will find my faults are few.
> I've brought a gift of honey, bright as sun and sweet as wine.
> And as pure as all the love I hold inside my heart for you.

Celia paused, and Giula looked up at me, her eyes wide. "Everyone's talking about this song. I hadn't heard it sung yet."

Celia began to sing the verses. Six children tasted the honey and embraced their stepmother. Then the seventh son rejected the honey, and was murdered by his own father for his insolence. Then one by one the other six children died, poisoned by the lethal gift. In the end, the father wept over the graves of his children, but was at the mercy of his new wife and his two stepchildren. In the final verse, the bones of the dead children cried out for vengeance; apparently this was left up to the listener.

There was a knock on the door of our practice room. I opened the door; it was Bella, her trumpet in her hand. "Did you hear Celia?" she asked.

I sighed. "I gather we aren't the only students here who aren't rehearsing."

Bella waved her hand—not the one with the trumpet—

dismissively. "I think I saw the person who brought the song."

"Really?" Giula set her violin down altogether. I resigned myself to the inevitable and put mine down as well.

Bella sat down on one of the practice stools, and Giula and I did as well. "I was watching down the hill for the messenger wagon, and I saw someone ride into town. I don't know horses that well, but it looked like a fast riding horse—not the sort of horse you'd hitch to a plow. The rider was wearing a cloak pulled over his face—" Bella gestured with the floppy sleeve of her robe.

"It's been a chilly autumn," I said. "Of course he wanted to protect his face."

Bella rolled her eyes. "I saw him dismount by the cottage where your teacher lives—Domenico. He was inside for less than an hour, and then he rode away."

"Did you see his face?" Giula asked.

"It would have been too far even if his face hadn't been covered," Bella said. "You should try asking Domenico about it." She shot a glance directly at me. Domenico would never gossip to Giula—not when she was so busy flirting with him—but he might talk to me. I nodded a little. It was worth a try.

"What do you think the song's about?" Giula asked.

"It's probably some stupid noble's feud," Bella said. "Some branch of the family got killed by treachery and now they want the whole world to help them get revenge."

"Wouldn't it help if the offending family were named?" I asked.

"People might not spread the song if they knew it was some petty feud," Bella said.

"They would if it was a good enough tune."

"So what's your theory?" Bella asked.

"I don't know. I don't think the poisoned honey refers

to literal honey, though. I think it's some sort of disguised danger, but it's disguised awfully well. I don't have any idea what it's talking about."

Giula didn't even venture a guess. "I wish it had been the messenger service, instead of a man with a mysterious song," she said.

"Honestly, so do I." For a moment, Bella's face looked worn. "The news from my family last time wasn't good." The news next time was unlikely to be better, but anything was preferable to uncertainty. And perhaps the harvest would be better than expected, if only by a little.

The supper bell rang, and we quickly packed up our instruments to walk over to the girls' meal hall. I had expected Mira to join us for supper, but she wasn't there. Celia was, though, repeating the words of the honey song to those who hadn't heard them yet. Giorgi, the cook's assistant, brought out heavy tureens of stew made from the vegetables we grew in the conservatory garden, and jugs of tea and wine.

Celia flicked back a curl that had fallen into her face and took a sip of her tea. Celia didn't like tying her hair back, probably because the curls framed her heart-shaped face so charmingly. Not that any of us were supposed to be trying to attract the attention of the boys, but Celia liked any attention she could get. "It's a lovely song," she said, "but I think it's just about some feud. Some noble family sent a bride to another family with poisoned honey. Their children ate it and died. Maybe there was a son who refused to eat it, but—"

This wasn't far off from Bella's theory, but her eyes narrowed. "Oh, come on, Celia," she said. "You don't really think the song is about literal *honey*, do you?"

Celia arched one perfect eyebrow. "Why don't you share *your* theory with us, Bella?" she said.

"Eliana thinks the poisoned honey is a symbol for some disguised danger," Bella said. "I think she's right, but I don't know what the danger is."

Flavia, a percussionist, looked up from her stew. "I think you're right about the symbolism," she said. "It's a ballad rhythm, or I'd say that the Fedeli wrote the song."

"The Fedeli." I put down my tea. "Why the Fedeli?"

"Don't you think the 'poisoned honey' could refer to a heresy of some kind?" Flavia said. "I could easily see the song reaching us well before we actually heard what heresy it was supposed to be about."

We considered that idea for a moment.

"But, like I said, the rhythm's not right. I would expect the Fedeli to write something that sounded like a hymn— not like something that sounds like a folk ballad." Flavia took a sip of wine.

"Eliana got a new roommate today," Giula said. "From Cuore."

That diverted the conversation entirely, and after checking to make sure that she wasn't standing behind me, I described Mira to the others and told what little I knew about her: born in Tafano, trained at a seminary in Cuore, and ignorant in the use of candles.

"Do you suppose . . ." Bella said.

"Why would you come *all* the way to the conservatory from Cuore if you were going to try to get pregnant?" I asked. Any pregnant girl student—and any boy student who was named as the father—was expelled from the conservatory. Clearly, if the Lady blessed your union, she wanted you to get married and settle down, not go off to join an ensemble.

"Maybe she's in love with one of the boy students," Giula said.

"How would she have *met* him?" I asked. We were kept

well separated from the boys at the conservatory. The only place we were even allowed in the same room with them was the chapel. This encouraged a high degree of religious observance among girls like Celia.

"That can't be it," Bella said. "Maybe she had a lover in Cuore, and she hopes she's pregnant by him."

"Why would she have left, then?" Giula asked.

"That's obvious," Bella said. "She was an initiate, wasn't she? Maybe the boy wasn't."

"Still," I said. "Why would she leave Cuore?"

"Maybe . . ." Bella closed her eyes and rubbed her forehead. "This is getting too complicated. Even if the relationship ended badly, if she has any reason to think she's pregnant, then coming back to Verdia would just be stupid."

Celia tossed her hair back. "Clearly, *you've* never been in love."

Bella's eyes narrowed and she smiled slowly at Celia, letting Celia's words hang in the air as a pink flush crept slowly upward from the gray wool collar of Celia's robe. "If I risk being expelled from the conservatory," Bella said, "I want it to be for a man—not a boy. But to each her own."

"What's *that* supposed to mean?" Celia said.

Bella had started to turn back to her tea, but when Celia got defensive, she took that as an invitation to twist the knife a little more. "Why would it mean anything?" she asked. "I think your devotion to the Lady is very touching, Celia."

Celia went white. Naturally, she attended chapel daily to flirt with the boys there, but Bella meant something else, and Celia knew it. Magery was the Lady's gift to humanity, but it decreased fertility. To counteract this tendency, the Lady encouraged Her children to try to make children of their own as frequently as possible. Of course, the Lady didn't want conservatory students having babies—our celibacy, like the sterility of the Circle, increased the fertility of everyone else. But, still. "Honoring the Lady" was a popular euphemism for the sort of thing that happened secretly on summer nights in the shadows of the practice halls—and that occasionally resulted in expulsions.

"The Lady rewards those who love Her with their whole heart," Celia said, her voice shaky and her face still white. "You should try attending Chapel sometime when it isn't required, Bella. The results might surprise you."

"Sure, Celia," Bella said, and returned to her tea. Celia stood up to go, and Bella caught her by the dangling edge of her sleeve. "Just be careful," she said. "You know what I mean." She released Celia, clucking her tongue, and Celia flounced out.

I tried to imagine Mira with a lover, and shook my head. Mira lacked the coy flirtatiousness it took to catch a boy's eye. She was like me—a little bit intimidating. Besides, if she'd stopped using magery that long ago, why wouldn't she have learned to light a candle by now?

Mira was not in the room when I returned from supper, but her cloak and violin were missing. She'd gone somewhere to practice, late though it was. She'd taken the candle. I slung my own violin over my shoulder and went out to see if I could find her. I was curious how well she could play, after all these years as a seminarian.

I listened carefully to the muffled cacophony in the corridor of the main practice hall. Two violins—but I recognized both. Not Giula, unfortunately—she *needed* the practice, but was probably studying for our music theory class.

I left through the back door, and as I crossed the courtyard, I saw the flicker of candlelight in the north practice hall. Many students used candles rather than witchlight while they practiced, but none of us used the north practice hall. It was cold, first of all, and so drafty that small drifts of snow actually blew across the floor in winter. And the acoustics were terrible. Bella once claimed it was haunted, though she was telling a ghost story to scare Giula and needed a creepy setting for it. In any case, the candle had to belong to Mira.

The front door of the north practice hall was ajar. I slipped in and paused in the shadow. Mira was playing in the ensemble hall rather than one of the side rooms; she had set her candle in a wall niche that protected it from drafts, but it still wavered, making her shadow dance on the wall. It occurred to me that sneaking around to spy on another student practicing was a little absurd, but I was curious about Mira. I put down my violin very quietly, sat with my cloak huddled around me, and listened.

Mira started off with very basic études—finger exercises. Her fingers were clumsy, and she missed many of the notes, which wasn't surprising for someone who'd spent the last few years in a seminary rather than a conservatory. But as she warmed up and the fluidity began to come back to her, she began to make the études sound like something I hadn't expected. She treated them as if they were music rather than a demonstration of technical skill; I realized, listening to her, that the world was slipping away around her, and nothing but each note existed. Her technique was raw, but the sound was beautiful. I wondered how she was able to bring herself to give this up, when she thought she had a calling—and if her calling was so powerful, how she had been able to give *that* up, now.

Then she finished with her exercises and began to play a melody—and I froze.

There were a few songs once used in old village ceremonies that still circulated at the conservatory. Playing ritual music from the Old Way was illegal, of course. And it would have been dangerous in a city conservatory, because of the Sudditi Fedeli della Signora, the Faithful Subjects of the Lady. But the Fedeli avoided backwater areas like Verdia, and most everyone shrugged off the danger. I certainly did. I knew a wedding song and a healing song, and I played them regularly. The Old Way music had an undercurrent that more recent music completely lacked. Most Old Way songs were in a minor key, but they were fast, with rhythms that felt like the heartbeat of the earth underneath me, and they stirred my blood like strong wine and cold wind.

I had never heard the song Mira was playing, but I recognized it as Old Way music from the peculiar rhythm: *da dat da da dat da wham wham wham. Da dat da da dat da wham wham wham.* Listening intently, I could see Mira throw her head back as she played, raising the violin like an offering, and I thought, *she* was studying to be a *priestess?*

Mira played the song through twice, picking up the tempo as she played. A cold draft touched my feet where I sat, and I curled my toes up inside my boots, clenching and flexing my hands. Then, midphrase, Mira stopped. She set her violin down carefully on the floor, and straightened for a moment, looking at the candle. Then she bent over and vomited on the floor, and vomited again, and then fell to her knees, still retching. I jumped to my feet. "Mira!"

She should have been startled by my presence, but she didn't even look up. When I reached her, she was curled up on the cold stone floor, clenching her fists and wrapping her arms around herself. "I'll get the physician," I said.

"No," she gasped, and grabbed the edge of my robe in her fist. "No, it won't do any good. Stay here. Don't leave me. This will pass. *It will pass.*"

I didn't believe her, but I was afraid she might be dying, and she might die alone if I left her. So I dragged her away from her vomit on the floor, then covered her with her cloak and sat down beside her. She was shaking harder than I'd ever seen anyone shake from cold. After a moment I covered her with my own cloak, as well.

"I'll be fine," she said, between spasms of shaking. "Don't worry about me."

"Lady's tits, Mira," I said. "Let me get the physician. Or Giorgi, the cook's assistant—he's the village healer."

"No," she said. "I just want you. Stay with me. Please, don't leave me."

"But I don't know anything about healing," I said. I touched her forehead with the back of my hand to test for fever, but it was cool, even chill.

"I don't need healing," she said. "Talk to me."

"What do you want me to talk about?" I asked.

"Anything," she said. "Just let me hear your voice, so I know I'm not alone."

So I talked. I told her about my family—about my favorite brother, the second-oldest, Donato, who taught me to fight and used to make me clay whistles. I told her about my friends at the conservatory—Giula and Bella and Flavia and Celia. I told her about the song that had arrived so mysteriously, about poisoned honey and dead children. I told her about my teacher, Domenico, how he was one of the handful of great teachers still left at the conservatory. Domenico had been educated at the Central Conservatory in Cuore and had actually spent several years playing at the Imperial Court before he gave it all up to come live in Verdia and teach at our conservatory. No one really knew why. Domenico told me he'd hated court, and from his descriptions of it I could understand why, though I still dreamed of playing there myself.

Mira shuddered, but this time she didn't stop. Her eyes rolled back in her head, and she shook as if invisible hands grasped her shoulders and wrenched her back and forth. I had seen one other person have a convulsion—one of my nieces, when she was a baby and had a high fever. My mother had poured cold water over her and she'd lived. But Mira had no fever; her skin was as cold as the stones underneath us. I grabbed her and tried to hold her still, but her jerks pulled her out of my grasp. Then a moment later it was over, and she lay still. I held my hand lightly over her lips; she was still breathing. I sat back silently, clasping her limp hand. Mira's hand was like carved marble—cold and impossibly smooth. I rubbed her palm with my thumb and suddenly my own blood turned cold. Mira had no calluses on her hands—not even the sort she'd have had from light garden work.

One of my brothers had trained for the priesthood for a while. He'd given it up after falling in love with a girl in the village, but I clearly remembered his complaints to our mother about the work. The elder priests and priestesses talked a lot about communing with the Lord and the Lady through reaping their bounty, but my brother thought that was just an excuse to stick the novitiates with all the heavy farm chores. I'd grown up on a farm and my brother was no stranger to hard work, but after a year at the seminary his calluses were thicker than my father's.

I touched Mira's soft hand again. She had never been an initiate priestess. That whole story was a lie.

Why would she make up a story like that?

I lit a globe of witchlight to get a closer look, and Mira threw her free hand over her face with a groan. "Hurts my eyes," she muttered. "Put it away."

I dispelled the witchlight with a flick of my wrist. Mira drew her hand away slowly.

"Play for me," she said.

Her violin was in reach and in tune, while mine wasn't, so I picked hers up.

"Play the funeral song," she said. "The song I was playing earlier. I know you were listening."

So it had been a funeral song. I added that mentally to my repertoire and began to play. I have always been able to pick out tunes quite easily, and I experimented a little as I played, adding a forceful downstroke to the strong beats and pairing them with the same note an octave up. Domenico had told me to hold still while I played, but Old Way songs always made me want to use my whole body, and I swayed back and forth with the music. I closed my eyes, watching the flicker of the candle against my eyelids. Then I opened my eyes.

For the first crazy instant, I thought a third person had silently entered the north practice hall, dressed in the uniform of a soldier. Then I thought I recognized my own face around the dark, riveting eyes. I started to my feet, and then realized that all I was looking at was a crumbling fresco. This was one of the oldest buildings at the conservatory, and had once been lavishly decorated.

I forced out a laugh. "I've been listening to too many of Bella's ghost stories," I said. Mira was silent. Slowly, I sat back down on the stone floor, more shaken than I thought I had any call to be. "The candlelight is making me jumpy."

I set down Mira's violin and took her soft hand again just as the candle went out.

I stayed beside her through the night, talking when she roused enough to ask to hear my voice. Mira seemed to waver from consciousness to unconsciousness like a sputtering flame, but when she woke she seemed glad to have me there. In the last part of the night, her tremors calmed, and I asked if she'd like me to help her back to the room, where she might be more comfortable. She sat up, still shaking a bit. "Thank you," she said. "I'd appreciate that."

I packed up her violin and slung both hers and mine

over my shoulder, then wrapped her cloak around her shoulders and slipped my arm under hers. If anyone was out and about at that hour, they were on their own business and pretended not to see us; I helped Mira up the long staircase and into our empty room, then helped her sit down on the bed. Mira lay down and pulled her blanket over herself, closing her eyes. Her shaking had finally eased.

There was an hour or so before I'd have to get up, and I quietly slipped my boots off. As I hung Mira's cloak up, something fluttered to the floor. I picked it up and kindled a tiny witchlight, hoping that it wouldn't disturb Mira; it was a letter of some kind. *You stupid fools,* it said. *We don't want your money. We want our daughter back.* I flipped it over; it was signed, *Isabella and Marino of Tafano, Verdia.* I slipped the letter under a musical score on her desk, ashamed of myself for reading it.

"What?" Mira said, and I jumped, flicking away my witchlight and nearly scattering the papers again. In the darkness, I lay down on my own bed, curling up under my blanket.

"I'm leaving," Mira said, her voice as clear as the bells we rang at the Viaggio service.

"What?" I said, but Mira went on without heeding me, and I realized that she was talking in her sleep.

"You're wrong, Liemo," she said. Her voice was contemptuous. "I'll break the chains you've bound me with. The Lady promises freedom and I'm going to *take* it. You can lock me up, you can even kill me, but you can't make me serve you again."

She was quiet after that, her breathing low and even. I lay awake, shivering. I told myself that I was still cold from the practice hall, but the fierce steel in Mira's voice had cut me to the bone. I didn't know whom she was speaking to, or what she was talking about, but I hoped

I'd never find myself standing against her. In the end, I didn't sleep at all that night. At dawn, Mira opened her eyes and looked over at me, giving me a slow smile that warmed me to my feet. "You will keep my secret?" she said.

I didn't even know what her secret was, but looking into her eyes, I would have done anything for her. "Yes," I said. "Yes."

CHAPTER TWO

*When the stranger comes among you, you shall not
abuse him; behold, I am a stranger among you,
yet I bring the greatest of gifts.*
—*The Journey of Gèsu, chapter 1, verse 1.*

$\mathcal{E}$ase up a bit on that first crescendo," Domenico
said. "And keep the tempo steady—you're speeding up." I nodded and flipped the music back a page to
start again. "Incidentally, I heard you got a new roommate
this week."

I lowered my violin. "Yes," I said. "Mira. She's also a
violinist."

"Is she really from Cuore?" Domenico pulled his chair
out from behind his desk and sat down. He gestured for
me to pull up a chair, then gave me a sheepish look. "We
really should be working on your part of the duet, but let's
face it; you're far ahead of Giula at this point. If you aren't
note-perfect on Viaggio, it won't be because *you* didn't
practice."

The Viaggio festival at the autumnal equinox celebrated
the beginning of the Lord's annual journey to fight and destroy the Maledori. Our autumn recital was held in the
afternoon the day of the festival.

Domenico gave me an easy grin. "Tell me about your roommate," he said.

"I think she really did live in Cuore," I said, sitting down. I hesitated, debating whether I should tell my teacher that she was lying about being from a seminary, and decided against it. "She says she was at a seminary."

Domenico shook his head, raking his fingers through his sand-colored hair. "That would explain why she's literate, but not where she got the money. Are her parents wealthy?"

"They're from a village in southwest Verdia," I said. "I can't imagine they're that rich."

"Maybe she had a rich friend from the seminary," Domenico said. "Do you know why she left?"

"No, but I think she probably got in some sort of trouble. Bella was speculating last night that it involved a love affair, but I doubt that." I paused. "You know, as far as I can tell, she doesn't use magery."

"Really?" Domenico looked up, startled and fascinated.

"Does that mean something?"

Domenico averted his eyes. "Well . . . probably not."

He was hiding something from me; that was obvious. I couldn't very well call him on it, so I folded my arms and waited silently.

"Have you made your list yet?" he asked. It was a lame attempt to change the subject. The Lord was known for handling the little things, the small requests that the Lady was too important to bother with. Making a list wasn't part of official church rites, but since the Lord was leaving on His journey, everyone tried to get in requests before He left.

"Sure," I said, continuing to glare at the floor.

Finally Domenico sighed and said, "Certain heresies hold that the use of magery is a sin."

"You think she's a *heretic*?" Trouble with the Fedeli would certainly explain Mira's departure from Cuore. "Although, you know, she doesn't know the first thing about getting by *without* magery, either. When I first saw her, she was trying to light a candle cold with flint and steel."

"That wouldn't be it, then," Domenico said. "I've heard of musicians who stop using magery because they say their music is *their* gift from the Lady—they want to use that power in their playing rather than to make lights to read by. That particular school of thought has been out of fashion for a few hundred years, but maybe Mira read something that mentioned the idea and adopted it."

"That fits," I said. "Well, at least it fits better than anything else."

Domenico nodded, still reflective. I leaned forward. "I heard you had a visitor yourself, this week."

Domenico's eyebrows shot up. "Who did you hear that from?"

"Bella saw someone on a horse stop in at your cottage," I said. "She thinks he's the man who brought the Wicked Stepmother song."

"Bella was watching?" Domenico shook his head. "I shouldn't tell you anything; you'll only repeat it to that gaggle of goslings you call your friends."

I shook my head. "Not if you'd rather I didn't."

"It hardly matters. I take my meals with Nolasco, Bella's teacher, and I'm sure she'll worm everything I've said out of him." Domenico raked back his hair again. "Bella was right. That was the man who brought the song. It was a very young nobleman, handsomer than anyone has a right to be but with a manner that could curdle milk. He invited himself in, sang me the song enough times for me to learn it by heart, then went on his way. No explanation, not even an apology for interrupting my meal. He acted like he was

doing *me* a favor by singing it for me." Domenico shook
his head. "But the song is a puzzle. I passed it on hoping
that someone would be able to explain it to me, but so far
no one has." He leaned forward. "Have you and the goslings had any ideas?"

"Flavia thinks that the 'poisoned honey' is some sort of
heresy, and that the song might have been written by the
Fedeli," I said.

"Interesting thought."

"Celia thinks it's literal—well, mostly literal. About some
stupid feud between noble families. That was Bella's theory,
too, till Celia picked it up."

"I'm dubious on that one. And not just because Celia
likes it."

"But with the young nobleman bringing the song—"

Domenico shook his head. "No. If it were a feud, they'd
have hired professional musicians to spread it. The man
who sang it for me could barely carry the tune."

"Do you have a theory?" I asked.

Domenico shrugged. "Not yet," he said.

• • •

Viaggio fell on a perfect autumn day, sunny and cool. It
was a shame to waste most of the day indoors, but we
were required to go to church in the morning. I refused to
drag myself out of bed before dawn to primp for the boys,
like Giula or Celia—but I did make sure I had a clean robe
to wear as we'd be playing publicly that afternoon. As a
fourth-year student, I was allowed to wear my hair long
enough that I could pin it neatly back. Mira combed my
hair for me, so that it could be parted straight. Her hands
were gentle as she eased out the tangles; she focused as
completely on my hair as she did on her music.

One sunny morning when I was eight years old, my mother had left the dishes unwashed after breakfast and had taken me down to a pond near our house where we could see our reflections in the water. She spent the morning teaching me how to braid hair, first hers, then my own—with four strands, or six, or so that the braid started at my temples. She braided her own hair so that it twisted in a dark wreath around the crown of her head. My hair was too short for that, but she let me braid and rebraid her hair until it was perfect.

When Mira had finished with my hair, she pinned it back for me in my clasp. Then I combed Mira's hair for her, though her hair was cropped so short that it hardly mattered. I spent more time on it than the job really justified, wishing that it was long enough for me to braid. Her hair was fine, and feathery soft. It curled just a little at the nape of her neck.

We filed into the chapel after breakfast, with most of the students vying for a spot near the center aisle that divided the boys from the girls. I sat by the far wall, next to Mira; Bella was in front of us. Despite the sun, the chapel was chill. I tucked my hands inside my sleeves. My brother, before he quit the seminary, spoke of the fire of devotion he felt inside. I never felt even enough fire from the church to warm my hands.

Once everyone was in place, Father Claro and Mother Emilia filed in with a few of the more devoted conservatory students acting as assistants. A cloud of rose-sweet incense smoke blew over me in a wave, and I stifled a sneeze. Mira stood with her head bowed, her eyes closed. The percussion instructor struck a large, deep drum twelve times, to dispel any Maledori that might be lingering near the doors, and we took our seats. I propped my chin on my fist, hoping that if I nodded off it wouldn't be too noticeable. Father Claro insisted on chanting most of the service, which was always painful to hear; he was tone-deaf.

At the midpoint of the service, we rose again and picked up the bells and sheet music that had been set by our seats before the service started. This was by far my favorite part of the service; even if most of the church music was honey-sweet and ploddingly predictable, the after-echoes of the bells gave it a faint savor of the Old Way music. I checked the keys on my bells and followed along with the music, Mother Emilia conducting. The sound of the bells hung in the air for a long time even when the song was done. Mira's eyes were closed again and she had a faint smile on her face. Then we sat down and the service became boring again. Father Claro led a long prayer to the Lord and the Lady, and Mother Emilia preached an even longer sermon. Then was time for silent prayer and meditation; I closed my eyes and meditated on the piece I'd be playing in the recital later, running the notes through my head like a stream of water.

Finally the service was over. The meal before the recital was rushed and excited. Giula and Celia picked at their food; Bella attacked hers with single-minded concentration. I ate quickly and thoroughly, forcing myself to finish at least one full bowl of soup. I was thirsty, but drank only one cup of tea. Too much and I'd want to go to the privy during the concert.

The autumn and spring recitals were a big deal, even in a village as small as Bascio; the entire village attended. Signs were posted at the gate saying who would be playing, and where; I'd heard that there were villagers who specifically sought out my performances, though I didn't believe it. Giula and I played immediately before one of the senior quartets, though, so I wasn't surprised that the hall was filled.

As Giula and I stood up to play, Giula looked out at the audience and her eyes grew wide. "Lady's tits," she whispered. "I've forgotten how the duet goes."

"Just close your eyes and don't look at the audience," I said. "You'll remember when you hear the opening notes." I looked out at the audience, searching for Mira. She was in the very back, but our eyes met and she gave me just a hint of her devastating smile.

Domenico nodded at us to start. Giula looked petrified, but tucked her violin under her chin when I lifted mine. The crowd grew silent.

I played the opening cascade of notes, hearing the audience let out its breath in a sigh. As I'd predicted, Giula remembered her part on cue, and even played through the full piece without stumbling. I could see Mira watching me, and I closed my eyes and poured my heart through the music. It finished far too quickly, and I ended my part with an improvised flourish that I realized too late I'd borrowed from the Old Way wedding music. Domenico's eyes narrowed slightly, but I could see the hint of a smile on his face. I caught just a glimpse of Mira's face again through the crowd, and she was giving me her quiet secret smile. The audience applauded with an enthusiasm that reassured me I'd done well, and Giula and I bowed. As we moved out of the way for the next performers, I looked back to see Mira again, to see if she knew that I'd been playing just for her.

Mira met my gaze immediately. She knew.

• • •

In the years before the war, the autumn concert was followed by a feast attended by students and faculty alike. Because the famine around us forbid that kind of waste, though, supper after the concert was now a simple, even haphazard affair, and Mira and I took our bread and soup and carried it down to the low conservatory wall to eat it. The wind had turned chill, and we both wrapped up in our cloaks, sitting on the wall and looking down at Bascio while we ate. Bascio was a hill town, the buildings clinging to the sides of the steep slope, the paths winding up to the top like gut around a tuning peg. The conservatory was at the very top of the hill, allowing us to see almost everything on our side of the hill.

In the cobbled streets of the town, the villagers were lighting bonfires to celebrate Viaggio, drinking wine and dancing. Like most of the festivals, Viaggio was believed to increase fertility, and many people took advantage of that. I vaguely remembered festivals that I'd celebrated in Doratura before I came here, but I was too young to participate so my parents gave me plenty of wine and then put me to bed.

"Thinking of home?" Mira asked.

"There's only one Viaggio I really remember," I said. "When I was nine years old, I knocked myself senseless the morning of the festival." Mira gave me a startled look over her soup bowl. "My second-oldest brother, Donato, had given in to my wheedling and boosted me up to the lowest branch of the chestnut tree that grew outside our house, so that I could climb it. I fell out." I dunked my bread into the broth and took a bite. "Donato felt just terrible, even though I was the one who'd pestered him to help me climb the tree. I didn't tell our parents that he'd helped me climb, and Donato did all my chores until the headaches went away. Which took *months*, of course. A bad knock on the head hurts for an amazingly long time. Kind of funny, though, that *that* is what I remember—a bad knock on the head." I scraped out the last of my soup bowl with the crust of the bread. "So what was Viaggio like in Cuore?"

Mira stared down at Bascio thoughtfully. "Bigger," she said.

I waited for her to go on. "No other differences?" I asked, when she didn't.

Mira set down her soup bowl. "There are other differences, of course." She considered for a moment. "In the city, the Fedeli are always close by. You never know when they might be watching you, especially during a festival, when they can shed those black robes they usually wear. So in Cuore things are a bit more—frenetic. It's necessary, you see, not only to express your devotion toward the Lord and the Lady, but to make sure that the Fedeli, should they be watching, see that you do so."

I had always daydreamed about landing a place in one of the Imperial ensembles, but right now that didn't sound very appealing. Mira saw my smile fade and touched my hand. "Sorry to make you sad."

"What do you want to do when you're done at the conservatory?" I asked. "Do you want to go back to Cuore?"

"Not a chance," she said. "I want to be a minstrel."

I swung my head around to stare at her. "With a *violin*?" I asked. She shrugged. "You should take up lute. Minstrels have to sing."

"Well, I suppose. I've been trying to work out a way to harmonize with the violin."

I shook my head. "My old roommate, Lia, wanted to be a minstrel. But she was always a little eccentric. And she played lute."

Mira shrugged again. "If that doesn't work, I'll come up with something else. But I'm never going back to Cuore. Not even if someone held a sword to my throat." Her voice had taken on a bitter edge that made me feel cold and strange inside.

"What's so horrible about it? Just the Fedeli?"

"There's more to it than that, but—" She broke off and turned her eyes back toward the bonfires in the Bascio streets. "I don't want to get into the dirty details of it. Maybe some other day."

"I don't know what to think of you, Mira," I said. "I know you were never a seminarian."

Mira didn't look up. "I know that you know. Thank you for keeping my secret."

"So what *were* you doing in Cuore? And why did you leave?"

"I can't tell you," Mira said. "Not now, not here."

"Mira—" I said, and broke off. I didn't know what to say. If not now, then when? If not here, then where? "Who's Liemo?"

Mira's eyes widened. "Where did you hear that name?"

"You spoke it in your sleep once."

"He's someone I knew in Cuore," she said. "He's not a nice man."

"Is that all you're going to tell me?" I asked.

"I'm afraid so," Mira said.

"Mira, I don't know what to think about you," I said. "Your secrets—" *Frighten me.* I stared into Mira's eyes. *How can I trust you when it's so clear that there are Maledori lurking just behind your shoulder?*

Mira took my hand and pressed it gently between hers. They were still impossibly soft. "You stayed with me in my weakness," she said. "You've kept my secrets. You are the truest friend I've ever had, so I'll swear this to you: I will never lie to you again." She released my hand. "I'll give you my vow as my grandmother would have." She picked up two twigs, held them in an X, and kissed them where they crossed. "I swear."

Swearing in the Old Way—and on Viaggio, no less. For a girl who had just been talking about her fear of the Fedeli, Mira was a puzzle. "Do you want me to swear anything?" I asked.

"No," she said. "I would never ask you to bind yourself to me."

"What if I said I didn't mind?" I reached out, tentatively, for Mira's hand. She let me lace my fingers with hers, and laid her free hand against my cheek.

"Listen," Mira said after a moment. "You can hear the drums in the Bascio plaza."

I closed my eyes. The drums were faint, like an echo of a heartbeat. Then they were lost in a gust of wind, but I could still hear my own heartbeat pounding in my ears.

"Eliana," Mira said. "I've heard that almost all musicians, sooner or later, learn some of the Old Way songs. Do you know any?"

"Yes," I said. "I know three. One is a song that was played at weddings, one is a song played for healing, and one—I heard you play."

"That's a funeral song," Mira said. "Would you like to learn more?"

I felt excitement flare inside me like witchlight. "I would love to learn more," I said. Since the music was illegal, it was never taught; I'd learned all three songs by eavesdropping. "How many do you know?"

"Lots," Mira said. "Do you know of others who would like to learn? Who might be willing to play the songs, in a group?"

I pulled back for a moment. That would be far more dangerous than simply playing the songs individually, secretly.

But—"Yes," I said. "Bella would. Flavia. Giula—I've heard
her playing the wedding song. Celia, the vocalist—I think
she would, too. It's true that everyone learns them, even if
they don't talk about them."

Mira nodded. "Can you ask them for me?" she asked.
"You know them, I don't."

"Sure," I said, thinking already about how best to approach each girl. "Although—I know Bella will ask this,
so promise me you aren't here as a spy for the Fedeli, to
uncover heretics?"

Mira's eyes sparkled and her smile was warm. "No, of
course not. I'm not here as a Fedele spy, and I'm happy to
swear that for anyone who asks." Mira leaped off the
wall. "Dance with me," she said. "Dance to the music from
Bascio."

So we clasped hands, and closed our eyes, and listened
to the faint drumbeats from the village piazza, then lost
ourselves in the crunch of the leaves under our feet, and
the pounding of our hearts, and the wind in our ears.

•   •   •

I approached Bella, Flavia, Giula, and Celia about one
week after Viaggio. I tackled each one individually, so that
they wouldn't talk each other out of the idea.

Bella raised one eyebrow when I asked her if she was interested. "Old Way music? What makes you think I know
any?"

"I learned the wedding song from eavesdropping on
you," I said.

Bella's eyes widened, then she gave me an easy grin.
"Fair enough, Eliana. At least you're as much of a heretic
as I am. Tell me where to show up and when."

Giula was a bit more difficult. "But we're not supposed
to play those," she said.

"Right," I said, rolling my eyes. "And nobody *ever* does. Kind of like nobody *ever* has a boyfriend, and nobody *ever* skips chapel services, and—"

"All right, all right," she said. "But having a boyfriend can't get you charged with heresy."

"When have the Fedeli even come to Verdia? You're a lot more likely to be caught with a boyfriend, and you can be thrown out for that."

Giula sighed sadly. "I've never actually had a boyfriend, Eliana."

"You've wanted one, though. I've seen you vying for an aisle seat in the chapel." I caught Giula's arm. "You want to play this music, too. Give it a try."

Celia gave me much the same argument that Giula did, except that she had actually had a boyfriend. "I'm not saying that I've lived a life of unblemished virtue," Celia said, flushing. "But my sins have at least been *small*."

"Are you telling me that you've never sung the Old Way music?"

"No, I'm not telling you that." Celia turned even more red. "But I see the difference between playing it alone and playing in a group as sort of like—"

"Sort of like the difference," I said, "between holding hands with a boy and meeting him at night behind the south practice hall for some—"

"I'll be there," Celia said hastily. "Tell me where."

I had all sorts of arguments ready by the time I made it to Flavia's room. Flavia listened to me carefully, then said, "I've been wishing for years I had the courage to do just this. Thank you—I'll be there."

Mira asked us to meet in the north practice hall. The weather had gotten colder in the last week, and no one used the north practice hall in winter if they could avoid it; it was even draftier than the chapel.

Giula walked over with me. "This was Mira's idea?" she asked. "No wonder she didn't fit in at the seminary."

I laughed, but didn't answer.

"Have you ever seen her use witchlight?"

"No. So far as I can tell, she doesn't use magery of any kind."

Giula looked speculative. "Do you suppose that she, you know, *can't*?"

"It's possible. There was a man in my village who couldn't. He was simple, though." I paused. "Domenico said that there used to be musicians who wouldn't use magery—they believed that abstaining from magic made them better musicians."

"Huh," Giula said. "Well, is there anything to that? Have you heard her play?"

Thinking about Mira's playing, I had to admit that there might be something to it. "Domenico said the theory's been discredited. But Mira's playing—" I shrugged. "Well, you'll see."

Mira had brought a large supply of candles, and lit them throughout the hall. Bella and Flavia were already there, but otherwise the hall was echoingly empty. Except for the night of Mira's strange illness, I'd never spent much time in the north practice hall; now I walked around to take a good look. It was one of the oldest buildings at the conservatory and had not been well maintained, but I could see the remains of frescoes along the walls. One of those frescoes had frightened me half to death the night I sat with Mira. Now, in the daylight, it was hard to see why. Almost all the frescoes had been torn out or had crumbled away; the best-preserved one showed a man clutching a faint light to his breast. I assumed that it was a depiction of Gaius with the Lady's Gift, but Gaius was generally depicted as looking triumphant rather than terrified.

Giula paced, her hands tucked into her sleeves and squeezed under her arms. I took out my violin and started tuning up. Mira, next to me, gave me a sudden flash of a smile, her gray eyes warming me.

"What are we going to play?" I asked Mira.

"I thought we'd play the prayer for healing," Mira said.

"I don't suppose you know a prayer for warm hands?" Giula asked.

Celia came in, peering curiously around the shadowed room.

"Everyone's here," Mira said. "Let's start."

I knew the tune for healing, as did Bella, but Celia, Giula, and Flavia did not. Mira sang the words for Celia: *"Rachamin, Arka / Rachamin, Gèsu. Refuya, Arka / Refuya, Gèsu."* Mira had a thin, high voice, like a boy's. Then she played the tune through once by herself. I joined in, harmonizing, and the others joined in, following her lead. It didn't work right away. Flavia had brought a small drum of wood and hide, which she tucked under her arm; she set a strong beat. After a few repetitions, it started to fall into place. The song was deceptively simple. Like all the old songs, it was eerie; we passed the melody around between violin, horn, and voice. "I like it," Giula breathed when we paused.

"Let's try it again," Mira suggested.

It had a simpler rhythm than the funeral song, but it was still infectious; I wanted to dance, but kept my feet still, self-conscious. We picked up the tempo. The melody was passed back to me; I started in, but an octave higher. We wound up in a rushing conclusion, and stopped to catch our breath.

"Well, I don't know about you," Bella said, "but *my* hands are warm."

Mine were, too. I'd forgotten about the cold. I looked

at Mira. To my surprise, Mira looked disappointed, even
forlorn. She saw my surprise and straightened up.

"Some of us have sectional rehearsals starting soon,"
Mira said. "We should probably head back."

"Let's meet tomorrow," Bella suggested.

Mira shook her head. "If we do this too often, someone
will notice, and just might decide to make a fuss. Next
week—same day, same time, same place. *Don't tell anyone.*"

Everyone drifted out. I lingered for a moment and caught
Mira's eye.

"Why were you disappointed? That was amazing." But
Mira shook her head and wouldn't answer.

I'd worried that someone—Giula, particularly—would
let slip what we were up to. But at supper, our heresies
were the farthest thing from her mind. "I heard the postman came today!" Giula told me. She was glowing, despite the cold.

"Who'd you hear it from?" I asked. The postman had
been due several days ago; this was the third time I'd heard
the rumor and I didn't want to get my hopes up.

"Flavia says she saw him come in with his horse."

"Well, it's about time," I said, trying to act unimpressed,
but my heart was racing. Sure enough, when the midday
meal was over, the Dean's assistants came out with bulging
sacks.

"Sit!" the Dean bellowed. "No one's getting their mail
unless they are *seated* and *behaving themselves.*"

Giula bounced up and down in her seat. "It's been
months and months," she said.

"Two months, same as always," I said, "plus four days,
since he's late."

I had a letter; so did Giula and Bella. "You all have until tomorrow morning to finish any letters you want to

send," the Dean announced. The room was quiet as people broke the seals and unfolded their letters. Not everyone's news was good. Across the table from me, Bella went ashen, then stood and ran out of the hall.

Dear Eliana, my mother's handwriting said, *we're all healthy and doing fine.* I sighed in relief. *We hope this letter finds you equally well. The harvest was good, thank the Lady.* She went on to enumerate the village gossip. Doratura was fine; more than fine, Doratura was beginning to thrive again. *But all these hungry people!* she added. Refugees from the devastated southern parts of Verdia were streaming north, and many had passed through Doratura. *All this desperation . . .*

Near the bottom of the letter, she added, *Good news! Donato and his wife have had another child, a fine little boy.* I suppressed an exclamation; Donato's daughter was almost eight years old, and he and his wife had been unable to have another since then. Donato couldn't write, but tucked into the folded letter was a thin sheet with an ink drawing of a sleeping baby: Donato's son. I smiled as I smoothed the drawing, careful to keep even a corner of the paper away from the damp spot where I'd spilled my tea.

Giula started babbling about the news from her village—several dozen weddings, funerals, and infants of people I'd never met. I excused myself to go find Bella; Mira followed me. We found Bella and Flavia by the wall at the edge of the conservatory, Bella weeping against Flavia's shoulder.

"My sister died," Bella said when she could speak again. "My youngest sister. She was just a baby when I left."

"I'm sorry," I whispered.

Bella wiped her eyes with her sleeve. "My brothers are leaving the village and going north to look for work. My father wants to go, too, but my mother is almost mad with grief—Erucia was her favorite." She paused. "When my father wrote the letter, he said they have food enough to last a few more weeks, and then they will have nothing. 'Pray for us,' they said." Bella's hand tightened over the letter, crumpling it. "If the Lady is listening to our prayers, why did every seed my parents planted die in the ground? Why did this *happen* to us?"

Flavia tightened her arm around Bella's shoulder.

"Well," Bella said, and wiped her eyes again, impatiently. "Tell me your news. I don't want to be the only person sharing my letter."

"I didn't have any mail," Mira said. "That's what comes of moving around. People don't know where to find you."

Bella laughed a little at that, the sound catching in the tears still in her throat.

"Everyone in my family is fine," I said.

Flavia unfolded her own letter. "My family is also well," she said. "But soldiers have been marching through our village, heading south. No one knows why. We know that the Vesuviani were well and truly beaten, so what does the Emperor have to fear now? Besides, no one has seen a Circle detachment, and how would the soldiers fight without magefire?"

I shook my head. Bella's head was still bowed, and Mira's eyes were fixed on Bella's face.

"Also," Flavia said, folding her letter again and putting it away, "this is kind of interesting. You know that song about the wicked stepmother with the poisoned honey—the song reached our village sometime in the last month. My mother mentioned it in passing." Bella looked up at that, and Flavia gave her a sympathetic smile. "And before you ask, Bella, no—they don't know what it means, either."

We all comforted Bella as well as we could, though we had no answers to offer her, and she didn't want our prayers. Back in my room, I took out the box where I kept my letters from under my bed, opened the lid, and put the newest letter on top.

"How is your family?" Mira asked.

"They're all fine," I said.

"Any new nieces or nephews?"

"One nephew." Mira was acting interested; I sighed, resigned myself to the change in subject and started telling her about the news from my village. I'm sure I sounded just like Giula, babbling on about a bunch of people Mira didn't know.

"So your village isn't affected by the famine, then?" she asked.

"No," I said. "The war never came to our part of Verdia. Some of the men were conscripted to fight in the army, but even then, they got by."

"What does your village think caused the famine?"

"They say that the retreating Vesuviani soldiers sowed salt in the fields," I said. "That's the prevailing theory, at least."

"Have you heard any others?"

"There are some who believe that the Maledori poisoned the land. Others think that the Lord and the Lady are punishing them, though of course the priests say that the Lady never wishes ill upon Her children."

"What did your family think of the war itself?"

I sighed, trying to think back to the letters my mother had sent as it was starting. "There had been raids from Vesuvia, coming across the border to steal crops and burn fields—not into my village, but still, close enough to feel as if the wolves were at our neighbor's door, if not our own. The story that went around right before the army marched—about the farm family burned with their crops—hit my mother hard. I remember one letter where she talked about how it could have been her and my father and brothers, even though they were a few days' walk from the border and not really that vulnerable to raids."

Mira nodded, not saying anything.

"What were things like in Cuore during the war?" I asked.

"The food shortages didn't hit us as hard," Mira said. "You probably would have guessed that."

"What do people in Cuore say caused the famine?" I asked.

Mira's voice was heavy. "Salt." She didn't seem to want to say anything more.

After Mira blew out her candle and we lay down, I lay awake for longer than usual. After a long time, Mira thought I was asleep, and in the darkness, I could hear her choking back wrenching, wracking sobs.

The next morning, the priest and priestess announced a prayer service, for Bella's sister and all the other relatives we'd just found out we'd lost. Lessons and rehearsals were canceled, and I trudged reluctantly to the chapel.

"Lord and Lady," the priest intoned. "Look down upon us, thy servants, and have mercy. May the hungry be fed; may the grieving be comforted. May the dead find peace in thy eternal garden."

"So may it be," we said. I stopped listening. Giula sat to my right, sitting on her hands to keep them warm; she'd been distracted enough by Bella's sad news that she hadn't even scrambled for an aisle seat. Mira sat on my left; she had a glazed look, like she wasn't listening any more than I was. Bella sat in the pew in front of us. Her eyes were red from crying, and she did not look comforted.

As we left the chapel service, Bella caught Mira's arm. "Our ensemble plays *today*," she said.

Mira nodded as if she'd been thinking the same thing.

We met after the midday meal. Bella reached the north practice hall first. "You know the funeral song," she said to me. "Teach us."

It worked better this time. I played the song through, then played it a line at a time, the group playing the line back to me. *Da dat da da dat da wham wham wham. Da dat da da dat da wham wham wham.* I stamped out the rhythm with Flavia's drumming. Everyone else was stamping with the beat, too. We passed the music to Bella, and she began improvising, taking the music higher and higher and higher. There was an odd feeling in the air. It was like a swarm of bees in my head, or like standing on a wooden floor right over the percussionist sectionals, *feeling* the rolling bass more than hearing it. Like I was *inside* a cello. I was breathless; *something was going to happen.*

Then Celia stopped singing and stepped out of the circle. Her face was very white. "This is wrong," she said.

Bella opened her mouth to say something scathing, but Mira put a restraining hand on Bella's arm. Celia went on. "We've crossed the line," she said. "It's one thing to play for the sake of the music, but you can't say anymore that that's what we're doing. I'm not going to turn away from the Lady. Worshipping the old gods is wrong."

In the silence, she put on her cloak and left the hall.

"We'd better not play anymore today," Mira said. Her voice was gentle, and she was speaking to Bella. Bella shook her head, not saying anything.

The door to the practice hall swung open. We looked over, expecting Celia, but it was Giorgi—the cook's assistant and the village healer. "We need to talk," he said.

Bella stepped forward. "About what?" she asked.

"I don't think you realize the sort of trouble you could get into for what you're doing," Giorgi said. "Celia's right; you've crossed the line. The Dean and the teachers know that students play the Old music—they did the same, when they were students—but alone, and in secret. Not like this."

"This is the way the music is *supposed* to be played," Bella said.

"Of course," Giorgi said. "That's why you need to stop."

Bella was shaking her head and I said, "I don't understand."

Giorgi gave me an exasperated look. "You probably have grandmothers who bless themselves to ward off the evil eye, don't you?"

Flavia touched her forehead, heart, left shoulder, and right shoulder. "B'shem Arka, v'barah, v'nehora kadosha," she said in the Old Tongue. "Like that?"

"Yes. For a long time, the Fedeli have carefully ignored some small amount of Old Way practice, mocking it as superstition instead of treating it as a serious threat. But that's changing—in Cuore, and elsewhere. Conservatory students are kept deliberately isolated, so you had no way of knowing that." He turned to Mira. "You, however, had an obligation to warn these children what you were getting them into. And you did not."

I glanced at Mira, expecting her to look defiant. Instead, she looked crushed.

Giorgi went on. "If Celia decides to make a fuss, the Fedeli could be summoned to the conservatory, to look for heresy, apostasy, disloyalty—anything and anyone they could find. You could get far more people killed than just your little group. Do you understand what I'm telling you?"

Now even Bella had lowered her eyes.

"This is not the time for this music," Giorgi said. "This is not the place. You are children, and you are playing with fire. I just hope you don't all *end* in fire." He turned his back on us and left the hall.

"I'm sorry," Mira whispered.

"Don't be sorry," Bella said. "This was the right way to pray for my sister." She packed up her trumpet and put on her cloak. Giula slipped out after her, her face white.

Flavia wrapped her drum and put on her cloak. Mira was still staring at the floor, her face bleak, and Flavia took Mira's chin to lift her face. "I knew we could get in trouble," Flavia said, "and I've never believed that conservatories are somehow invulnerable to the Fedeli. And I chose to play with you. Take heart."

Alone with Mira in the north practice hall, I touched her hand gently. "I'm not sorry, either," I said. "Come on. If we're not going to do something illegal, let's go somewhere warmer."

A few days later, I overheard Bella talking to Giorgi, and paused to listen. And to warn them, of course, if anyone else tried to overhear their conversation. "Teach *me*, then," Bella said. "I don't care how dangerous it is. I don't care what the Fedeli could do to me."

"You have to promise me that you won't play the songs anymore," Giorgi said. "Faith is more than music—and faith is more important."

"I swear," Bella said.

Giorgi had her swear in the old way, kissing the crux of an X. Then Bella blessed herself: "B'shem Arka, v'barah, v'nehora kadosha."

"That blessing means *In the name of God, and Her son, and the Holy Light*," Giorgi said. "It's not a prayer, exactly—it's a blessing, a dedication."

"Teach me a prayer," Bella said.

"*Rachamin, Arka. Rachamin, Gèsu,*" Giorgi said, and I

recognized the words of the healing song we'd played together. "It means, *God, have mercy; Gèsu, have mercy.*"

"Protect us from the Maledori," Bella said. "How do I say that in the Old Tongue?"

"There are no Maledori," Giorgi said. "All that happens is the will of God."

I felt a sudden cold uncertainty in my stomach. *Everything?* The priests and priestesses taught that the Lord and the Lady wished only good for us; all suffering came from the Maledori. What sort of God would send pain to Her followers?

"B'shem Arka," Bella said. "God's will be done."

You really are an apostate, I thought. But that night, staring into the darkness, I whispered Giorgi's prayer— "Rachamin, Arka. Rachamin, Gèsu."

CHAPTER THREE

If two among you quarrel, then clasp hands
and make amends. You have not time to
waste on enmity.
—The Journey of Gèsu, chapter 15, verse 9.

Today we're going to work on dancing," Domenico said. "Pair up."

Mira and I grabbed hands without so much as looking around the room; Giula cast a longing look at Domenico before partnering off with Bella, who was rolling her eyes at Giula's wistfulness. Celia danced with Flavia. There were other girls in the conservatory class on courtly graces, but Mira's arrival meant there was an even number now, so no one had to dance with the teacher. Not that Domenico had ever picked Giula as his partner, but that didn't stop her from hoping.

As the teacher who'd spent the longest time in Cuore, Domenico had for years been stuck teaching this class. Few of us (if any) would ever play in Cuore, but certain etiquette would be expected among the nobility even in Pluma.

"You'll take turns dancing the woman's part," Domenico said, and reviewed the steps to the dance. "One-two-three, one-two-three, left-right-left, right-left-right, got it?"

I didn't have it. Mira was supposed to be dancing the man's part, but I was so busy watching my feet that I failed to follow her lead and we collided. Mira laughed. "How are you going to flirt with your partner if you're staring at your feet, Eliana?"

"Would it be better if I batted my lashes at you while stepping on your toe?"

"You're supposed to trust me to keep my feet out of the way."

I tried looking up at Mira, and she gave me a look of mock gallantry. "You look lovely this evening, my dear," she said in a husky voice, and I started laughing again and tripped over the hem of my robe.

Mira actually knew how to dance court-style, which startled me a bit; I wondered if she was worried that the other girls would notice. I was fairly certain that dancing was not taught at most seminaries. Still, when I managed to relax enough to actually follow her lead, I found that I didn't step on her feet, or trip over my own. Domenico stopped counting and started playing his violin for us to dance to, which was distracting enough that I fell out of step again. "Hey," Mira said, and let go of my hand to punch my arm. "Pay attention to your *partner*, not the music."

"Again," Domenico said. "One-two-three, one-two-three."

Mira cupped her hand lightly against my waist and gave me a grin. "You're allowed to smile while you're dancing, you know."

I grimaced at her, knowing that if I tried to answer I'd fall out of step again.

"You're supposed to be *enjoying* yourself, or at least convincing your partner that you're enjoying yourself." When I didn't answer, Mira pulled a solemn face and said,

"Oh, the horror, the horror! I could be practicing my violin, but instead people are making me dance!"

That did it. I started laughing again and fell out of step. Domenico stopped playing. "Do I need to separate the two of you? Mira, why don't you dance with Giula; Eliana, you and Bella can partner up."

Bella was a more competent dancer than I was, but not as skilled as Mira; I had to watch my feet again. She was preoccupied and didn't make much eye contact. I wished I knew what she was thinking about.

"You aren't telling us what *some* of us most want to know," Giula said when Domenico called for us to stop. "How do we get young men to *ask* us to dance?"

Domenico returned her pout with a wry smile. "You flirt, Giula! Do you really need instructions?" Giula blushed and pouted some more. "Well, all right, then. There are a hundred ways to flirt, but one of the most popular these days, or so I hear from my friends still at court, involves flowers."

Giula was now paying rapt attention, as was most of the rest of the class. Bella still looked preoccupied; Mira caught my eye and made a face to get me to laugh again.

"Many of the ladies and gentlemen at the Imperial Court carry flowers, either in their hands or fixed to their clothing," Domenico said. "They're used to cover up unpleasant smells; fresh flowers are preferred but expensive, and sachets of dried flower petals the less pricey alternative. If you find a young man attractive, you can buy a flower—a rose, ideally—and drop it when he's nearby; with luck, he'll pick it up and bring it to you. If a young man wants to approach you, he might buy a flower, then bring it to you saying that he thinks you might have dropped it."

"And if I'm not interested?" Bella asked.

"Then you say—" Domenico put on a squeaky falsetto voice " '—You must be mistaken, signore, that isn't mine.' "

"What if you drop your flower, and the wrong man picks it up for you?" Celia asked.

"Then you're probably out a flower," Domenico said. "And the man who brings it to you will probably be quite embarrassed, just as you'd be in his shoes."

Domenico moved on to talk a little about proper forms of address if we happened to want to flirt with a member of the Imperial family, or high-ranking members of the Fedeli or the Circle. "The Emperor rules," he said, quoting an aphorism we'd all heard before. "The Circle protects, and the Fedeli guide."

Bella stirred. "I've heard that it's common knowledge outside the conservatory that the Circle and the Fedeli rule, not the Emperor."

Domenico raised one eyebrow. "Bella, you're going to get yourself in trouble someday if you're not careful," he said, and ended the class.

That evening, I bent my head over my music theory assignment while turning Bella's comment over and over in my mind. Domenico was typically quite frank about life at court, so why would he repeat something he knew wasn't true? Unless *he* feared getting in trouble. But then, why would Bella—or Giorgi, who undoubtedly was the person who'd told her this—be any more reliable? I pushed my stool back finally and looked at Mira, who sat cross-legged on her bed, her head bent over a book. "I suppose you'd know," I said, setting down my pen.

"Know what?" Mira said, looking up. A lock of hair had fallen over one eye, and she twitched it back behind her ear.

"Who really rules. Like Bella said, we're always told

that the Emperor rules, the Circle protects, and the Fedeli guide—that the High Circle and the High Priest and Priestess of the Fedeli advise the Emperor, but he makes the decisions."

Mira gave me a steady look. "Bella is absolutely correct. It's the Circle and the Fedeli who rule, and everyone in Cuore knows that. Even in the provinces—if you'd been older when you left your home village, the Emperor's place in the ensemble of power, or his lack of one, would probably be known to you."

"Oh," I said, and lowered my eyes, disappointed. Bella could be such a know-it-all, and her relationship with Giorgi had only made this worse. It was a disappointment to find out that she really did know what she was talking about.

"When I say the *Circle* and *Fedeli*, of course, I mean the Circle Council and the High Priest and Priestess. There are about two hundred mages in the Circle, not counting initiates, and there are thousands of priests and priestesses in the Fedeli. Of course it's not *all* of the Fedeli and the Circle who rule; that would be absurd."

I laughed a little, though Mira wasn't really smiling. "This should stand me in good stead if I ever *do* get to play at Court," I said. "I won't be quite as ignorant as they'd like to keep me."

"Playing at court really is what you want?" Mira asked.

"Why else would I be here? It's what almost everyone here wants. There's no higher position for a musician."

"Domenico gave it up," Mira said.

"That's true. He didn't like court. That doesn't mean I wouldn't."

Mira was silent for a long moment, looking into her candle. "There's an old saying I've heard: 'The one who pays the piper, calls the tune.' I wouldn't want to play the tunes the Circle calls."

"Well, if you want to get technical about it, they're paying for my 'piping' now, in a way. They pay my scholarship. And Bella's, and Giula's, and Flavia's, and Celia's. They paid Lia's until she left. We're all beholden to the Circle, since we're sponsored by them. And thus so is Domenico, even if he left court years ago."

Mira wouldn't look up at me. "And none of you wish to speak ill of your benefactors?"

"It doesn't stop Bella," I said. I wanted, desperately, to lighten the mood, but I wasn't sure how. "I've met only one mage in my life, anyway, and he was nice enough."

"Really?" Now Mira looked up. "Tell me about it."

"It was when I was six. You know how the Circle sends people down into the provinces to find children who are particularly good at magery? Well, I was good enough as a child that my father took me up to the next village to be tested."

Mira leaned forward, putting her book down. "How good were you?"

"Honestly, it wasn't so much that I was *good* at magery as that I was precocious. I started making witchlight when I was barely more than a baby, and when I was six I could light a fire with damp wood. That's why my father thought I had a chance." I smiled ruefully at the memory. "But the man from the Circle wanted me to set fire to *stone*. He gave me a little pebble and asked if I could make it burn. I tried and tried, but I couldn't even warm it up."

"Too bad," Mira said.

"Yeah, well. It was worth the trip. The mage was very kind; he gave me an apple for trying so hard, and a dozen more to my father for bringing me in." I shrugged and smiled at Mira, but her face had gone hard. She ducked her head down to look at her book again. "What? Mira, was your trouble in Cuore with the Circle?"

"I don't want to talk about it." Her voice was hard.

I looked down at my music theory work; I had dripped a great big inkblot onto the paper. I muttered a curse and blotted it up as well as I could. "I'm sorry, Mira. I shouldn't have brought it up."

"Don't worry about it," she said, but she didn't want to talk more that evening.

Mira was still being distant with me the next morning at breakfast, and I felt terrible about it, but didn't know what to say to mend the rift. Thinking back to our class with Domenico, I thought that maybe I could offer her a flower, as if I were a young man approaching a young lady at court; that would make her laugh, and everything would probably be all right after that. Finding a flower would be difficult, though. It was late November, and the roses and most of the other flowers around the conservatory had gone dormant for the winter. That had to be true at court, as well, though; Domenico would know an appropriate offering for late November. I could ask him at my lesson, later that morning.

But that lesson, at it turned out, was canceled. As all of us (except for Mira) lingered over our tea, the Dean came in and knocked the floor with his staff to quiet us. He was trailed by three of the teachers; none were smiling. "There is solemn news," the Dean said. "The Emperor is dead. His son, Travan, has ascended to the Imperial throne. May the Lady shelter the soul of Emperor Iago; may the Lady guide and defend Emperor Travan."

"So may it be," we chorused, stunned to near-whispers.

"Classes and lessons are all canceled for the rest of the day," the Dean said. "Father Claro and Mother Emilia are convening a prayer service in one hour to mourn the old

Emperor and pray for the new; I expect to see you all there." He nodded to all of us and stomped out, presumably going to tell the same thing to the boys. A few minutes later, we heard the chapel bell tolling.

I went looking for Mira, hoping that she'd have gotten over her anger enough to sit next to me, but I couldn't find her. She wasn't in her favorite practice room, not in the north practice hall, not by the wall that bordered the conservatory grounds. I even tried the bell tower, which was where I'd normally have looked for Bella—of course, neither Mira nor Bella was there that day. In the end, I sat with Flavia, since Giula had managed to score a seat next to the aisle. When we rose for the priest and priestess to come down the center aisle, I saw that Mira and Bella were both sitting in the very back row.

It was a strange service. In form, it closely resembled the service of prayer and mourning that we had observed a month earlier, after so many students had received bad news through the mail—but there had been a bitter edge a month ago that was missing today. The death of an Emperor was a solemn occasion, but it was an impersonal sort of mourning. None of us, except possibly for Domenico, had ever met the Emperor. I stole a look at Domenico, standing with the teachers near the front; his face was grim and inscrutable, and I couldn't tell if he was grieving over the Emperor's death, worried about the new Emperor, or thinking about something else entirely.

But because the ascension of a new Emperor to the Imperial throne was an occasion for celebration, even as the death of the old Emperor was a cause for mourning, we were supposed to have a festival meal after the prayer service, with meat, wine, and fruit pies. With the famine around us, though, the conservatory's larder couldn't permit much of a celebration. Our cook planned very carefully in order to have meat in the stew on festival days, and an unplanned festival was not part of his calculations. Our midday meal was the same bean soup as always. We did each receive a small serving of stewed apples. Mira still didn't seem to want to look at me, so we let Giula babble on about the Emperor's death and the Dean's announcement and the prayer service and which boy students had managed to snare aisle seats on short notice.

"How old was Emperor Iago, anyway?" Celia asked as we ate our fruit.

"Not that old," I said. "My father's age." I remembered my father noting this once. "Too young to die of old age. I wonder how he died?"

"A sudden illness?" Flavia said. "Or maybe an accident. Even if he wasn't old, things happen."

"They certainly do," Bella said, and raised one eyebrow.

"What's that supposed to mean?" Celia asked.

"I'd better not say anything," Bella said. "Like Domenico said, I could get myself in trouble one of these days."

Mira scraped up the last of her fruit and excused herself, still avoiding my gaze. "Lessons or not, I'm going to go practice," she said.

There was a pause as she left, and then four pairs of eyes turned toward me. I didn't really want to try to explain to Giula, Flavia, Celia, and Bella why Mira was angry at me, so I shoved my plate away as well and left the hall.

I picked up my violin and went to practice for a while, but my mind kept returning to Bella's comment. Finally I sighed and put my violin back in its case, and went to find Bella; if I asked her what she meant, she probably *would* tell me, despite her claim about wanting to avoid trouble. She just wanted to be asked, and I was curious enough about what she knew (or thought she knew) that I was willing to give her that satisfaction.

I found Bella in the library, her head bent over a musical score, brown from age. "Hey," I said, and pulled up a chair across from her. "Is that for one of our classes?"

"No, actually." Bella slid the score gently across the table toward me. "I'm doing some independent research."

I raised my eyebrows. "On what?"

"Honey." She grinned at my puzzlement. "You remember that song that showed up last fall? The wicked stepmother with the poisoned honey? Well, I've been trying to figure out what the song is talking about."

"And you think that's in the library?"

"Sure, why not? I'm looking up old folk songs that mention honey, to see whether any of those songs have double meanings. Also stepmothers, and treacherous gifts."

"I can't believe that the person who wrote that song would have been referring to an old, forgotten folk song, anyway," I said.

"True, but I could still get ideas," Bella said.

"So have you?"

"I've found lots of great stories, but none that answer my question," Bella said. "No songs about poisoned honey. I did find a song about someone who slew their lover for rejecting their gift. And I found another song where someone got a poisoned garment that killed her."

"Any underlying meanings?"

Bella sighed. "No. Not really. Well, unless you count the moral, 'Don't accept gifts from people who hate you, even if they seem perfectly innocent.' "

"Seems like a good rule to live by," I said. I glanced down at the score Bella had been studying. "So what does Giorgi say about the song?"

A look of annoyance crossed Bella's face—annoyance at

Giorgi, not at me. "Just that it's a waste of time to worry about it."

"You don't agree?"

"Obviously not."

I couldn't keep myself from smiling a little, and Bella noticed. "Oh yes," she said, and gave me a wry smile back. "I still keep my own conscience, even if Giorgi is my teacher."

"I rather thought he was more than your teacher," I said. "You always said that if you were going to risk being thrown out of the conservatory, it would be for a *man,* not a boy. Giorgi's a man."

"True enough, but I'm not saying," Bella said, and gave me a smile that told me everything I wanted to know.

"So what has Giorgi told you about the Emperor's death?" I asked. "If you aren't worried that by telling me, you'll get yourself into trouble."

Bella laughed. "Oh, I just said that to annoy Celia. She's going to tie herself in knots for a week before she breaks down and asks me what I meant. Giorgi said that there have been rumors for a while that the Circle, or maybe the Fedeli, were angry at the Emperor. The story is that he was poisoned; whoever did it thinks Travan will be easier to manipulate."

"Things happen, huh?" I said.

"They certainly do. Especially at court."

I found myself wondering if *Bella* still wanted to play at court, given all the stories she was hearing from Giorgi, but I didn't quite dare ask. I changed the subject, instead. "Any idea where I could get a flower?"

"Any particular kind?"

I shrugged. It probably didn't really matter. "Something pretty, that smells nice."

"Some of the herbs in the garden flower this time of year. Ask Giorgi. He should be able to help you."

I went from the library to the back door of the kitchen. The door was standing open, to let in the cool air; I poked my head in but didn't see Giorgi. The kitchen was damp and yeasty and very warm, despite the open door.

"May I help you?" It was one of the other assistants.

"I'm looking for Giorgi."

The assistant nodded; a few moments later, Giorgi emerged, wiping his hands on his apron. His sleeves were rolled up past his elbows and his face was flushed from the heat. "Is anyone sick?" he asked.

"No, nothing like that," I said. "But Bella said you might be able to help me."

Giorgi stepped outside the kitchen. "Is this about—"

"It's nothing about the music," I said. "I want a flower, just one flower. Bella said you might have a flowering herb you could give me a cutting from."

Giorgi looked a little surprised. "Sure," he said. "I could do that." He stepped back into the kitchen to hang up his apron and grab a small knife; rolling his sleeves down, he slipped a cloak over his shoulders and we walked down to the kitchen garden.

The conservatory did try to grow at least some of its food, and the kitchen gardens spread out along the slope of the hill that led down from the back door. This time of year, nearly everything was dormant. Withered bean plants hung slack from their trellises, and bits of rock marked out beds where parsnips, cabbages, and onions would be planted in the spring. The herb garden was in a sheltered spot next to a stand of apple trees. The rosemary and parsley twined as green and fragrant as ever, but Giorgi reached past them to a plant with a profusion of yellow blossoms. "Winter jasmine," he said. "How much do you need?"

"Just a sprig," I said.

Giorgi snipped off a piece and gave it to me. I inhaled

the scent—it was delicate and heady all at once, perfect for my plans. "Thank you," I said.

"Is there anything else I can do for you?" Giorgi asked.

It occurred to me that if I wanted to ask him to teach me about the Old Way faith, as he was teaching Bella, this was the right time to ask him. We were alone; no one would overhear us. His manner was reserved but kind, and I thought that if I did ask him to teach me, he would probably agree. I knew nothing about the Old Way beliefs, and what I'd overheard Giorgi telling Bella didn't sound terribly appealing—but there was the *music*. I knew I wanted to know more.

But I was afraid that if I asked, Giorgi would expect me to commit myself to it wholeheartedly, like Bella. And I wasn't sure I was willing to do that. Besides, Giorgi seemed to believe that just playing the music was a terrible risk, and I suspected that if I asked him to teach me about the Old Way, he would insist that I stop playing the songs. Our subversive little ensemble may have been broken up, but I still played the music on my own. In fact, Mira had taught me the other songs she knew—a song to celebrate the return of spring, a song for safety during childbirth, and a song of praise to God. The music was part of the bond I had with Mira, and I wasn't giving that up.

"The flower is all that I needed," I said. "Thank you."

I wondered, as I walked back from the garden with the jasmine clutched in one hand, if I was playing the tunes the Circle called, after all.

• • •

I had intended to find Mira and bring her the jasmine with the line Domenico had suggested in class: "Excuse me, signora, but I believe you dropped this." I had imagined myself saying it in a husky, deep voice like Mira had used when teasing me while dancing, and generally playacting the part of a lovesick nobleman. But I couldn't find Mira, and the longer I looked the more the idea seemed stupid. Still, I had the jasmine, and after asking Giorgi for it, I couldn't just throw it away. Finally, I went back to our room, left it on her bed, and went to practice.

It was late afternoon, almost time for dinner, when someone knocked on the door of my practice room. I answered it, expecting Bella or Giula, but Mira stood in the doorway, the jasmine in her hand. I fell back a step, not knowing what to say.

"Excuse me, signora," Mira said. She held the jasmine sprig to her nose and inhaled the scent for a moment. "I believe you must have dropped this."

I looked down at my feet, then back up at Mira. "Why yes," I said. "That does look like mine."

"I'm so glad I was able to return it to you," Mira said. She took my hand and folded it around the flower. "It's a lovely flower and it would have been a shame for it to get lost."

I nodded, not certain of what to say.

"Signora, I was just going to dinner," Mira said, and struck a gallant pose, offering me her arm. "Would you care to accompany me?"

That was easy. "I'd love to," I said, and took her arm. And everything was all right again.

CHAPTER FOUR

Rise up, daughter, and dance with me; and in the dancing, know the glory of God.
——*The Journey of Gèsu, chapter 2, verse 11.*

During the week before Mascherata, the Midwinter festival, it was bitterly cold. None of us spent more time outside than we had to; even Bella abandoned her usual vigil for the postman. Still, as I huddled next to Mira at the midday meal, cupping my hands around my soup bowl, I was in a good mood. Mascherata, even the watered-down version celebrated by the conservatory, was a fun holiday, with music and dancing. My lesson day fell on Mascherata itself, which meant that Domenico and I would trade places and I would teach the lesson; I was trying to come up with insults to hurl at him if he decided to be a recalcitrant student who didn't spend enough time practicing.

Then the Dean of the conservatory came out to the center of the dining hall, slamming a staff to the floor for attention. At first I assumed it was the postal delivery—then I saw the two black-clad strangers beside him and felt Mira go rigid beside me.

The Dean's voice was strangely flat. "This is Father

Cassio and Mother Galeria, from the Sudditi Fedeli della Signora. They have honored us with a visit to observe our celebration of the Mascherata festival."

The room went suddenly very quiet, as if a dropped wine cup had just shattered on the floor.

"There will be a special chapel service tomorrow morning, in their honor," the Dean said. "I expect everyone to be there."

Cassio stepped forward. His hair was black, and he smiled too easily. "We are looking forward to celebrating the Lord's Victory with you," he said, and if I hadn't known what he was, I might almost have liked him. "The Fedeli are making a special trip through Verdia this winter, to pray for the Lady to restore the land. People often greet us with fear, but I hope that you will all soon learn better. As the Lady has told us, 'Innocence doesn't need to hide.' We are the servants of the Lady, here to teach and to encourage. The Lady's faithful children have nothing to fear from us."

Cassio and Galeria swept out of the room, the Dean in their wake; there was a sudden hushed burst of conversation, but I didn't dare say anything. Bella was as white as the winter sky and Giula looked as if she were about to throw up. I gulped down my soup, wondering as I did it if anyone would tell the Fedeli that I was the first to leave the dining hall after they left, as if I had some secret I needed to discuss—but there was no help for it. "Meet in my room," I whispered. "As soon as you can get there."

Mira joined me first. She wrapped herself up in her cloak and sat down on her bed. "Have you ever encountered the Fedeli before?" she asked me.

"No. They usually leave Verdia alone. I've heard stories about them, of course, but that's all." The moral of the stories was always the same: stay on their good side, and if you can't, stay out of their way. "You have, though, haven't you?"

"They're all over, in Cuore. Like cockroaches, but with black silk robes."

I smothered my giggle in my cloak. "Be careful, they might hear you."

"They're not in the dorm," Mira said. "They're in the Dean's study right now, sitting by a warm fire and drinking hot wine."

"Are you afraid of them?" I asked.

Mira was silent for a long time. "Of course I'm afraid," she said. "If the Fedeli find out that I recruited students and taught them an Old Way song—*that's* what they're here to find, Eliana. I could be executed. Of course I'm afraid."

There was a knock at the door—Flavia. She came in and sat down, and Mira fell silent. Flavia tapped her hand lightly against the edge of my bed, drumming out a rhythm as she waited. She gave me a wry smile when she saw me watching. "I'm afraid I'll tap out an Old Way song without even realizing it," she said. "I could be betrayed by my own hands."

"Be careful," Mira said. "Don't think they wouldn't notice."

Bella arrived next, then Giula, and finally Celia. The room was very crowded, with so many people. I sat beside Mira; Flavia and Bella sat on my bed. Giula and Celia pulled out our work-stools to sit on.

"We have to turn ourselves in," Celia said as soon as the door was closed. "They'll go easy on us if we confess, if we're penitent."

I looked at Mira. "What will they do if we all turn ourselves in?"

"If you seemed sorry, and did whatever penance they

assigned, you would almost certainly be pardoned," Mira said.

"What about you?" I asked.

"It's hard to say. Since I was the instigator, they would probably go harder on me. They would assume that I had been a member of a secret Redentore group before coming here. They would want names." Mira was next to me, and I could feel the shudder that went through her body. "If I was cooperative, they might choose to show me mercy."

"What are Redentori?" Flavia asked.

"It's what the people who practice the Old Way call themselves," Mira said. She shook her head. "If you think it's best to turn yourselves in, do it. Don't worry about me. I'll run."

"In winter?" Flavia said. "In weather like this? Even if they don't catch you, you'll freeze to death."

"And if you run, they'll know you have something to hide," I said.

"I'll be all right," Mira said. She had stopped shaking, and I found myself certain that she was right, that she could run and survive—*but I'd never see you again*, I thought, and found myself desperate to think of another way.

"Then are we agreed?" Celia said. "We turn ourselves in?"

"No," I snapped. "We aren't."

Bella hadn't said a word, and I turned to her. "What do you think, Bella?"

Very deliberately, Bella said, "I'm not saying anything that *she* can use to curry favor with the Fedeli." She jerked her head toward Celia. "But I'm not turning myself in. The Fedeli would not find me as repentant as I imagine they would require. And while dying for your faith is an honor, it's an honor that I would rather forgo."

"Are you saying I'd turn you in to the Fedeli to make

myself *look* good?" Celia said. Her cheeks flushed as red as if she'd been slapped.

Bella didn't answer.

Celia's lips tightened. "If that's what you think of me, why did you even get me into this?"

"Keep your voices down," I hissed. "Look. We're all on the same side. Celia, it's clear that your plan won't work— if we go to the Fedeli, it's entirely possible that Mira and Bella will die. I'm sure you aren't willing to sacrifice their lives for your own, any more than they'd be willing to let you die to save themselves."

Celia shook her head.

"Outside of this room, does anyone know we have something to hide?" I asked.

"Giorgi," Bella said.

"Well, *he* isn't going to go to the Fedeli and turn us in, is he?" I asked. Bella shook her head. "Then we're safe as long as we all stand together. The six of us *have* to be able to trust each other." I crossed my index fingers and held them up. "I swear—"

"Wait," Mira said. She clasped her hand over mine, and I could feel her shaking again. "The Fedeli will use torture if they suspect that you know something you're not telling them. Don't swear an oath that you won't be able to keep."

Outside, someone was running down the hallway. It was probably just someone late for a lesson, but the anxious sound of the footfalls made my heart leap into my throat. My own hands shaking, I crossed my fingers again. "I swear that I will not go to the Fedeli to save myself," I said. "I will not offer to name names, and I will do everything in my power to avoid betraying you." I kissed my crossed fingers, then added, "I make no promises about what I might say under torture."

Flavia crossed her fingers and made the same oath; so did Mira. Her hands and voice shaking, Giula did the same. We looked at Bella; Bella looked at Celia.

"I'm not taking an Old Way oath," Celia said. "That's a sin in itself."

"Swear by the Lady, then," Bella said.

"Take any oath you like," I said. "Anything we can trust."

"I'll give you my word," Celia said, and tossed her curls back. "I'll give you my word that I won't go to the Fedeli to betray you. If that's not good enough for you—well, keeping this a secret wasn't *my* idea." She shoved the stool back under my table, and walked out of the room, slamming the door behind her.

We were silent for a moment. Then Bella said, "I'll give you my oath, now that she's gone." From under her robe, she took out a carved wood cross. "I will not betray my faith, nor will I betray any of you," she said, and kissed the cross. "God will give me the strength I need. She would give you the same strength, too, if you asked and believed."

"You shouldn't be wearing that," I said. "The Fedeli could see it. If they decided to search you—"

"I am in God's hands," Bella said, and deliberately tucked the cross back under her robe.

Lady's tits, I thought. Given half an excuse, Celia might betray us; given a moment's bad luck, Bella might betray herself. Flight was looking more and more appealing, but if anyone vanished abruptly, her friends would be investigated and questioned—guaranteeing Bella's discovery as a secret follower of the Old Way.

Flavia was watching my face, and she gave me a wry smile. "It looks like we're all in God's hands," she said. "Whether we want to be or not."

That night, Mira and I lay side by side for warmth. "Were you accused of heresy, in Cuore?" I asked her. "Could the Fedeli recognize you?"

"No, I wasn't accused of heresy. I didn't have the courage to take these sorts of risks in Cuore," Mira said. "And I don't recognize Cassio or Galeria, so I think it's safe to assume that they don't recognize me. Cuore is a big city."

I closed my eyes, though I didn't feel like sleeping.

"Giorgi was right," Mira said. "I put all of you in danger, and I should have known better."

"No," I said.

"I didn't think that the Fedeli would ever come here—to the province of war and famine, desperation and starvation. The Fedeli like the comforts of Cuore. I thought that here, if nowhere else, would be a safe place to play that music."

I slipped my arms around Mira, cradling her like a cat, but she refused to be comforted.

"You haven't ever seen someone die from fire, have you?" Mira asked after a little while.

"No," I said.

"I have," Mira said. She was quiet again, then added, "It's a terrible way to die. People scream until the smoke chokes them. Flesh doesn't burn easily—it takes a lot of wood. There's a square in Cuore where the Fedeli execute unrepentant heretics; it smells like cooked rotten meat. I wandered there by accident once, and I had nightmares for weeks."

"Don't think about it," I said, stroking Mira's hair. Mira smelled a little like smoke, because of her candles, but it was a delicate smoke, not like the smell of greasy meat that came from the kitchen on festival days. "Everything will be all right."

Mira nodded wordlessly.

"Mira," I said. "Whatever happens, I want to face it together. Promise that you won't leave me."

"I can't promise that," she said. "And neither can you."

We didn't talk after that, but stared into the cold darkness.

We rose early for the chapel service. For once, no one was tempted to skip. Apparently even Bella had an understanding with her Old Way God, because she filed in to the chapel with the rest of us, sitting beside me with an impassive face.

Like all chapel services, it started with drumming, to drive away the Maledori. This close to Midwinter's Eve, there shouldn't be many Maledori around anyway, but it was always good to be on the safe side. Then Mother Emilia and Father Claro processed down the aisle, with the black-robed Fedeli behind them. I thought that Mother Emilia looked oddly pale, though it was hard to tell.

We went through the standard morning prayers. Celia, in front of me, spoke the prayers loudly and clearly—she knew every prayer by heart from attending chapel so often. Partway through the opening prayer, I began to worry that the Fedeli would notice my mumbling. When I ducked my head to listen, though, I thought there were probably enough enthusiastic show-offs like Celia to render my own stumbles inaudible.

Mother Emilia delivered a sermon. I tried desperately to pay attention—fearful that we'd be quizzed on it later—but it was rambling and disjointed, and my thoughts kept wandering. Would Celia keep her word? I wanted to believe that she would, but part of me wondered. And Giula—what if she lost her nerve? What if she lost her nerve somewhere *public,* like the chapel service? She was sitting somewhere behind me and I couldn't see her; I listened for hiccuping breaths that would tell me someone back there was on the edge of hysteria, but heard nothing.

When Mother Emilia sat down, Galeria—the Fedele priestess—rose to deliver a second sermon.

Galeria started by talking about the Lady's limitless love for us. Nothing we could do, she assured us, would make the Lady love us any less. It was precisely for this reason that the Fedeli existed—to deepen understanding of the Lady's love.

I thought, *You mean, to punish us because you don't trust the Lady to do it,* and wished I could whisper that to Mira.

Then Galeria talked about the Maledori—the dark spirits that worked constantly to undo the good that the Lord and the Lady worked in the world. The Maledori would tempt us to evil; they would offer us their darkness in a pleasant guise, to deceive us. I remembered the song about the poisoned honey and wondered if the Fedeli had written it after all.

Sometimes, Galeria told us, someone would fall under the influence of the Maledori and not even realize it.

Beside me, Bella stared ahead, utterly impassive.

"As Fedeli, we are taught to cast the darkness out of the Maledori's victims, and to bring them back into the light of the Lady's love. If the Maledori have control over someone, it's not that person's fault. We can *help* them. But sadly, it's the people who most need our help who are least likely to ask for it.

"Sometimes we can sense the darkness just by looking into someone's eyes—but it is each of you who know best who needs our help. If you have seen a friend slip away from you into the darkness, you *owe* it to that friend to try to help them. You *owe* it to your friend to come to us.

When someone is truly in darkness, they can't save themselves, and *you* may not be able to save them—but we can.

"If you suspect that a friend has fallen into the darkness of sin, blasphemy, heresy, or apostasy—if you care about that friend—you *will* come to us."

The chapel was silent. Ahead of me, I could see Celia's shoulders, but not her face; at least she wasn't nodding in enthusiastic agreement, but I stared at her chestnut curls and shivered. Beside me, Bella was still impassive. She probably still believed that she was in God's hands, and that God would protect her or not, as She chose. I stared at Celia's back, wishing that I had Bella's certainty, and wondering if I should have suggested that we all flee.

Galeria finished exhorting us to turn in our friends, and began to list the heresies that our friends might have foolishly been taken in by. The belief that the Lady's love was conditional. The belief that the Lord was not the equal of the Lady. The belief that magery was not truly the Lady's gift. Then Galeria reached the Old Way.

"The so-called Old Way is perhaps the greatest darkness threatening to swallow the faithful today," Galeria said. "The Old Way apostates hold that the Lord and the Lady are not true Gods, and that in fact a dark and cruel God rules the world. A God who rejected Her children for disobedience; a God who once condemned the world to darkness and famine."

Famine? I refrained from stealing a glance at Bella.

"Even the practices that you may think of as harmless open the door to the Maledori. We're not here to find everyone who has ever sworn an oath over crossed twigs, but it's important that if you've done such things, you turn away from them now. This service will include the rite of purification, and minor sins will be forgiven. If you've done something, and you aren't sure if this service has purified you, come and talk to us. We're here to help."

For the purification, Mother Emilia and Father Claro burned rose-petal incense; I fought back the urge to sneeze, afraid that this might constitute a heresy of some kind. There was more drumming, and water was sprinkled over the crowd. Then we filed back out of the chapel and went to lunch.

During the midday meal, I could tell that Celia wanted to say something; when we were done, she followed me back to my room. "I think the Maledori have Bella under their influence," she hissed as soon as the door had closed.

I raised one eyebrow. "Just Bella? Not me, or Mira, or—"

"I think playing Old Way music falls into the category of a minor sin. At the conservatory, anyway. But Bella! You know perfectly well she's gone a *lot* further than that."

"So what are you going to do?" I stepped closer to Celia, so that she had to look up at me. "Are you planning to turn her in to the Fedeli?"

"Well, don't you think we *should*? After what they said—they can *help* her."

I grasped Celia's wrist and yanked her over to the window. Below, we could see the Fedeli's black wagon. "The Fedeli will 'help' her by torturing her until she renounces her faith. I know you haven't always gotten along with Bella, Celia, but would you wish that on *anybody*?"

Celia jerked her wrist away. "Is it better to leave her in the hands of the Maledori?"

"Are you joking? Do you think Bella would give in easily? They *burn* unrepentant heretics." I picked up one of Mira's candles and lit it with a flick of my fingers. Then I grabbed Celia's hand again and held it over the candle flame, so she could feel the rising heat. "Imagine Bella burning, Celia. Imagine hearing her screams—"

"Let me *go*!" Celia shrieked, jerking away from me and the candle.

"Did that hurt? Imagine the pain Bella would feel, with flames devouring her body and no way to escape. Imagine the stench of the smoke, the way it would hang in the courtyard for weeks. I've heard that burning human flesh smells like cooked meat. Imagine how it would turn your stomach, every time there was mutton in the stew—"

Celia turned away, her face pale. "Fine," she said. "Have it your way."

"You gave your word, Celia. I want you to give me your word, *again,* that you will *not* go to the Fedeli."

"Fine," Celia said again. "You have my word." But she wouldn't meet my eyes as she slipped out of the room.

Mira came in a moment later. "I don't think Celia's going to want meat for weeks," she said.

"Do you think she's going to tell the Fedeli about us?"

"Not today," Mira said. "I think you've convinced her for today."

"Maybe we should have all run when we had the chance," I said.

"No," Mira said. "I think by myself I could probably have gotten away. As a group, we'd have been caught within hours."

"Why would you have been able to get away?" I asked.

Mira shrugged. "I'd have stolen a horse."

"You know how to *ride*?" I said.

"It's not all that hard," she said. "But it's a skill that's best learned *before* your life depends on it. Besides, there weren't enough fast horses for all of us."

I shook my head and gave her a grin. "You're full of surprises, Mira."

The whole conservatory was on edge that evening. If anything, Bella was the calmest person at the table. Giula's eyes were red; Celia's jaw was so tense that her neck muscles stood out like tree roots. Before the meal, Father Claro and Mother Emilia came in to lead us in the traditional offering of a portion of food to the Lady. I wondered if they were trying to pretend to the Fedeli that we *always* did this.

As I picked at the last of my food, the Dean came in with Galeria and Cassio—and my teacher, Domenico. Domenico was chatting easily with Cassio. I felt my eyes go wide and my face go slack; I'd always liked Domenico, and the idea that he would be on the side of the Fedeli had never crossed my mind. Domenico glanced in my direction and gestured for me to turn my face away. I looked down and carefully rearranged my features. Domenico had lived in Cuore; it was a big city, but it was possible that he'd known Cassio.

"I have an announcement," the Dean said. "Under the guidance of Mother Galeria and Father Cassio, I have decided to expand our Mascherata Festivities, to better honor the Lord and the Lady. In addition to the chapel observance, there will be dancing in the courtyard all night." He paused, and cleared his throat. "I would like to remind everyone present that other rules still stand." He turned and strode brusquely out of the meal hall.

Other rules. We looked at each other, baffled. "Do you suppose he means that the boys will be at the same dance?" Flavia said.

Celia's eyes went wide. "That must have been what he meant," she said. "Where else would the boys go to dance, if we were in the courtyard?"

Bella wanted to say something snide to Celia, I could tell, and I kicked her shin under the table. Making Celia mad at Bella right now was not a good idea. With any luck, she'd be so distracted by the idea of getting to dance with her boyfriend—*openly*—we wouldn't have to worry about her reporting us to the Fedeli at least until she'd slept off her hangover.

Mascherata honored the Lord's victory over the Maledori. Because of the Lord's victory, Midwinter's Night was considered safe from all supernatural threats, and the Lord and Lady's faithful could pass the night in wild revelry. Except for conservatory students, who normally attended a chapel service and then danced in the hallways of the dormitories while the Dean turned a blind eye. It was customary to wear a costume—a mask—to the Mascherata festivities, but I hadn't had the chance to do that since I had last celebrated the holiday in my village as a child.

Conservatory students all wore the same gray robes. We had nothing we could wear as costumes, and no way to make masks. But in the morning, we discovered that the Dean—or the Fedeli—had bought yards and yards of black wool from the village seamstress. We were each issued a rectangle of black fabric from which to cut a simple mask. Mira helped me with mine. The wool made my cheeks itch, and I imagined I looked pretty silly. Mira certainly looked silly in hers.

"The point is to look like everyone else," Mira said. "The point is to not stand out."

As I tied Mira's mask to her face, there was a knock at the door. I opened it to find an irate Domenico, violin case in hand.

"Were you going to skip my lesson today?" Domenico said, his voice a high querulous whine. "Don't you care about my progress on my instrument?" He stomped into the room and started laying out his music.

On Mascherata, students and their teachers traded places for the day—but I had completely forgotten about our lesson. Mira caught my eye and grinned. "The room's all yours," she said, and slipped out.

"Did you want to go back to the rehearsal hall?" I asked tentatively.

"No! You've wasted enough of our time already," Domenico said. "I'll take my lesson in here." He unpacked his violin and went through an elaborate show of tuning it up with great difficulty. He was going to be a difficult student, I could tell. I wished I could remember some of those cutting remarks I'd started to think up. I pulled out my own violin and tuned up myself. Domenico looked at me expectantly.

"Let's hear the concerto," I said.

Domenico launched into a piece I'd never heard before, stumbling midway through the tenth measure. "I forget how it goes," he said, and looked at me expectantly.

"Well," I said. "You don't have a recital coming up, so it's all right if you don't have it memorized yet. Why don't you get out the music?"

Domenico began to root through the papers he'd brought to my room. "I must have left it in the practice room," he said.

"You left it in the practice room?" I rolled my eyes elaborately. "Domenico, this is becoming an unhealthy pattern. Last week it was the music for the étude, and the week before, it was your bow. When are you going to learn to keep track of your belongings? Or is it just that you haven't practiced it and don't want me to know?"

"Of *course* I practiced it," he said. "It's just that I've lost the music."

"Well, you can go copy the score out again," I said. "In

fact, after our lesson is over, I think you should go copy the score *twice*. You can leave the extra copy with me, for the next time you lose it."

"So what do you want me to play?" Domenico asked.

"Let's hear you drill on your arpeggios," I said.

Domenico started an arpeggio drill; I half listened to his intentionally clumsy arpeggio, trying to think of an appropriately scathing remark, or—failing that—something to make him play next. After a moment I realized that he'd segued from the arpeggio into something else. He'd segued into the Old Way healing song.

I snatched his bow out of his hand. "Are you completely out of your mind?" I hissed.

"What's wrong, teacher? I heard someone playing that song and thought it was pretty."

"Well, you shouldn't play it," I said. "It's an Old Way song. It's wrong to play it."

"So you've never played it?" he asked.

"Never," I said.

"Then how come you recognized it, teacher?" Domenico tipped his head to look at me and gave me a half-wit grin.

"Everyone has heard them played," I said. "But no one *plays* them. It's forbidden."

"Ah," Domenico said. "I think I understand now." He took the bow back and played an arpeggio. Still playing, he said, very softly, "Teacher, some strangers came to the conservatory this week. Who are they?"

"The Fedeli," I said.

"Why are they here?"

"To make sure that we're good," I said. "So long as you're good, there's no reason to be afraid."

"I've noticed that whenever someone tells me there's nothing to be afraid of, it's usually because there is,"

Domenico said. "And they've told us an awful lot of times now not to be afraid of them." Domenico switched to a different key. "One of those strangers says he knows an old friend of mine. Did you know that I used to live in Cuore, teacher?"

"I'd heard," I said.

"You make all sorts of strange friends in Cuore." He stopped playing arpeggios and started playing scales, up and down, up and down. "You learn all sorts of strange tricks there, too. Like if you try to listen in on someone talking, and there's music in the room, you can't hear what the people in the room are saying."

"Is that so," I said. I picked up my own violin and joined him in the scales.

"Eliana," Domenico said, and the half-wit student was gone. "Be careful tonight. The Fedeli want to make an example of *somebody*. I'd really rather that it not be you."

I said nothing.

"Mira's avoidance of magery will put her under suspicion. As her roommate, you'll also be under suspicion. It wouldn't take much more than that to convince them that you have something to hide."

"What should I be careful of?" I asked.

"Don't give them that look of horror you gave me at the evening meal yesterday. In fact, it's probably best if you don't make eye contact." Domenico sighed. "I'll keep you out of trouble if I can, but my friendship with the Fedele priest in Cuore will get me only so far. So watch your step."

When the lesson was over, Domenico packed up his violin and left, complaining that my demands were unreasonable, my teaching was uninspiring, and my breath stank. As he hoisted his violin to his shoulder, he winked at me and said, "Actually, you aren't a half-bad teacher. You should consider going to work at a conservatory, once you're done here."

We ate the evening meal early that night, so that we could start the festivities as soon as the sun went down. Mira and I tied on our masks and wrapped our cloaks around us, because a bitter wind blew across the courtyard. From our room, I could hear the drums beginning—a slow, deep rhythm like the earth's heartbeat. I wondered if Flavia was one of the drummers. Down in the courtyard, Mira and I found a bonfire; people were already dancing to the drumming, their bodies jerking in unison. There were boys in the courtyard, though few actually seemed to be dancing with girls. Mostly the boys were on one side and the girls were on the other. I didn't see Celia, and I wondered if maybe she was over on the boy's side.

In the firelight, with the crowd and the masks, it was surprisingly difficult to tell who was who. Mira clasped my hand, and we joined the dancers. No one was smiling, which was strange; one week ago, most of the girls would have traded their boots for the opportunity to spend a night dancing with the boy students. Now, though, everyone's attention was focused on Galeria and Cassio—and everyone wanted to be sure to look devout. The drummers took turns so that they didn't get tired, but the dancers didn't have that luxury. Out of breath, Mira and I slumped briefly in the shadows, out of sight. "I can't keep this up much longer," I whispered.

"Yes, you can," Mira said. "We'll take breaks. You'll make it."

We rose and rejoined the dancers. Flavia was drumming now, and some other instrumentalists were joining in. I spotted Bella taking a spot beside Flavia and getting out her trumpet; as I forced my tired feet to move, I felt a surge of jealousy. Violins weren't well suited to this sort of thing, but trumpet music carried over the crowd.

Dancing to honor the Lord and the Lady was supposed to be spontaneous. The Lady asked us to pray with our bodies as well as our voices and our hearts, according to Mother Emilia; a scripted prayer was not sincere. That might be true, but sometime during the long, cold night, we began to move in a sort of unison: bounce to the right, bounce to the left. Right-bounce, left-bounce. It was all our exhausted bodies could manage. I could hear Bella playing the trumpet again—something appropriately syrupy—and then, suddenly, I felt a strange warmth surge through the crowd. For a moment, I thought I'd wandered into the bonfire's warmth without realizing it. But the wind was still as cold as ever; it was a different sort of warmth that I felt—as if I had drunk hot wine. I touched my cheek, wondering if my face was flushed. Bella's trumpet music was loud in my ears, and when I looked at her, I saw that her eyes were wide and bright behind her mask. I thought I saw light shining through her—shining out of her. And then Cassio snatched the trumpet from her hands and threw it to the ground.

Bella stumbled back a step. Behind her, Flavia's eyes were wide, but her face was rigid. Mira squeezed my hand tightly.

Galeria stepped forward. "What is your name?" she asked.

"Bella." Bella knelt to pick up her trumpet, then rose to face the Fedeli.

"Bella," Galeria said. "The Lady has spoken to me, Bella. She has shown me the darkness inside you. There is a terrible, terrible darkness there." Galeria's voice was high, almost frightened. "A darkness that threatens to spill out of you, to infect others."

Bella said nothing.

"You can still be saved, child," Galeria said. "Swear your loyalty to the Lady, and all shall be well."

For a moment, I thought that Bella was going to do it—that she would say whatever they wanted her to say. Then she threw back her shoulders. "I bear witness that the Lord and the Lady are false gods," she shouted as loud as she could. "In the name of God, and Her Son, and Her Holy Light, I pledge my life to the truth, and nothing else!" She flipped the cross out from under her robe. "I am Redentore. If I must die for the truth, then so be it."

Cassio yanked the cross from around her neck and threw it to the ground. *This is it,* I thought, and wondered if Mira would have a chance to steal a horse and get away, since Bella would be tortured and would undoubtedly name every one of us. But instead of binding Bella and taking her away, Cassio pushed Bella to her knees, then drew his knife and cut her throat.

Bella fell forward, and the students who had been dancing near the front leapt back from the gush of blood. Because of the crowd, I couldn't see Bella as she died—I couldn't see if she tried to make a cross on her breast, or if she grabbed for her throat as if she could stanch the blood. I clasped my own hands over my mouth, smothering my own cry of anguish. *This isn't happening,* I thought. *This isn't real. That isn't Bella they just murdered—not Bella.*

"In the name of the Lady," Cassio said, looking down at Bella, "I commend your soul to Her."

I shuddered. The warmth I'd felt a few moments ago was gone, as thoroughly as a doused flame.

Cassio turned back to us. "Dance," he said. "Tonight, we honor the Lord and the Lady."

I might have fallen, but Mira clasped me around the

waist. "Do as he says, or we'll all follow Bella," she whispered. "Move your feet. They don't expect enthusiasm—just obedience."

I managed to shuffle my feet to the music. Around me, others did the same. Through the crowd, I saw Celia; she had turned her face to hide from the Fedeli, and her mask was wet from her tears.

I wasn't crying, because I still couldn't believe that Bella was really dead.

At dawn, the fire had burned down, and we were sent to rest for a few hours. The Dean announced that all lessons and rehearsals were canceled for the day. Mira and I made our way back to our room, and I collapsed onto my bed.

Moments later, there was a knock at the door. It was Flavia. She hadn't taken her mask off, and her hands were shaking. "I saw them do it," she whispered. "I was standing right there. I saw Bella die."

I let Flavia sit down on my bed. "After they cut her throat, she was struggling to speak," Flavia said. "Her body convulsed, and when she saw me, her lips moved. She wanted to tell me something. But I can't read lips."

"She probably just wanted to tell us to believe," I said. I put my arm around Flavia, and she pulled off her mask, leaned her face against my shoulder, and cried.

There was another knock at the door. Giula, this time. "I can't sleep," she said. Her voice was flat and toneless; her face was expressionless. "I've been trying, and I can't sleep."

"Come lie down on my bed," Mira said. "We'll talk to you, if you need company."

"Are they going to do that to all of us?" Giula asked.

"No," I said. "They're not going to hurt you, Giula. I promise."

"How can you be so sure?" she asked.

I wasn't, really—it just seemed to me like reassuring Giula as much as I could would increase the chances that we'd get through this without her losing her nerve. "Domenico told me that he thought they wanted to make an example of someone. Bella was their example. They don't need to hurt anyone else."

Giula shook her head, sinking down on Mira's bed. "I can't believe it," she said, and I wasn't sure if she meant that she couldn't believe me, or if she meant that she couldn't believe what had happened.

There was another knock at the door, and then Celia opened the door before Mira could let her in. Her mask dangled from her limp fingers, and her eyes were swollen. She closed the door and leaned against it. "They weren't supposed to do that," she said.

Flavia's head snapped up. "Did you turn Bella in?" she hissed.

"No!" Celia said. "How could you *think* that? I haven't told them *anything*!" She sat down on my stool. "But it doesn't matter. They were supposed to give her a chance to recant—"

"They did," I said.

"They were supposed to try harder than that," Celia said. "They *wanted* to kill Bella!"

"Keep your voice down," Mira said.

"I don't understand it. Why would the Lady *want* Her servants to do that? Why?"

None of us said anything.

Celia looked at me, her red eyes meeting mine. She crossed her index fingers. "I swear that I will not go to the Fedeli to volunteer information," she said. "I will not offer to name names, and I will do everything in my power to avoid betraying you." She kissed her crossed fingers.

"Thank you," I said.

Celia nodded once, then stood up and left.

After she had gone, Flavia sat up. "You know, she has a point," she said. "If the Fedeli really thought that Bella was a heretic, why wouldn't they have questioned her?"

I looked at Mira.

Mira shook her head slowly. "I don't know."

"They must have been afraid of something," Flavia said. "I wish I knew what."

We managed to sleep a little in midmorning, Flavia beside me and Giula beside Mira. We slept right through the bell summoning us to the midday meal. Shortly after the meal ended, there was a loud rap at our door. "What?" I called, raising my head from the bed.

"The Fedeli have ordered that everyone at the school report to the courtyard," said a voice—one of the teachers, I thought. "Immediately."

We piled out of bed, pulled on our boots, and grabbed our cloaks. Bella's body had been removed from the courtyard; all that remained was a dark stain on the stones. The ashes of the bonfire had been swept away. The Dean and the teachers organized us into lines, as if we were in chapel— the boys on one side of the courtyard, the girls on the other. Mira, Flavia, Giula, Celia, and I stood together. At the end of the courtyard, Domenico stood with the Fedeli. I could see him smiling and joking, and my blood ran cold, even though I knew he wasn't really on their side.

Once people had stopped coming out of the dorms, the teachers counted us twice, to be sure that everyone was there. Someone was missing—one of the boys—and it was determined after a few minutes of looking that he was in the privy, throwing up. He was escorted down to the courtyard with the rest of us. A freezing cold wind blew through the courtyard. I hugged my cloak around me, but it didn't help. Despite the sick fear in my stomach, I was very hungry. I had eaten nothing that day.

The Fedeli approached the first of the boys. "Make a witchlight in your hand," Cassio said. Puzzled, the boy cupped his hand and summoned a feeble light. Galeria held out the symbol of the Lady, two linked circles worked in gold, and said, "Swear your loyalty to the Lady."

"I swear that I am the Lady's humble and obedient servant," the boy said, and kissed the gold circles.

They moved on to the next boy, and made the same request.

Beside me, I felt Mira go rigid, though her facial expression didn't change.

The Fedeli worked their way through the boys; no one balked at the request. Bella would have, though, I realized. Bella would have refused to swear loyalty. Even if she'd survived Mascherata, she would have been caught here, in the courtyard.

They made their way up and down each line of girls. The wind blew through the courtyard, whistling a little against the stones; I heard a door blow shut somewhere.

To my left, they had reached Celia. "Make a witchlight in your hand," Cassio said. Celia made a light, her eyes staring straight ahead, past Cassio's shoulder. "Swear your loyalty to the Lady."

Celia took the symbol in her hand. "I swear that I am the Lady's humble and obedient servant," she said tonelessly, and kissed the circles.

Flavia. "Make a witchlight in your hand," Cassio said. Flavia made a witchlight, and swore loyalty to the Lady.

Now it was my turn. "Make a witchlight in your hand," Cassio said. I made a witchlight. "Swear your loyalty to the Lady."

I took the circles. They were warm from all the hands

that had held them, all the lips that had touched them. "I swear that I am the Lady's humble and obedient servant," I said. My voice rang oddly in my ears, and I felt a sudden surge of shame that I didn't have Bella's courage—even though I didn't really believe in her god, either. I kissed the circles.

Mira. "Make a witchlight in your hand," they said.

Mira raised her right hand in front of her. Her expression never changing, she summoned a tiny light. Beside her, I could feel a sudden warmth radiate from her body.

"Swear your loyalty to the Lady," they said.

Mira dispelled the light, swore her loyalty, and kissed the circles.

Giula. "Make a witchlight in your hand," they said.

Giula held out one trembling hand. She closed her eyes, cupping her hand slightly. "I—" she said, and stopped. She squeezed her eyes tighter. No light formed in Giula's hand; I could see Galeria's eyes flicker.

"I can't do it!" Giula cried. "I want to, but I can't! You have to believe me!" She fell to her knees, grasping Galeria's sleeve and kissing the symbol of the Lady embroidered to the side. "I swear that I am the Lady's servant," she sobbed. "I swear it! I'm loyal!"

Galeria pulled her sleeve away from Giula. "Make a witchlight, daughter," she said. "Show that you are unafraid to use the gifts that the Lady has given us."

Giula cupped her hands together, weeping. "Sweet and gentle Lady," she choked out, but no light formed.

Domenico threaded his way through the crowd and grasped Cassio's arm. "Father Cassio," he said. "Giula is my student. Really—she's not very bright, and panics easily under pressure. I can assure you that she uses magery on a regular basis—I've seen her use witchlight."

Cassio patted Giula on the shoulder; his voice became a

comforting croon. "The Lady accepts your profession of loyalty," he said. "Don't be afraid."

Cassio and Galeria moved on, leaving Giula still sobbing on her knees. No one else failed—or refused—to summon witchlight. When every student at the conservatory had proved that they were not Redentori—or at least that they didn't have enough faith to die for it—we were herded into the chapel for another prayer service. I sat down in the pew, lightheaded from fear and hunger. Giula still shook with occasional hiccuping sobs; Mira's cheeks burned with a strange heat, as if the witchlight she'd summoned had kindled a fire inside her.

After opening prayers, Cassio preached a sermon about Old Way apostates. I might have learned a lot about what Bella had believed if I'd been able to pay attention. Instead, despite the danger, I kept almost dozing off. I had stayed up all night and slept only fitfully that morning, and I was exhausted. My mind kept running through the bedtime prayer Giula had started to recite when she hadn't been able to summon the witchlight.

Sweet and gentle Lady
Hear my little prayer
Hold me in your arms tonight
I know that you are there.
Sweet and gentle Lady . . .

My hands were ice cold, and I clasped them between my knees, trying to listen to Cassio. He was talking about the Redentori sexual practices—apparently, they believed in picking their own marital partners, rather than letting the Lady pick for them. This was yet another way that they went against the Lady's will and rejected Her love. I thought that was kind of funny; I mean, normally—in my village—

young men and women would make their choice, then keep trying until the Lady blessed their union. It wasn't like anyone *really* let the Lady pick for them. I tried to imagine a village where the young women slept with each young man in turn, to see whom the Lady liked best.

When Cassio had finished, Galeria led us in a long, long prayer. For the death of heretics and blasphemers, for the protection of believers, for the peace of Bella's soul. After each line, we repeated, "So may it be." I stopped listening after a while; I didn't want to hear anymore what I was praying for.

Then, to my surprise, Domenico stood up to speak. "After investigation, the Fedeli have determined that Bella was seduced into apostasy by a servant at the conservatory named Giorgi," he said. "Unfortunately, Giorgi fled sometime last night; rest assured, however, that he will be found and brought to justice. You all know Giorgi, so it may come as a surprise to you that he was an apostate. If Giorgi ever attempted to sway any of the rest of you to apostasy, please know that you are welcome to submit a deposition with Father Cassio and Mother Galeria; this will be used as evidence against him when he is caught."

As soon as Domenico said that Giorgi had fled, relief swept through me like a warm wind. While a group of six conservatory girls would have stuck out like a six-toed foot in the area around Bascio, Giorgi would be able to disappear. There was nothing about him that was so unusual that the Fedeli would be able to identify him from a description. If they blamed Giorgi, but couldn't *find* Giorgi, then the rest of us were—probably—safe.

"If you have anything to tell Father Cassio or Mother Galeria, please come by my quarters tonight," Domenico said. "They will be leaving early tomorrow morning."

Domenico sat down, and after a final prayer, the service

ended. As we filed out, a bell rang—it was time for the evening meal.

Bella's space at the table was painfully empty. Flavia and Celia sat a little closer together, trying to make it less obvious. I was too hungry to think about much of anything other than food. Knowing that the Fedeli were leaving had made the mood almost festive; the conversation around us was loud and boisterous, if still a little nervous. The soup had meat in it—technically, this was a festival meal, but I suspected they hadn't planned to give us meat until the Fedeli showed up. I was surprised that I was able to get it down.

After the evening meal, I took my violin and a candle to go practice. I had barely had time even to tune my instrument in the last few days, and I ached to spend some time playing. I was fairly certain that I didn't need to convince Celia not to turn us all in, nor to convince Giula that she wasn't going to die.

Besides, I wanted to mourn Bella alone.

As I closed the door of my practice room, I wished that I had the courage to play the Old Way funeral music. That was what Bella would have wanted—a Redentore funeral, or the closest thing to it that I could give her. With the Fedeli still at the conservatory, though, I didn't dare. Instead, I played some music that Bella had liked—first an achingly sad violin piece that I'd played in recital a few years earlier, then the tune of her favorite trumpet serenade. "Rachamin, Arka," I whispered when I was done, very quietly, my eyes closed. "Rachamin, Gèsu."

I remembered Bella's fascination with the Wicked Stepmother song and plucked the tune gently on my violin.

I've come to wed your father but I want to make you mine.

If you'll take me as your mother, you will find my
     faults are few.
I've brought a gift of honey, bright as sun and sweet
     as wine.
And as pure as all the love I hold inside my heart for
     you.

The door to my practice room slammed open, and I
stared into Galeria's furious face.

"How dare you!" she shouted.

For some reason, the first thing that came into my head
was a terrible fear that she would throw my violin to the
ground, as Cassio had thrown Bella's trumpet. "Please
don't break my violin," I said, backing up. "Just let me put
it down, *please.*" All I could think was, *the Lady told them
that Bella was an apostate, and now she's told them that I
am, too,* but I was too busy defending my violin to say
anything incriminating.

"Where did you learn that song?" Galeria demanded.

It took me a moment to remember that I hadn't been
playing an Old Way song—I'd been playing the song about
the poisoned honey. "It was all over the conservatory a
few months ago," I said. "I don't remember whom I first
heard it from." Celia, I remembered a moment later. "We
thought that the 'poisoned honey' referred to a heresy—
something that looked sweet, but would rot you from the
inside. Some people thought that the Fedeli wrote the
song."

The fury on Galeria's face had eased, and now she gave
me what was doubtless intended as a reassuring smile.
"No, daughter," she said. "Your own innocence is clear,
but that song doesn't do justice to you. It was written
by apostates, to turn people against the true faith. The

Redentori believe that the Lady's gift of magic is evil—like poisoned honey. That's what the song is about."

"I'm sorry," I said. "I'll never sing it again."

"The Lady understands that you played it without malice," Galeria said. She stepped forward, her eyes searching mine. I forced myself to meet her gaze.

"I can see that you're afraid of me," Galeria said.

I didn't dare deny it. "Bella was a friend of mine," I said.

"I see," Galeria said. "Kneel, daughter."

I knelt at her feet, and she clasped my head in her hands. Then she raised my chin so that I was looking up at her face, and her eyes were full of tears. " 'Innocence doesn't need to hide,' " she quoted. "Daughter, the Lady assures me that your heart is as pure as Bella's was black. Be at peace, and remember that the Lady loves you." She raised me to my feet and left, closing the practice room door behind her.

I discovered that my hands were shaking too hard to play anymore tonight. I waited long enough to feel sure that she was gone, then packed up my violin and headed back to my room.

When I reached it, Mira wasn't there. She might have been practicing, as I'd been, but I was struck with the sudden fear that she had run away from the conservatory. Her cloak was gone, and her violin. I knelt to look under her bed for personal belongings—there was a box under her bed, like the one where I kept letters from my parents. She wouldn't leave without her letters, I thought.

Still, I couldn't shake my fear that she'd vanished like Giorgi. Grabbing my cloak again, I went back out to the practice hall, but the halls were quiet. I tried the north practice hall next, crossing the courtyard and finding my way to the crumbling building beyond the chapel. I didn't see the flicker of candlelight, but it occurred to me that Mira might have feared that the Fedeli would see a candle and grow suspicious. I opened the door and stared into the cold darkness. "Mira?" I said.

There was no reply, but as my eyes adjusted to the darkness, I could see a shape huddled on the floor.

"Mira?" I said again, and knelt beside her. It was Mira; I took her hand. I had expected her hand to be cold from the wind and the damp stone floor she lay on, but it was so hot I wondered if she was running a fever. I made a witch-light to see her face, and she cried out as if I'd burned her.

"Put it away," she said, and I flicked away the light.

"Mira, do you need help getting back to our room?" I asked.

"No," she said. "I need to stay here."

"I'll stay with you, then," I said. I lay down on the floor beside Mira, wrapped in my cloak. Heat radiated from Mira's body like a fire.

Mira was silent as I arranged myself beside her. Then— "Do you know why I left Cuore?" she asked.

"So that you could play the forbidden music?" I said.

She shook her head. "That's why I came *here,* not why I left Cuore."

"Why, then?" I asked.

"My grandmother died," she said. "She was the person who'd taught me to play the violin. My parents sent her violin to me in Cuore, along with a letter. And that was when I knew I had to leave."

"Was she executed by the Fedeli?" I asked.

"No," Mira said. "She lived in Verdia, like my parents. She died from the famine."

"I'm sorry," I said.

"It wasn't your fault," she said. "It was my fault."

I didn't know how to answer that—how could the famine be her fault? So I touched her hot arm with my hand and said, "I was afraid you had run away."

"You thought I'd lose my nerve now?" she asked. "After all this? If I were going to leave, I should have gone when we first saw that they'd come."

"Galeria heard me playing the poisoned honey song," I said. "She was furious. She told me that heretics wrote it to slander the Lady."

"But she let you go?"

"I told her that we'd thought the poisoned honey referred to a heresy. She believed me." I laughed bitterly. "She made me kneel, and then she told me that the Lady had told her that I was pure, just as the Lady told her that Bella was an apostate."

"They're liars," Mira said. "The Lady doesn't talk to Her followers." She rolled away from me and coughed. The heat from her body was fading.

"Mira—"

"You should leave me alone," Mira said. "I don't deserve your loyalty." She pulled herself to her knees and retched.

When she had finished, I drew her away from the pool of vomit, and covered her with her cloak. "Mira, you're my friend. I'll stay with you."

Mira was silent for a while; then she retched again. Her body began to shake. The warmth she had radiated before was gone. "I can't do this again," she whispered.

I wrapped my arms around her, as I had in bed, and said nothing. I could hear her weeping; then her body stiffened against my arms, and I realized that she was having a convulsion, as she had when she first arrived. I tried to hold her, but the convulsion wrenched her out of my grasp. When the convulsion ended, she slipped into unconsciousness, and I pulled her into my arms again.

"My fault," she muttered suddenly a while later.

"No," I said, and stroked her hair. "It's not your fault."

"I could have stopped them," she said. "The Fedeli. I could have stopped them."

"You would have been one against all of them—Galeria, Cassio, all their guards," I said. "There wasn't anything any of us could have done."

"No," Mira said. "When he drew the knife. I should have—" She broke off. "I can't tell you," she said. "You shouldn't know."

I clasped her tightly. "It wasn't your fault."

"I can't do this again," she said. "I won't be able to let another friend die."

"The Fedeli leave at dawn," I said. "They won't come back."

Mira fell silent, then began to weep again. I pressed my hand against her wet cheek, wiping her tears away. "Mira," I said.

"Don't say it," she said. "Whatever it was you were going to say, just don't say it."

So I waited until she was asleep again. The moon was up, and shining through the cracks in the walls enough that I could just see Mira's face when I sat up. The warm flush had drained out of her face, leaving her as pale as polished bones. I touched her cold forehead with my lips; she didn't wake.

"I know you don't want me to bind myself to you, Mira," I whispered. "But even if you don't hear me, I want to tell you that I'm not going to leave you." I crossed my forefingers. "Whatever you fear, I will face it with you. Whether we face Maledori or Fedeli, I'll stand beside you. If it's in my power, I'll protect you." I kissed my fingers, sealing the oath. Mira's eyes never flickered.

"I love you, Mira," I whispered.

I slept, toward the end of the night, my body tucked around Mira's. I dreamed all night of the soldier I'd seen in the old practice hall before, and of Mira's eyes, watching me across a vast chasm filled with fire.

At dawn, I peered out through a crack in the wall to see the Fedeli leaving. Once I was certain that they were gone, I went to stand in the courtyard, where Bella had died. It was the earliest dawn, and the courtyard was empty. As I started back toward the old practice hall, to see if Mira would wake for breakfast, something caught my eye.

Between two paving-stones, stained with blood, was a small wooden cross on a broken cord. Bella's cross. I looked around quickly to see if anyone was watching, but the Fedeli had gone and the courtyard, in the cold dawn, was empty. I snatched it up and slipped it into the sleeve of my robe. *Bella would have wanted me to have it,* I thought, then went to wake Mira.

CHAPTER FIVE

Look out of your window and wonder at the world—
God's creation! Do not forsake it, or you
forsake the glory of God.
—The Journey of Gèsu, chapter 5, verse 8.

The rest of the winter passed too quietly. No one spoke of the Fedeli, and no one openly said Bella's name. As the first heavy rainstorm turned the roads to impassable mud, Mira fidgeted and paced until I set aside my music and pulled her down to sit beside me. "The Fedeli can't come back," I said. "No one can travel in this."

"But I can't leave, either," Mira said.

"Do you want to leave so badly?" I asked. My hand, clasping Mira's, trembled slightly.

"I came here to play the forbidden music," she said, dropping her voice even though we were alone. "To teach it. But after what happened . . ." She turned her face away from me.

"Where would you go, if you left?" I asked.

"I don't know," she said. "Farther south, maybe. Back to my home village."

"I thought you wanted to become a minstrel. That's what you said, once."

Mira glanced up at me with a faint smile. "Want to try

to work out a minstrel style on the violin with me? Sing and play at the same time?"

"I can't sing," I said.

She rolled her eyes. "It's really not as hard as Celia makes it out to be."

"I know what a voice should sound like," I said. "My voice doesn't sound like that."

"Stand up," Mira said, hopping off the bed. I stood, and she touched my back lightly. "Stand up straight." I straightened. "Now, pretend I haven't heard 'The Wicked Stepmother'—and you're the only person who can sing me the words." She sat back down on the bed and looked at me expectantly.

I started to say that I really didn't have a good singing voice—but Mira just waited, still smiling, so I took a deep breath and started the song.

I've come to wed your father but I want to make you
     mine.
If you'll take me as your mother, you will find my
     faults are few.
I've brought a gift of honey, bright as sun and sweet
     as wine.
And as pure as all the love I hold inside my heart for
     you.

When I was done, my face was hot, and I stared down at the floor. "I don't know why you say you can't sing," Mira said. I looked up, surprised, and she met my gaze with a smile that struck me like an arrow. "You have a lovely voice. All you need is to be able to accompany yourself with the violin."

The violin worked reasonably well for a minstrel performance, as it turned out. We couldn't tuck our chins down while singing, of course, and it took some practice, but we were able to work out a way to play and sing at the same time. The violin was louder than a lute, and two violins sounded really good together. Mira and I started digging up old folk songs to play together—it wasn't Old Way music, so we couldn't get in trouble for it, but at least it was something *different* and a little strange. And the project seemed to dispel Mira's restlessness, just a bit.

During the worst of the rains, we celebrated the birthday of Aelius, brother of Gaius. Gaius was the prophet who brought the Lady's Gift of magery to the rest of us; Aelius was not a prophet, but he was honored by musicians because he had started to teach musicians to play in ensembles, and had created the Central Conservatory in Cuore. The legend said that he also created the first violin, though in the library I'd seen drawings of similar instruments that had predated Aelius. His birthday was not a sacred day, so we didn't have to go to the chapel; instead, we had the day off from lessons and classes and threw a party in the meal hall.

Bella had always loved celebrating Aelius's birthday. At the party, we played games—trying to name ensemble pieces from a line of harmony, or racing to play a tune named by the musical archivist. Bella had a superb memory and always won every game until the teachers disqualified her to give someone else a chance. This year, nobody felt much like playing anything.

When the rains stopped and the roads hardened again, the mail came. People scrutinized their letters in silence and compared notes privately later. Several villages had had visits from the Fedeli, and others, like Flavia's family, had seen soldiers—hundreds of soldiers, marching south. None had seen Circle detachments. Everyone wondered the same thing—if we're going to war with Vesuvia again, where are the mages? How can the army fight without magefire?

And why had the Fedeli come? They were driving out the Maledori that had caused the famine, some letters said. There was nothing to fear. Other letters were fearful or angry. There had been a burning, in one village, or so I heard.

The Fedeli had not come to Doratura, my home village, nor had my family heard these rumors. Instead, my mother wrote about a new ritual they did each week to honor the Lady and ensure the fertility of the land. Singing, with drums and dancing. *This is an older way to honor the Lady,* she wrote. *Sometimes it's the older ways that are the best.* I shuddered, and added to my letter back: *Be careful, all of you. The Fedeli came to the conservatory, and we found that they take a dim view of certain "older ways."*

At Equinox, we would celebrate Ritorno, the Lord's return from His battle with the Maledori. Chastened by the visit from the Fedeli, the conservatory was planning an extensive and elaborate observance. I helped halfheartedly with the preparations, thinking of home—they would be planting the early crops, onions and wheat and beans. They'd celebrate Ritorno with a bonfire in the piazza, and rites to ask the Lady to bless the fields and the planting. On our first beautiful day, the week before the Equinox, I slung my violin over my shoulder—so that I could pretend to myself that I was going to practice—and made my way to the conservatory wall to watch the festival preparations in Bascio. I sat down on the wall and swung my legs to dangle into forbidden territory.

Two—no, three summers earlier, Bella and I slipped out of the conservatory one night on a dare. *Bring us a pebble from the Bascio piazza.* It had been Celia's idea. Bella and I had jumped over the wall and crept down the hill; the moon had been full, and we'd jumped at every noise, convinced that someone from the conservatory had seen us. We each grabbed a smooth pebble, white in the moonlight, and ran back to the conservatory, smothering our giggles.

Pushing down the grief that rose up into my throat, I stared down at a stray goat that was winding its way around the cottages of Bascio, filching stray vegetables. Someone spotted it and started beating it with a stick, shouting words I could almost catch. I wondered how Doratura would look from this perspective. Probably much the same.

I tried to remember when I had last been down to Bascio. Seven months ago, I decided, shortly before Mira arrived—for my new boots.

I opened my violin case, but couldn't bring myself to play. Tucked in with the extra gut and the rosin, though, was a tiny clay bird whistle, which my brother Donato had made for me while we were walking to the conservatory. He'd tried to make it so that I could use it to tune my violin, and it hadn't really worked, but it had a pure sweet sound, and I blew through it gently to pick out the tune to the song about the poisoned honey.

I heard a twig snap and turned around; Mira had crept up behind me. She also had her violin slung over her shoulder. I started to swing my legs back to the legal side of the wall, and she laughed. "Don't get up on my account," she said, and sat down beside me. She gestured to the whistle. "You've been hiding one of your talents."

"Not really," I said. "A bird whistle isn't exactly a flute. My brother Donato made this for me."

"Can I see?" Mira asked. I handed it to her, and she blew on it, a little too hard; the sound was harsh. She laughed and handed it back. "Well, it takes *some* sort of talent, anyway."

"Just a little practice," I said, and put it away. I would

make a whistle for Mira, I decided; not clay, that would be too hard to get on the conservatory grounds. I'd carve a wooden whistle for her. We looked down at Bascio for a few minutes. The troublesome goat had been corralled and tethered to a post, where it had started to chew on its rope again.

"Are you homesick today?" Mira asked.

"No," I said.

"Letters make a lot of people homesick," she said.

"I'm feeling restless," I admitted. "I wish I were graduating this spring, instead of next spring—I'm ready to get out of here."

"Where do you want to go?"

"Today? Anywhere that *isn't* the Verdiano Rural Conservatory."

Mira flashed me a smile. "We should go on a trip," she said. "Right now."

"Where? Bascio?"

"No, farther than that. We should run away. You've got your violin with you, I've got mine. What more do we need? We could just jump over the wall and go." She grinned broadly. "What do you say?"

"Keep talking. You might convince me."

"We could play at taverns," she said, "the two of us together. Those songs we've been learning—we sound good."

"I don't know," I said. "Minstrel life is hard. Never knowing if we'd sleep in a bed or under a bush—never knowing if we'd eat or go hungry—"

"We'd eat," she said. "We'd sleep at the inns where we played. Think, Eliana! Freedom. Adventure. We could see the whole *world* together." She clasped my hand and fell silent, looking into my eyes, and I realized that she wasn't joking.

My heart started knocking in my ears as I returned her

stare. I realized that I was holding my breath. The warmth of her hand felt like it was scorching mine; my grip tightened. *Leave the conservatory?* I thought. It was a crazy idea. But—

There was a crash from behind us and we both whirled, leaping to our feet. It was Giula, looking sheepish. "Sorry," she said. "Mira, your teacher sent me looking for you. You're late for your lesson."

Mira smacked herself on the forehead. "I can't believe I did that." She turned and whispered in my ear, "Think about it." Giula gave me an apologetic look and followed Mira back up the hill.

I broke a small branch from one of the trees that grew along the wall, and started carving a whistle for Mira, thinking about her offer as I let the sun soak into my skin. What if she truly was planning to leave? *I'd go with her,* I thought. *If I had to.* But I preferred to stay, as long as I could persuade Mira to stay with me; I wanted to finish my last year at the conservatory, audition for ensembles, and see how I did. It occurred to me that Mira had said repeatedly that she didn't ever want to go back to Cuore, and of course I'd be auditioning for ensembles there . . . Well, there was no guarantee that I would get into *any* ensemble, let alone one of the ensembles in Cuore. I'd worry about it if it happened.

I blew into the whistle to test it, and was pleasantly surprised by the sweet, clear note. Mira would like it, I thought. *I would go anywhere, if it meant being with Mira. Or rather, if the alternative meant* not *being with Mira.* I slipped the whistle into my violin case and started walking back to the room we shared.

Mira wasn't there, so I left the whistle under her pillow, then leaned out the window to stare up again at the clear blue sky. *I need to get out,* I thought, *just for a day. Maybe*

I can convince the Dean I need new boots. No, a new cloak. I fingered the fabric thoughtfully.

The next day, giddy with my temporary freedom, I managed to keep myself from skipping down the road from the conservatory to the village. The Dean had looked over my shabby cloak and given me coin and permission to go get myself a new one. The cloak I wore had been cut with a generous hem that could be let out as I grew, but no one had known I'd grow two inches taller than most men. It was too short for me, and wearing badly at the edges. I slipped a bit in the mud as I reached the village; it had rained the night before, leaving the stones of the Bascio piazza glittering in the sunshine.

The village seamstress was a tiny, aged widow named Marietta; she lived alone in a cottage filled with bolts of gray cloth. Outside her cottage, rose bushes were coming back to life; in the summer, the walls of her cottage were covered with a cloak of red flowers. "How old are you now, dear?" Marietta asked me as she climbed up onto a chair to measure the breadth of my shoulders. "Just hold the measure there, now, on your shoulder," she added, and let the tape fall, climbing off the chair to check my height.

"I'm sixteen years old," I said.

"So almost ready for an orchestra." She clucked her tongue. "Well, you'll be wanting another new cloak soon enough, then. It's too bad I can't give you something a bit more stylish now."

"Can I see your other fabrics?" I asked.

Marietta smiled. "Surely. There's no harm in looking, is there?"

The teachers, and the students leaving to play in orchestras, bought their clothes from this woman as well, and in her back room she had a fine selection of dyed wool flannel. "I think this one is my favorite," I said, fingering a swatch of dark red.

Marietta clucked her tongue again. " 'Tisn't quite the color for you, dear; you'd do better in a dark blue. Still, not too bad." She held it up. "Not bad at all; I'd have thought you too pale for the red, but you'd carry it off, anyway." She sighed and put it away. "Next year, yes? In the meantime . . . I think I actually have a cloak on hand that might fit you. Made it for a boy who got himself into trouble and had to leave the conservatory, and I was left with the stock." She fetched it from her back room. "Here now, try that on."

Much to my disappointment, the cloak fit perfectly. "Thank you," I said.

Marietta saw my wistfulness, and gave me a smile. "Now then, you'll be off on your own soon enough, won't you? What's an extra trip to Bascio when you'll have the world?" I tried to smile back. She patted my hand and said, "Just one more moment."

She vanished into the back room again and returned with a strip of the dark red cloth. "Since I had the cloak anyway, I'll give you a discount," she said, "and with the difference you can pay for this. It's just a scrap, but it's big enough for a scarf, or even a sash." I made a token protest, but she insisted. "Just don't let that Dean of yours see it, and if he does, don't tell him where you got it!" I promised, and she folded it neatly and tucked it inside the cloak.

Despite being denied a second trip to the village, I was in a fair mood when I returned. Mira would like the scarf, I was certain, so I headed back to our room, whistling one of the folk songs we'd been learning. I swung open the door.

Witchlight flared, blindingly bright. I leapt back, but

hands seized my arms and jerked me inside. The door slammed shut behind me. I blinked in the dazzling light, staring into the rigid face of the man who had grabbed my arms. He wore the uniform of the Circle Guard. Beyond him, I could see four more men in the same uniform, seated on the beds, crossbows leveled.

At the very end of my bed sat an older man in a scarlet robe, with chill yellow eyes. He rose, his lips tight, his head tilted back to stare down at me even though I was taller than he was. "It's the roommate," he said, and sat back down. "Bring her here." He indicated the floor directly in front of him.

"Sit," the guard said, shoving me toward the man in scarlet. "And be silent."

My knees shaking, I sank to the floor. I could hear my heart pounding. With a flick, the man in scarlet dispelled the witchlight. We waited, in silence, staring at the door in the fading daylight.

Mira. They had to be here for Mira. *Why?* My first thought was that somehow, they'd found out about Mira teaching the Old music—but these men were not Fedeli. I could hear the man in scarlet behind me—his breathing was calm and even, like this was something he did every day. Who was he, with his white-hot witchlight? He wore no uniform. Was he a mage from the Circle, all the way down here? What could Mira have possibly done that would require the *Circle* to come for her? The man shifted slightly; I heard the rustle of movement. If I had ever met someone who could be a Maledore in the guise of a mortal, he was it. I had only looked at him for an instant, but his yellow eyes were burned into my mind. I shuddered, and felt his hand close briefly over my shoulder like a claw, ensuring that I wouldn't move again. *Maybe this is a dream,*

I thought, but the growing ache in my legs from sitting still assured me that I wasn't sleeping.

Time passed; the room went from dim to dark as the last of the light faded. I tried to guess the passage of time from the noises outside. It must be almost time for the evening meal; Mira would be back soon.

We heard footsteps approaching the door. I felt a gloved hand cup my throat. My stomach lurched with the desire to escape the touch of his hand, but I bit my lip and remained still. "Be silent," the man in scarlet whispered. I could hear the soldiers tense, then rise. The door started to swing open.

"RUN!" I screamed to Mira, and the man clapped his hand over my mouth.

"That was very stupid," he said into my ear—but Mira still stood in the doorway, in the blinding flare of witchlight. She stepped inside, and the door swung closed to trap her. The man released me and shoved me aside to stand up. "Hello, Miriamne," he said.

Mira leaned back against the door, eyeing the man with defiance and disgust. "Hello, Liemo," she said.

There was a long pause. Mira gently set her violin down on the floor. "You certainly brought enough guards. Were you planning to have them drag me bodily back to Cuore?"

"Miriamne—"

"Mira," she snapped.

The man winced. "I've come to tell you that you can come back."

"Really."

"Miriamne, we *understand*. You were under strain, ten times over—just being the youngest full member of the Circle in ten generations would have been enough. The death of your grandmother—we understand why you left.

Why you felt you had to stay away, *hide* from us here. But you can come back, Miriamne—your chair is waiting for you."

"Mira," she said. "My name is *Mira,* and I will never sit in the Circle again." My head was spinning. *Mira? Circle? The girl who couldn't—wouldn't—even summon witchlight?* I stared at her; her eyes were locked on Liemo's. My mouth had gone dry. Would she have ever told me? I felt like I should feel betrayed—or horrified—or frightened, but all I could think was that I wished we'd run away the other afternoon, when she suggested it.

"Don't be hasty," Liemo said. "I know you need time to think—"

"I made my decision before I left Cuore."

Liemo's voice softened. "Miriamne . . . Mira. Don't you miss magery?" With a flick of his wrist, his witchlight flared brighter, danced in his hand like flames in a wind. I could see Mira flinch. "The energy drawn by the full Circle with *you* as the focus . . ." His voice dropped to a whisper. "Miriamne, don't you miss it?" He held out his hand, as if offering her the globe of light.

When Mira spoke, her voice was a whisper and her face was lowered. "More than you could imagine. I think of it every day—every time I see witchlight, or see someone start a fire. I remember the elation—the rush of power flying through my body. I miss it more than you could imagine—" Her breath caught. "That is why I don't summon witchlight. That is why I will *never* go back." I saw her straighten her shoulders and look Liemo in the eyes. "Liemo. We can talk all night, but I will not change my mind."

"Perhaps." Liemo's voice was almost too soft to hear. "You are one of the strongest, Mira. One of the best."

Silence.

"We need you."

Mira's eyes widened. "I don't care how much you think you need me. *I would burn Cuore to the ground myself before I'd help to kill more of the land!* You know we're the cause of the famine. You *know* it, even as you mouth the lie that the Vesuviano army sowed our land with salt. Our magefire drained the Verdiani borderlands of every drop of energy they had. *We* killed the land. *We* caused the famine. It's *our* fault, Liemo."

I sucked in my breath. *Magery* caused the famine? The Circle—our protectors—had killed us? Killed Bella's sister? I felt a pain in my chest like a knife, and I stared at Mira with blinding anger—but whether it was at the Circle for what they'd done, or at Mira for keeping their secret from me, I wasn't sure.

"I'm sorry about your grandmother . . ." Liemo looked down, almost ashamed. Almost.

Mira shook her head. "I don't care if you're sorry. I won't share magery with you again, Liemo. I would rather die."

There was silence. Then Liemo spoke, very softly.

"I am sorry, Miriamne. But we truly do need you."

The room went dark. Hands seized my arms; someone stuffed a cloth into my mouth to stifle my scream. Light flared again. I was dragged up against the door. There was horror in Mira's eyes as she struggled against the soldiers who now held her fast. I tried desperately—uselessly—to break free, or to spit out the gag.

The last soldier was cocking his crossbow.

"I am sorry, my dear," Liemo said to me. "But you did try to cry out, when I had told you not to." He turned to Mira. "It would be immoral, of course, to kill an innocent simply to test your resolve." He nodded toward the soldiers holding me. "Violinist? Left hand, I think."

I screamed; the sound caught in the gag. I tried again to

tear free. One soldier held me against the door; the other held my left arm, palm out, flat against the wall.

"You can stop this at any time, Mira. I will give you a few moments to think about it."

I tried again to tear free. *No, not my hand, not my hand—*

"Bowman, fire."

I heard the snap of the bowstring and tried to brace— my eyes followed the blur of the bolt—

—and, in a flash, it was gone.

Mira's hands were outstretched as if she were praying to the Lady, and there was a wild, terrifying ecstasy on her face. She stood a moment more, frozen in silence. Then she fell limp to the floor. The soldiers released me, and my own knees gave way. I tore the gag out of my mouth.

"Come, Miriamne," I heard Liemo say. "We're going."

"No," I said. I tried to stand, bracing myself against the wall, but my legs were still shaking too hard. My mouth was almost too dry to speak. "Mira, don't go with him!"

Mira held one hand over her eyes, and her shoulders were shaking. She didn't answer.

I couldn't take her arm, so I grabbed the edge of her robe. "Mira, you don't have to go with him!" Liemo gestured, and one of the guards shoved me away from her. "Mira! Look at me! *Please,* Mira!" Liemo was lifting her to her feet; she straightened slightly.

"You see, Miriamne?" Liemo murmured. "You are one of us, after all." He smiled at me, a patronizing, triumphant smile that knotted my stomach. He had an extra cloak, made of a fine black wool, which he flung over her shoulders, covering the drab gray robe. "Let's go."

As the last of the soldiers left my room, I found that my legs would hold me again and I stumbled to my feet. The hallway outside was empty. Liemo was striding down the stairs, Mira following in his wake; I stumbled down behind them.

The other girls from the dormitory were clustered at the bottom of the stairs, just inside the door, a teacher standing watch over them. Someone must have told the Dean to keep people out of the way. "What's happening?" Giula asked. "Who are they? Where are they taking Mira?"

I shook my head. Seeing how hard I was shaking, Giula offered me her shoulder for support as I stumbled after them. The teacher reached to stop us, but I brushed him away, and the rest of the students followed me silently as I ran out the door.

"Mira!" I shouted again. "Mira, *don't leave.*"

"I don't understand," Giula said, flushed with frustration and worry. "Who are they?"

"The Circle," I said. "Mira is a member of the Circle."

"What? That's impossible, she's not a mage, she doesn't even summon witchlight."

"*Doesn't* summon witchlight. Not *can't. Won't.*"

"I don't understand," Giula wailed again, almost losing her own footing as I stumbled. Someone steadied me from behind. I realized that people were spilling out of the buildings—students, then teachers, staring bewildered at Mira and the guards.

Eight black horses pawed the ground in the courtyard. Liemo had brought an extra for Mira. *Miriamne.* He had said the name like a curse, like a threat. They were mounting the horses. *"Mira!"* I cried out.

This time, she met my eyes, looking down from her horse. Her face was anguished, choked with despair, drowning, and I reached out the last way I knew how.

"*Rachamin, Arka,*" I sang—the words to the healing song. "*Rachamin, Gèsu.*"

Giula, next to me, clasped my hand. "*Refuya, Arka.*"

she sang. *"Refuya, Gèsu."* Behind us, Flavia took up the song, as well. Then someone clasped my other hand—Celia. Looking straight at Mira, she took a deep breath and joined the song.

In the hush of the crowd, the courtyard rang with the voices; our sharp rhythm echoed off the walls. Mira closed her eyes, and for a moment she almost seemed comforted. Liemo started and stared at us, with an expression almost like fear in his eyes. Then he took the bridle of Mira's horse and spurred his horse to a gallop, fleeing us, fleeing the school. The soldiers wheeled and followed. Slowly, our singing died.

My knees gave way again, and I fell to the stones of the courtyard.

PART TWO

Let Me Be the First to Salute You

CHAPTER SIX

If you would journey with me, turn your back on your home, on your comforts, on all that you know. Then follow me.
—The Journey of Gèsu, chapter 5, verse 17.

I'm leaving," I said.

Domenico looked at my travel sack and the red wool knotted as a belt around my waist. "You aren't thinking of going after her, are you?"

"No," I said. "I want to go home."

"I know you've always hoped to play in Cuore," Domenico said. "Don't think that you wouldn't have other options."

I shrugged. "As a scholarship student, I am supported by the Circle." I paused for a moment to steady my voice. "I don't want their money. And—" I paused again. "I want to tell my family what caused the famine."

Domenico nodded slowly. "Be careful," he said. "There were people executed last fall in Cuore for their heresy against the Lady's Gift."

I nodded and started to leave.

"Wait," Domenico said. He took a small leather pouch out of his desk drawer and dropped it into my hand; it had a meager but solid weight. I started to refuse, but he closed my hand over it. "You'll need this to get home," he said. "You'd have gotten a stipend next year, anyway."

"Thank you," I said.

"Tuck it well out of sight when you pass through cities," Domenico said.

"I will," I said. I started to leave again, then turned back. "Did you know?" I asked.

"No," Domenico said. "We all knew that Mira had never been a seminarian, but we also knew that she paid in coin. No one wanted to look too closely." He rubbed his forehead with the heel of his hand. "Do you think we should have tried to find out?"

I felt the tears I'd been holding back rise to my eyes. "No," I whispered. "I just think she should have hidden better."

Domenico turned his face away. I started again for the door, but Domenico reached out and pulled me quickly into a rough hug. He whispered something in the Old Tongue, and then let me go. "Be careful, Eliana," he said. "I don't want anything bad to happen to you."

I left Domenico's study before he could make me cry again.

An hour later, I had food and a blanket; my spare robe was tucked into my sack, along with the letters from my family and a few other personal things, and my violin was slung across my shoulder. I took one other thing—the box of Mira's letters. I told myself that I had to take them so that no one else would find them. Her violin was gone. I checked under Mira's pillow; the whistle was gone, too.

It was almost noon when I shouldered my pack and turned toward the gate. The road sloped down the hill, past the dorm, the chapel, and then the north practice hall. I stepped briefly inside the north practice hall, standing in the ensemble hall where I'd played the Old Way songs with the others, and where I'd sat with Mira those two nights when she was ill. Sunshine filtered in through the cracks in the walls, illuminating the one fresco that hadn't crumbled away. I studied the image—a terrified-looking young man clutching a faint glow to his chest. I assumed it was Gaius with the Lady's Gift, though again it seemed a strange depiction of Gaius. "You had it right, though," I whispered. "You were right to be afraid. Damn you for bringing us that sort of gift at all."

Back outside, I heard someone shout, "Eliana, wait!"

I turned to see Giula running toward me. She carried a pack as well, and I could hear the jingle of a coin pouch from somewhere under her robe as she ran across the courtyard. "I'm coming with you."

"Giula, don't be—"

"I'm coming *with* you," she said. "My family deserves to know about what caused the famine, just as yours does. Even if you don't care for company, would you leave me to travel alone?"

"You'd be a fool to leave," I said.

"And you aren't?" she asked.

"You don't have my reasons."

Giula shook her head, stubborn. "I have my own reasons." She shifted her pack on her shoulder. "Our villages lie in the same direction. I'm coming with you."

"You'd better not slow me down," I said.

She snorted. "You're just as soft as I am. Don't worry. I won't slow you down."

The brown dust road wound out of Bascio and around the curve of the hill, and then the conservatory was hidden from view. Bascio's silver-green olive groves spread out before us, with the deeper green of evergreen forest beyond.

The sky overhead was blue, fading to white at the horizon. We could just make out the next village, rising on a hill far ahead. Maybe we could walk there by evening.

Giula and I sat down under a tree after what we reckoned to be about an hour. It probably hadn't been that much; wishful thinking was making the sun seem lower in the sky. "I think my boots don't fit right," Giula said. "They're giving me blisters."

I was starting to get blisters, too, but I wasn't going to admit it. "You'd just better not slow me down," I said again.

"Tell me when you're ready to start walking again, and I'll be ready." Giula rubbed her shoulders. "My violin never seemed this heavy before."

"I'm ready," I said, standing up, and Giula groaned and pushed herself up, bracing her back against the tree we'd been sitting under.

"Eliana?" Giula asked as we started walking again. "When did you realize that Mira was a member of the Circle?"

"Yesterday," I said. "When they came for her."

"I still can't believe it," Giula said. "Why did she leave with them, if she hated them so much?"

"I don't know," I said. I brushed at my eyes. "After she used magery, she just folded in on herself."

"What happened in your room?" she asked.

"I don't want to talk about it," I said, but Giula looked so sad and hurt when I said that, I hunched my shoulders and gave her a brief version.

"I still don't understand," she said when I had finished.

"I don't either."

"You must have known more than any of us," Giula said. "She was your best friend."

"I knew that she'd never been a priestess," I said. "That's all."

Giula gave me a look of hurt surprise—that I would have known, and not told her—and I looked away.

"Magery causing the famine," Giula said, when we paused to rest again. "Do you suppose that's what the Wicked Stepmother song was about?"

I thought about it for a moment. "The stepmother would be the Lady, I suppose. The poisoned honey kills each child—" I blinked, and counted verses quickly. "Each child represents one of the provinces," I said. "You're right. That is what it's about."

Giula laughed shakily. "Whoever wrote the song sure didn't want anyone figuring that out."

"They wanted a song that people would be able to sing," I said, thinking of Domenico's warning about the people executed for slandering the Lady. "I bet it spread a long way before the Fedeli figured it out."

"It's too bad I didn't think of it before we left," Giula said. "I bet Flavia would have liked to know that."

"It doesn't matter," I said. Isolated at the conservatory, it hardly mattered whether Flavia knew or not.

As the afternoon light faded, we stopped to ask for hospitality at a farmhouse. A big bearded man threw the door open wide. "Welcome, strangers," he said. "You've picked a good night to stay with us."

"Why?" I asked.

"It's the night of the planting festival. Come in and rest your feet for a while. The boys are building a bonfire in the piazza. We can join them once it's dark."

A festival celebration was the last thing I wanted that night, but it was too late to go back to the last village. And besides, that would have been rude. The village's name was Bosco. The planting festival was one of the not-quite church-sponsored festivals that so many villages had, asking for the Lord and Lady's blessings on the just-planted crops.

Our host's name was Persco. He led us to the piazza as night fell, enthusiastically introducing us to his neighbors. Wine flowed freely, and we were quickly made to feel welcome.

"Hey," a young woman said to me, gripping my hand and drawing me to my feet. "The dancing's starting."

"I have blisters—" I said.

"It's easy, don't worry," she said, pulling Giula to her feet as well. She led us over to a circle of young women. The older women—mothers and wives, I suspected—surrounded our circle and sang for us, clapping. "Blessed Lord. Blessed Lady. Send us sun. Send us rain. Send us children, send us husbands. Blessed Lord, Blessed Lady." I listened intently. The words were new—but the tune was an Old Way melody, I was certain. I wondered if the Fedeli had skipped this village, or if it just hadn't occurred to them that they were dancing to the Old music.

"Come on," the girl next to me said—I still didn't know her name. She pulled me to the right, and I stumbled as the dance started. I craned my neck to stare down at her feet, trying to match my movements to hers. Giula followed behind me, even more clumsily.

"Right-behind. Right-behind," the girl said as we stepped around the circle. "It's easy. Just run in the right direction." That was easy enough, and I started listening to the music instead of watching the dancers. "Now in," the girl said abruptly, and I was lost again. She hauled me along unsympathetically, two steps toward the center of the circle, then back out. Everyone else seemed to know the dance; Giula and I were the only odd ones out. I tried to follow along, clumsy and off the beat. At least I hadn't stepped on anyone's foot yet.

"I'm just getting in the way," I said.

"No, you're not," the girl insisted. "It's easy. Now to the right again."

Following along now, I felt a bit better. The dance was sinuous and hypnotic, with the scores of young women stepping in unison around the circle. Dancing in Bascio had always looked a bit more free-form. Giula was catching on more quickly than I was, smiling as she spun through the circle like a spindle of thread.

"Good dancing!" the girls around me said encouragingly when the dance ended. They clasped my arms and passed me a wineskin.

"Do you think this is all right, Eliana?" Giula whispered. "The music—the Fedeli—"

The girl who had brought us into the dance overheard Giula. "The words honor the Lady," she said. "How could it not be all right?"

Giula ducked her head.

"Go sit down if you want," the girl said, and Giula withdrew timidly. "What's your name?" the girl asked me.

"Eliana. Yours?"

"Tercia." She gave me an easy smile and tipped her head toward the circle. "Let's go dance some more." Despite Giula's worries, she rose eagerly to dance when she realized boys would be dancing too, this time.

A circle of men and women danced around the fire next. The village priestess threw rose incense into the bonfire, and the smoke billowed out sweet and sticky over our dancing. None of the dances were terribly hard, once you had the rhythm right. "Just keep on the beat and go in the right direction," Tercia said, and my mistaken steps didn't seem to interrupt the dance. Finally my feet hurt too much to continue, and I sat down at the edge of the circle, Giula dropping out as well to sit beside me.

"Hello," a young man's voice said. I looked up. Two boys, one fair and one dark, stood looking down at us.

"Hi," Giula said, looking up with a shy smile. I averted my eyes nervously and said nothing. They both grinned at Giula; she was prettier than me, anyway.

"What's your name?" the dark-haired one asked her.

"Giula," she said, tucking her chin down and looking up past her lashes. "What's yours?"

"Marco. What's your friend's name? She's acting shy."

"Her name's Eliana."

My cheeks flamed. I couldn't bring myself to look up, although I knew that the fairer-haired boy was still looking at me. My shyness was ridiculous, which only embarrassed me more. If I'd stayed home, I would probably be married by now. Listening to Giula giggling, I half-wished I'd tried flirting a few times. I didn't even know what I was supposed to *say* to a boy.

"Eliana? Hello, Eliana." The fair boy's deep voice sounded almost taunting. I gave him a quick glance up and a tight smile. He was handsome enough, in a freckled sort of way. "Nice to meet you."

"Hello," I said. I was trying hard not to sound nervous, and I realized as soon as the word was out that I sounded hostile instead.

"My name's Gino," the fair boy said. He sat down close beside me; I fought the urge to edge away. "Are you from the conservatory?"

"Yes," I said.

"We just left today," Giula said.

"We thought so," Gino said. "Because of your clothes." Giula laughed and tilted her head so that her short-cropped curls spilled over her shoulder. "Where are you going?" he asked.

"Home," Giula said. "We live south of here."

The boys' faces grew sober. "Are you sure you want to go there?" Marco asked. "Most people are trying to leave." He caught her arm, gently. "You're better off up here."

Now Giula ducked her head. "I have to go back." She sighed, and looked at me, but I stared at the ground. "I have to."

There was a nervous pause. Then Giula gave Marco one of her sweet smiles that showed her dimples. "But not until tomorrow," she said, and looked up at him, doe-eyed.

As Giula flirted with Marco, Gino slipped his arm around my shoulders. I froze rigid under his elbow, and after a moment he withdrew his arm awkwardly. "Are you enjoying the festival?" he asked me.

"I'm a bit tired," I said, and he nodded, looking relieved. After a few minutes, he excused himself to find someone else to flirt with; I looked around to find that Giula and Marco had slipped away. Gone to honor the Lady, no doubt. I wondered if she'd come back here if she got pregnant, and wed Marco.

From the other side of the fire, another boy was looking me over. I felt my cheeks flame again and looked down, then slipped back into the shadow of one of the cottages. It was too early to go back to Persco's house; he would be dancing here for hours yet. I was tired and wanted to sleep, but mainly I wanted to dodge the advances of the local boys.

I watched the piazza from my shadowed corner as couples paired off. The bonfire was burning down; Persco and some of the other men threw more wood on it. The girls were still dancing, but their dance was faster now, and their feet moved in a complicated pattern of steps that I was certain I'd never be able to follow. Watching Tercia's intent face as she concentrated on the dance, I was suddenly reminded of Mira; the wrenching pain in my stomach took me by surprise. I decided to go for a walk, away from the piazza and the boys and Tercia and the dancing. As long as I walked slowly I wouldn't hurt my feet any worse.

I took the path out to the new-plowed fields, lighting my way with witchlight and keeping my eyes on the path. There would be couples out in the fields, honoring the Lady, and I had no wish to watch. The path led over a hill, with an olive grove beyond. As I reached the crest of the hill, I heard something—the beat of a drum. *Wham. Wham. Wham. Wham.* Somebody banishing the Maledori? I listened for a moment and heard the unmistakable rhythm of an Old Way song.

The drumbeat was coming from over the next hill. I stepped off the path and let my witchlight go out, picking my way quietly through the olive grove. The path led up a steep slope; I crept to the top of that hill and lay down on the damp earth, resting my chin on my arms as I looked down at the people below. They were also dancing, but the words they were singing were *not* to the Lady.

"Arka, v'Bara, v'nehora kadosha. Arka, v'Bara, v'nehora kadosha." The chant was low and breathy. I didn't recognize the tune.

There were perhaps twenty dancers in the circle, both men and women, with a violinist and a drummer in the center. The violinist wasn't very good; he kept falling behind the beat and having to skip a note or two to catch up. The dance was simple, not too different from one of the dances I'd done earlier. Moving left: *skip, slide-skip, slide-skip, slide-skip.* Then right: *skip, slide-skip, slide-skip, slide-skip.* "*Arka,*" skip, "*v'Bara,*" skip, "*v'nihora,*" skip, "*kadosha.*"

I caught my breath, realizing what I was watching. *Dancing*, I thought. *Of course.* The Redentore music had always made me want to dance. *But the Fedeli. Didn't the Fedeli come here, as they came so many other places? How did they keep this secret?*

The dance stopped and one of the women from the circle stepped forward. She signaled, and in unison each person knelt to touch the ground where they stood, then rose and crossed themselves. "B'shem Arka, v'barah, v'nehora kadosha," the woman said, and everyone murmured, "Amen."

She continued in the Old Tongue, but I couldn't catch individual words. Everyone in the circle had clearly done this many times—they crossed themselves, knelt, and stood on cue. The woman—priestess?—leading the service raised her palms to the sky as if she were praying to the Lady, then gripped them into fists and pulled them down through the air.

One of the others from the circle stepped in to the center and picked up a white bundle from beside the violin player. The priestess lifted off the white cloth, revealing a silver platter with a chalice and a loaf of bread. She took the bread in one hand and the chalice in the other, and lifted them to the sky. "Iyt gufay," she said, in a clear voice that rang across the misty field. "Iyt damay. Achal. Ashti. V'chaya ad alam-almaya."

"Amen," the others in the circle said, and crossed themselves.

The priestess took a sip from the chalice, then set it down and broke off a piece of the bread.

Behind me, in the olive grove, I heard the unmistakable high-pitched peal of Giula's flirtatious laughter.

The dancers heard it, too, and froze. "Scatter," the priestess hissed, and the dancers melted into the shadowed fields. The priestess hesitated a moment longer, pouring out the wine onto the ground where the violinist had stood. "B'shemah," she said. She looked up, and for a moment I thought she saw me; she looked straight in my direction. Then she followed the rest into the darkness.

"Giula," a boy's voice called from the olive grove. "Where'd you go?"

"I'm right here, Marco," Giula said. She giggled again, then shrieked; Marco must have found her. Turning quietly, I could see them in the olive grove. Marco reached to circle Giula's waist with his hands, and she dodged aside with another giggle, running over the crest of the hill and down to where the dancers had been. "I'm *sure* this isn't the way back to the village," Giula said.

Marco slid carefully down the hill after her. "What makes you think that was where we were going?" he asked. He drew her toward him and dipped his face down to kiss her.

Giula pulled away briefly, still teasing him, then kissed him back. Marco dropped his cloak to the ground, spreading it out, and reached to loosen the drawstring at the neck of Giula's robe.

This was exactly the sort of thing I had wanted to *avoid* watching. I stood up quietly to head back through the olive grove and met Persco on the path.

"What are you doing out here?" Persco asked.

"I—" The explanation was too long to get into. "I went for a walk," I said.

Persco gave me a careful smile. "I'm heading home now, if you're ready for bed."

"I am," I said, and fell into step beside him. "I don't know if Giula's coming back tonight."

Persco laughed lightly. "The door stays open on festival nights. Giula can follow in her own sweet time or watch the sunrise with Marco, if she prefers."

I trailed Persco back out to his house, and he made up a bed for me by the hearth. "Sleep well," he said. I fell asleep quickly, but roused several times during the night as the door opened and closed. I woke at dawn to find Giula curled up next to me. Persco's wife was awake and making breakfast. I got up to join her. We were alone; on mornings after festivals, even farm families kept irregular hours.

"Good morning," she said. "I'm Rafina; I don't think we met last night."

"I'm Eliana," I said as Rafina served me a bowl of porridge. She looked familiar. When she looked into my face to give me my porridge, I realized who she was—the Old Way priestess I'd watched last night.

"You've come from the Bascio conservatory, haven't you?" Rafina asked as she sat down to eat her own porridge. I nodded. "But you're in robes, not new finery—why did you leave?"

"We were caught with boys," I said.

Rafina looked up sharply, and I could tell that she didn't believe me. I lowered my eyes and looked at my porridge.

"The Fedeli came to the Conservatory at Mascherata," I said. "We've heard they went elsewhere in Verdia afterward. Did they come here?"

"Yes," Rafina said. She said nothing more, but when she took my bowl, she stole a quick look at me with narrowed eyes, and I realized that she suspected *me* of being on their side. Her hostility was palpable, and for a moment, I was tempted to take out Bella's cross and confess my own heresies to her. On the other hand, if the Fedeli returned, Rafina might well be arrested, and I didn't want my name on the list they might tear out of her.

I wondered, if the Fedeli *had* been here, how the villagers had kept them from finding out about the Redentori. Perhaps the entire village was made up of apostates, who all stood together and protected each other. If that was the case, they must have been able to justify pledging their loyalty to the Lady, or they'd all be dead.

It occurred to me that perhaps the practice had spread *after* the Fedeli came through.

In any case, Rafina seemed unlikely to discuss it with me. In the dawn sunlight through the windows, I stole another look at her, and she turned and looked me full in the face, as she'd looked at me last night. For a moment, even knowing how foolish it would be, I nearly told her everything. But then there was a rustle and a groan from the hearth as Giula started to get up. "Thank you for your kindness, signora," I said.

"It's nothing." She rose, picking up a second bowl to fill with porridge for Giula. "The Lady has taught us hospitality. We know our duty."

Giula moved slowly that day. I would have pushed her harder, if I hadn't been so tired myself. My violin case felt like it was filled with sand, and I was tempted to eat all of my provisions right then to lighten my load. "We aren't covering enough ground," I muttered. It had only taken five days to walk from my home to Bascio when I came to the conservatory with my brothers; it was going to take me at least a week to get home now, maybe more. Hearing me, Giula quickened her pace for a few minutes, but we fell back to a slow trudge soon enough.

We were worn out by midafternoon, and started resting at every opportunity. "Where did you stay at night, when you came to the conservatory?" Giula asked.

"Houses. My brothers asked for hospitality." Donato and Rufo had escorted me out; whenever we were well out of earshot of anyone, Rufo had made elaborate mock-threats about what he'd do if anyone refused us a comfortable bed.

"Did you ever stay at an inn?"

"When we passed through Pluma. They didn't trust city folk."

Giula smiled. "My father paid for an inn, every night." I must have looked shocked. "We'd had a really good harvest that year. Also, he kept talking about how once I got into an orchestra, I could support them, send some of my stipend home." Her face grew sober. "I hope he isn't angry."

"Are you the only musician?"

"The only good one," she said with a giggle, cheerful again. "But, you know, I have a cousin who's headed for the Circle. She's . . ." Giula calculated for a moment. ". . . almost twenty. She just became a provisional member of the Circle; she'll probably be a full member in another few years."

I shivered; the air was growing chill.

"My mother was always jealous, of the money they got," Giula said. "And my cousin didn't have to go nearly as far away for her education."

We don't want your money; we want our daughter back. The furious words of Mira's mother's letter echoed in my head.

"I'm the best in my family at magery," I said.

"Me too, except for that cousin," Giula said. "Why do you think that is?"

"Concentration," I said. "We know how to concentrate. That's all it really takes."

"Is that really it? And they make it sound so hard and impressive." Giula sniffed.

"Any sisters or brothers at the seminary?"

"Well . . ." Giula dropped her voice. "Actually, you know, my oldest brother was once a priest."

"Really?"

"Yes, and it really looked like he might have prospects.

His first posting, well, it was a small town but it was close to Pluma. The word was, it was a posting that could lead to other things, if you know what I mean."

"So what happened?" I asked.

"He and the priestess fell in love," she said.

"So was this a problem?"

"It was a problem when the priestess got posted to the other side of Verdia."

"Oh," I said.

"And the new priestess was old, and ugly, and smelled like onions. He said. So he quit. And so did the priestess he was in love with. It was a bit of a scandal; it kind of embarrassed the people who'd done him favors, they were quite put out. So he moved away, and they settled down quietly. It's been all right; they have four children now." She smiled happily. "I thought it was terribly romantic, even if it was scandalous."

I smiled too, thinking of Giula's brother, wondering if he was as silly as she was. Probably not, if he'd been a priest with "prospects."

Late in the day it started to rain, and we sought shelter in a roadside chapel. It was dimly lit and smelled of stale incense. We sat down near the door, trying not to drip water on the smiling icon of the Lady. Giula wrung out her skirt on the stone floor by the door. "What did you think of Rafina?" she asked.

"She was nice enough," I said.

"I got the feeling she didn't like me," she said. "Do you think maybe Marco was her daughter's sweetheart or something? I'd hate to think I made trouble."

I was pretty sure that wasn't the problem, but I rolled my eyes anyway. "Maybe you should have thought of that *before* you slept with him."

"Why do you assume I slept with him? Just because you saw me flirting—"

"I overheard you in the olive grove," I said.

"Well, what were you doing there?" she demanded indignantly. "Spying on me?"

I rolled my eyes again and tried to wring some of the water out of my robe. "The rain's slacking off. We should get moving again," I said.

"Oh, come on," Giula said. "Let's just sleep here."

"I was hoping for a host who could feed us dinner," I said.

"But I'm tired of walking," Giula said. "I *know* you don't want me to slow you down, but we're not getting much farther today *anyway* and I don't want to go back out in the rain just to *look* for a house."

"Why don't you pray to the Lady," a man's voice said from near the altar, "and if She sees fit, She will arrange shelter for you."

We turned around. Our eyes had adjusted to the gloom, and now we could see a man sitting in the front of the chapel. He glared at us with dark, sharp eyes, and I shivered.

"Of course," I said, edging away from him without meaning to. *What did he overhear?* I thought, trying frantically to remember exactly what Giula and I had said to each other. I raised my hands to the shadowed ceiling of the chapel and closed my eyes. "Lord and Lady, if You see fit, please see to it that we have a roof over our heads and food to eat tonight."

"You see?" the man said. His voice was like the low, steady drone of a bass string instrument, smooth and silky. "She only wants what's best for all of us. And tonight She must want for you to have food and shelter, for I will be happy for you to stay with me."

Liemo—he reminded me of Liemo, the mage who had come to collect Mira. I was too frightened of him to refuse, and Giula gladly accepted—she was willing to go back out in the rain if his house was as close as he promised. Back in the last of the daylight, I got a good look at him. He wasn't tall for a man—shorter than me, with no gray in his hair. Not at all like Liemo, really, but there was something in his voice, something in the way he carried himself, that said that he was a man accustomed to power. This was not a village priest. *No,* I realized as I recognized the insignia on the sleeve of his tunic. Fedele. He was one of the Fedeli.

Giula looked stricken as we trailed behind the man on the muddy path. I clasped her hand, trying to send her the message, *just smile and tell the same lies I do and everything will be fine.* Only one night, I thought. Let him do the talking.

"My name is Aviro," he said, glancing over his shoulder at us.

"I'm Eliana," I said, and since Giula was still staring at him nervously, added, "and this is Giula."

"You came from the conservatory," he observed. I nodded. "I'll have Frugia lend you some clothes."

"Is Frugia a priestess?" Giula asked.

"No," Aviro said. "Frugia is providing me with hospitality."

He'd offered us hospitality in someone else's house? That seemed rather rude to me, but just then I was more concerned about Giula's look of open terror. If Aviro turned around, he'd *know* we had something to hide. I jabbed her in the ribs. "Smile," I whispered.

Frugia met us at the door, a pale, nervous widow who looked older than she probably was. She ushered us up a ladder to the second-floor loft, to let us change into some dry clothes. "You can borrow one of my daughter's dresses until your clothing dries," she said to Giula, and then looked me up and down. "You're very tall," she said. "I think we'll have to get out some of my husband's old clothing for you."

"How long have the Fedeli been in your village?" I asked softly.

Frugia glanced toward the ladder. "Aviro is here to ensure the purity of our worship of the Lady," she said, pitching her speech to be heard downstairs. "There are villages near here who have slipped into superstition or heresy. Aviro is here to find them and to show them their errors." Her eyes showed fear and suppressed anger. "He has been here for two weeks," she said in a softer voice. "I don't know how much longer he'll stay."

From a shelf beside the bed, Frugia took out a dress and held it up. "This should do for Giula," she said, and laid it across the bed. Then she opened a trunk by the window and took out a tunic and trousers, shaking them out and holding them up to me. "They won't quite fit," she said, "but they'll do. Bring your own clothing downstairs when you've changed, and we'll put it by the fire to dry." She went back down the ladder to give us privacy to change.

It wasn't until I pulled my robe over my head that I remembered Bella's cross, on its ribbon around my neck. "Lady's tits," Giula hissed, her eyes going wide. "Are you mad?"

I hurriedly clasped my fist over it, as if Aviro might be watching from under the bed. "No harm done," I whispered, giving her a reassuring grin, but she didn't looked reassured. I slipped it over my head and hid it in my boot.

"I want to leave," Giula whispered. "Now."

"We can't," I whispered back. "We'll look guilty."

"So what? We won't *be* here anymore."

"Don't you think he'll come after us, if he thinks he should? We'll eat dinner, sleep on the hearth, and leave at dawn. Just tell the same lies I do." I considered for a moment. "And if you get a chance to use witchlight when he can see you, do it."

Giula's dress was made of a heavy linen fabric, dyed yellow. It fit her quite well, and I stepped back for a good look, impressed by the embroidered scooped collar and the narrow waist. My clothes were less decorative. I had a linen tunic over black wool trousers. It was loose in the wrong places, and Frugia had forgotten to get out a belt, but my red wool sash was only slightly damp, so I belted it with that.

"You don't look half bad in boys' clothing," Giula said. "Anything but the robes, I guess." She smiled gamely. "Might as well make the best of it." We combed our hair and climbed back down the ladder.

Frugia took our wet clothing and half-soaked cloaks and spread them by the fire. "Have a seat," Aviro said, and gestured at the bench across the table from him.

We sat down.

"Why did you leave the conservatory?" he asked.

"We were expelled," I said. "We were caught talking to boys. One too many times."

Giula stared at the floor, feigning shame. "Did you have to tell him that?" she wailed.

"Giula, he's with the *Fedeli*. Didn't you see his insignia? We can't lie to *him*." I gave Aviro the look I'd seen Giula give male teachers, when she was trying to suck up. Giula was better at it, but Aviro preened anyway, and I felt mildly disgusted with myself.

"You were at the Verdiano Conservatory?" Aviro asked.

"Yes," I said.

"There were members of my order there a few months ago," Aviro said.

"Yes," I said. "During Mascherata."

"They executed a girl about your age for apostasy," Aviro said. "I read the report."

"Yes," I said.

"Did you know her?"

I dug my fingernails into my knees to keep my face impassive. "Of course I knew her," I said. "We were students together for four years."

"Was she a friend of yours?"

"No," I said. "Just someone I knew."

"There was a servant, as well," Aviro said.

"Giorgi," I said. "He disappeared."

"How much contact did you have with him?"

"Not much," I said. "He worked in the kitchen."

"How about you?" Aviro said to Giula.

"Not much," she squeaked.

"And Bella? Were *you* friends with her?"

Giula shook her head.

Aviro turned his attention back to me. "Who is Rafina?" he asked. "The woman you spoke of in the chapel. Who is she?"

Giula was weakening—I could feel her trembling next to me on the bench. I dropped one hand under the table to squeeze her arm tightly. I needed to divert the conversation; Rafina was clearly guilty of apostasy, and sooner or later Giula would blurt something out. "Are we under suspicion of something?" I asked.

"Is there something on your conscience that would arouse my suspicions?" Aviro asked.

"No," I said. "But you're asking us questions like you think there is."

" 'Innocence doesn't need to hide,' " Aviro quoted.

I licked my lips. " 'When you welcome a guest,' " I quoted back, " 'you shall first bring wine, that he might refresh himself from his travels.' Do you intend to meet the Lady's obligations of hospitality?"

Aviro's eyes narrowed and Giula sucked in her breath. "Are you quoting the Book of the Lady to *me*?"

"I shouldn't have to," I said.

Aviro slammed his fist down onto the table. "You—"

There was a crash from across the room. "Oh, Lady," said a timid voice. We turned; it was Frugia's eldest daughter, gathering up shards from a broken bowl. "It slipped out of my hands, signore. I'm so clumsy—I'm sorry." She stared at us meekly in the silence. "Mother is almost done cooking dinner," she said. "Why don't we get ready?"

Aviro made the ritual offering to the Lady before the meal, then said a long, involved prayer, thanking the Lord and the Lady and their servants and everything short of the house sprites. Frugia and her children sat, backs straight, eyes closed. Even the youngest child, who couldn't have been more than seven years old, sat perfectly still until the meal was served. By then, of course, it was lukewarm. Such is the price of piety.

Frugia's eldest daughter sat to Aviro's right, and I noticed as the meal progressed that she was keeping his wine cup filled to the brim. I glanced at Frugia and saw her giving her daughter an almost imperceptible nod.

When the meal was concluded, Aviro took out a worn, heavy copy of the Book of the Lady to read aloud. "Lift up your voices to give eternal praise to the Lady and thanks unto Her," he read. "For She will never turn Her back on you, nor turn a deaf ear to you in your time of need. She asks not blind faith, but places Her light in your hand, dispelling the darkness and the Maledori." Aviro stumbled over *Maledori,* slurring the syllables. "Ever loving and ever faithful, She waits with open arms for all who seek Her warmth." He stumbled again and yawned. "Excuse me. She watches us as we slumber. She—um." He closed the book. "My apologies; I'm very tired. We'll continue this in the morning." He went up the ladder. Apparently Aviro slept upstairs; Frugia and her children slept in beds around the hearth.

Frugia's oldest daughter cleaned up from dinner silently. Frugia went to look up the ladder, then returned and shook her head, and gestured for Giula and me to spread out our cloaks by the hearth.

"What were you *thinking?*" Giula hissed as we lay down.

I shrugged, not wanting to explain that I had been trying desperately to steer the conversation away from Rafina before Giula blurted anything out. I was too worried to be sleepy, and watched as Frugia put her younger children to bed. She peered up the ladder again, and nodded once to her eldest daughter. The daughter opened the door and peered out, then felt our robes, which had been moved out of the way of the bedrolls. She shrugged.

Frugia came down to sit beside Giula and me; her daughter followed.

"If you have anything to hide," Frugia whispered, "then you should go now."

"Won't that make us look guilty?" Giula asked.

"Yes," Frugia said. "But he already suspects you of something. You're better off guilty and *gone.*"

"Will you get into trouble?" I asked.

Frugia's daughter gave me a slight smile. "No," she said. "He'll sleep well into the morning, and we'll tell him you left at dawn."

"What about your clothes?" I asked.

Frugia looked us over. "Give me a coin and we'll call it even."

Giula took out a coin to give to Frugia, and we gathered up our cloaks, violins, and packs. We pulled our boots on.

I paused in the doorway to look back at Frugia. "Thank you," I said.

"Don't mention it," Frugia said. "*Some* of us are faithful to the Lady's obligations of hospitality. Now get going."

It had stopped raining, and the moon was out. "Not a bad night for travel," Giula breathed, and we headed down the road by moonlight.

CHAPTER SEVEN

*I can cure the sick and cleanse the leper; I can
give sight to the blind and strength to the crippled. But
I cannot help those who will themselves to blindness,
and turn away.*
—The Journey of Gèsu, chapter 11, verse 30.

We walked through the night and through the next
day, and made it almost to Pluma. We were so
tired we couldn't even walk in a straight line; as evening
fell, we found a spot off the road to camp. I wanted to try
asking for hospitality—what were the odds of running
into the Fedeli *twice*—but Giula refused, and we were
close enough to the city that people were less likely to be
hospitable. We could see the flicker of firelight through the
trees. We hadn't seen many refugees yet; the north-south
road and the east-west road crossed just east of Pluma, a
few hours' walk from where we were.

Giula scraped out a hole in the ground for our fire while
I gathered up firewood. We were fortunate that I was skilled
at magery, or we'd never have gotten the damp wood lit.
We spread out our cloaks and lay down; except for the
tree root poking into my back, the ground was softer than
the hearthstones had been.

"You were studying minstrel techniques, weren't you?"
Giula asked. "With Mira, before she . . . left?"

"Yes," I said.

"How well was it working?"

"Better than you'd expect," I said. "Mira claimed she liked my singing voice."

Giula laughed. "Could you teach me the techniques? How hard were they?"

"Not hard. Here, let's tune up. I'll show you a few tricks." I sat up and took out my violin.

As Giula and I tuned our violins, I heard a footstep behind me and felt as if someone were staring at my back. I turned around slowly, afraid for a moment that it would be the Fedele.

It was not Aviro. Standing just outside our camp, staring at us, was an old man wrapped in a ragged cloak.

"So you're here already," he said hoarsely, still staring at me.

"Excuse me?" I said. "I don't believe I know you." Maybe he was someone from my village I'd forgotten? I felt a brief pang of worry. "But you can share our fire, if you like."

He laughed, the gravelly chuckle rattling in his chest like pebbles, then hopped over a fallen branch to join us by our campfire. "Let me be the first to salute you, Generale!" he said to me, and thumped his bony chest, then held his fist out, a soldier's salute to his commander.

Giula and I exchanged shrugs. This diverted his attention to Giula.

"Ah, yes," he leered. "And you as well." He sidled up to Giula, and without warning, grabbed her breast. "Sweet young thing, aren't you?"

Giula shrieked and smacked his hand; I shoved him away from her and stood between them. He pouted at us. "No fun; you're no fun at all. You're *all* like that. No fun at all. You'll see—you'll see what I mean."

"Go away," I said. "We don't want to share our fire with a crazy man."

"Go away," he said sadly. "I'll go away. No one wants to share their fire with me. I'll sleep under a rock—don't mind me." He shuffled off into the night.

Giula brushed her dress clean, shaking and looking disgusted. "I can't believe it. What a disgusting old man. Do you think we need to take turns watching?"

I closed my eyes. "Probably. You go ahead to sleep; I'll take the first watch."

I woke Giula midway through the night to take over watching—but when I woke at dawn, Giula was slumped over asleep under the tree she'd been leaning against. Fortunately, no one had robbed us, and the madman hadn't come back. I sighed and shook Giula awake.

The road became much more crowded as we neared Pluma. I wondered how many of the people around us were refugees from the famine areas. The merchant caravans with their heavily armed escorts obviously weren't. But looking around at the other people on the road, I wasn't sure where "traveler" stopped and "refugee" started. Some of the travelers looked like us, footsore and dirty but with packs clutched tightly against potential thieves. There were families that huddled together, resting by the edge of the road with small crying children. There were people who wore rags and carried nothing. I thought that Giula and I were obviously travelers, rather than refugees, but I saw one woman close one hand protectively over her necklace when she saw me approaching.

I smelled Pluma before I saw it. Smoke, road dust, incense, horse shit, perfume, fried meat, and the sour smell of rotting garbage mingled in the air. The city was surrounded by a high wall; we could see the ragged edge that had been filled in with newer stones after the war. The old wall that had remained standing after the war was dirty and worn; the new parts were cleaner, the rocks still rough.

Everyone around us seemed to be trying to get into the city; the press of people around me nearly pulled me away from Giula. I clasped her hand and tucked my violin under my arm to keep anyone from stealing it off my back, and we headed for the city gates.

"Name?" a city guard asked me.

"Eliana."

"Business in Pluma?" he asked.

"Just passing through," I said.

"Uh-huh," he said. "Got coin?" I nodded. "Let's see it." I dug my coin purse out from its hiding place inside my tunic and held it open for his inspection. He gave it a cursory glance and waved Giula and me inside the gates.

Pluma was the largest city in Verdia. It was sort of our province's extension of Cuore; there were government offices, an army detachment, seminaries, a training school for children with magical talent, even a conservatory. The Pluma conservatory would have been closer to my home than the rural conservatory in Bascio, but my parents didn't want me attending a conservatory in a city. The Pluma conservatory had many more students who paid fees, instead of being sponsored by the Circle; merchants sent their children there for the prestige of having a musician in the family.

"Do you remember where you stayed when you came through Pluma before?" Giula asked. I shook my head. "Me either."

"I had two of my brothers with me then," I said. Giula and I pulled out of the crowd and backed into an alley, leaning against a wall. I had never tried to make my way through such a crowd; when I had been here before, the city had been less crowded, and Donato and Rufo had pushed through the crowd on my behalf. "They chose the inn," I said. "I don't even remember the name, let alone where to find it."

"At least it's early in the day. We've plenty of time to find something."

I shook my head. "We could move on, too." We paused for a moment. Pluma was where Giula and I would part ways. Her parents lived south from here; mine, to the east. "But there's no harm in resting a little," I said finally.

"And seeing the city," Giula said, her eyes lighting up. I shook my head. "We could buy you a dress," she suggested.

"I rather like the tunic," I said. "Maybe I should have been born a boy."

She laughed. "You're certainly tall enough."

I wasn't ready to move out of the alley yet, but then I heard a whisper from just behind my feet. "Signora. Pssst, *signora.*" I jumped and jerked away. Two eyes stared at me from a tiny gap in the crumbling brick wall, looking terrifyingly malevolent in the shadows.

"Let's go," I said, grabbing Giula's arm. "Do you know what you need to buy?"

"I still think we should buy you a dress," Giula said. "But if you really don't want one—provisions, I suppose. We don't have much food left."

I didn't know where the market was, so we followed people who looked like they were heading to haggle. Pluma was a maze of narrow streets, and there were far too many people here; the town had never been meant to hold so many. "They've certainly rebuilt since the war, haven't they?" Giula said, staring around us at the tall buildings.

Pluma was the farthest north the Vesuviano army had come. They had attacked the city, then been pushed back south by the Circle. Last I'd heard, there were still soldiers stationed there. During the battle, apparently, half the east

wall had been blown away and a number of Pluma's in-
habitants killed. Rumor said that nothing in Pluma would
grow, either, but the city-dwellers were better off than the
farmers, since they could at least buy food.

"We aren't even in the parts of the town that were damaged," I said to Giula.

"Oh, I suppose not. Do you suppose they've rebuilt
those parts?"

"Signore?" I felt a hand grasp the edge of my tunic and
looked down to see a scrawny, shrill-voiced child. "Signore—
signora," he corrected himself, "—please, signora." He held
out his hands, cupped upward. "I'm hungry." He wore the
remains of a shirt, stained and badly torn.

Giula paled and looked away, horrified. I wondered if
she was thinking about her family, in the famine areas, or
if she was trying hard not to. I dug in my pouch for a piece
of cheese. "Here," I said, putting it in the child's outstretched hands. He stared for an instant, amazed, then
stuffed the whole piece into his mouth and ran off like a
frightened rat.

The market square was watched by guardsmen who
looked us over before standing aside to let us in. This
square was in part of the town that had been damaged
during the war, and only parts of it had been rebuilt. The
houses ringing the open area had new stone in part of the
walls, but the ruins of a fountain stood in the center of
the square. The rising curve of what was left of the fountain edge was now used by merchants to show their wares.

We made our way toward the cheese merchant. Standing in the line by his stall, I saw the flash of silver from the
corner of my eye and turned my head to see that I stood
shoulder-to-shoulder with a Fedele priest. I instinctively
ducked my head, but it wasn't Aviro, and he ignored me as

he haggled for his cheese. I listened attentively while I waited; either the cheese merchant was badly cheating the Fedele, or prices in Pluma were shockingly high.

"May I help you, signore?" the cheese merchant said. It took me a moment to realize that he was addressing me. I decided not to bother telling him I wasn't a boy. I ended up paying the same price for my cheese that the Fedele priest had paid for his; when I tried for a lower price, the merchant just laughed.

I turned to the next woman in line. "Is cheese particularly expensive here?" I asked her.

She snorted. "The cheese is cheap, girl," she said. "You won't see a better price than he's giving you."

I sighed and dug out my coin pouch, weighing the cheese with my hand after the merchant gave it to me. Giula and I each bought several pounds, then stocked up on hardbread and wine. There seemed to be no shortage of food here, but the woman at the cheese stand had told the truth—all the prices were high. Everyone around me looked hungry; I was no longer certain I wanted to spend the night here.

"The wine merchant told me where we could find a good inn," Giula said. "He said sleeping on the road near here wasn't a good idea—we could be robbed." She led me through a long maze of streets and alleys with complacent certainty until we came to a dead-end against the edge of the city wall. "Huh," she said. "This *should* have had a left turn onto the street that was going to lead to the inn."

"Maybe it did before they rebuilt," I said. The wall here was lower, and half crumbled, leaving footholds. On impulse I climbed up to peer over. "Lady's tits," I whispered, looking out over a field of tents, as far as the eye could see. "Giula, climb up here, you need to see this."

Grumbling, she did her best, catching her foot on her skirt at one point and nearly falling. Finally she pulled herself up to lean over the crumbling edge, and her eyes grew wide as she looked. "Who are they?"

"Refugees. They must be. Who else would live like that?"

"Why do they stay here?"

A breeze gusted across our faces, and I smelled rotting meat and cooking fires. "There's food here," I said. "At least a little." Staring out, I realized that there were tents in the areas closer to the wall, but that past those, there were people in the open, wrapped in blankets or just sitting. I had never seen so many people gathered in one place in my life, nor had I ever seen such poverty. In my village, no one was rich, but no one starved. Even when the town drunk died suddenly, his wife and children were taken care of—sometimes grudgingly, but always taken care of—until the children were old enough to run the farm. They were pitied, occasionally scorned, often resented, but they were never left to starve, never shut out of shelter, never—

"Get off of there!"

Giula and I jumped down off the wall and turned to face two soldiers. "Sorry," Giula gasped, cringing.

"What were you doing up there?"

"We're lost," Giula said. "It's my fault. I thought I could find us an inn. The wine merchant gave us directions. I've never been in the city before without my brothers . . ." I let her babble on; she was doing a better job of it than I would.

"Do you have coin?" one of them asked. We nodded. "Let's see it."

I took out my pouch slowly, wondering if they were

going to steal it, or demand a bribe. I stood up as straight as I could, glaring at them as they stared at me coolly. Digging my hand into my purse, I closed my fist over every coin I had, holding my purse half closed so that the soldiers couldn't tell it was now empty. They stared at the scant coins in my palm skeptically, then shrugged and gestured for me to put it away again.

"Go back to the last street and turn left," the taller soldier said. "Stay on that street. After a few minutes of walking, you'll find an inn called Agostino's. It's comfortable and cheap, or as cheap as you'll find in Pluma without going into areas we don't recommend for ladies."

They escorted us back to the previous corner. "What are you doing in Pluma?" the shorter soldier asked Giula.

"We're going home," she said. "We've been at a conservatory. Her village is east of here, and mine is south."

The soldiers glanced at each other, then back at us. "Signora, we don't recommend heading south from here," the tall one said. "Not at all, not for anyone."

"Why?" Giula said.

"It's hungry and dangerous down there."

"East is all right, though?" I asked.

The shorter soldier looked at me with something like pity. "East is better," he said finally.

"We can't stay *here*," I said.

"No," he said. "Once you ran out of coin, we'd have to escort you from the city."

"Thank you for your time," I said. "And for directing us to an inn. Good day."

Next to me, Giula was near tears; I was angry at them, for upsetting her, and for telling us that what we were doing was stupid without being able to offer a better alternative.

"Let's go," I said, and urged her down the street.

"Hungry and dangerous," she said. "How dare they talk like that about my home!"

"That's right," I whispered soothingly.

"There are good people in my village. The war *never* came there."

"Here's the inn," I said. "Agostino's."

Agostino was surly, but he had plenty of rooms, and the inn did seem to be clean. If the price he charged us was cheap, I didn't want to know what a pricey inn would cost. We were left with one coin each. "Dinner's in an hour," he said. "You can sit in the common room until then if you like."

The common room was crowded and noisy; we were almost the only women there. We found an empty corner and slipped our violins under the table. I could see a few people sneaking glances at us, but fortunately Giula was too distraught to flirt.

"Your family is fine, Giula," I said, squeezing her hand. "You'd have heard if they weren't, wouldn't you?" She nodded. "Didn't they tell you the harvest was all right? Didn't they say there was enough food?" She nodded again, still not answering. "How many brothers and sisters do you have, Giula? I forget."

"Twelve living," she whispered, finally answering. "Four brothers and eight sisters."

"Your mother must be one tired lady."

Giula sniffled and then laughed a little. "My mother can't make witchlight. She's almost a little simple—she never would have gotten married if she hadn't been so pretty when she was young. But she can't make a witchlight, and has to use a flint and steel to start a fire."

"So she couldn't keep from having babies that way," I said, nodding.

"She used to call my father in from the fields to start fires for her. 'Elmo, could you start this for me?' 'Lina, didn't I *just* start a fire for you?' 'Yes, but you know me, I'm so clumsy, I spilled the dishwater on the hearth, and put it out.' Over and over again, to try to make it so that my *father* wouldn't be fathering any babies." She chuckled, then sighed. "He did finally catch on, and he went along with it. She still had three more babies, though."

"Which one were you?"

"The first of those last three." She smiled. "So I suppose I can't complain too much about all those children."

"You must have a lot of nieces and nephews."

"Hordes," she said. "I've lost count. There were twenty-five when I left home. I forget how many since then."

"Are any of them any good with a violin?"

"There's a nephew who's supposed to be good at drums. He's almost twelve now."

Someone was glaring at me from across the room. I turned to look, half expecting to see the crazy old man, but it was a boy, not a lot older than I was, with a shock of dark hair and violet-blue eyes. I gave him a long, direct stare, and he went back to staring at his drink. "Check out handsome," I muttered to Giula.

"Oh!" she said. "I don't think I like him. He doesn't look very nice."

He glanced up to give us another malevolent glare, and I rolled my eyes. "Maybe we're sitting in his spot."

Giula giggled. "Maybe he's actually from your village, and you've forgotten him. You slighted him when you were nine and he's hated you ever since."

Now I started giggling. Lots of people were staring at us now, along with the boy, but I was so glad to have something to laugh at that I didn't care. "You never know," I said.

Dinner was skimpy soup with bread and half-sour wine, but no one else seemed to view this as unusual fare, so we dug in and made the best of it. The soup was tasty, despite being thin, and the bread was fresh, so I concluded that we'd done fairly well by our money. It just wasn't what we were used to. "I'm still hungry," Giula said when we went up to our room, so we broke out our provisions and had a little hardbread with cheese.

There was a single wide bed. I hoped Giula wouldn't steal the blankets. Since I'd had no sisters, I'd only rarely shared a bed even before going to the conservatory. The door had a heavy bar, which we swung into place before lying down.

The room had a barred and shuttered window. Giula was asleep within minutes, but I lay for a while with my eyes open, listening. In the street below I could hear voices, feet splashing through puddles, occasionally the steady tromp of a horse. Downstairs, there were voices in the common room, and I heard the occasional thump of an emphatic cup being banged to the table. I could hear snatches of music, probably coming from next door or down the street. Maybe someday I could find a job playing for a tavern, as a minstrel. Maybe. I closed my eyes, and fell asleep.

I woke with a start; the night was chill and very quiet. I had been dreaming about the boy from the common room; I'd been furious at him, and he'd been shouting that *he* was the one in charge, not me. I shivered, and then realized that the bed was cold because it was empty. Giula was gone.

She's probably just gone to use the outhouse, I thought, and tried to go back to sleep. I closed my eyes, but my nervousness increased. *How could she get into trouble going to the outhouse? This is ridiculous.* I swung my legs out of bed and sat up with a groan. Giula was going to laugh at me. Still . . .

Her boots were gone, but everything else was still here, implying that I'd guessed her intentions correctly. I left my boots off, closed the door behind me as quietly as I could, and tiptoed down the stairs.

I could see firelight under the common room door, and I could hear voices. I pressed my ear against the door.

"She's a *spy,* Cilo."

"Don't be so hasty."

"Don't be a *fool.* Look at her!" Boots stomped across the floor, and I heard a smack and a shriek. "We know you're from the Fedeli. Tell us what you heard!" the voice shouted.

That was enough. I slammed the door open. "Leave her alone!" I shouted.

Five men turned. Giula collapsed against the wall, crying. "Eliana! Oh thank the Lady. Eliana, they've been shouting at me, and they won't believe me, and they say I'm a spy and you are too, and, and, and—"

The boy who'd glared at me during dinner stood over Giula, his hand raised to hit her again. I strode straight to him. Even barefoot, I was slightly taller than he was; I drew myself up to my full height to stare him down. "*You.* I don't know what *your* problem is, but you clearly decided we were spies the moment you laid eyes on us. I don't know who the hell you are or *what* you think you're doing that would be worth spying on, but if you can spot a spy from across a crowded room, the Fedeli could certainly use *your* talents." I turned away from him and knelt next to Giula, trying to reassure her.

"You see, Cilo?" The violet-eyed boy turned furiously to the older man. "I was *right.*"

I lifted Giula up, one hand around her waist. "If I *were* one of the Fedeli," I snapped, "I'd have you drawn and quartered by my men-at-arms for hitting my friend. *Bastardo.*"

One of the men, not Cilo, blocked the door.

"We're not spies," I said. Across the room, I could see a loaf of bread and a carafe of wine on the table, and on impulse, I flipped Bella's cross out from under my dress. The man who had blocked our way stared at it for a moment, then slowly moved aside. "Can we go now, please?" I asked.

"That proves nothing," the young man shouted.

Cilo turned on him and said mildly, "It explains why the girl was listening to us, does it not, Giovanni?" He turned back to us and bowed slightly. "Go in peace. We apologize."

Giula's cheek was flaming red where the boy had slapped her. She continued crying as I helped her up the stairs and back to our room. "What happened?" I asked as I barred our door.

"I went to the outhouse," she whimpered. "On my way there, I heard music—singing. Old Way music. So I stopped to listen. Then they opened the door and dragged me in. The boy who was glaring at us, he wouldn't stop yelling. I told him I wasn't a spy but he didn't believe me—" her voice went quivery and she sniffled, wiping her nose on her sleeve. "I'm so glad you came."

I helped her sit down on the edge of the bed, but she didn't take off her boots. "I still have to go to the outhouse," she said, looking up at me pathetically.

I escorted her back downstairs. The common room was empty and silent as we passed. We slipped out the back door; I was still barefoot, so I waited in the doorway while she ducked into the outhouse. As I waited, I heard someone behind me. It was the boy with violet eyes—Giovanni.

"May we have your permission to relieve ourselves, *signore?*" I whispered.

"*You* were never going to the outhouse," he said.

"You're right," I said. "I came looking for my friend. Now would you be so kind as to go *away,* so that she doesn't start crying again when she comes out of the privy and sees you?"

"I'm sorry your friend is such a fragile little flower—" he said.

"You *hit* her," I said, furious. "You decided we were spies because we were strangers. It never crossed your mind that we might just be *strangers,* trying to get home to our families. Spies for the Fedeli! Unbelievable. Now go *away,*" I said again, because the outhouse door was starting to open.

With a final muttered insult, Giovanni slipped away, and was out of sight when Giula padded up the stone walk. "Come on," I said to her. "Let's get back to bed."

The next morning, I walked Giula to the south gate. "Do you think you can make this last bit on your own?" I asked. She nodded. Giula's family lived only a day or two south of Pluma, and another five miles east of the main road—the war really had gone right past them. Giula was still shaken from the confrontation in the night, but once she was out of the city, I was fairly certain she'd be all right. I gave her a long hug.

Giula sniffled. "I don't know when I'll see you again," she said.

"Soon," I said. "We're friends. We'll find each other."

Giula hesitated for a long moment, and I smiled at her encouragingly. "Bye," she said finally, and walked away down the road. I watched her go for a few minutes. She did not turn to look back. After a while, I turned east.

I knew it should be faster to go through the city, but I'd

have to find my way through the streets. I decided to just walk the extra distance around the edge.

As had happened when I approached the city, I smelled the refugee camp before I saw it. Gusts of wind brought the smell of death as I circled the last of the wall. I hesitated, but the road east led directly through the encampment. There was no way to go but through.

Giula had turned away from the boy begging for food yesterday, but there was nowhere to look here that was "away." Filthy children with huge hungry eyes swarmed around me as I walked through the camp; I could feed one or two, but how could I feed all of them? There were hundreds—no, thousands of people here.

As I'd noticed the previous evening, the tents were toward the city wall. As I moved outward, it grew worse. There were people dying, fevered and alone. There were people too weakened by hunger to move, who stared at me as I passed, arms wrapped around bony legs.

There was nothing I could do. Nothing I could do. After what seemed like a thousand years of walking, I passed the last sprawling bodies, and walked out into open fields.

●   ●   ●

The road was quiet without Giula, but I made better time. By the end of the day, I'd covered half again as much road as I would have with Giula. I tried not to think about how much my feet hurt; once I was home, I'd be able to rest.

Heading south and west, I passed through territory that had seen battle. This wasn't truly famine area; crops were stunted and shrunken, but they were at least growing. Some of the farms I saw were clearly abandoned—many had been destroyed during the war, and had caved-in roofs and burned-out barns.

Even in the worst areas, the land was returning to life. It was only early spring, but weeds and grasses grew knee-high in the abandoned fields, and honeysuckle worked its way through the fallen stones of the empty houses. There were no trees here, though, just a few stunted shrubs. I passed what had once been an olive grove; every tree was twisted and black, burnt skeletons frozen in place, arms raised in surrender.

I spent the first two nights in abandoned farmhouses, but came to an inhabited farm on the third evening and knocked on the door. The woman who answered was young, not much older than myself, and carried an infant. "Good evening, signora," I said. "I'm traveling to my family's home in Doratura and I need a place to stay. Can you provide me with hospitality?"

"Come in," she said, stepping out of the doorway. "You're welcome to stay with us. My name is Herennia."

The cottage was small, but clean. I put my packs by the door and sat down at the table. Herennia balanced the baby on her hip as she added a bit more water to the soup and then poured me a cup of wine.

"My husband, Metello, will be back soon," she said, sitting down across from me. "Where are you coming from?"

I told her I'd been at a conservatory and described my travels. Herennia listened with interest, rocking the baby. "We came here last summer," she said. "The farm was abandoned, and no one seemed to expect that the family that had lived here would come back. The neighbors didn't mind if we settled here, so we did."

"Are things very bad where you came from?" I asked.

"Terrible." Herennia didn't elaborate. "We were very surprised that anyone would leave this farm. We got some planting in, late last summer. I hadn't had the baby yet then. We grew just enough to last us through the winter. They say the plants here are stunted, smaller than they should be, but . . ." She shrugged. The baby took a handful of her sleeve and stuffed it into its mouth. She pulled the sleeve away gently and leaned across the table toward me. "We've heard recently that people in the famine areas aren't being allowed to leave." Her voice was tinged with horror. "We heard soldiers were sent to keep them from leaving."

The baby grabbed again, at something around Herennia's neck, and I realized that he'd grabbed a tiny wooden cross on a ribbon. Herennia followed my shocked gaze and her smile tightened. She started to turn away, to tuck it back under her dress.

"Wait," I said, catching her arm. "I'm just surprised. With the Fedeli in Verdia—aren't you afraid?"

Herennia didn't reply; her fist closed over the cross. I stared at her rigid face, floundering for something I could say that would make her trust me.

"At the conservatory," I said, "we always played Old Way music—secretly. Then the Fedeli came last winter. One of my closest friends had become Redentore; they killed her when she refused to renounce her faith."

Herennia's face softened, but she still said nothing.

I pulled out Bella's cross. "This was Bella's. I've worn it since she died."

Herennia raised her eyebrows. "That was foolish of you," she said. "The Fedeli could have seen it."

"But you wear one," I said. "Haven't the Fedeli come here?"

Herennia bent her head briefly to her baby, then looked up at me again, and I could see that she'd decided to trust me. "The Fedeli don't come this far south."

"How can you be sure? Maybe they just haven't come yet."

"They won't," Herennia said. "There are too many of us here. They're frightened of us, and they're frightened of the famine. They won't go past Pluma." She touched Bella's cross gently. "You can wear that openly here," she said. "Don't be afraid."

I nodded and touched the cross uncertainly. It felt very strange not to have it tucked under my robe.

"Do you know what this means?" she asked, seriously.

I shook my head. "Another one of my friends—" I couldn't say Mira's name. "She got several of us to play the songs together. Bella actually became Redentore, but the rest of us just played the music. It's beautiful."

Herennia's smile warmed. "It is, isn't it? Do you know any of the dances?"

"Dances?" I said, then remembered the group I'd spied on in Bosco. "No."

"Do you know the creed?"

I shook my head.

"Have you been sealed?"

I shook my head again.

The door swung open, and without meaning to I clapped my hand to my chest to hide the cross. It was Metello, Herennia's husband. "Metello, this is Eliana," Herennia said. "She is one of us."

"Evening, signora," Metello said with a slight bow. "Glad to have you here."

They said a prayer before dinner; I bowed my head when they did and crossed myself as they finished. Herennia passed the baby to Metello for a while, so that she could eat, then took him back so that Metello could eat some more. The soup was thin; I would be hungry later.

"Why did you leave your conservatory?" Herennia asked. "Shouldn't you be going to join an orchestra?"

I shook my head, bending my head over my soup to stall for a moment. I didn't want to tell her the lie I'd been using, that I'd been caught with a boy. For one thing, I liked Herennia and her husband, and for another, I wasn't sure she'd believe me. But I really didn't want to tell the whole story about Mira, and what she turned out to be. "I found out that magefire caused the famine," I said, and looked up from my soup, to see how they reacted.

The baby was squirming; Herennia offered him her breast, stroking his soft dark hair as he nursed. Metello had looked up sharply at my words. "So the Lady's Gift *is* poison," he said.

"Yes." I looked back down at my soup. "I'd always hoped to play with an orchestra in Cuore, but after I found out about magefire—I didn't want to have anything to do with the Circle. So I left."

"Let's hear you play," Metello said, so I finished my soup and tuned up my violin. I played one of the ballads I'd learned with Mira, to warm up, and then played the music for the Redentore healing prayer. The fire had burned down, leaving the room deeply shadowed; I couldn't see Herennia's reaction to my playing, or Metello's.

When I finished, they were silent for a moment, Herennia rocking the baby. Then Herennia said, "God is with you, Eliana, even if you don't know it." Her voice was distinct in the darkness, and I wasn't sure if she meant to reassure me or to frighten me.

Metello was gone when I got up in the morning; Herennia gave me a small bowl of porridge for breakfast, then said, "Wait a while. There's something that must be done before you go on."

We sat on the doorstep of the house, in the sunshine,

Herennia's baby in her lap. Her cat sauntered over and rubbed against my leg; I picked it up and it purred vigorously, butting its head against my chin. The morning sun dazzled my eyes. Staring across Herennia and Metello's fields, I could almost see my own mother striding along the path, a basket over her arm and a jug of water balanced on one hip. Normally she would bring out a snack of bread and cheese in midmorning to whoever was working in the fields, but one day when we were planting, the basket contained bread and cheese and a kitten. One of the cats had had kittens a few weeks earlier, and my mother had finally found them, and she'd brought one out to the fields for us to play with. Donato had set the kitten on his shoulder; it had squeaked a protest and tightened its claws, but Donato had just laughed, gently detached it, and handed it to me.

Metello returned with an old woman, one of the grannies who had probably never given up the Old Way. She kissed Herennia's baby and then squinted into my face. "What's your name, boy?" she asked.

"I'm not a boy," I said. "My name is Eliana."

She looked startled, squinted into my face again, then let out a rusty chuckle. "Very well then, Eliana. Have you received God's seal?" she asked.

"I don't know what you mean," I said.

She motioned for me to kneel and took a cup of water from the well. "This will give you God's seal upon your soul," she said, as if this explained everything. She muttered briefly in the Old Tongue, finishing off with the familiar *Arka, v'bara, v'nehora kadosha*. With the water, she drew a cross on my forehead, each eyelid, my lips, my hands, my stomach, and my feet. "May your soul be filled with the glory of God. May your eyes be opened to see the world of God," she murmured, "May your lips be opened to speak the word of God. May your hands be strengthened to do the work of God. May your womb be opened to have children for God. And may your feet carry you along the path God has laid out for you." She poured a little water into her cupped hand, then splashed it over my head. It dripped down the back of my neck as she kissed me on the forehead with a loud *smack*. "Welcome, daughter," she said, and then sniffled, her eyes filling.

Herennia and Metello were smiling happily as they helped me to my feet. "There," Herennia said. "Now God will *definitely* be looking after you, wherever you go."

I was baffled, but I was afraid that if I asked for an explanation, it would be lengthy, so I thanked all of them and took my leave.

My eyes, opened by God or not, didn't see anything different as I continued south and west. I cringed a little, thinking back over the ritual. "May your womb be opened"? Maybe if I'd stayed home and gotten married I would want children. All my sisters-in-law seemed happy enough to have baby after baby, even if they discreetly tried to space the pregnancies a bit. I was certainly old enough for a husband and children, but when I tried to imagine a husband, I blushed and found myself wanting to think of something else.

In late afternoon, I stopped to rest under a tree for a little while. My feet were blistered, and I tried not to think about how much worse I was making them by pushing myself. I took off my boots for a few minutes, just to give my feet a little air, and shrugged off my pack and violin case.

I needed something to occupy my mind for a time, to keep me from fretting about my lack of progress while I waited. As I set down the pack, I heard a bump that reminded me that I still had the box of Mira's letters. I opened my bundle; the box was near the bottom.

I suspected that the letters at the top were the most recent, so I tipped them out into my hand and read from the bottom up. *Dear Miriamne,* read the first letter. *We miss you so much.* It read much like a letter from my own mother. Mira had been taken away from her parents; this was unusual for a child with mage ability. Normally, promising children stayed with their parents until they were twelve. They attended academies close to home, where their parents could visit, for four years after that. Mage-talented children might be taken from their homes, though, if their parents were troublemakers—which Mira's parents were, that was clear from the letters. *You stupid fools.* I remembered this letter. *We don't want your money. We want our daughter back. Isabella and Marino of Tafano, Verdia.*

I should have realized when I read this—parents of mage-talented children were paid a stipend when their children left home. Parents of seminarians received a stipend as well—my parents had been supportive of my brother's decision when he left the seminary, but mildly depressed at the loss of income. Parents of conservatory students received nothing, although most professional musicians sent some of their money home, so the investment was generally considered worth it.

Mira—Miriamne—was exceptionally talented. Liemo had called her a focus, and reading the letters, it became clear what he meant. Any mage could raise a great deal of power and unleash it; mages working in concert could raise enough power to rain fire down on an entire army. A focus, though, could direct that power with the precision of a seamstress's needle. Burning, for instance, a crossbow bolt even as it sped toward its target. Miriamne was so skilled that as a test of her abilities when she demanded admittance to the full Circle, just before her sixteenth birthday, she had burned her name into the side of a flying bolt. And sent the bolt to her mother, apparently, as a gift, because Isabella thanked her for it and complimented her skill, though she sounded a bit like my mother the time two of my brothers had presented her with the biggest frog they'd ever found.

During the war, the tone of Isabella's letters grew both fearful and reproachful. Miriamne served on the front lines during the war, and Isabella was clearly very worried about her. At the same time, she pointed out repeatedly how close Miriamne was to her home; surely, during a break in the fighting, she could visit? Then the fighting intensified, and Isabella was simply worried. *Please, my daughter, remember that as skilled as you are, there may be one just like you on the other side of the battlefield. Please try to stay out of that person's sight.*

The first letter after the war ended was openly angry and reproachful; Miriamne had not come. *I would have thought that you would have liked to see your grandmother, at least,* Isabella wrote. *You and she were so close once, and she is an old woman now. And she is not getting any younger.*

I wished I could see Mira's letters; I wondered if I would recognize my friend in them. Some of the early letters sounded as if Mira's mother was trying to take her down a peg. *Don't think this makes you better than your parents,* Isabella had said in one letter. And in another, *They're telling you that you're better, you're theirs, and you're alone. They're lying on all three counts.* Mira's father had never written to her; I assumed that this was because he couldn't read or write. Most of my brothers couldn't.

The letter that started with "you stupid fools" had not

been written to Mira; I wondered how she had come into possession of it. I could imagine someone like Liemo flinging it down before the child-Mira, taunting her with her mother's impotent anger. I imagined the child-Mira picking it up when he was gone, keeping it secretly with her other letters. I could see her reading it over as tangible proof of her mother's love, that Isabella would risk the wrath of the Circle by raging at them for taking away her daughter. That was the letter I had knocked off her desk at the conservatory. She must have taken it out sometimes to read it. Maybe she was trying to draw strength from her mother's anger.

My own mother was not a firebrand like Isabella. Still, I remembered one time that I had been unjustly blamed for something by a neighbor—she had cursed at me for picking her roses, when it was actually the squirrels eating them. My mother had overheard, and had come to my rescue, her face flushed and her fists clenched. I had been relieved that my mother didn't believe I was guilty, but also frightened by her anger. She seldom got really angry.

I had missed her terribly my first year at the conservatory.

Dear Miriamne. We have terrible news for you. Your grandmother has died. This was the final, most recent letter. *We are all doing poorly from the famine. Not even weeds grow in our fields these days, and any reserves we had before are gone. The money from the Circle helps, as much as I hate to admit it, but we have to share with the rest of the village. Even if they do not expect it, we feel an obligation.*

Your grandmother grew ill from a fever. It was not a terrible sickness, and she was once a strong woman, but weakened by hunger, she died. She asked for you in her delirium. We told her you'd come if you could.

*We don't know how much longer we can stay here, but
we don't know where else we can go. There are rumors
that we won't be allowed to leave, that the Circle will do
whatever it takes to keep us here. Do you know if that's
true? They would starve us to death willfully?*

*Do you know if they will let you come for a visit soon?
You said that once the war was over, you'd be able to visit
again. We'd love to see you, Miriamne. Please. You can't
truly have turned your back on us. Take care of yourself
and don't let them frighten you. God bless you. Love, your
mother.*

I folded the letter. This must have been the letter that
arrived in Cuore, with Mira's grandmother's violin—this
must have been the letter that convinced her to run away. I
tried to imagine Mira in Cuore, weeping over the letter
and saying to herself, *No more.* It occurred to me that she
could not have left immediately; to make good her escape,
she would have had to do some planning. Maybe she told
the Circle that she intended to visit her family, headed to
Verdia, and never returned. It occurred to me that the
Circle had probably sent people to visit Isabella, looking
for Mira. I found myself hoping that Isabella hadn't gotten
herself in trouble when the Circle came. Reading over the
letters, I'd started to like her.

"Signora."

I jumped up, still barefoot, and turned to stare at the
person speaking; the letter fluttered from my hand. It took
me a moment to realize that it was the madman who had
accosted Giula and me outside of Pluma. "Go away," I
said. Had he followed me? How had he known where I
was going?

Instead of leaving, he fell to his knees. "Pray for me,"
he said in a husky voice.

"Pray for you? Why?"

"Anointed of God," he said. "Pray for me!" I came over to stand beside him and he pulled me down to kneel, facing him. "In the name of the Mother and Her Son and the Light," he said, and looked at me expectantly.

"I don't know what you want from me," I burst out.

"Not like that!" he said. "How will you ever reach your destination if you say such stupid prayers?"

"You're crazy," I said.

"Of course I am!" he said. "That's why I want you to pray for me."

I sighed in frustration, but he had a good grip on my sleeves, and showed no inclination to let me back up. Finally, I sketched a cross on his forehead. "B'shem Arka, v'barah, v'nehora kadosha," I said. "Rachamin, Arka. Rachamin, Gèsu. Refuya, Arka. Refuya, Gèsu." I had come to the end of what I knew, so I drew another cross on his forehead.

"Thank you," he said. He now wore a beatific smile. "God opened my eyes. She opened my *eyes*. But what I see isn't always what everyone else sees." He stood up slowly, dragging me after him. I stood barefoot in the road, wondering if he were ever going to let go of me.

"Do you want to know what I see when I look at you?" he asked.

"No," I said.

"I see the soldier," he said. "I see the fires. I see—" He released me abruptly and I stumbled back a step. "You don't need me, Eliana," he said. "You can see clearly enough for yourself." He turned and headed down the road, back the way I had come, humming to himself.

How had he known my name? I stared after him, terribly shaken, and eventually concluded that he must have listened to Giula and me talking, back when he first harassed us in the woods. I watched until he was out of sight—I really didn't want him following me again. Then I gathered up Mira's letters, put them back in the box, and pulled on my boots. I continued down the road as fast as I could go. I didn't want to have to sleep outside that night. Tonight I didn't even have Giula to watch over me.

To my distress, I found no occupied farms before night fell. I finally pried a shutter off one of the abandoned houses and lit a fire in the hearth, so at least I'd be inside and have walls between me and the old man. The house was dark and empty, and the leaping fire cast eerie shadows on the walls. There was no furniture. I leaned against the wall by the fire, wrapped in my cloak.

Back when I was just twelve or thirteen, Bella used to tell Giula and me ghost stories, preferably when we slipped out of our rooms late at night and met in the grove behind the chapel. Bella was a superb storyteller, and even though I wasn't as gullible as Giula, she had been able to make my hair stand on end. Snatches of Bella's stories came back to me now, watching the shadows on the walls. If I'd ever been somewhere that might be haunted, this was it.

Don't be ridiculous, I thought. *Herennia and Metello set up house in an abandoned cottage just like this one and they don't spend their nights sitting up, staring at shadows.* I broke out my provisions and bit into a piece of cheese. Suddenly I was absolutely certain that the people who had lived here were dead. And then I was certain they were watching me, just like the girl Bella talked about who'd hanged herself from the last bough of the apple tree . . .

A log in the fire split with a snap and I nearly jumped out of my skin. *This was ridiculous.* I was not the sort of person who got jumpy. Still, I crossed myself like a granny, muttering the Old Tongue words under my breath, to keep away the evil eye. The ritual made me feel a bit better. Finishing my cheese, I banked the fire and curled up to go to sleep, staring into the darkness.

• • •

I stood in the doorway of the farmhouse. To the west, on the hill, I could see five figures silhouetted in the last of the afternoon light. Fear stabbed me through like a spear and I started to shout warning, but it was too late. Fire was falling from the sky. I could hear screams around me and I realized some of them were mine—

• • •

I woke with a gasp. Lady protect me. No, that wasn't right. God protect me. The fire had gone out and I could see *nothing* in the darkness. I was trapped and dying—no, my cloak was wrapped around me, that was all—the house was haunted—

I pulled one hand free of my cloak and cupped it to summon witchlight. I needed light to banish the spirits; what had my village priest and priestess taught me, when I was just a child? *Light will banish the Maledori. Now that you can make witchlight, you can always chase the Maledori away.* I concentrated, focused—

Darkness.

I *concentrated*.

Darkness.

My hands were shaking. Witchlight finally gleamed through my fingers, dim and greenish. Shadows leapt along the walls. I saw a woman, as tall and narrow as a spear, holding a violin, dancing in a circle of flame—I cupped my witchlight against my chest, willing it not to go out.

There was no way I could stay in here. Could it possibly be almost dawn? Still cupping my witchlight in my shaking hands, I grabbed all my belongings into my arms and scrambled out the broken shutter.

As soon as I was out of the house, I felt calmer. The sky was just turning violet in the east; the morning star gleamed like a candle against mist. The air was frosty and it was still too dark to travel. I wrapped my cloak around me and sat down on the low wall around the abandoned farm to wait for dawn.

I was almost home now. Starting as early as I did, I could cover the final distance by late afternoon. My feet and shoulders were raw, but that wouldn't matter if I were back with my family. Besides, as I walked, I traveled back into more fertile lands. Seeing lush fields again, I almost felt that I could draw my own strength from the renewed land. It was a beautiful day, with a clear blue sky and sunshine that warmed as the day went on. The light of the day almost dispelled the shadows of the night.

Doratura was a small village, just a cluster of houses and farms on the other side of a low hill. I recognized the hill as I drew close, in the deep shadows of afternoon. The trees on the ridge were stark against the blue sky.

Climbing the hill, I smelled something—ash, and old cooked meat. I suddenly remembered Mira's description of the square in Cuore where the Fedeli executed heretics at the stake. *It smells like cooked rotten meat.* I shuddered— had the Fedeli been here? Executed someone in Doratura? I broke into a run, scrambling up the hill until I could see down into the village.

"Lady—" I whispered.

My village was gone.

I shook my head, unable to believe what I saw. The houses were charred foundations, the fields black, the trees twisted. *Magefire.* Mages had done this. This had to be somebody else's village, I thought. I had forgotten my way and wandered here by mistake. This had happened during the war, except that the ash was still fresh, the stench still potent.

"No," I heard myself saying. "Lord and Lady . . ." I started running, stumbling and nearly falling on the damp grass of the hillside. There were charred bones in the streets, bones in the doorways and courtyards of the houses, child-sized bones that had uselessly sought shelter behind trees, behind houses, in their mothers' arms. I fixed my eyes on the ground under my feet, unwilling to look up. My family could not be—they couldn't.

My house was on the far edge of the village. I could see it from the hill, but somehow I could refuse to believe until I stood among the charred ruins of my home, stared at the empty skeleton of the barn, the blackened fields. The stone foundations of my parents' house still stood, and I stepped slowly over the threshold.

"Mother?" I whispered.

Doratura's dead had been left where they fell; some had been blasted to ash by magefire, others had been picked over by scavengers. There were bones scattered through the house and yard, and as I stared around me, unable to believe what I saw, I realized that I didn't even know whose bones were whose, where one body stopped and another started.

A breeze ruffled my hair and stirred the ashes around me like sand. I need to bury them, I thought. If I couldn't be here to warn them—to die with them—I could at least bury their bodies. I let my violin and pack slip from my raw shoulders onto the stone doorstep. Tools were kept in the barn; if there was a shovel to find, it would be in there.

The animals had met the same fate as the people. As I

sorted through the wreckage, I found a small skull that had probably belonged to a cat. It had hidden itself under a low shelf, uselessly seeking safety. I wondered if there were mouse skeletons in there as well, or if they'd managed to get away. Near the shelf, I found the scoop of a shovel. The wooden handle had burned away, but with effort, I could use the scoop to dig a grave.

I had to kneel to use it, in the yard outside the house. I decided to dig where the herb garden had been, because the soil would be softer there. It bruised the heels of my hands as I worked; I settled for scraping out a single shallow grave, then went to gather up the bones.

Since I could hold only a few fragments in my hands, I used my spare robe to gather up what was left. The task would have been easier with a broom, the fragments were so small and so scattered; what I scooped up with my hands was as much dust and ash as bone, but then, the ash was probably my family, too. I piled everything onto the robe and carried it to the grave.

Before I covered over the bones with dirt, I took out the wooden box of Mira's letters. I was tired of carrying this. I set the box on top of the bones. I thought for a moment about shaking out the spare robe, but I couldn't imagine ever wearing it again. After staring for a moment at the small heap of bone, rubble, and ash, I used the shovel to close the grave.

I still couldn't believe that this was my village—my home—my family, until I returned to the doorstep, to gather up my violin and my bag. Nestled in the corner, between the doorstep and the foundation wall, was a tiny clay bird whistle, like the ones Donato used to make for me. I knelt to pick it up, and grief tore through me like a knife. Donato would have made this for his daughter, I knew. Now he was dead, and his wife and children with him.

My hand shook, and the whistle fell to the ground and cracked. "Oh *no!*" I screamed. I fell to my knees and picked up the two pieces, trying uselessly to fit them together again. "No, no, *no,* why did I have to drop it? Why? *No.* Please—" I pressed the pieces back together. "Please don't be broken. Please, please don't be broken."

I don't know how long I wept in agony over the shards of the broken whistle, but when I stopped, it was quite dark. I would have to spend the night here, with the ghosts of my family. I spread out my cloak and sat down, wishing I had wood for a fire; the spring night was turning cool, but everything burnable in Doratura had already been consumed by the magefire.

Staring into the darkness, I realized there was one more thing I needed to do for my family. I took out my bow and tightened it, then tuned my violin and tucked it under my chin, rising to stare out over the broken fields into the darkness around me.

Da dat da *da* dat da *wham wham wham. Da* dat da *da* dat da *wham wham wham.* The rhythm of the funeral music didn't echo against the dirt and ash that I stamped my foot against, but it echoed in my head, and as I closed my eyes, I imagined that Bella and Flavia were here to play with me.

I played the music through. Herennia had mentioned dances; my feet were too sore to dance as vigorously as I had that night in Bosco, but I moved in a slow circle as the girl there had shown me. *Right*-pause-*behind*-pause. *Right*-pause-*behind*-pause. At least there was no one here to see me.

I'd had seven brothers, all married, all with children. Donato was the second oldest. He'd been delighted by the prospect of a younger sister after all those boys; in addition to making me whistles and helping me climb trees, he'd taught me to fight well enough to beat any boy my age, even the one boy who was bigger than I was. Donato was less of a ruffian than our eldest brother, Agrippo; Donato's wife, Imelda, was gentle and sweet with a wry sense of humor, the kind of woman who was impressed by kindness, not the ability to intimidate all other prospective suitors.

Gone, the song echoed.

My father was a big, quiet man. I'd gotten my height from him; he was taller than I was, taller than any man in the village except for Agrippo, who was a hair taller. My father had always been a little bewildered at the idea of a daughter; I'd catch him blinking at me like I was some sort of lost exotic bird that had flown to Verdia by mistake. When I was little, he would take me into his lap to tell me stories about Lugo, my grandfather's youngest brother, who was blindingly stupid but always seemed to have things work out in his favor anyway.

Gone.

My mother—I realized I was crying, my hands shaking. I could barely hold my violin. I remembered my mother's touch, gently combing the tangles out of my hair. Each year in late summer, when we celebrated the Birth of the World, she would snip off a lock of my hair to keep in a pouch that she wore around her neck, along with a lock of hair from each of my brothers. That way she could pray for us, even if we were far away. The night before I went away to the conservatory, I asked to see the contents of the pouch—I wanted to be certain nothing had happened to the lock of my hair she had cut the previous summer.

She unlaced the soft circle of fabric and spread out the pouch on our table. There were ten locks of hair. "This one is yours," she said, pointing to a soft fawn-brown curl. "Agrippo's, Donato's, Rufo's, Erucio's, Lorenzo's, Berio's, Fiorenzo's."

"Who do these two belong to?" I asked, pointing at two tiny locks of silvery hair.

"I had two other children," she said. "One between Agrippo and Donato, one just before you. They died when they were just babies." She sighed and looked away. "I shouldn't keep these—those children are with the Lady. But I can't bear to give them up."

Gone.

I couldn't play anymore. I paused, lowering the bow, trying to keep back my sobs.

Somewhere beyond me in the darkness, I saw the faint outline of a figure. For a moment, I thought it was Donato's ghost, but the shadow was far too tangible, and I realized that it was the madman from the road. His eyes were calm and he didn't look at me. Half closing his eyes, he raised his hands as if to grasp invisible hands on either side of him, then began dancing, moving in a slow circle around the clearing. *Step-pause-step step step turn, step. Step-pause-step step step turn, step.*

Instead of feeling frightened, this time I felt oddly comforted. I lifted the bow again and began playing. *Da dat da da dat da wham wham wham. Step-pause-step step step turn, step.* The madman danced silently, except for the soft crunch of leaves underfoot. My hands were shaking again, but I was able to hold the violin steady enough to play the music through twice more. When I finished, I almost dropped the violin as I bowed my head, my body shaking with sobs. When I looked up, the madman was gone. Still shaking, I put the violin away, and curled up in my cloak. I had no one to watch over me, but the madman didn't frighten me anymore.

This is all a dream, I told myself, as I stared up at the stars. *If only I go to sleep, I will wake up, and find myself back in that empty house, or with Herennia and Metello. Or at the conservatory, with Mira beside me.* But I was too cold to sleep. And too alone.

At dawn, I rose and walked to the next village, Gervala, which was a few miles away. I don't know what I would have done if I'd found another burned-out dead village, but Gervala was untouched. I went to the door of the first house I came to and knocked.

A woman opened the door a crack and peered out. "Who are you?"

"My name is Eliana—I'm from Doratura—"

She slammed the door closed. "Go away," she said, her voice muffled behind the door.

"What happened?" I cried. "What *happened*? Everything's *gone*." There was no response, and I pounded on the door. *"Open the door!"* I screamed. "Tell me what happened to my village!"

The door opened again, and I half fell into the doorway. "Come in, then," the woman hissed, and I limped inside.

She did not invite me past the threshold. "There were refugees from the wasteland," she said. "They came up, trying to go north. *Doratura* took them in." Her voice was scornful. "This was just a place to rest, they weren't going to stay here. But soldiers came to meet them on the road, to turn them back. The refugees wouldn't go home. The soldiers pushed them back to Doratura, the refugees fighting them the whole way. So then two weeks ago, the mages came." She shuddered involuntarily. "Just five of them. They stood on the hill that overlooks the village and . . . they burned everything. They killed everyone."

"Everyone?" I whispered.

"There were a few survivors. They took them south, to

Ravenna—it's an encampment for refugees, deep in the wasteland. And a prison, I guess, for the ones who make trouble." Her eyes hardened. "Now leave. I've told you everything I know."

"My family," I said. "Regillo and Marisa. Do you know if—"

"Go away!" she said, and struck me, shoving me out the door. She slammed it in my face.

I was alone in the damp morning. I tried knocking on another door, but this time no one answered. Eventually, the Gervalesi would have to come out to do their morning chores, but so long as I was there, apparently, they would sit inside with their doors barred.

• Very well then, I thought. I needed more food; most of the provisions I had purchased in Pluma were gone. I could steal from the Gervalesi without feeling particularly guilty about it. I pried open one family's storehouse and stole grain and dried fruit, and refilled my wineskin from their wine barrels. Their early spring stores were low, but not too low. I was quite certain they were watching me, but no one came. They were afraid of me, I knew—an angry orphan with nothing to lose, but worse, a symbol of their own shame. When I had taken all I could carry, I left the village.

Back on the road, I realized I had no idea where to go now. But the woman had said that they took the survivors south. I had not been able to identify the bodies as I buried them. Maybe someone in my family had survived. Limping from the pain of the blisters on my feet, I turned away and headed south.

PART THREE

*The Weapon You Know
How to Use*

"Enough. I don't know anyone from Doratura. It may be that only refugees survived. That happens sometimes." He patted my shoulder apologetically. "Good luck to you, though."

We reached Ravenna in late afternoon. Ravenna itself was a valley of blackened earth and ragged makeshift tents made of blankets and stitched-together cloaks. Three buildings stood in the center of Ravenna: a keep, a barracks, and a stable.

A fence ran along the hills surrounding the valley, golden in the setting sun. Sticks had been planted in crossed X's, set close together; it was the sort of arrangement used to block a cavalry charge, but in this case it had been designed simply to keep the Ravenessi from leaving. The fence could not possibly be all that sturdy—it would be easy enough to work one of the sticks loose—but I could see patrols of soldiers along the edge as well.

"They shoot on sight if you try to leave," the refugee whispered to me. "So if you make a run for it, do it after dark, on a moonless night, and hope the soldiers don't see you."

Just beyond the valley, draped with shadows, I could see a wall, winding past the camp like a gray river until it was hidden from view by the rise of another hill.

"What is that?" I asked.

"That's the wall," the refugee said. "That's what Ravenna is for. The Circle wants a wall built along the border, to protect us from the Vesuviani." Below us, the workers had finished for the day; I saw no signs of life by the wall, but a long line had formed below us in Ravenna, and I could see a large pot over the flicker of a single fire.

The soldiers led us down into the sea of tents. The camp looked worse close up; many of the "tents" were simply cloaks staked up, barely waist-high. Except for the single road that passed through to the keep, the tents were crammed together so tightly I'd have to turn sideways to pass between them. People came out of their tents to stare as we passed. Their eyes and cheeks were hollow. I could feel their eyes burning into me, and I tried to stand up straighter, to show that I was not afraid.

"Hey," one of the soldiers said. "Here." He handed me a string, with fifteen chips of wood strung along it. A small star had been burned into each, and a hole cut in the center for the string. "Ration chits." I stared at the wood chips stupidly, and he sighed. "One chit gets you breakfast, one dinner. This is a week's worth. Once you start working you'll be able to earn more, but—I thought I'd let you get settled in."

I slipped the string over my head and tucked the chits inside my shirt, next to Bella's cross.

"Stay out of trouble," he continued. "Anyone tries to steal from you, or tries to make trouble with you—well, you can come find me. My name's Mario. Don't get into fights—Teleso doesn't give a rat's ass who started it, if you're found fighting."

"Who's Teleso?" I asked.

"The camp commander, and you don't want to piss him off—got that?" Mario clasped my shoulder briefly. "They're serving dinner now," he said. "You should go line up and get some."

The light was fading from the sky. "I gather I am not permitted to leave?" I asked.

"No one is allowed to leave," he said.

"I thought slavery was against the Law of the Lady," I said softly.

"You're not a slave," Mario said. "No one will make you work."

"But I'm not allowed to leave," I said. "And if I don't work, I don't get any food."

Mario looked wounded—I was a bit startled, as I hadn't honestly expected my snide comments to make much of an impact. "I'm sorry," he said softly. "I hope you find your family."

I joined the long line of people, shuffling slowly forward. The bravado I'd felt earlier had evaporated like the last of the life from the fields around me. Whatever I was going to do now, I could do after I'd eaten. I'd finished the last of my provisions that morning.

As the twilight deepened into night, I realized that I had never been anywhere so dark in my life. Torches burned near the front of the line, but that seemed to be the only light in Ravenna. I cupped my hand and tried to summon witchlight, just to be able to see the people around me, but nothing happened.

"Doesn't work," the person behind me grunted. "No magery works here."

Even on moonless nights on my parents' farm, I had been able to summon witchlight to light my way. Anywhere but the wasteland, a crowd this size would be lit with hundreds of tiny lights, cupped to illumine conversations and to keep people from tripping over the uneven ground. Here, the torches cast only a small circle of light, and there was almost no moon.

It was a long, chilly wait. I pulled my cloak around me, but still could not get warm. The food, when I finally reached the head of the line, was a thin gruel. I surrendered a chit and they filled my bowl. I was ravenous, and moved only a little way from the soldiers serving the food to take out my spoon and eat it. I scraped the bowl clean with my fingers, but was left hungry, even so.

As I watched, scraping out my empty bowl, a boy dodged in between the soldiers, grabbing a handful of wooden ration chits from the barrel by the cauldron of food. "Hey!" one of the soldiers yelled, giving the boy a cuff to the head that sent him sprawling.

"Let him go, Niccolo," the other soldier urged in a whisper. "Just get the chits and let him run. He's only a boy."

"Not bloody likely," Niccolo hissed back, hauling the boy up by his collar. "I'm turning this runt over to Teleso. They're all thieves, and I've had enough of them." The other soldier watched helplessly as Niccolo stalked off into the darkness, hauling the boy behind him. I watched a moment longer, then went to find somewhere to sleep.

In the darkness, there was no way I could navigate the sea of tents. I continued down the path, past the keep and toward the far edge of the valley. I finally came to an edge where there was a little space and lay down, wrapped in my cloak. I was exhausted, but I couldn't sleep. The ground felt harder than any hearthstone. I rolled onto my back and looked at the sky.

The sky was very clear that night, and the moon was a narrow crescent. It occurred to me that there were more stars than I could normally see. When I went out at night, I usually held some witchlight to see my way, and that clouded my night vision; here, I couldn't make witchlight at all, so there was nothing to keep me from seeing the stars. In places, I couldn't see individual stars, but there was a misty white glow. The sky was beautiful, but oddly threatening. I thought of the Redentore God, who Giorgi said sent pain as well as joy; I could imagine Her creating such a sky simply to impress upon me how small I was. I stared at the stars for a long time before my weariness pulled me down into restless sleep.

I was stiff and cold when I got up in the morning, and damp with dew. To my relief, no one had stolen my violin or my chits. Everyone seemed to be heading to the food line, so I joined in the slow shuffle. I had risen early, so I got my breakfast—more gruel—a bit faster than I'd gotten my dinner. When I'd finished the last of it, I wandered around Ravenna a bit, hoping to see a familiar face.

There was a little bit more to Ravenna than I'd seen the previous night. In addition to the keep and the sea of tents, there were occasional bits of stone walls. Ravenna had been a town once; destroyed in the war, bits and pieces remained and were used to hold up some of the tents.

Things were packed so tightly that anywhere I went off the main road, I felt that I was trespassing on someone's territory. People were still staring at me, and an old woman glared as I stepped over the edge of her tent. Finally, I returned to the piazza next to the keep; at least this didn't seem to belong to anybody.

A thick pillar of wood stood in front of the keep; iron rings were screwed to the sides, on level with my head. It looked like a permanent installation, but I'd missed it last night in the dark. As I studied the pillar, a door in the side of the keep swung open, and four soldiers led out a struggling boy. It was the boy I'd seen yesterday trying to steal ration chits. One of the soldiers unbelted the boy's tunic and tried to pull it off, but he continued to struggle and almost slipped out of their hands, so the soldiers bound his hands to the iron rings on the pillar and then tore his tunic open to bare his back. One of the soldiers read from a parchment: "For attempted theft of ration chits. Fifteen lashes." The boy cried out, though the lash hadn't touched him yet.

Three of the soldiers returned to the keep; the fourth picked up a long whip and brought it down on the boy's back. The snap echoed across the piazza and the boy screamed. His cry was echoed by a woman watching—his mother? She clapped her hands over her mouth and moaned in anguish, watching the lashing.

I didn't want to see this, but I stood frozen, counting the blows. The boy went limp as they finished. They cut the bonds and pushed him away from the whipping post; the woman rushed forward to gather him up. I could hear a low moan from the boy. The soldiers coiled the whip and went back into the keep. No one else in Ravenna seemed to have noticed.

With my week's worth of ration chits, I had no need to go work on the wall, but within a few hours, I realized that I was terribly, stunningly bored. There were a surprising number of other Ravenessi who didn't seem to be working, either. I found out later that many fed themselves some other way—begging, prostitution, theft, or the largesse of family. The children, elderly, and ill were forced to rely on this, but there were other able-bodied young people as well, sitting around and killing time. We had no fields to tend, no crafts to occupy our hands, nothing to do at all except stand in line for food twice a day and wait for death by slow starvation. By midmorning, I was hungry again. I drank some water to give me the feeling of fullness for a little while.

It had been a few days since I'd played the violin. At least practicing would give me a way to pass the hours until dinner. Sitting in the spot where I'd slept, I took out my violin and tuned up. I played my half of the duet I'd played with Giula, then my section of the ensemble piece we'd been working on right when I left the conservatory. Around me, people ducked out of their tents, staring at me. I flushed slightly, but ignored them and kept playing. Some settled down in the dirt across from me, and others began to clap time with my playing. I realized, with no little surprise, that they were listening to me for pleasure.

I hadn't played for such an uncritical audience since my mother became a sophisticated enough listener to evaluate my technique, back when I was just a child. At the conservatory, I never listened to another violinist without quietly noticing every mistake, every fumble, every note I could have played better, and I knew the other violinists returned the favor. In Ravenna, though, people seemed to view my playing as high entertainment. An old woman closed her eyes, a slight smile on her face, and one or two people got up to dance. Nothing formal like the Redentore dance I'd seen; they just wanted to move to the music. I almost started enjoying myself; it was nice to feel like a concert star. I segued into some of the folk songs I'd played with Mira, and people sang along. There was some inconsistency in the words they sang, but no one seemed to notice.

I scanned the faces of the audience as I played, hoping to see someone I knew. I caught a glimpse, in the late afternoon, of a young man who looked familiar, but he was gone before I could place him. My first impulse was to race after him, but I couldn't just leave my violin case and bag behind, and by the time I gathered everything up, he'd be long gone. Besides, thinking it over, I was fairly certain he wasn't from my village. If I knew him, I knew him from somewhere else.

People began lining up for dinner just before the work crews were expected back, in late afternoon. I joined the line soon after that; I was ravenous. The soldiers hadn't started serving the food yet, so the line wasn't moving, but at least close to the head of the line, I'd get fed sooner.

"Hey," a voice said behind me. "You're new here, aren't you?"

I turned. The young woman behind me in line was as

thin and ragged as anyone else here, but she had an inner warmth that lit her eyes with life. She smiled kindly, the first welcoming look I'd seen in weeks. "You are new," she said, without waiting for my response. "I'd know you, if you weren't."

"You're right," I said. "I am new here."

"My name is Lucia," she said.

"Eliana."

"Where did you come from? You haven't been living in the wasteland."

"Doratura. I'm looking for my family."

"Doratura," she said. "Where were you before that?"

"Conservatory."

"Ah, yes. That explains the violin case." She touched my arm gently. "Doratura was destroyed by the Circle— you knew that, yes?"

"Yes." My voice nearly caught, and I cleared my throat. "A woman in the neighboring village told me that soldiers took the survivors south, to Ravenna."

Lucia nodded. "That's right. There were ten survivors from Doratura who were brought here, plus three of the refugees that they had sheltered."

Hope leapt in my throat and blinded me. "What were their names? Can you tell me?"

She closed her eyes a moment. "From Doratura—Bino, Adria, and their children Idi, Pamfilo, and Masina; Eleanora, and her son Duilio; a man named Alessandro; and two orphan children, Neri and Balbo."

I remembered Bino and Adria, Eleanora and Alessandro. Bino had been a good friend of my father's. Alessandro once brawled with my eldest brother Agrippo over a girl; they'd both wound up with cracked heads, and the girl decided they were both louts and married someone else. I realized dimly through my sobs that Lucia was holding me up; I had not even realized that she'd slipped her arm around my waist to support me.

"Let me go," I choked. I wanted to get away from the crowd, to cry somewhere more private, where no one could stare at me.

"Stay here," she said. "You don't want to lose your place in line." I struggled, against her and against my own uncooperative legs, but she held me firmly. "You need to eat," she said. "You'll need all of your strength. And don't give up hope. Those were the survivors brought here. If any of your relatives were gone from the village when the Circle attacked, they might have fled and avoided both death and capture."

"Perhaps." I could almost stand again. "Alessandro and the others. Where are they now?"

I could feel her arm tighten around me again. "They escaped a few nights ago," she whispered. "All of them. Your village sticks together."

My knees held, this time, and I found myself laughing. "So now I'm truly alone."

"You're not alone," she said. "God is with you."

I stiffened, then straightened up slowly and turned to look carefully into her face. Lucia looked steadily back at me. After a moment, she let go of my waist and took my hand. "You're one of us, aren't you?" she said, and traced a cross on my skin. I jumped, starting to pull away, and she squeezed my hand. "Don't be afraid," she said. "The Fedeli don't come to Ravenna. This is perhaps the safest place in all the Empire to be a Redentore." She smiled at the irony and I gave her a tentative grimace back.

"Why do you know everyone here?" I asked.

Lucia smiled, and again her eyes lit like candles behind

a screen. "It's not such a big valley, really," she said. "I try to meet people as they come in."

"Where are you from?" I asked.

"Varena," she said, and my face must have shown my surprise, because she shrugged and added, "It's a long story." Varena was weeks north of here—even further north than Cuore. "Where did you go to conservatory?" she asked.

"The Verdiano Rural Conservatory. In Bascio."

The line began to shuffle forward. "Hey," Lucia said. "Why don't you join me while we eat? There are some friends I'd like to introduce you to."

In the torchlight at the head of the food line, I noticed that Lucia's eyes were a beautiful deep blue. Where had I seen eyes that color before? I couldn't remember. "I'd love to," I said.

The tent Lucia led me to was a little larger and more solid-looking than the tents around it. The residents seemed to have claimed at least one solid wall and pulled down their canvas over the edge. Lucia stuck her hand through the flap and waved. "Rafi," she said. "It's Lucia. I've brought a friend."

Rafi flipped the tent flap back and peered out. He had a shock of curly black hair and long black lashes. "Come on in," he said.

There were four people in the tent: Rafi, a beautiful young woman, and two men. "Move over, Giovanni," Lucia said to one of the men.

"For what?" he demanded. "Some other bloody stray you've picked up?" Giovanni looked up to glare at me and I realized with a sickening drop of my stomach who he was.

"You," I gasped. *This* was who I saw while playing earlier.

"Giovanni of Cuore," he said, looking at me nervously. "What do you mean, 'you'?"

It was the violet-eyed pretty-boy from the inn in Pluma. The louse who'd slapped Giula. "Never mind," I said. "If you don't remember, there certainly isn't any point in reminding you."

He continued to stare at me for a moment, and I gave him my most threatening glare. "Oh!" he said suddenly. "From Pluma."

"Yeah," I said. "From Pluma."

"This is Eliana," Lucia introduced me, completely ignoring Giovanni's outburst. I realized where I'd seen her blue eyes before. They were the same color as Giovanni's. "She's the one I heard playing violin earlier today." There was an approving murmur through the tent, though not from Giovanni.

"I still don't see any reason that *I* should move over," Giovanni said.

"Shut up, Giovanni," the other man said, rising slightly to bow to me. "My name is Beneto, and this—" he gestured to the beautiful woman, "is Jesca. It's a pleasure to welcome you to our tent, although we could choose more hospitable surroundings." He gave me a charming smile, then glared at Giovanni, who moved out of the way to let Lucia and me sit down.

Beneto was startlingly clean, cleaner than anyone I'd seen since I'd arrived at Ravenna, and his clothes were cut just a little too nicely—as if he had gone to the best tailor in a substantial city and said, "Make me peasants' clothes." Jesca was Beneto's quiet shadow, with a gentle smile that could melt marble. She was just dusty enough not to stand out like a duck in a henhouse, but the worn elbows of her dress were carefully mended and her long, straight hair was brushed smooth.

"Tea?" Rafi asked. "It's not exactly the best Verdia has to offer, but it'll be hot." Rafi, at least, looked like an ordinary Ravenesse, and it was clear that this was his tent. He wore a cross openly on a leather thong; it dangled over his dishes as he bent to get cups.

"Yes, please," Lucia said, and Beneto and Jesca nodded, so I nodded as well. Giovanni was still busy sulking and didn't answer.

Rafi lit a tiny fire, using flint and steel, and set a pot over it. Beneto was studying me. "Do you think this is the one Amedeo spoke of, Lucia?" he asked.

"Well, he was speaking pretty, ah, poetically," Lucia said. "But she seems right."

Beneto nodded, giving me a long, meditative look. I met his eyes with a glare. I don't like being stared at, especially by someone who's talking about me as if I'm not there. He looked slightly surprised, then smiled warmly. "She's the one."

"The one *what*?" I demanded.

"Your arrival here was not entirely unanticipated," Beneto said. "Amedeo is a prophet. He's a little, well, unstable. I don't know if you've met a prophet before—"

"No."

"They say that the Light is too bright for anyone to hold by himself," Rafi said.

"Which is a polite way of saying Amedeo is crazy," Giovanni said, poking at the fire. "Rafi, did you make enough tea for me?"

Rafi rolled his eyes. "I should say no. But yes, I did." He checked the pot. "And it's ready." He filled the cups and passed them around. I cupped my hands around my tea. It smelled good, but it was weak and bitter. At least it was hot.

"Amedeo said you'd be coming. Or rather, he predicted a musician, 'as tall and straight as a tree in winter,' and he said you'd have the Gift," Lucia said.

"What gift?"

Beneto shrugged. "We don't have the slightest idea. Amedeo seemed to think it was very important, though."

Lucia shrugged as well. "Although, as Giovanni noted so tactfully, Amedeo is crazy. Sometimes what he says is inspired, and sometimes it's just ravings. He's not an especially easy man to be around." She looked a little uncomfortable. "In any case, I think it is God's will that you're here."

"Whatever," Giovanni said. "I think it's the Circle's will that brought her, like the rest of us, to this godforsaken desert of a valley. And it's Lucia's will that brought her to Rafi's tent." He turned to glare at me again. "Peasant." He said it as an insult.

"May I remind you whose tent you are in?" Rafi said. "My origins are also somewhat humbler than yours."

"If *you* aren't a peasant, then what are you doing here?" I asked Giovanni. "I saw you in Pluma. But you claim to be from Cuore. So what are you doing *here*?" For a heartbeat, I wondered if he was another runaway mage.

Giovanni opened his mouth to answer but Lucia cut him off. "Shut up, Giovanni," she said. "Get out of here. Go for a walk. I want to talk to Eliana without your constant interruptions."

"Why can't *you* go for a walk then?" he said.

"That's an order, Giovanni," Jesca said. It was the first I'd heard her speak. She had a deep, melodious voice. Giovanni stomped out with a curse word. "Charming boy," Jesca said. "Beneto and I will go, too, Lucia. I think Eliana is probably feeling a bit overwhelmed." She smiled at Lucia, then turned to me. "It was a pleasure to meet you, Eliana," she said. She clasped my hand briefly, and I noticed that her hands were as soft and delicate as a baby's. Beneto clasped my hand as well; he had calluses, but they were in the wrong spots for farm work. Beneto and Jesca ducked out of the tent, leaving me alone with Rafi and Lucia.

In the silence that followed, I picked up Lucia's hand and flipped it over to study her palm. Her hands were callused, like a peasant's, but small and slender. Her skin was brown, her hair bleached to straw from the sun. "But you come from Varena," I said. "What are you *doing* down here?"

"I came down before the war," she said. "Several years before."

"Why?"

"I got into a bit of trouble." There was a hint of satisfaction in her voice. "The Fedeli wound up not at all pleased with me. Fortunately, I skipped town before they could arrest me."

"But all the way down here?"

"I came to learn the Redentore music," she said. "And the dances."

My heart quickened when she mentioned the music, and I felt my cheeks flush slightly. Lucia watched me carefully, gauging my reaction. "You also feel their power, don't you?" she said.

I nodded, not speaking.

"Do you know songs, or dances, or both?" Lucia asked.

"In the conservatory, many people played the music secretly. I know six songs. I don't know any dances. Or, actually—I passed through a village while I was traveling.

They had a festival and sang songs to the Lady, but they used an Old Way melody. And they danced."

"That's very common," Lucia said. "There are also towns where they dance, but with different music. Or sing, but without dancing. That's why I came to Verdia. To learn everything, to piece it together." Her eyes sparkled in the dim tent.

"How many songs are there?" I asked.

"Hundreds," Lucia said, and she smiled at the flush that rose to my cheeks again. "I can teach you the songs, if you'd like."

"But there's nowhere private here to play," I said. "If I play the music, everyone will hear."

"Teleso likes to say that the Fedeli don't rule here, he does," Lucia said. "And when it comes to Redentore practice, he doesn't give a rat's ass, as long as it keeps people quiet."

Rafi laughed bitterly. "Just wait till the next time he needs an excuse for a massacre." I jumped—Rafi had been so quiet I'd almost forgotten he was there.

Lucia looked at him sharply. "This is Jesca's theory, not mine," Rafi said. "Come on! Everyone knows that he gets a set amount of food to ration to everyone in Ravenna. Are you saying that some of those riots weren't provoked?" Lucia didn't answer, and Rafi went back to cleaning out the teapot.

"Through the music and the dances, God pours out Her light into the world," Lucia said. "I will teach you the songs, if you will play them for our rituals." Lucia looked across the tent at Rafi. "God has not forsaken us; She dances with us, even here." She looked back at me. "And don't worry. You can play them openly in Ravenna."

"All right," I said. "You teach me, I'll play."

Lucia gave me a brilliant smile. "Good," she said.

Neither of us spoke for a minute.

"You still haven't answered my question to Giovanni," I said. "What's he doing down here? And Beneto and Jesca. They aren't peasants either."

Lucia drained the last of her cup of tea and wiped out the cup, then studied the ground for a moment. "Had you and Giovanni met before?" she asked.

"Yes," I said. "When I was passing through Pluma, he accused a friend of mine of spying on him, and slapped her. He *terrified* Giula."

Lucia sighed. "Giovanni has all the charm of a leashed dog that's been kicked too often," she said. "He's hostile and suspicious with everyone. Which is basically why he's down here."

"I don't understand."

Lucia didn't elaborate right away; she looked at Rafi, who checked outside the tent, then came back in and nodded. "I think you should tell her," Rafi said. "If she's to be playing for you, she has every right to know."

Lucia nodded, then took my hand again. "Beneto, Jesca, and Giovanni are the local leaders for the organized reform movement," she said.

"The what?"

"There is a group, organized from Cuore, that is trying to restore the Empire as it was before the Circle," Lucia said. "Do you know what caused the famine?"

I nodded. "Magefire."

"More and more people are realizing that," Lucia said, "but to say it aloud in Cuore invites a death sentence. The Circle will never relinquish their power voluntarily, and they will never stop what they do, no matter what the price. Through their magic, and their cruelty, they have condemned everyone in Ravenna to slow death by starvation." She flushed with anger, and paused to collect her thoughts. "The reform movement began at the university. That's where Beneto, Jesca, and Giovanni met."

"So they were sent down to Ravenna to organize the people here?"

"Beneto and Jesca were sent to Ravenna to organize," Lucia said. "Giovanni was sent to Ravenna because no one in Cuore could stand him." She sighed, her eyes on Rafi. "It's my fault, in a way. The organizers in Cuore used me as an excuse; I'm his cousin. 'You already have family down there.' So of course Giovanni blames me, and so do Jesca and Beneto and Rafi . . ."

"That's not true," Rafi scolded. "I don't think Jesca blames you."

Cousins, I thought. That explained the eye color.

"He's harmless, really," Lucia said. "Useless, but Beneto and Jesca keep him in line."

"On a short leash, you might say," Rafi said.

I laughed. My head was spinning.

"So," Lucia said, and clasped my hand more tightly. "Now you know. I hope we haven't misjudged you—you aren't going to run off and tell Teleso?" I shook my head. "But we need you, Eliana," Lucia said. "We need you on our side. We need you to be one of us."

"Why?" I asked. "What is it you want from me?"

"Your music," she said. "And—Amedeo believes you're important. We don't know why, not yet, but—I know we need you."

"I said I'd play for you," I said. "I haven't changed my mind."

Lucia smiled at me, and again her face lit like the evening star. "Thank you," she said.

I spent the night in Rafi's tent, squeezed in between Lucia and Beneto. Giovanni slept on the other side of Jesca, as far away from me as he could get. Despite the crowding, I slept later and more soundly than I had outside, where I was woken by the light and activity at dawn.

Beneto and Jesca were up and gone by the time I woke; I found out later that they did not work on the wall. Giovanni had just begun to stir as Lucia and I got up, glaring at us from below his drooping lashes. Lucia and I left him rubbing the sleep out of his eyes while we lined up to get breakfast. "You can leave your violin and your cloak here," Rafi said. "I'll take care of them." I left my cloak and bag behind, but took my violin with me. I liked Rafi, but I wasn't leaving my violin anywhere.

"We're celebrating Mass this afternoon," Lucia said.

I gave her an uncertain look. "Celebrating what?"

Lucia was startled. "You haven't celebrated Mass before? But you are one of us, I know that. How much do you know about the Old Way?"

I shook my head. "I learned some songs and prayers at the conservatory, before the Fedeli came and scared everyone too badly to play Old Way music even in secret. While I was coming home, I saw a little bit of a ritual in the woods—and one of the farmers I stayed with had a woman come to 'seal' me."

"That's all?"

I nodded. "There's no way you could play a song here without everyone hearing. How can you do an Old Way ritual in the camp?"

"The Fedeli don't come here," Lucia said.

"You said that before," I said. "How can you be so sure?"

Lucia grinned broadly. "*Nobody* comes down here if

they can help it. And the followers of the Lady are afraid of the wasteland, because magery doesn't work."

"There must be priestesses and priests here," I said.

"Of course," Lucia said. "But they're refugees, and stuck here just like the rest of us. Even if they complain to Teleso, he's happy enough to have us squabbling among ourselves." The food line had stopped moving, and Lucia craned her neck to see what had caused the holdup. She turned back to me with a shrug. "So. We're celebrating Mass this afternoon, and if you haven't ever received God's Light, it's high time you did. I'll teach you the dance after breakfast."

"I thought you wanted me to play the music," I said.

"You need to know the dance, too," she said. "You should learn that first." Lucia craned her neck again, then settled back into the line. "We don't celebrate Mass as often as I'd like," she said. "You need bread and wine, and as you might imagine these aren't the easiest things to come by here."

"How do you get them?"

"We have a few friends among the soldiers, and there's always the black market . . . If you know so little about the Old Way, Eliana, do you know about the Journey of Gèsu, at least?"

"I recognize the name. *Rachamin, Gèsu. Asaya, Gèsu.*"

"Gèsu is the son of God, healer of the earth." She sketched a cross. "When you say, *B'shem Arka, v'barah, v'nehora kadosha,* that's, 'In the name of God, and Her son, and the Holy Light.' Gèsu is Her son."

I nodded, although this didn't make a whole lot of sense to me.

"Gèsu was killed and His blood was spilled upon the sands. Where His blood fell, flowers bloomed, even though the land had been dead before. The Journeys say that we shall be redeemed through blood; the blood of Gèsu will give new life to the land." Despite her words earlier about how the Old Way wasn't secret here, she had lowered her voice to a whisper. Habit, perhaps. "Each time we celebrate Mass, we help to bring that day closer."

I nodded again.

"Before He left for the last time, He broke bread and shared wine with His disciples and said, 'This bread is My body, and this wine is My blood. Eat, drink, and live forever; dance with Me and know the glory of God.' So that is the Mass."

I nodded again.

"I'll teach you the dance after breakfast. It's not hard." Lucia peered around the line again. "Almost there," she said.

We did finally make it to the front of the line for our gruel. Lucia led me through a maze of tents, bowl in hand, before finally sitting down in a tiny clearing, a miniature piazza formed by a gap in the tents. We sat down to eat. As soon as we were done, she put away the bowls and pulled me to my feet. "Right," she said. "Time to learn the dance."

I laid my violin aside and stood, feeling nervous. I had been dragged through those dances in Bosco, but I felt much more exposed in the bright daylight with just me and Lucia dancing. People started coming out of their tents to watch. "Don't mind them," Lucia said, which didn't make me feel any better.

"What do I do?" I asked.

"It has a three-beat rhythm. One two three one two three one two three one two three. And the steps go like this: side hop step side hop step side hop step side hop step." She showed me. "Now, slowly," she said. "You try."

I took a tentative step to my left, then hopped, then

took another step. My feet got tangled up and I flushed. Our audience laughed, not unkindly, but I could feel my face flush hotter.

"It's all right," Lucia said. "Most of them can't do it either. Come on. *One* two three."

It took several repetitions to get the steps down. "During Mass, you hold hands with the people around you," Lucia said. "I'll teach you the song now, so you can play it next time." She sang it for me; she had a very pure soprano voice that sounded almost like a violin. I took out my violin and played the song through several times; I was tempted to harmonize a bit with Lucia's voice, but I was afraid that Lucia would disapprove of alterations to music that was sacred to her.

At around noon, she led me toward the edge of the camp, to the side of a hill guarded by a soldier. Rafi joined us a bit later, along with a dozen other men and women. Rafi produced a chalice, filled it with water, then added a few drops of wine; someone else produced a small piece of bread and gave it to Lucia.

We joined hands in a circle around Lucia. She closed her eyes and started chanting in the Old Tongue. On some cue that I didn't see, we started to dance, stepping in a circle to our left. "Arka, v'barah, v'nehora kadosha. Arka, v'barah, v'nehora kadosha."

On another signal I missed, the dance stopped, and everyone around me knelt briefly to touch the ground. I caught up with them and crossed myself with everyone else. "B'shem Arka, v'barah, v'nehora kadosha," Lucia said, and everyone said, "Amen."

I didn't catch much of the ritual; it was all in the Old Tongue. Finally, Lucia raised the bread and the chalice to the sky. "Iyt gufay," she said. "Iyt damay. Achal. Ashti. V'chaya ad alam-almaya."

"Amen," we said, and crossed ourselves.

Lucia took a sip from the chalice, then a bite of the bread. Then she stepped into the circle and crossed to face me. "Gufa d'go'el," she said, and broke off a tiny piece of the bread. "Eat it," she whispered when I hesitated. It was stale bread, terribly dry; I was thirsty from dancing in the noon sun, and was barely able to choke it down. "Dam d'go'el," she said, and gave me a sip from the chalice. The wine was a faint aftertaste in the bitter wasteland water.

"Cross yourself," she whispered, so I did.

She went around the rest of the circle. When she finished, the bread was gone, but there was still liquid in the chalice. "Dam d'go'el," she said. "May the blood of the Redeemer bring life and purity to the earth that God created," and poured the rest of the water onto the ground at the center of our circle.

We danced and chanted a bit more, then we each knelt to touch the ground and she spoke a few words of blessing. "Go, the Mass is ended," she said.

"Thanks be to God," said Rafi, next to me, and I muttered the words a heartbeat late, again.

The group dispersed quickly, Rafi lingering with Lucia and me.

"What did you think?" Lucia asked, and her eyes sparkled.

"I don't know much of the Old Tongue," I hedged.

"You'll need to learn, sooner or later . . . but the Mass?"

"It was . . ." Watching Lucia lead the Mass was like watching my priestly brother in church. "The music is beautiful."

Her eyes showed no disappointment, so I must have said something close to what she wanted to hear. Rafi squeezed my shoulder again; he understood. "It will make more sense as you learn," Rafi said. "I think you were meant for playing, not for dancing."

"So," Lucia said to Rafi. "Were we going to take Eliana to watch Giovanni at work?"

Rafi raised his eyebrows. "If you think it's wise." He turned to me. "Would you like to go watch Giovanni?"

Watch him do what? "I'd love to," I said. There was no way I was letting Giovanni get away with thinking that he scared me. Not a chance.

CHAPTER NINE

*Knock, and the door will be opened. Sing, and you will
be heard. Dance, and you will be received.
I am ever with you.*
—*The Journey of Gèsu, chapter 9, verse 2.*

Giovanni's training ground was mostly concealed by
two of the highest walls anywhere in Ravenna. It
had probably once been the corner of a blacksmith's shop;
I could see the remnants of the furnace. The two open
sides were screened by a couple of taller tents. I couldn't
believe that Teleso didn't know this was here, but maybe it
served some purpose for him, like riots and Old Way rituals.

It was a cramped space to use for physical training. A
half dozen skinny young men stood pressed against one of
the walls, watching as Giovanni shouted at a seventh.

"Severo! You're holding it wrong. It's a *sword,* you
turnip, not a hoe. No, not like that! How can you be so
stupid?" Dropping his guard, Giovanni strode over and
readjusted the boy's grip on the wooden stick he held.
"Left hand here, right hand here. This isn't that hard, you
idiot. Now, defend yourself!" The boy swung the stick up,
holding it clumsily at one end, trying to mimic Giovanni's
stance. Giovanni also wielded a wooden weapon, carved a

little more artfully. "No! Not like that! Oh, you're hopeless. Give it to Michel. Michel! It's your turn."

Severo returned to the wall with obvious relief, passing the stick to Michel.

"No!" Giovanni howled. "You just handed him the blade, you idiot! Michel, give it back to him. Severo! *This* is the hilt. *That* is the blade."

"That's a stick," I said.

"You *stay out of this,*" Giovanni snapped without turning; he must have noticed us as soon as we came in.

I fell silent for a moment, then turned to Lucia. "What is he doing?"

"Training them to fight with a sword," she said.

"Where are they going to get real swords?" I asked. Lucia shrugged. "Giovanni! Why are you training them on swords?"

"What business is it of yours?" he said, but Michel, grateful for any distraction, had dropped his guard and was waiting with interest for the answer. "What other weapon would I train them on? Crossbow?"

"You were a university student, weren't you?" I said to Giovanni. Dueling was something of a gentleman's art; conservatory students were warned about this in passing during the lectures on courtly etiquette. Young men from that class were tutored in fencing from an early age; even the physician at the conservatory had a sword, though he seldom carried it.

I stepped onto the training ground. Michel was about the same age as my eldest brother Agrippo had been when I left home. Agrippo was the brother who brawled over the girl and wound up with the cracked head. At least, he was the first of my brothers to brawl over a girl and wind up with a cracked head. I gave Michel a tentative smile and he smiled warmly back.

"Give me your 'sword' a moment, Giovanni," I said.

"Get out of here!" he said. "What right do you have, coming in here like—"

I held out my hand stubbornly. He reversed his grip to pass me the "hilt" with a sullen glare. "Thank you," I said. "Now Michel. You're holding a stick. Let's see if you know how to use it." I slapped the "blade" into my opposite palm and swung the staff at Michel.

Giula and Bella and the other girls at the conservatory could probably not have done this, especially after five years of sheltered conservatory life. But I had grown up with seven brothers, and Donato had taught me to fight.

Michel grabbed his stick like a stick and deflected my swing effortlessly; his grin grew wider. "You swing a staff like a girl."

"In your dreams, big brother," I said, returning the grin. I hooked his staff with mine and nearly jerked it out of his hand. He swung the stick to knock my wind out but I dodged aside.

"Lovely," Giovanni said. "But the soldiers he'll be fighting won't be swinging sticks."

"Fine, then," I said, and handed the "sword" back to Giovanni, hilt first. "Michel, show Giovanni how you'd deal with a sword."

Michel was still grinning; he dodged Giovanni's first two thrusts, then hooked the sword and sent it flying. He swung the staff again, to clip Giovanni across the head. I had a feeling that Michel had put up with quite a few smacks on the head from Giovanni's sword. Giovanni stumbled back a step and then snapped, "Hold." He turned around to glare at Michel and the other six boys. "Out," he ordered, and they left gladly, still grinning. He turned on me.

"I'll thank you," he said icily, "to stay out of the way during training exercises."

"What are you trying to do?" I demanded. "They aren't university students. They aren't gentlemen. You're trying to teach them to fight, aren't you? Don't you want them to win?"

"I suppose *you* think I should be teaching them to swing plows and pitchforks," Giovanni said. "I'm teaching them to fight with real weapons."

"A real weapon," I said, "is the one you know how to use." I turned to Lucia. "Let's go, Lucia," I said. "I think I've seen plenty." Besides, I'd had the last word, and I wasn't sure I could come up with another retort.

"Don't come back here!" Giovanni shouted as we left. "Don't you *dare* come back here!"

"You're right," Lucia said, once we were out of earshot. "Why make them learn to fight with swords when they already know how to use another weapon?"

"Lucia," I said. "Is Giovanni planning to train six boys at a time until the whole camp knows how to fight? We'll be dead of old age before he's half done."

Lucia sighed. "Beneto and Jesca don't have much faith in the arms training—that's why they put Giovanni in charge of it. Our real strength is our sheer numbers. There are thousands of refugees here, and only 122 soldiers. If we decided to *walk* out tomorrow, they'd run out of crossbow bolts before they could kill all of us."

"So why don't we? I suppose they could kill a fair number of us."

"Yes. And so many people have lost hope . . . Beneto thinks that our best chance is to wait until people are really angry, then try to direct their anger. We could tear the crossbows from the soldiers' hands and use them against them, and only a handful of Ravenessi would die. We just have to get people angry enough."

I shook my head. "I don't know, Lucia."

"Beneto's convinced we could make it work. But we'd need an incident, first."

"What about the massacres Rafi referred to? Those must have involved 'incidents.' "

"Yes. And yet here we are. Beneto thinks that *next* time, he can make it work."

I shook my head. "I don't know. I'm angry already. I bet other people here are, too. If he *organized* people— trained them *properly*—"

"So tell Beneto. Maybe he'll listen to you."

As the sun neared the horizon, Lucia and I got into the line for dinner. As we waited, I heard a voice rasp behind me. "Signora," the voice said, and I felt someone tugging at my sleeve. "Signora!"

I turned and sucked in my breath. It was the madman from the road. "Welcome, signora," he said, gravely.

Lucia turned. "Amedeo," she greeted him. "Is this the one you spoke of?"

The madman looked offended. "Have there been any *other* musicians who've arrived this month?"

"No—"

"Then she's *her*. Don't be ridiculous." He turned to me. "The tune of the piece is not going quite as you expected, is it?" I tried to stare him down, but he refused to look away, grinning at me broadly. "Don't worry. We know what we're doing."

"Piss off," I said, shakily.

He laughed. "Welcome, signora. Enjoy your stay in Cuore." He wandered off down the line of people, weaving and stumbling like a drunk.

"So," Lucia said. "That's Amedeo."

"I've met him before," I said.

"He gets around. Like Rafi said, the Light is too bright . . . he's cracked."

"I don't like him."

"Well, he's a nuisance," she said. "It's even worse that some of what he says is inspired. You actually have to pay attention to his ravings. And fret about them."

The line inched up. We had barely moved, although more people had joined the line behind us. "What did he mean, 'enjoy your stay in Cuore'?"

Lucia shrugged. "Who knows? He might have meant that you're going to go to Cuore sometime. Or maybe he meant that in some sense, this is Cuore. Or maybe he was just raving." She shook her head. "You never know with Amedeo."

"Lucia. Eliana." We turned; this time it was Beneto and Jesca who'd come up behind us. "How did today go?" Beneto asked Lucia.

"Well, I think," Lucia said.

Beneto took Lucia aside to confer with her in a low voice, and Jesca gave me a conspiratorial smile. "I heard about your confrontation with Giovanni." Jesca squeezed my shoulder. "Good for you."

"So what do you think?" I asked. "About training peasants in the weapons of the gentry?"

Jesca shook her head. "It doesn't matter all that much. Our strength is in our numbers, if we could only . . ." She shrugged. Her voice was crisp and chill, like a bell through evening mist. "Sooner or later, Teleso will make a mistake. When people are angry enough, they won't need weapons. They'll fight the soldiers with their bare hands, grab the crossbows away, and tear the keep to the ground. It *will* happen."

I shivered.

Beneto was done with his conference with Lucia, and Beneto and Jesca moved off down the line. They spoke briefly with almost everyone, squeezing peoples' hands or shoulders, offering commiseration and comfort. They reminded me of the priest and priestess back at the conservatory.

We took our gruel back to Rafi's tent. Giovanni was there. I hadn't seen him join the food line, but he'd gotten his gruel somewhere and beaten us back to the tent. He moved over to make room for us, but it was clear he wasn't happy about it.

"So," Rafi said. "Did you have a nice day?" He sounded just like my mother, and I started laughing, then crying, and Giovanni stared at me like I had gone completely mad.

The next morning, Beneto took me aside after breakfast. "I heard what happened at the training ground yesterday."

"Uh-huh?" I said.

"I'd appreciate it if, in the future, you left Giovanni to his own devices there. That's his territory."

I felt my face grow hot. "Jesca said—"

"Jesca is my lieutenant. I am the Generale here."

"Ah," I said, and looked down.

"Think of it this way," Beneto said placatingly. "If you were conducting a musical ensemble, and Giovanni came up and started complaining about the way you were going about it, how would you feel?"

I looked up. Beneto was searching my face with his eyes. He *really* wanted to convince me that he was right, which was strange to me; if he was "Generale," why did he care what I thought? "Beneto," I said, "there are many different ways to conduct an orchestra. However, any conductor who started off by making the brass players take up violin would be *replaced*. By his superiors."

"Ah," Beneto said, and now he flushed. "Well, you know, this military training—"

"Is just to keep Giovanni busy," I finished. "Irrelevant in the larger scheme because once people get angry enough, they'll break out by sheer force of numbers. Doesn't it seem to you that more of us will *survive* this breakout if we've learned a bit about fighting *together* first?" Beneto wasn't listening—I could tell—and I grabbed his arm. "Everyone comes to the conservatory knowing how to play an instrument. And most of the men here—and quite a few of the women—know how to fight, even if it's just brawling or fending off wolves with a bow. But just as conservatory students must learn how to play in an *ensemble,* the people here need to learn to fight as an *army*. Isn't that what you want?"

Beneto extracted himself from my grip gently, the smile never leaving his face. "I'll think about it," he said. "For now, leave Giovanni alone. That's an order."

My jaw dropped as he walked away, and I ducked back into Rafi's tent. Giovanni was long gone, but Lucia sat drinking some of Rafi's "tea." "I never signed on to your movement," I said. "Why does Beneto think I take orders from him?"

Rafi glanced at Lucia. "Told you," he said to her. He turned back to me. "Right then. *I'll* tell you to stay out of Giovanni's way when he's training. You'll do it because you sleep in my tent, and I want some peace under my roof, even if it's a cloth one." He gave me a menacing glare, but I could see the glint of amusement in his eyes.

"Yes, signore," I said.

"You see?" He was speaking to Lucia again.

"Don't tell me," Lucia said. "I was on your side all along."

I looked at Lucia. "Lucia, he—"

"We heard," Lucia said. "Tent walls are thin. And you may be right, but give it some time. Beneto is a reasonable man, but you've only just joined us. Give it some time."

Lucia took me for a walk later along the hillside around the entire camp. "This is as far as we can go," she said. "Any farther, and they'd have to shoot us." She indicated the soldiers who patrolled the edge of the hill.

"Do you know any of the soldiers?" I asked.

"Many of them. By name and reputation, at least. I can't say I've ever exchanged many words with Niccolo." Her lips tightened. "And I try to keep out of Teleso's way."

"Niccolo." The name rang a bell. "I think I saw him. He was serving food, and caught a boy trying to steal the ration chits. The other soldier wanted to let him go, but—"

"Niccolo turned him in. I know. He'd have volunteered to flog the boy himself, if he'd been on duty then. Charming man, Niccolo."

"Not all the soldiers are like that."

"No." She waved as we passed one soldier along the hill. He glanced around to see if anyone was watching and then trotted down the slope to greet us. "Most of them come from Verdia, just like the rest of the people here. They joined the army for the duration of the war, and most of them feel that they've been double-crossed . . . being sent down here instead of getting their bonus and being released from their oath to the Emperor. *Nobody* wants to be here. Even Niccolo."

"Hey," the soldier said, joining us. "You've settled in fast." I realized it was the soldier who'd brought me here—what was his name?

"Mario," I said. "It's nice to see you again."

"Did you find your family?" he asked me.

"No."

"I'm sorry." He looked genuinely bereaved. There was an awkward pause.

"I heard you playing your violin for the Ravenessi the other afternoon," Mario said. "I was wondering, could you come play in the barracks some evening? I can't promise everyone would stay awake for you, but I would."

"I'd be honored to play for you," I said.

"Good. Tomorrow night? After sunset?"

I nodded. "Tomorrow night would be fine."

"I'll meet you in the piazza. You'll need an escort to get into the barracks."

Belatedly, I threw a glance at Lucia, worried that I'd just made a mistake, but she didn't seem concerned. There was a threatening shout, and Mario jumped. "I need to get back to patrolling," he said. "I'll see you tomorrow night!"

We continued around Ravenna. I had seen Ravenna from the hillside before, but it had been quiet and almost calm in the twilight. In the bright light of midday, Ravenna crawled with activity like an anthill, even though few of the people could have had anywhere to go. The tents were a garish assortment of ragtag colors, muted by the accumulated dust; few of them were more than shoulder height at their tallest point. The keep stuck out jarringly, like a giant boulder in a burned-over prairie.

"In a way," Lucia said, "the soldiers are prisoners here as much as we are, even if they're fed better." She gazed at the keep. "Except for Teleso. He has friends in Cuore; he could go home if he liked, but he's happy to play Emperor here in his own little capital." She pushed her hair back behind one ear. "The Fedeli don't come here because they fear what it means when they can't use the Lady's Gift; the Circle doesn't come here because they fear their own powerlessness. And the rest of the world is happy enough to forget about us, which is just fine with Teleso."

"Why are *you* here?" I asked. "Even if the Fedeli in Varena are after you, you must have other options. Is it because of Beneto and Jesca and their reform movement?"

Lucia shrugged. "Not really. Maybe a bit. I'm here because I think that God wants me to be here."

"How did you get in trouble with the Fedeli?"

"Can't you guess?" She grinned. "That's not fair. I'm sorry. I'll tell you sometime, I promise, but it's a long story and right now I want to finish our walk. Are you really going to go play for the soldiers tomorrow night?"

"Is there a reason I shouldn't?"

Lucia shook her head. "I try to steer clear of Teleso, and that's not always easy in the barracks or the keep. But you should be fine with Mario looking after you. He's a nice boy."

As we were finishing our circle, Michel—the young man that Giovanni had been trying to train on sword—trotted up. "Eliana," he said.

"Michel," Lucia said. "You're supposed to be in training."

Michel shrugged and gave me a broad grin. "Yeah," he said. "Might as well go rabbit hunting in the Ravenna piazza, for all the good it'll do me." He hooked his thumbs on his belt, an extremely worn brown sash. "I like being told I can fight the way I'm used to. I wasn't so bad at it, back before."

"Yeah," I said. "You were probably a brigand that preyed on travelers to Pluma, weren't you?" I glared at him mildly and he gave me a grin back. "Where are you from?"

"Merela." My expression must have been blank, because Michel shrugged. "It was a pretty small village."

"Michel," I said. "The key isn't just learning to fight, it's learning to fight *together*. Like the army already knows how to do."

"Can you teach us that?" he asked.

"I'm a musician. You need somebody who knows *fighting* to teach you that."

"You seemed to know something about fighting yesterday."

"I know something about *sticks*," I said. "And unlike certain people, I'm not completely devoid of common sense. But fighting like an army—" I spread my hands wide. "I might be able to teach you to play like an orchestra."

Michel laughed. He had a nice laugh. "I'd still take you as an arms master over Giovanni."

"Give me a couple of weeks," I said, and he grinned again and hiked off back down the slope.

Later that afternoon, Lucia started teaching me her Old Way songs, beginning with a prayer for rain. It had a strong beat, like all the Old Way music I'd heard, and shifted between a sweet and a sad sound.

"Maybe I shouldn't play this one," I said. "I sure don't want rain right now." Ravenna in the rain would turn from a bowl of dust and ashes to a sodden mud-laden heap. I didn't even want to think about what winter must have been like here.

"Don't worry about it," Lucia said. "God knows we have to practice sometimes."

I played the piece through, and Lucia showed me the dance steps, though she didn't try to make me learn them. "You said you learned songs and some prayers at the conservatory," she said. "Did you ever participate in a true ritual?"

I laid my violin aside gently. "No," I said. "But my roommate, Mira, formed a group to play the songs together.

One time another friend of mine, Bella, got word that her sister had died, and we played the funeral music. Bella went on to become Redentore. The Fedeli killed her."

I'd expected more questions about Bella, but instead Lucia asked, "Who was Mira?"

I pulled away, startled. "Why do you want to know?"

Lucia looked at me steadily. "Something in your face when you mentioned her name."

I shrugged and lowered my eyes. "My roommate. I told you."

"All right, then."

I wanted to change the subject. "How did Beneto and Jesca end up here? Did someone up in Cuore not like them?"

"Oh, no." She shook her head. "Everyone likes Beneto and Jesca. For them, it was a choice between being third or fourth somewhere more comfortable, or being leaders here. They're idealistic. They thought they could make a difference."

"Do they still?"

"I think they do, yes."

I hugged my knees and rested my chin on my arms. "What do you mean by being third or fourth somewhere else? Like Giovanni is here?"

"More or less. There are cells, you see. Each place. Each cell has a leader, and that leader has a second, and there might be a third, and fourth, and so on. Here it stops with Giovanni. They have a general, Beneto; his second-in-command, Jesca; and their lieutenant, Giovanni."

"What about you and Rafi?" I asked.

"You can't command among the reformers unless you were a student at the university. Rafi was a farmer, and I was never a student. I'm in the right class, so if I made a fuss, they'd probably make me a fourth, under Giovanni. But I'm not that desperate to be an official leader."

"Why would you need to go to the university for *this*?" I was astonished.

"It was university scholars who realized the connection between magery and the famine. When the Circle tried to stifle that knowledge, it was students who started the reform movement." She glanced at me. "It's much more complex than I've made it sound." She sketched in the dust. "There are twenty different 'armies' that basically consist of a bunch of officers and whomever they can round up and convince to follow them. They all report to a centralized committee. Beneto and Jesca aren't supposed to do anything other than recruit unless they get orders, or at least permission, from the high committee."

"Lady's tits," I said. "They've organized the movement like the messenger service."

Lucia grinned. "In theory, anyway. In practice . . . well, like everyone else, the reformer leaders don't like to come down here, and there's no real good way to get messages back and forth. Sometimes Beneto sends Giovanni to sneak out and go to Pluma to send a message, but that's risky and Giovanni's not willing to do it that often. So in practice Beneto is pretty much on his own."

I shook my head. "How many of these other armies have any actual followers?"

"Maybe a few."

"And somehow, they're going to overthrow the Circle?"

"That's the idea," Lucia said.

I stared at her for a long moment. "Giovanni's not the only one of you who's crazy. What do you think of all this?"

"I believe that God wants us to win, so we will." She met my eyes and smiled slowly, and once again her eyes sparkled with light from within. "Somehow."

Lucia and I lined up early for dinner; once we were done, I picked up my violin and went to the keep to meet Mario. The piazza was almost deserted. "We're all still eating dinner," Mario said as I walked up. "I've arranged some for you, too. Come on."

The army barracks was a long narrow building next to Teleso's keep. Inside, it was spare and crowded, just one long room lined with bunk beds. A narrow table ran the length of the room, and the soldiers sat on the benches, finishing their dinners. The room was brightly lit with torches, and noisy with conversation. Mario made one of the soldiers scoot down the bench, clearing a spot for me on the end, and set down a bowl of soup and a slice of bread, the first bread I'd had since leaving the conservatory. "You can eat before you play for us."

The soup smelled delicious, of meat and carrots and onions. I downed it in minutes, mopping up the last of the broth with the bread, and was left feeling vaguely guilty for not trying to find a way to take some home to Rafi and Lucia. "Done?" Mario asked. "Do you want any more?"

"I'm full," I said. I was.

"Right, then," he said, and stood up. "May I present," he said, making a grand gesture, "Signora Eliana, Premier Concert Violinist of Ravenna." Most of the soldiers applauded; some of the men sitting at the table moved over to their bunks and got comfortable to listen, pulling off their boots and flopping down. I spotted Niccolo on a bunk in the far corner; he watched me through half-lidded eyes.

I pulled one of the unoccupied benches over to the end of the room and hopped up on it, so that everyone would be able to see me. I started off with one of the folk songs I'd learned with Mira. Everyone recognized it, and joined in on the chorus. "Any requests?" I asked when I was done. Someone shouted out another folk tune, and I started off on that.

I played for hours, with Mario filling a glass of wine for me when I got thirsty. "Lights out is at midnight," he said finally. "We should call it a night."

"You'll come play for us again, won't you?" one of the younger soldiers asked.

"Yes," I said, returning his smile. "The food's better here." I stepped down off the bench and started to pack up my violin.

"Wait," Mario said. "Aren't you going to pass your hat?" I looked at him blankly. "They didn't teach you that at the conservatory? I suppose they expected you to join an ensemble. When you entertain, you should pass your hat. Here, I'll lend you mine." He handed me his helmet, then pounded on the table to get the attention of the audience. "This is Eliana's hat," he announced, "and she's *passing* it." He took it back, fished something out of his pocket to drop in, and passed it along. When it had made the rounds, he deposited the contents into a cloth sack and handed it to me, reclaiming his helmet. "Let me know the next time you want to come play," he said as he escorted me out. "We'll be waiting."

I was fairly certain I knew the way back to Rafi's tent, but all the same, I was relieved to see Lucia waiting for me in the piazza. "They passed a hat," I said, holding up the sack.

"Let's see," she said. In the slight moonlight, I poked through. Several dozen ration chits. "Why do soldiers have ration chits?" I asked.

Lucia shrugged. "Ration chits here are as good as

money," she said. "People steal them, trade them, forge them . . . the soldiers are issued a few to use as bribes and rewards, when necessary. But, you know, there's a black market. How do you think we got the wine for Mass?"

Two loaves of bread. A sachet of tea. A flask of wine.

I felt rich. "Let's go home," I said. "I want to show Rafi."

Rafi met us at the entrance of the tent, in tears. "Thank God you weren't here," he said. "They've arrested Beneto and Jesca."

CHAPTER TEN

Daughter, why do you seek me in darkness? I am here, as I am everywhere, but why fight your way through darkness when I will come to dance with you in the light of the sunrise?
—*The Journey of Gèsu, chapter 8, verse 31.*

Arrested?" Lucia sucked in her breath. "Why?"

"Disloyalty—conspiracy—everything." Rafi was visibly upset. "They came here. To my tent!"

"Did they take Giovanni, as well?"

"Don't you think I would have told you that? No. Just Jesca and Beneto. Giovanni was here, but they didn't seem to want him. But I'm afraid they'll come back. Lucia, Eliana, you need to hide somewhere. Not here; this is where they'll come back to look. Isabella's tent—go there. Hurry! I've sent Giovanni into hiding as well. It's best you don't know where."

"Here," I said. "You should take this." I thrust the sack at him. "There's tea and ration chits. The soldiers passed the hat after I played."

Rafi paused in his panic to take the sack and give me a hug. "You're a good woman, Eliana. Now go!"

Lucia dragged me back through the sea of tents. "Arrested!" In the starlight I could see that her face was streaked with tears. "*Arrested.*" Her voice dropped and I couldn't understand what she was saying; after a moment I realized that she was praying in the Old Tongue.

Isabella's tent was on the opposite side of Ravenna from Rafi's, and we had to go around the piazza rather than through it. "Isabella!" Lucia hissed, poking her hand in through the folds of the tent and waving. "Isabella, are you awake?"

"Yeah," a voice muttered. "I'm always awake in the middle of the night."

"Isabella, it's Lucia and Eliana, and we need somewhere to stay!" There was a pause, and a rustle inside the tent. "Now!" Lucia hissed.

"Come in, then."

We crawled into the tent. Isabella's tent was made from sewn-together grain sacks; it was smaller and lower than Rafi's, and very crowded. In addition to Isabella, there were four other people asleep in the tent already. They rolled out of the way and pulled the edges of their cloaks over their faces with half-asleep surliness. Isabella flipped her cloak back from her face and propped herself up on one elbow to light a candle. "What's going on that you're waking me up in the middle of the night?" Isabella was an older woman, perhaps my mother's age; she wore her gray-streaked hair in long braids. As she lit the candle, I noticed that she had broad peasant hands, tanned and callused, with the scattering of small scars that came from being careless with the kitchen knife.

"Beneto and Jesca have been arrested," Lucia said. "We weren't there. Rafi was afraid they'd come for us next."

"If they want you, they'll find you," Isabella said. "You can't hide for long in Ravenna." Lucia started crying again and Isabella patted her shoulder. "There, now. This means they aren't interested in arresting you, doesn't it?"

"But Beneto and Jesca—what will they do to them?"

"How long do you think we'll have to stay here?" I asked.

"I don't know," Lucia said. "Giovanni got detained once, but it was just so Teleso could put a scare into him." She lowered her eyes, looking worried again.

"Are you and Giovanni really cousins?" I asked. If I could change the subject, maybe Lucia would feel better.

"Yes." She sighed. "Our fathers are brothers. And we're both from Varena, even though Giovanni likes to style himself 'of Cuore' because that's where he studied at the university."

I didn't understand this obsession that the university students had with being university students. Before Ravenna, I had met one person who'd been to the university: the physician at the conservatory. In lectures at the conservatory they'd explained that university scholars staffed the civil service, keeping things running smoothly so that the Circle could concentrate on keeping us safe and the Emperor could concentrate on ruling. Peasants didn't go to the university; it cost too much and it just wasn't done. Bright peasant children might go to the seminary; talented ones went to the conservatory.

"Is your father a government official?" I asked.

"No," Lucia said. She rolled onto her side and held out her hand. "Give me your sash for a moment."

I untied the strip of red cloth and handed it to Lucia. She stroked the wool gently, then rubbed it against her fingers and checked for a stain. She closed her eyes and smelled it, breathing deeply. She folded the cloth tightly and creased it, then allowed it to unfold. "The wool is from Verdia," she said. "The cloth is of average quality; the wool was probably spun in one cottage and woven in another. The red is quite a high-quality dye, imported from the East." She gave me back the sash and winked. "That's

"Get some sleep, Lucia. You too, Eliana. You're up far too late for clear thought." Isabella moved over to make room for us to lie down. I wrapped up in my cloak and squeezed in between Lucia and Isabella.

The tent emptied out quickly in the morning. Lucia and I each gave Isabella a ration chit, and she brought us back bowls of gruel. "You're the musician, aren't you?" she asked me. "I've heard you play. You're good."

"Thank you."

"And don't think I don't know what I'm talking about, like the rest of your audience." Isabella gestured toward the tent flap. "My own mother was quite a musician, though she never played in an ensemble. I can't play a note, but I know what to listen for."

"Did your mother go to a conservatory?" I asked.

"Never," Isabella said. "Stayed at home her whole life. But she played *beautifully*. Taught all my children to play, too."

"Did any of them go?"

Isabella shook her head again. "One of my daughters showed promise. But she died, during the war." She sighed, and brushed some of the dust from her dress. "I should go see Rafi. He's probably more upset about the arrests than anyone, and with you two gone, he's got no one to distract him. You stay here. Keep each other company. I'll be back before sundown." Isabella ducked out of the tent.

Lucia and I were left alone. I leaned back against my rolled-up cloak. "Is Isabella a reformer?" I asked Lucia.

"Not exactly," Lucia said with a flash of a smile. "She sympathizes, but she won't take orders from Beneto. She kind of has her own faction of old-guard troublemakers. Sometimes she comes by to tell Beneto that he's just a child who doesn't know what he's doing. They've had some disagreements. We can trust her, though."

The Emperor rules, the Circle protects, the Fedeli guide. I could hear Domenico's even voice, and Bella's challenge, and I wondered if Domenico really believed what he'd told us. And whether he still believed it now.

During the war, I'd felt a new respect for the Circle, and for the protection they offered us. We had gone to war with Vesuvia after their cross-border raids had led to atrocities, with families burned with their crops. The war had raged for two full years, with neither army advancing more than a few miles except on rare occasions. In the end, the border was left more or less where it had been before. Army detachments were left to keep an eye on things and the Circle retreated to Cuore. *The Circle protects.* Opening my eyes again, I stared up into the dark rafters. Some birds had gotten in and built nests; I could hear the squawk of squabbling fledglings, and see the flutter of wings. Who had been there to protect my family? What the Vesuviani had done was nothing compared to what the Circle had done. My mouth turned bitter and I almost retched. I closed my eyes again.

I briefly considered returning to the conservatory. The Dean wasn't supposed to take me back, but he'd bent the rules before. And under the circumstances . . . but no. If I became a student at the conservatory again, it would be under the sponsorship of the Circle. *I'd rather starve,* I thought. Besides, I couldn't imagine being sequestered again. I was part of the world now, for better or worse.

I sat up after a while, and eased my boots off to take a look at my feet. I had worn away big strips of skin, and those parts were raw and bloody. I wet the edge of my cloak and wrapped my feet in it; the cold water might bring some of the swelling down. I hoped the cloak would dry by evening.

I stayed at the abandoned farm for almost a week,

CHAPTER EIGHT

The children of the Light must stand together,
for all others will stand against them.
—*The Journey of Gèsu, chapter 11, verse 26.*

By morning, I had moved on, but I could barely walk. By midmorning I had reached an abandoned farm. I broke into the barn—I felt like it would be less likely to be haunted—and decided I'd spend a day or two there to let my feet heal. Now that I was alone, really alone, my thoughts were deafeningly loud. I tried to find tasks to occupy myself—getting water to wash my feet, mending a ripped seam in the edge of my bag, tuning my violin—but nothing seemed to drown them out.

Except for the day that my father took me to see the mage who'd given me apples even though I couldn't burn stone, I had rarely thought much about the Circle before the war. To play for the Circle was the highest position a musician could hold, and back at the conservatory I had sometimes imagined myself playing in Cuore, closing my eyes as I practiced and imagining the glitter of a banquet hall in place of the gray stone walls around me. In the shadowed barn, I lay back and stared at the rafters, then closed my eyes, imagining myself back at the conservatory.

eating the provisions I'd stolen from Gervala. I stayed in the barn during the day, limping out at night to fetch more water as necessary. I was afraid that someone from Gervala might see me and bring a group of people down to punish me for stealing food. At least the former residents of the farm refrained from haunting me. Perhaps they were satisfied that I was staying in the barn, or perhaps they felt sorry for me.

I thought about the Circle a great deal, and Mira, and Bella and Giula. I managed not to think about the ashes of the house, the wreckage, the bones of my family.

As soon as I had skin on my feet again, I padded my feet carefully, gathered my belongings, and moved on. I passed through villages that day, but no one would meet my eyes. My first thought was that they could tell I was a thief, but I realized quickly that my ragged clothes and hopeless wariness marked me as a refugee. Refugees brought danger; they knew what had happened to that village just to the north. A young child asked her mother why I was walking south—"Nobody goes south, do they?"—but she was quickly hushed, and her mother made a sign to ward off the evil eye as I passed.

The land died around me as I walked. That first day, I had been in territory that had never seen war. The second day, I saw farms that had been burned in the war, but had since been rebuilt; the landscape was scarred, with dead trees, but the spring flowers were in bloom and the fields were green. The third day, I saw shrunken weeds and withered flowers; when I knocked on the door of a farmhouse, no one answered.

On the fourth day, I came to the wasteland.

The wasteland was just on our side of the border with Vesuvia. The war had raged there for more than a year, with each army pushing forward just a few miles, then falling back again. The people who lived in that part of Verdia fled the fighting during the war, trying to get out of the way of the armies. Some of them never came back. They made the right choice.

Not even weeds grew in the wasteland. The fields were black, or baked sand-brown by the sun. I felt as exposed as a rabbit on the treeless plain, and quickly grew hot in the sun. Streams still ran through the wasteland, but the water tasted strangely bitter, and I found myself wanting to rinse my mouth with the last of my wine, just to get rid of the taste.

As I rested in the shade of a ruined barn, a column of refugees passed by. Guarded by soldiers, they were being marched south.

"Hey there!" one of the soldiers called when he spotted me. "Where do you think you're going?"

"Ravenna," I said.

The soldiers laughed. "You don't *go* to Ravenna," one said. "You get *taken* there."

"So, do you have any other recommendations?" I asked.

"You're pretty much out of options, at this point," he said with a shrug. "Our orders are to bring in anyone we find, no matter where they say they're going."

"What if someone wants to stay with their farm?" I asked. That was really hilarious; the soldiers laughed again.

"Where are you from, girl?" one of the refugees asked as I joined the column of marchers. "Not from around here, that's obvious."

"I was at a conservatory until recently," I said. "I came home to find my village burned. I heard that the survivors were taken to Ravenna. I'm looking for my family."

He sobered. "Which village?"

"Doratura. Have there been so many?"

the sort of vastly useful information you learn as the daughter of a textiles merchant and importer."

I gave her a skeptical look as I retied the sash. "You could have made all that up and I'd never know."

Lucia smiled, tipping her head to look at me sideways. "You could show your sash to Giovanni. He ought to be able to tell you the same thing. It's the family business— my father does the imports, his father does the sales."

I took her hand, flipped it over. It was small and delicate, but deeply tanned and heavily callused. "You don't look like a city girl."

"Thank you."

"What happened in Varena? You said it was a long story. We've got plenty of time."

Lucia leaned back, resting against her own rolled-up cloak. "When I was fourteen, I decided I had a vocation; I wanted to become a priestess of the Lord and the Lady."

"Why?"

"I felt . . ." she gestured, then dropped her hands back into her lap. "I felt an emptiness inside that wanted to be filled. I thought that the Church would fill it. I thought that was what a vocation meant."

"How long did you stay at the seminary?"

"Three years." She sighed heavily. "Three years of porridge and living in a bunk room with fifty other girls and owning no more than would fit into the pockets of my robe."

"As opposed to now?"

A smile lit her face. "As opposed to now, when I have all I could ever need." She looked at her tanned hands and her smile faded slowly to a wistful gaze. "The emptiness grew worse and worse, those three years. I thought if I believed *enough,* if I prayed and worked hard enough, I would feel the joy of the Lady and the peace of the Lord that my teachers spoke of. I used to—" her hands began to twist her skirt. "It got so that I rarely slept, but I could barely rouse myself from bed, even so. I felt like I was being walled inside a room with no door—" She took a deep breath, let it out again. "The end came when I spent four solid days and nights in vigil, praying in the chapel. It was this cold stone building, and I spent my vigil in this tiny room in the cellar, in almost complete darkness. Truth was, my teachers were tired of my sad eyes and bad attitude. They sent me down there and told me that if it turned out I *didn't* have a vocation, I should just say so."

Lucia's eyes were closed now. "The first day and night I spent on my knees. The next I spent pacing. Oh, I was fasting, too—water but no food—so then the third day I was too weak to pace or to kneel. I lay in front of the altar and tried to pray. The fourth day I couldn't even do that. I lay on the floor in the darkness, because I was also too weak to summon witchlight."

"No one even came to see if you were all right?"

Lucia shook her head. "That wasn't how it was done." She paused and collected her thoughts for a moment. "While I was lying there, I felt a burst of light, like sunlight breaking through a cloud. I felt the darkness inside me recede, although the emptiness was still there. And I heard a voice say, 'Daughter, why do you seek me in darkness? I am here, as I am everywhere, but why fight your way through darkness when I will come to dance with you in the light of the sunrise?' "

"You weren't dreaming?"

"No," she said. "I wasn't dreaming." Lucia opened her eyes to meet mine. "I wasn't dreaming. And I said to the voice, 'Why do you leave me alone?' And I heard, 'You are never alone. But if you come into the light, I will dance with you.'

"So somehow I found the strength to stand up and stumble out of the chapel. It was dawn, the sun was rising, and no one was in sight. And when I came into the sunlight, it was as if my mind exploded into light. The emptiness was filled. And I knew this was what I had been seeking all my life. I shouted, 'Dance with me, dance with me!' There aren't words to describe how this felt. But for the first time, God was truly with me.

"The ironic thing is, I thought it was the Lord and the Lady, finally showing up to tell me that I truly had a vocation. But when I shouted, the teachers came running and saw me dancing. I was singing this tune that came into my head—" she hummed a few notes, and I recognized the music from the Mass. "And they grabbed me and hustled me inside and started shouting that I had lost my mind, that only someone as twisted and evil as me would sing that inside a seminary of the Lady. I didn't understand what I'd done wrong at first, but finally I realized that I was singing an Old Way song and dancing the dance that goes with it. But the problem was, I wasn't sorry." Once again, a smile lit her face.

"So that's why the Fedeli don't like you?"

"Not quite," she said. "The teachers finally decided it was the fact that I hadn't eaten or slept in days that was causing me to be so obstinate. Up until then I'd always been this meek, sad girl, you see, and terribly eager to please. So they gave me something to eat and told me to go sleep for a bit. But instead, I went out to tell all the other initiates that we'd been looking for the wrong gods in the wrong places, and that if they'd follow me—I didn't know the first thing about the Old Way at the time, of course—we'd find the true God and the true worship and dance together in the light. I'm sure I sounded as cracked as Amedeo." She laughed, genuinely amused. "Fortunately, I had friends who warned me that the Fedeli were on their way, and so I left, barefoot, with nothing but my robe. It was early summer and I headed south. I remembered from classes on the spread of the Faith that Old Way superstition was most prevalent in the remote regions, particularly among peasants, so I headed to Verdia. And that's why I can't go back to Varena. They'd get me for apostasy and blasphemy and spreading evil doctrine. Back then the Fedeli weren't going after the Old Way followers that much—mainly they were trying to root out heresy within the Church—but they made exceptions for crazed ex-seminarians who tried to recruit their classmates."

"So how did you survive, barefoot and penniless?"

"Oh, I got by. People fed me here and there. Once I got to Cuore, I tracked down Giovanni and blackmailed him into giving me some money to go away. He was horribly embarrassed by me. I used that to head deep into Verdia. That was about a year before the war started. I've been learning dances, and teaching them to others ever since." She stretched, cracking her back. "So that's what happened in Varena."

"I can see how you got on the Fedeli's bad side."

"Yeah," she said, and grinned. She was tremendously proud of her notoriety, I could tell. We sat in silence for a moment. "Your turn," she said. "Why did you leave the conservatory?"

I shook out my cloak and rerolled it to make a better backrest, then leaned back again. "Well," I said. "I was at the Verdiano Rural Conservatory, which is in Bascio." Lucia nodded. "Last fall, a new student showed up . . . Mira." I told Lucia about Mira, and Bella and the Fedeli, and what Mira's secret turned out to be.

"Why did she leave the Circle?" Lucia asked.

"She found out what had caused the famine," I said.

"All the Circle knows what caused the famine," Lucia said.

"And her grandmother died."

"Ah." Lucia looked at me speculatively.

"How secret is it that magefire caused the famine?" I asked. "I mean, I didn't know until I heard Mira say it. But at the conservatory, we're so isolated—"

Lucia sighed. "In Cuore, it's something that everyone knows but nobody says, because to say it aloud is heresy, and the Fedeli are always listening." She rubbed her forehead. "I told you it was discovered at the university? The Circle tried to cover up the knowledge by killing the ones who knew. Fortunately, they missed a few. The survivors started the reform movement. This is part of why Giovanni is so suspicious. Some of his friends died in that purge." She looked up again. "So, I'm sorry. I interrupted your story. The other mage came for her?"

I found my voice shaking as I told Lucia about waiting in my room as the light slowly faded, Mira standing in the doorway, Liemo forcing Mira to use magic to save me. "After that—" I clenched my fists; I still didn't understand this. "Mira just seemed to collapse in on herself. She started crying, and she followed him downstairs. They got on horses, and they rode away."

There was a long silence. "Don't be too hard on your friend," Lucia said softly.

"She saved me—how can I hold that against her? But I don't understand why she just *left* like that. Just because she'd used magic once. She could have refused after that."

"It's not quite that simple," Lucia said.

"What do you mean?" I asked.

"It's difficult to explain." She shook her head. "I'm not sure I entirely understand it. But it is very difficult for mages to stop doing magery. Imagine that you were dying of thirst, and someone offered you a cup of water. Even if you knew that the water was poisoned, you might drink it, because it would satisfy your thirst. And once you'd taken the first sip, it would be even harder to stop." She looked into my face, searching for some sign of understanding. "As I said, I don't entirely understand it, either. But don't judge Mira too harshly."

"I trusted the Circle, once," I said.

"All of us did. Don't judge yourself, either." Lucia studied her hands. "I was in Verdia when the war broke out. Few people questioned the Circle's story about the border raids that were leaving farm families dead." Lucia sighed. "I didn't even have to be a Redentore to know the real cause of the war—just a merchant's daughter who had seen where certain crops went after they left Verdia."

I sat up straight. "What are you saying? What caused the war?"

"A great deal of trade comes through Varena. We buy and sell commodities from people across the sea—spices, dyes, certain drinks that are like very strong wine, fruits, and sweet things that no one down here has ever seen. Of course, we need things to sell to them in order to have the money to buy the goods they bring."

"Of course," I said.

"There's a flower that grows—or used to grow—in the southern parts of Verdia and northern parts of Vesuvia. It smells very nice, and with some work can be distilled into perfume. A few years ago, demand for this perfume suddenly shot up—who knows why, a court fad on the other side of the sea, most likely—and merchants from Vesuvia were cutting into Varena's profits. I'm sure they felt the same way about us. Both sides wanted the war; it was a gamble, but they hoped to destroy the other side's ability to make the perfume."

I felt sick, but not really surprised. "Are you saying that the Circle *meant* to drain the land?"

"Oh no," Lucia said. "I think that was an accident—I think even the Circle didn't realize that would happen. But certainly they meant to burn the Vesuviani fields, to do what they could to keep the Vesuviani from growing those flowers."

I shook my head and leaned back again. "I think right now you could tell me that they drained the land for the sheer joy of destruction, and I might believe you."

"Don't say that. They're still people, even if what they do is wrong. Some of them even have family down here, like your friend, Mira."

We were quiet for a while. Outside the tent, we could hear two old women arguing. They were arguing over a goat—someone had traded a goat for some chickens, but the goat died the next day. I looked at Lucia, baffled. The only evidence of goats in Ravenna was the meat in the soup at the barracks. Lucia grinned and shook her head. "I've heard these two at it before. That trade took place eight years ago."

"Why would you fight over something like that here?"

Lucia shrugged. "Entertainment?"

"Do you ever feel like those women?" I asked, then flushed, realizing what an insulting question this could be. "With the movement and the Old Way, do you ever feel like there's no real purpose in it? I mean—" I was in a hole, but I kept digging. "All my life I've trained to become a member of an orchestral ensemble. When I left the conservatory, I slammed that door shut. I still play and practice, but sometimes I feel like I'm just doing it because that's what I've always done. Do you ever feel that way?"

I was afraid to look at Lucia's face, afraid that she'd be furious at me, but she took my hand gently. "There are some things that are never meaningless. God's love is one. Music is another."

I finally looked up, but she wasn't looking at me. "There is power in the music of the Old Way and there is power in singing and dancing together—power that can't be stopped by the Fedeli, Teleso, or the Circle," Lucia said. "One of the villages I went to had lost every dance but the one they called the Dance That Turned the Storm. This was a village in Marino, just on the coast of the sea. A fishing village. Years ago, a terrible storm was coming from the ocean, the kind that can destroy houses, and they had nowhere to go to hide from it. As the storm approached, the whole village went to the piazza and joined hands to dance. When they stopped dancing, the storm had turned and headed back out to sea. There is power in the dances. Even here." Lucia looked up to meet my eyes. "That's what you were getting ready for, all these years, Eliana. Even if you didn't know it. Not to play in an ensemble. To play the Dance That Turned the Storm. Someday."

Isabella returned to the tent in late afternoon. "Teleso has ordered the whole camp to the piazza at sundown."

"How will everyone fit?" I asked.

"The tents on the edges of the piazza will be taken down until the assembly is over," Isabella said.

"Does anyone know why?" Lucia asked.

Isabella shook her head. "No. But I heard that they're building a scaffold."

Lucia covered her face with her hands. "How is Rafi?" she asked after a moment.

Isabella sighed. "He blames himself. You know Rafi." She patted Lucia's shoulder. "Give me one of your ration chits and I'll go get you some dinner. They're serving it early so that we'll be done by sundown."

We each gave her a chit and she ducked back out.

When evening came, Isabella gave us each a scarf to partially obscure our faces as we headed for the piazza. "Stay near the back," she warned us.

"Beneto and Jesca—"

"Will know that your thoughts are with them. It will be nearly dark. Even if you were in the front row, they wouldn't be able to see you."

Despite this warning, Lucia dragged me nearly to the front of the piazza; it wasn't difficult, as most people seemed to prefer to be farther back. I tucked my violin case under my arm, trying to hide it with my cloak, since we didn't want to be recognized. The violin made me pretty distinctive.

As we reached the front we got a clear view of the scaffold. Two nooses dangled, slack in the evening calm. "Oh no," I heard Lucia murmur; her hand turned cold.

The setting sun lit the black hills to the west with an orange fire, but I don't think anyone else noticed. As the colors began to fade, the front door to the keep opened. "Teleso," Lucia said. "No one else uses that door."

A squadron of a dozen guards marched out. I recognized some of the faces. Teleso was making his men work extra shifts. Behind the guards was a slender man with dark hair and cold eyes. I knew without asking that this was Teleso.

Escorted by the soldiers, Teleso strode up the steps onto the scaffold. He gestured for silence and a hush fell over the crowd. "People of Ravenna," he said. He had a strong voice, as clear and deep as a church bell, and it rang through the valley on the still evening air. "You know that my first duty and desire is to keep you all as safe and comfortable as possible. Ravenna offers refuge, shelter and sustenance to anyone who comes here willing to work. But to become part of our community, you must be willing to allow others to live in peace. Thieves will be *punished*. Marauders will be *punished*. And those who would destroy what we have built here will be *cut off* from our community."

Teleso gestured to the soldiers who still stood in the doorway, and they came forward, dragging Beneto and Jesca with them. Beneto blinked in the torchlight, trying to see past the glare to our faces; Jesca looked dazed and sick. The soldiers dragged them up the steps to the scaffold.

"Beneto and Jesca," Teleso said, "have committed extortion, treason, and disloyalty."

Beneto stirred. "Lies!" he shouted. One of the soldiers standing beside him slapped him across the face; the sound echoed through the piazza. A rustle of fear and anger wound through the crowd.

"They have entered into a deliberate campaign of terror against the people of Ravenna," Teleso continued. "This community has no place for them." He looked slowly around the crowd, and for an instant, his eyes met mine. I felt like a field mouse in the shadow of a hawk. "The sentence is death," he said. He stepped down from the scaffold, and the soldiers shoved Beneto and Jesca under the nooses. I realized that one of the soldiers on the scaffold was Mario; he averted his eyes as he held Beneto's arms. Another soldier slipped a noose over Beneto's head, tightened it around his neck. Next to him, I recognized Niccolo tightening the other noose around Jesca's. Mario and most of the others stepped back.

Beneto closed his eyes and shouted, "For the glory of God, and Her son, and the Light!" Niccolo shoved him off the scaffold. The crowd went rigid; I could see people around me touching their collars, their throats, watching Beneto's desperate struggle for air. The soldiers had left his hands untied so that he could claw desperately at the noose, legs kicking frantically to find purchase. Lucia stood rigid, hands pressed against her lips.

Jesca cried out, "Death to the ones who have left us to starve." Niccolo shoved her off the scaffold. Her face contorted as she tried uselessly to suck air past the noose, but through a supreme act of will, she clenched her arms at her sides, refusing to claw at the rope like Beneto. She would die with dignity. I touched my fist to my chest, then held it out, a soldier's salute to his commander.

"Live with God, Jesca," Lucia whispered. "Live with God, Beneto." The woman on the other side of me turned away; others wept openly. As the last of the golden sunset faded in the hills, Beneto's struggles finally ended; Jesca's body became limp and still. Lucia's hand found mine; she was as cold as ice, and so was I. People began to drift out of the courtyard. "Who will lead us now?" Lucia whispered.

"Come on, Lucia," I said. As I started to help Lucia back toward the tents, I felt someone staring at me. I looked up to glare, and met Teleso's cold eyes. I turned away hastily, but from the corner of my eye I could see him gesture to someone. As we tried to slip past the edge of the keep, a soldier blocked our path.

"Signora Eliana," he said.

"Yes." I looked up unwillingly.

"You're to come with me," he said.

"What?" Lucia cried.

"He's not looking for you, Lucia," the soldier said. "He just said to bring him the violinist." More kindly, he added, "It's all right. I think he just wants to hear her play." Glancing around, he gestured sharply to someone, and I saw Isabella coming over. "Take Lucia," the soldier said to her. "I don't think she's in any shape to get home by herself. I'm to take Eliana to the keep." Isabella looked at me for a moment, wide-eyed.

"I'll be fine," I said to Isabella, having no idea whether I was telling the truth or not. "Tell Lucia I'll be fine."

"Come on," the soldier said to me, and he had a sword, so I followed him into the keep.

CHAPTER ELEVEN

They can stop us where we stand, but more will come.
They can kill us, but more will rise. They can blind us, but
more will see with open eyes. They cannot stand against
us, any more than they can stand against the tide.
—*The Journey of Gèsu, chapter 27, verse 4.*

*T*eleso waited just inside the door of the keep. "Signora Eliana," he said. "What a pleasure to meet you at last. I have heard a great deal about you."

Forcing myself to meet his eyes, I drew myself straight and raised one eyebrow silently.

"After your performance last night, half my soldiers were singing your praises. The rest were on duty at the time, and were thus denied the opportunity to hear you." He gave me a smile that never reached his eyes. When he reached to touch my arm I jerked away without thinking.

"Don't be afraid," Teleso said. "I only want to converse with you, and to hear you play." He held out his arm, crooked slightly at the elbow. "Take my arm, signora," he said. I stood motionless for a moment. "Take my arm!" he said impatiently.

Awkwardly, I slipped my hand under his arm. The last time I had practiced this gesture was with Mira.

"Good," Teleso said, tucking my arm snugly against his side. "Now, if you will join me for supper, I would appreciate the opportunity to demonstrate the advantages of friendship with me. Come."

Teleso led me down the corridor and up a staircase, through a door into a room with a long table, and finally to a chair at the table. "Where are you from, Eliana?"

"Doratura," I said. Teleso released my arm and pulled a chair out for me, slipping it neatly under me as I sat.

"If you'll excuse me for just a moment," he said, "I need to speak to my lieutenant about a few details. The servants will be in shortly with our meal." He went out, closing the door behind him.

With Teleso gone, I took a deep breath and looked around. An iron circle of candles swung by a chain from the ceiling, lighting the room. There was a thick rug under my feet; I could feel the plush pile even through my boots. The table itself was long enough to seat twelve, but only two places were set, one at each end.

The door opened and I jumped, but it was only a servant. He poured wine into a cup made of glass as thin as an eggshell, then set it by my hand. It looked as if it would shatter if I picked it up, so I decided not to; I didn't want to spill wine on the tablecloth. The plate was also made of a thin, fragile-looking material. I tapped it gently with my fingernail; it made a *tink* noise like a bell. A knife and spoon were laid next to the plate, but there were two spoons and several items I had never seen before and had no idea what to do with.

The door opened again; this time it was Teleso. He sat at the other end of the table. The servant filled his wineglass, then left and returned a moment later with a platter of food.

"Serve the Lady first," Teleso said as the servant approached him. He looked at me apologetically. "I wasn't able to bring servants with me from Cuore, so I've had to make do. They're all refugees, you understand—they work for me instead of building the wall—so we're not even really up to the standards of Pluma."

"Ah," I said. I watched the servant as he cut a thin slice of meat and raised it over his head, then set it in the center of the table as an offering to Her.

"Now serve the guest," Teleso said patiently when the servant started toward him again. Without looking up, the servant piled several slices of meat onto my plate, and suddenly I was ravenous. Ignoring the funny-looking implements by my plate, I speared the meat with my knife and took a bite.

Teleso chewed methodically as he watched me dig in. Several times he gestured to the servant to serve me more food. "You're not drinking your wine," he said as I mopped up the last of the juices with a piece of crusty bread.

"That cup it's in," I said. "I'm afraid I'll break it."

Teleso chuckled, not unkindly. "They're sturdier than they look," he said. "Just don't drop it on the floor or throw it across the room."

I picked it up carefully and took a sip of wine. The glass stayed in one piece. "From Cuore," he said proudly. "Excellent vintage." I nodded politely, although Doratura's wine was better, or even Bascio's.

The servant brought us tea when we were done, and Teleso leaned back in his chair to sip his, cupping his hands around the mug to warm them and looking at me thoughtfully. I met his eyes in a glare and he chuckled again, unoffended.

"So," Teleso said, after a while. "I heard you came here voluntarily."

"I was hoping to find that a member of my family had

survived the destruction of my village," I said. "None had."

"How unfortunate," he said, with what sounded like genuine regret. "Where did you learn to play the violin?"

"Originally, from a man in Doratura. Then I spent five years at the conservatory in Bascio."

"Of course, the peasant conservatory," he said. "No offense."

"None taken," I said. "Signore." It was common knowledge that the peasant conservatories had higher standards than those that admitted the children of gentlemen for a fee.

"Call me Teleso," he said expansively. "Are you any good? My men thought you were quite something, but they're not exactly musical experts."

"I like to think so," I said.

"How old are you?"

"Sixteen."

"Why did you leave the conservatory so close to finishing?"

I looked down and took another sip of tea, debating how to respond. I didn't think I wanted to tell him the lie that I'd been caught with a boy; on the other hand, I wasn't sure it was a good idea to share my opinions of the Circle.

"Come now," Teleso said. "This can't be such a difficult question. Surely you had your reasons."

"I wanted to see my family," I said.

"Homesickness? After all that time?"

I met Teleso's eyes in a fierce glare. Teleso looked as though he were about to press the issue, but his gaze faltered and he dropped the subject.

"Let me see your violin," he said. I picked up the violin from where I had set it next to my feet, and took the case down to his end of the table. Teleso set his tea down carefully, then pushed his chair back and set the case on his lap. He unfastened the largest buckle, then unlaced the leather thongs to open the case. "Lovely instrument," he said. "Where was it made?"

"Mivera."

"Of course," he said. He took out the violin, stroked his hands along the smooth wood. "There is no instrument more lovely, is there?"

"No." I had seen violins made with inlaid wood of different colors, or mother-of-pearl accents, but mine was very simple. Still, even the simplest violin was beautiful to my eye, and mine was of a dark wood with a strong grain.

"Let me hear you play." He offered me the violin and bow; I took them and went back to my end of the table, sitting back down to tighten the bow hairs and tune the violin.

"Any requests?" I asked, standing up again.

"Whatever you like," he said.

I pushed my chair in with my foot and backed into a corner of the room, tucking the violin under my chin. Teleso seemed like someone who would be more impressed by virtuosity than singability, so I played one of the more technically impressive solos I'd learned at the conservatory. He applauded enthusiastically when I was done.

"Bravo," he said. "Another."

I played a long selection of pieces from my days at the conservatory; he clapped for each. "I have a request," he said finally. "I don't know what it's called, but it has a catchy rhythm." He tapped it out on the table. *Da* dat da *da* dat da *wham wham wham*. The Redentore funeral music.

I flinched slightly, pressing my back against the wall behind me. "I don't know it, signore," I said.

His cold eyes narrowed. "The Fedeli do not run Ravenna, Eliana. I do."

I pulled myself up and gave him a long, measured look across the violin. He smiled slowly; this time, it almost reached his eyes. "My youngest sister went to a conservatory," he said. "Our father paid the tuition; he thought having a musician in the family would give us a bit of culture. I know from her that *all* musicians learn the Old Way songs, sooner or later. So don't tell me you don't know this song." He leaned forward across the table and his eyes narrowed again. "You should want to stay on my good side," he said gently. "And I want to hear you play this piece."

I closed my eyes and picked a key, drawing my bow slowly across the first note. As I began the piece, I could almost hear the low rustle of feet on ash and rubble, remembering Amedeo dancing as I mourned my family. I held my tears in check tonight, and kept my feet still.

Teleso was silent for a long time when I finished. Then he poured himself a cup of wine and drained it. "Not bad," he said. "You will stay as my guest in the keep tonight. The maidservant will show you to your room."

She was a girl a year or so younger than me, dark-eyed and painfully thin. She avoided meeting my eyes as she led me up a winding staircase and through a heavy oak door. "Is this satisfactory, signora?" she asked as I caught my breath and looked around the room.

"Yes," I said.

I surveyed the room slowly from the doorway. It was easily three times the size of my room at the conservatory. The floor was covered with deep rugs woven of a dark red wool. In the center of the room was a vast soft bed, piled high with pillows and quilts. A linen nightdress was laid neatly across the bed, along with a robe and slippers.

"Pull this cord—" the maidservant touched a silk rope by the door "—to summon me if you need anything. Do you require anything now?"

I shook my head.

"Good night, then." She started to close the door.

"Wait—" I said. She froze, her hand still on the doorknob. "What's your name?"

"Arianna," she said. She looked up for a moment and I caught a flash of brown eyes and long lashes. "May I go now, signora?" I nodded and she closed the door.

I didn't want to tread on the rugs with my boots on, so I leaned against the wall by the door and pulled them off, then padded across the floor in my stockings.

A few amenities were missing from the room. There was only a tiny slit of a window, high along one wall. There was also no way to bar the door. I wasn't sure why I felt the need to shut the people in the keep out of my room, but suddenly this lack disturbed me intensely and I dragged one of the heavy chairs to the door and wedged it under the knob.

In the flickering candlelight, I caught a sudden glimpse of a strange man across the room, and nearly jumped out of my skin. The man jumped, as well, and I realized that I was looking at a mirror.

There were few mirrors at the conservatory, and the opportunity to see my reflection was rare. I had seen my reflection in water, of course, and in polished metal dishes, but I had never seen myself in men's clothing. When I spotted the mirror, I went for a closer look, and decided that I really did look like myself—just different.

I was a mess. My hair was tangled and my face was thin and dirty. My clothes were dirty, too, although I liked the way the tunic looked on me, especially with the red sash. Much better than the conservatory robes. I didn't think I looked that much like a boy, except for maybe all that dirt. There was a basin in the room, so I undressed and sponged off my body, then washed my hair. The soap was perfumed, a sweet, heavy scent. I didn't like it, but it was an improvement over the dust and grime.

It took me a long time to comb out my hair. It had tangled badly in the wind and dust, and washing it had removed the dust but set the tangles into a sodden mess. It was just as well it was short; if I'd had to comb such tangles out of long hair, I probably would have lost all patience and cut it off with anything handy.

I was tempted by the linen nightdress, but decided after a few moments that wearing it would be accepting more of Teleso's forced hospitality than I really wanted. I put my tunic and trousers back on, dirty though they were, then folded the nightdress neatly and laid it across a chair. I suppose if I'd really wanted to demonstrate my reluctance to accept Teleso's hospitality, I would have slept on the floor instead of in the bed, but there was no point in being a damn fool about it. I crawled under the covers and was asleep almost instantly.

I slept heavily; when I woke, for a moment, I didn't know where I was, and I thought wildly that I was back at the conservatory, since it had been so long since I'd slept in a proper bed. This bed was much too soft, though, and after a moment, I remembered where I was. I got up and made up the bed, then dragged the chair away from the door. I was tuning my violin to practice when Arianna arrived with my breakfast—a bowl of porridge, sweetened with honey, and a mug of tea. I sat down and ate everything she'd brought, scraping the sides of the bowl with my spoon to get the last remnants, although if I'd pulled on the cord by the door and asked, she probably would have brought me another bowl.

Setting the bowl aside, I looked up at the window, high on the wall. It was over my head, so I pulled the chair over to the window and stood up to peer out. I could see down into the piazza, and to the tents beyond. The scaffold was still standing. The tents that had been taken down for the execution last night were back up, but the piazza was empty. No one wanted to set foot there. I climbed off the chair and pushed it back to where it had been.

I took my violin and went back to the mirror, checking my posture in the reflection. I closed my eyes as I played a set of scales, trying to imagine myself back in a practice room at the conservatory. Even with my eyes closed, the sound was strange, muted and gentled by the rugs and tapestries. This room was kept scrupulously clean; instead of dust, I could smell the lingering scent of tea and porridge. But when the breeze came into the room, it carried the sour smell of rot, like decaying corpses. I shuddered.

There was a knock at the door and I opened it. It was Arianna. "Excuse me," she said, flinching.

"Come in," I said, backing away from the door. "What is it?"

Arianna carried a colorful bundle in her arms. "Dresses," she said, holding them out toward me. "Signore Teleso sent them for you. You can pick out whichever one you like." I didn't make any move to take them, so she laid them on the bed, shaking each one out and smoothing the fabric.

"I want to keep the clothes I have," I said.

"He said for you to wear what you like," she said.

"Good."

Arianna brushed out the last dress, then looked up at me hesitantly. "You have not been in Ravenna long, Signora Eliana?"

"No."

"Be careful," she said. "Your life will be easier if you

don't make him angry." Arianna looked back down at the dresses. "These are nice dresses. They would look lovely on you." I didn't respond, and she excused herself, closing the door behind her.

I went back to practicing.

Teleso swung the door open without knocking. "Good morning," he said amiably, and closed the door behind him.

"Hello," I said, lowering my bow but not my violin.

Teleso looked me up and down, then glanced at the bed. "Were none of the dresses satisfactory to you?"

"I like these clothes," I said.

Teleso walked over to the bed, held up one of the dresses. It was a wine-red velvet. "How about this one?" he asked.

"I like these clothes," I said again.

"At least let the servants wash them." He ambled back over to stand in front of me. "You can wear one of these in the meantime." He laid the dress across my hands.

I stroked the fabric as I held it up against myself. It was almost as soft as cat's fur. "It's made for a smaller woman," I said with a relieved smile. "There's no way this would fit me."

Teleso scowled and took the dress back. "We'll see if we can find something your size."

"I'm very tall," I said. "For a woman."

"Indeed." Teleso looked me up and down again, slowly, then abruptly ordered, "Sit." He gestured toward the chair.

I sat. Teleso remained standing, pacing over to the bed to toss the dress down.

"You're likely to be here for a while," he said, "so please understand that this advice is for your own good." He glanced back at me. "That girl, Lucia. She's trouble, she's *in* trouble, and she's likely to get in *worse* trouble. Steer clear of her." He glanced at me again. I tried to keep my face bland, but I could feel a flush rising to my cheeks and I knew I was glaring at him. "There is one person here who can make your life significantly easier, and that's me. You should *want* to stay on my *good* side."

"Am I on your good side now?" I asked.

"Of course," Teleso said. He picked the dresses up from the bed, shook them out, and draped them across his arm. "I'll see about finding something that might fit you better," he said, and went back out.

Arianna returned sometime later with a new set of dresses. "These are larger," she said, unfolding one and holding it up.

"It's still too small," I said. It was velvet, like the other, but midnight blue, with gold brocade along the neckline and sleeves. What would it feel like to wear cloth like that?

"It will *do*, signora," she urged, biting her lip. Her eyes were wide and alarmed, and that, more than anything else, persuaded me to comply.

"I'm not letting you wash my clothes," I said. "I'm keeping them here."

"Of course, signora," she said, her face flushing with relief. I took the dress and waited for her to leave, but she just stood there. When I looked at her questioningly, she bit her lip again and said, "I'm to help you dress."

I hadn't been helped to dress since the last time I'd had a bad fever, almost three years ago, and I felt terribly self-conscious. Arianna averted her eyes as I slipped off my tunic and trousers, folding them neatly and laying them on the bed. They could use a washing, but I didn't trust her to give them back. "Here," she said, and I realized that the dress buttoned up the back; I would need her help, after all. I shrugged on the sleeves and she buttoned it up. It took a long time. "I'll comb your hair," she said when it was done.

"I can do it myself," I protested, but she sat me firmly down in the chair and undid my hair clasp. Arianna combed it out carefully, much more thoroughly than I had the night before, then braided it, winding a ribbon and a strand of blue glass beads through the braid. "This is ridiculous," I said, squirming as the comb caught in a tangle. "You're pasting peacock feathers on a sparrow. I don't wear clothing like this."

"You look lovely, though," she said, and led me to the mirror.

If seeing a strange man in the mirror had been a shock, this was even more disturbing. The dress was cut low in the front, showing the tops of my breasts, and the fabric hugged my waist, stretching over my hips to flare in a long, full skirt. I had the body of a woman, which was something of a surprise to me. I ran my hands slowly over the fabric. I was disappointed; it wasn't nearly as soft inside as out, and the brocade was scratchy. In the mirror, my face was pale and nervous. "I look like a child in borrowed clothes."

"No," Arianna said. "You look like a beautiful woman."

I snickered at that, and my reflection looked slightly less nervous. I drew myself up straight. "Well," I said.

In the mirror, I saw the door swing open behind me. "Much better," Teleso murmured, and gestured to Arianna. She bowed and slipped out silently. I continued to stare into the mirror, unwilling to turn to face Teleso.

He beamed at me over my shoulder. "Beautiful," he said, and I blushed like a twelve-year-old.

"No," I muttered.

"Yes," he said, and stepped up behind me, resting his hand lightly on the small of my back.

"What time is it?" I asked, whirling abruptly to walk back to the hearth and pick up my violin.

"Just before noon," Teleso said.

"I need to practice," I said.

"You sounded fine to me yesterday."

"Maybe," I said, "but if I don't practice every day, my skills will deteriorate. I don't just practice to get better at playing, I practice to keep from backsliding, getting worse. Your sister must have told you that." I knew that I was babbling, but tried to straighten my shoulders and meet Teleso's eyes, though it was harder to do that in this dress.

Teleso did not follow me, although he watched me, a slight smile on his face. I backed into the wall with a thump. He still hadn't moved.

"Eliana," he said. "Relax."

"What do you want from me?" I asked. My voice sounded high and thin, like a violin string about to break.

"Your company at the midday meal," he said. "Nothing more. Was there something else you were expecting?" I gulped and I knew that my eyes showed fear. He smiled, and his cold eyes creased. "So if you will return from the corner, and take my arm, I will escort you to my study, where we will have a nice meal, and good wine, and pleasant conversation."

"Yes," I said. "Thank you." I took his arm, and he tucked my hand snugly against his side. He led me back down the stairs, through a series of corridors and finally into his study.

The meal was silent and uncomfortable. Teleso sat behind a massive carved desk, staring at me for most of the meal. I sat on the other side, my bowl on the very edge of the desk. I stared at my food to avoid looking at Teleso, eating quickly to get through the meal as soon as I could. The dress made me feel exposed.

There was a sharp rap at the door as I was finishing the last of my bread. It was one of Teleso's officers, a dark-haired man with a face like a weasel. Teleso stepped over to the door for a hasty quiet conference. "Duty calls," he said, returning to the desk. "I'll have the maid show you to your room." He rang for Arianna.

Alone in my room again, I alternated between practicing and pacing. Struck by a sudden worry, I checked the bed, but my tunic and trousers were where I'd left them. They really were filthy. There was a basin of water in the room, along with a bar of perfumed soap, so I decided to wash them. The midnight blue velvet was not exactly suited to washerwoman's work, but wearing it hadn't been my idea. Still, I rolled up my sleeves and worked carefully so as not to splash water on myself. It was awkward and slow, but I managed to get out the worst of the dirt. I wrung out most of the water, but needed to leave them to dry somewhere that Teleso wouldn't see them and order them removed. I checked under the bed—no dust. Arianna was a thorough housekeeper. Hiking the velvet over my knees to avoid crushing it, I spread the belt, tunic, and trousers under the bed to dry.

I was arranging the trousers when there was a knock at the door. I jumped, knocking my head on the underside of the bed before managing to crawl out, gritting my teeth and rubbing the back of my head. "Come in," I said, trying to smooth out the dress with my other hand.

I was expecting Arianna, but it was a soldier, wearing a cloak with the hood pulled up to half cover his face. He closed the door gently behind him and flipped back the hood. It was Mario.

"Hello," I said, startled.

"I have a message for you," Mario said in a low voice, and held out a folded slip of paper. I hesitated. "Take it!" he said. "I can't stay here. It's from Lucia."

Still rubbing my head where I'd bumped it, I took the note, staring at him. "Are you all right?" he asked, lingering a moment longer.

I shrugged. "The food is better and the bed is softer. But—" I shook my head.

Mario gave me a crooked smile. "It will all be all right." He slipped the door open a crack and poked his head out to look for anyone coming. He gave me one more reassuring smile and left, closing the door behind him.

Alone in the room again, I sat down on the bed to read my letter. It was just a tiny piece of parchment, folded neatly. Lucia had drawn an X at the top. The letter was written in a beautiful, graceful script, but with the flourishes cut short. *Eliana,* the letter read. *You must persuade Teleso to allow us to hold a funeral, and to allow you to play. This is our* chance. *This is what Beneto was waiting for. I have faith in you. By the grace of God, Lucia.* In smaller letters at the bottom: *Burn this when read.*

I held the note a moment longer, as if by pressing it I would somehow feel Lucia touching my hand. Then I burned it to ash in one of the candles, and washed my hands in the basin.

The room was big enough for me to pace. What was going on outside these walls? I wished Lucia had sent me a longer letter. Was Rafi doing better? She hadn't said. I shook my head, wondering how I ever spent all those years at the conservatory. I'd only been shut up in here for a day and I was going mad, not knowing what was happening outside the walls.

I pulled over a chair and climbed up to look out the

window again. At the very edge of the piazza, I saw Lucia. She stood quietly, her hands clasped, looking at the keep. Looking for me—I was sure of that, but there was no way she could see me through my tiny window, not from that distance. I tucked my violin under my chin and played for her, hoping that the notes would carry. Lucia remained where she was, silently keeping her vigil.

Who will lead us now? Lucia's question from last night rang in my ears. After staring across the piazza at Lucia for a long time, I climbed down off the chair. Giovanni was next in line to lead, I realized, and shuddered. God help us all. I tried to concentrate on some études, but my mind kept wandering. Lucia would be a far better leader than Giovanni, but I knew that she wouldn't do it—she believed that her calling was elsewhere. Isabella, perhaps? Rafi? None of them would be able to claim the popular support that Beneto and Jesca had built up, I knew that much. Especially not Giovanni.

Ravenna was in deep shadow when Teleso swung my door open. "Good evening," he said with a smile. "Would you care to join me downstairs for supper?" He offered me his arm, then led me back down to the dining room.

The meal was more hectic tonight. The weasel-faced officer I'd seen before was in and out throughout the meal. Teleso spoke to him quietly, glancing at me a few times to see if I was listening. I lowered my eyes to my plate and tried to look uninterested, tipping my head slightly to hear as much as I could.

"—could be a good chance. They're all angry. Men couldn't object—"

"Yes, signore. As you say—"

"It's well past time."

"As you say, signore."

Teleso's deputy left, and Teleso gestured to the servant

to refill his wineglass. "Troublemakers," he said to me. "All of them."

I took a sip of my wine. "The refugees?" I asked.

"And the soldiers," Teleso said. He drained his wineglass. "Lucia is demanding to be allowed to hold a funeral, with everyone in Ravenna attending." He gestured to the servant, then jerked the wine bottle away and filled his own glass, banging the bottle down to the table. "I'll have to deal with her."

"A funeral—" I started to say. How was I supposed to persuade him to hold one?

"—Isn't a bad idea, really," Teleso said. "Make the refugees happy. What will they have to complain about then? You'll play the funeral dance for them, of course." He drained his glass.

"Yes, signore," I said. That was easier than I'd expected.

Teleso filled his glass again. "The trouble is," he said, "the bastards won't shoot unless there's trouble."

"Who won't shoot?" I asked.

"Bastards downstairs who call themselves soldiers. I'll have you play for them too."

"All right," I said. "Now?"

"No, not now!" he snarled. "Don't be ridiculous. You're supposed to play for *me* now. So stop talking. Did you bring your violin?"

"Not to supper," I said. "It's still up in my room."

"Well, go get it," he said. "Bring it to my study. I'll wait for you there." He rang for Arianna and rose, stumbling slightly. Arianna escorted me upstairs to get my violin, but when I brought it back down to Teleso's study he was snoring in his chair.

I edged over to his desk, treading softly on the rug. His eyes were shut, and he was drooling slightly in his sleep. I reached out one hand to shake him, then thought the better of it. As I was pulling my hand away, I noticed the papers on his desk. Teleso had pulled some papers out to work on while waiting for me. I glanced at him again, but he was still drooling, his eyes closed. I hesitated for a moment, afraid he'd wake suddenly. He seemed pretty drunk, though. I picked up the papers.

The top paper was difficult to decipher; it seemed to be a page from a ledger, with calculations scribbled down the side. I realized after studying it for a moment that it was a reckoning of how much grain Ravenna had left, and how much this allowed per person until the next shipment. I could barely make out the numbers, but I could tell there wasn't much grain to go around. I slipped the paper back onto his desk and went onto the next one.

It was a letter from his superiors in Cuore. *In receipt of your letter . . . Regret to say that supplements will be impossible at this time.* Supplementary food? No, reading further, they meant supplementary soldiers. *Advise you to make the most of the men currently under your command.* The letter became steadily more patronizing. At the bottom, in the cramped handwriting of the ledger scrawl, was the single word, *bastards.* Teleso's frustrations, most likely.

The final page was a list: *Beneto. Jesca. Lucia. Isabella. Rafi. Michel. Giovanni. Mario.* There were other names on the list, people I didn't know. *Tomas. Regillo. Petro.* There was a small check mark next to Beneto and Jesca's names. Lucia's name was circled.

Teleso snorted loudly and I shoved the papers back and reached across the desk as he opened his eyes. "Signore?" I said, touching his arm. "Are you sure you want me to play for you? I think you need sleep more than music right now."

"Surely," he said. His eyes were bleary as he stood up and rang for the servant. "You're right. Good night, then." I gathered up my violin and headed for the door.

"Eliana," Teleso said, and I froze in my tracks. "Tomorrow night. We'll hold the funeral. You'll play." Arianna appeared in the doorway, and Teleso waved me off. "Sleep well," he said.

Arianna had to help me undress for bed. She was less shy in the flickering candlelight as she unwound the beads from my hair and unbuttoned the long row of buttons down the back of the dress. "This dress is ridiculous," I said.

"It's a lovely dress," she said.

"It's a ridiculous dress. I can't *do* anything in it." I craned my neck to look over my shoulder at Arianna.

"You managed," she said, glancing significantly toward my still-damp laundry hidden under the bed.

"This dress is making me miss those stupid robes we had to wear at the conservatory," I said. "Those sleeves just got in the way. These don't want to let me move." I paused, but she didn't answer. "Are you almost done?"

"Yes, signora." She helped me step out of the dress, then hung it up neatly as I pulled the linen nightdress over my head.

"I can put this on by myself," I said, when she turned to look at me.

"Yes, signora," she said, but didn't leave.

I straightened the nightdress as she stood looking at me. Finally I asked, "Is there something you need?"

"Would you play your violin for me?" she asked, then bit her lip and looked down. "I haven't gotten to hear you play."

"Oh!" I blinked in surprise. "Of course."

"I'm sorry to ask you so late at night. During the day, I'm busy all the time, so I never get to sit and listen. I'm sorry, I shouldn't have asked."

I took her by the shoulders. "Arianna. Sit down. I'll play for you." I pushed her gently into the chair she'd sat me in earlier, to braid my hair, then took out my violin and tuned up. "Any requests?"

"Something old," she whispered, so I nodded and played the Redentore healing music. She didn't dance, but closed her eyes to listen, rocking back and forth with the music. The minor notes echoed off the stone hearth; the sweet chords were swallowed by the tapestries on the walls. I closed my eyes, hearing something I didn't quite recognize in my own playing, just a faint echo, like the lingering taste of honey.

When I finished, Arianna sat with her eyes closed for a bit longer, and for a moment I thought she'd fallen asleep. "Thank you," she said, her eyes still closed. "Good night." She left without another word. I realized suddenly how tired I was. I put my violin away, then curled up under the covers of the bed. The room seemed quieter tonight than it had last night. I slept soundly, except for the sense that I needed Mira, or Giula, or Lucia sleeping near my side.

Arianna arrived the next morning just as I was getting up. She had a tray with porridge—a larger bowl than yesterday—and tea. While I ate, she brought in hot water for me to wash myself, along with a soft robe to put on when I had finished. "I'll come back to help you dress," she said.

"Not the damn dress again," I said, but she was gone.

I finished my tea and porridge, and considered resisting. Arianna couldn't physically force me to put the dress on; she was smaller than I was, and anyway it would ruin the dress. Then I thought about her fear yesterday and wondered if Teleso would punish her for my rebellion, if I refused to put it on. I checked under the bed; my clothes were still there, but damp, since they weren't hanging up. I turned them over to give the damp side more air, then shrugged and stood up. I had washed myself some yesterday, but she'd brought enough water for me to wash much more thoroughly, and sleeping on white linen sheets had made me realize how dirty I still was. Besides, steam rose invitingly from the basin. I washed my hands and face, then pulled my nightdress over my head to wash the rest of my body.

The door banged open and I whirled, snatching up the robe to hold it in front of myself. Teleso stood in the doorway, smiling slyly. "Go away!" I said.

Instead, he closed the door behind him. "Good morning, Eliana," he said. Unfortunately, he did not look hung over at all.

Since I'd have to expose myself to put the robe on properly, I slipped it on backward, then tied it in the back. "Go away," I said again. "I'm still getting dressed."

"I can see that," he said. He advanced on me, and I backed away. "You know," he said, "the Redentori have the most curious customs. They believe that a girl shouldn't lie with a man until they're married. Now, how do they know if the Lady approves of their marriages? But you aren't Redentore, are you? You just like the music."

"Yes I am," I said. "I've been sealed. I'm one of them."

"But you haven't been for long," he said. "Their customs are not yours."

"I have been at the conservatory," I said. "I wasn't even allowed to talk to boys, Lady's blessing or not, not even at Midsummer."

Teleso had backed me into a corner. "Eliana, I could make your life here a great deal easier," he breathed.

"No, thank you," I said.

"You should want to be my friend."

"I'm not sure I like the price of your friendship," I said. Teleso might not look hung over, but he smelled it; his breath reeked of stale wine.

He was about to reply when the door flew open. "You rang, signore?" Arianna said from the doorway.

"No," he snapped, but she came in anyway.

"Lovely morning, isn't it?" I hadn't previously seen Arianna quite so relentlessly cheerful. She started making up my bed, apparently oblivious to the fact that Teleso still had me trapped in the corner. "Signore Teleso, Lieutenant Romolo says he needs to see you."

"Thank you, Arianna," he said. "Tell him I'll be right down." She hesitated and he turned to glare at her. "Go and tell him I'm coming."

It was clearly a dismissal, and she backed slowly out of the room. I tried to pull farther back into the corner as he turned slowly around to face me again, but he said only, "Think it over." He straightened, turned around, and left.

I still wanted to wash, but I was afraid he'd come barging into the room again. I shoved a chair over to block the door and did my best to wash without ever taking off the robe. My face was hot, and it wasn't from the water. When I was done, I pulled the nightdress and robe back on and tied them securely before I moved the chair away from the door.

Arianna was back shortly after that, biting her lip and avoiding my eyes. My hands shook as she buttoned me into the dress. "I don't want to wear this," I said, but she didn't answer.

She sat me down when she was done buttoning me up,

and braided my hair. "Arianna," I said, "what does he want from me?"

"I don't know," she said.

"Have other women stayed here?"

"One other."

"What happened to her?"

"He tired of her company."

"And?"

"And she returned to Ravenna," Arianna said, but I shook my head, not sure I believed her. "Hold still," she said. "I'm almost done."

"Do you know Mario?" I asked.

Arianna paused for a moment. "Yes," she said. "I've met him." Her manner was guarded, but she couldn't quite hide the softness that came into her voice when she spoke about the kind soldier. I sat back, satisfied to have gotten that much out of her. Arianna finished tying the ends of my braids, and came around front to inspect the results. "Teleso wants you to join him for dinner again," she said. "He'll be here soon."

"At least I'm dressed now," I said, and she nodded, still not meeting my eyes.

Dinner was quiet. I sipped wine from the fragile-looking glass and nibbled. I didn't have much of an appetite today. Weasel-face didn't come in. Teleso dismissed the servants as we finished the meal. "So," he said. "How have you been enjoying my hospitality?"

"You have been very generous," I said.

"Is the food to your liking?"

"Yes."

"And your room?" he asked.

"Very grand," I said. "Much grander than I'm used to."

"Do you like the dress?" He gestured with his wine-glass. He was drinking more slowly today.

"No," I said.

Teleso's face grew sullen. He took a sip of wine and brightened a bit. "I keep the guest room empty most of the time," he said. "You could have that room permanently, if you like." He looked at me expectantly.

"No, thank you," I said.

"What do you mean? Don't you want it?"

"Not without knowing the price," I said.

"There is no price," he said.

"Everything has a price."

"Really," he said. "Including you?" He stared at me across the table with his cold, hard eyes and I found myself flushing with fury and shame. I straightened up in my chair and returned the fiercest glare I could. He chuckled slightly and rose, advancing on my end of the table.

"Don't you want to be my friend, Eliana?" he asked.

"I'm afraid of what the price of your friendship might be," I said.

"Perhaps it's a price you'd enjoy paying." He moved to stand behind me, resting his arms on the back of my chair.

"I don't think so," I said.

Teleso dropped his hand to rest it against my waist. "You might enjoy my friendship more than you think."

"Take your hand off me," I said.

"Don't you find me handsome? Most women do."

"Take your hand *off* me," I said again.

Teleso stood behind me; I couldn't push my chair back and I couldn't stand up. As he began to slide his hand up my side, I jerked away, then ducked down and under the table, rolling beneath it and coming up to stand and face him. *"Don't touch me."*

"Don't be hasty," he said, moving toward me.

I grabbed my eating knife, sending the eggshell wineglass spinning off the table. It smashed between us; the wine splashed onto the edge of the tablecloth, making a stain like blood. *"Don't,"* I said, holding the knife out as threateningly as I could.

Teleso froze and anger flared in his face. He narrowed his eyes to stare at me. "That was a mistake," he said. Ignoring the knife, he reached out and grabbed my hand, twisting my wrist and jerking me toward him. "I am not interested in unwilling women," he hissed. "You have nothing to fear from me."

I didn't answer.

"You are throwing away quite an opportunity," Teleso said. "Think it over." He took the knife out of my hand, then released my arm and shoved me backward. He jerked on the bell cord with so much force he almost tore it off the lever. "Now get out."

One of his soldiers escorted me back up to my room. I rang the bell for Arianna, but she didn't come. No one else did, either.

The sun shone through the window high on the wall; when I pulled the chair over to peer out, I could see people assembling in the piazza for the funeral. I climbed up on the chair and tuned my violin, then started to play, still watching the people below. They could hear me; I saw an excited figure pointing up, then gathering other people to come stand under the window.

This is the dance that turned the storm. I played Lucia's dance now, from the window, and below me people clasped hands to step back and forth. *Side-together-side skip. Front-together-front skip. Side-together-side skip. Back-together-back skip.* I tried to spot Lucia in the courtyard below, but she wasn't there. *This is what Beneto was waiting for.* I could feel the nervous energy rising like steam from the dancers below.

Two soldiers came to the courtyard as I watched. They

sent the dancers away. One spoke quietly to each dancer, gesturing quickly and pointing toward the keep; the other grabbed one of the dancers roughly by the arm, shoving her out of the circle. Niccolo? No, Niccolo had fairer hair. I didn't know this soldier. At the sound of my playing, he looked up toward the window, shading his eyes with his hand. I imagined a venomous glare, but I couldn't see him clearly enough to tell. With the dancers scattered, though, I stepped down from my chair by the window, putting down my violin.

Who will lead us now? Lucia's question still haunted me. Those dancers under my window deserved a leader who believed in them. All the prisoners at Ravenna deserved a leader who believed in them. They deserved better than Giovanni—in fact, they deserved better than Beneto, for all his bright-eyed charisma. I paced the room, my violin in my hand.

I stopped in front of the mirror and tucked the violin under my chin. Closing my eyes, I played the funeral song as I'd played it for Mira, when she was ill the first time. I danced as I played—I didn't know the steps that Lucia knew, so I let the music carry me. As I whirled with the final cascade of notes, I opened my eyes and found myself facing the mirror. That night I played for Mira in her illness, I saw an image of a soldier with my face. Looking into the mirror now, I saw that soldier again, but it no longer frightened me.

Laying my violin down on the bed, I reached behind me to the buttons of the dress. There were scores of buttons, tiny and out of my reach. I unfastened the first few. Then, closing my eyes and gripping the collar of the dress, I tore it off my body. Buttons scattered across the floor like spilled stones, and I stepped out of the heap of velvet at my feet.

My clothes were still under the bed; they were slightly

damp, but I could live with that. I put on the tunic and
trousers, and belted the tunic with the red sash. The beads
and ribbons took some time to remove from my hair, but I
managed. The copper clip I'd used to secure my hair had
vanished with Arianna, so I used a single ribbon to tie it
back. Then I looked into the mirror again.

I was ready.

•   •   •

A soldier I hadn't seen before delivered my supper—gruel.
I ate it quickly, not really tasting it. I was too nervous to be
hungry, but as always before a concert, I forced the food
down. The door swung open as I scraped the last of the
gruel from the bowl, and Teleso froze, looking at me, my
clothes, the dress crumpled on the floor. "Why did you
take off the dress?" he asked. His voice trembled like a rejected child's.

"The price was too high," I said, and his face grew as
cold as his eyes.

"Come," he said, and turned away without offering me
his arm. I trailed him down the stairs. Just before we
reached the doorway of the keep, he reached back to grab
my hand, tucking it into the crook of his arm and pinning
it against his side. Soldiers joined us, and escorted us out
of the keep.

The light was fading from the edge of the hills; I stared
into the shadowy sea of faces, trying to make them out.
The area around the piazza had been cleared of tents again.
The crowd was quiet, frighteningly so. Teleso led me to the
scaffold, then up the steps and on to the platform. No ropes
hung tonight, but the cross-beam was directly over my head;
I wished fervently that there was some other platform for
me to stand on. Teleso let go of my arm and held up his
hands for silence.

"Enemies of Ravenna will be dealt with," he said. "Thieves and marauders will be punished. However, I am not without mercy. You may give them whatever funeral you wish. Their bodies have been returned to you." He gestured, and I looked down to see two shrouded bodies at the foot of the scaffold. He turned to me, smiling into my horrified face. "They're all yours," he said to me, and stepped lightly down the stairs, retreating to the keep. I was alone.

The crowd held its breath as I took a moment to retune my violin. My hands shook slightly as I tucked it under my chin, then started playing, sluggish in the damp air. *Da dat da da dat da wham wham wham. Da dat da da dat da wham wham wham.* The people were stamping their feet on the down beats, clapping their hands. "Come on!" I heard Lucia shout. "Step—wait—left behind left *turn,* left."

Slowly, like a vast mill slowly grinding to life, the crowd began to move. *Dancing. Da dat da da dat da wham wham wham.* My hands were warming; without meaning to, I sped up the music slightly. People responded. All around me, everywhere, they danced, moving in a slow circle around the platform.

The crowd was vast and packed shoulder-to-shoulder. Still, I could feel their energy, like a flame the moment before the log splits into fire. They were angry; their fury billowed around us like smoke. *Da dat da da dat da wham wham wham.* I started trying to hold the tempo back, but it wasn't working—they were speeding up, with or without me. The energy swelled. It vibrated behind my eyes like the wood of my violin, or the swarm of bees I'd felt when I played this with Mira and Bella and the others back at the conservatory. It was difficult to breathe.

The crowd's anger rose with the energy like an unstoppable tide, like an earthquake. They wanted to see Teleso's blood. My heart was beating loud enough to hear it in my ears. They were dancing faster. This was nothing like playing with Mira and Bella; *I* was the violin, played by the anger of the crowd.

A few paces from the scaffold, I could see Lucia and Giovanni dancing. Lucia's eyes were closed; Giovanni's were wide open, and riveted on me. *Our strength is in numbers,* I remembered Beneto's voice saying. *If you get people angry enough. We just have to get people angry enough.* This was what he had been waiting for, and now Giovanni was going to make it work. Lucia's lips were moving; she was singing the words to the song, which I could barely make out over the stamping feet. The dance was almost over. The anger was rising like a flooding river, waters that would smash everything in their path and carry the debris until the water was spent, soaked into the earth. I could unleash that against the camp—drown the keep in the anger like floodwaters would drown a hut— and my head spun with the power flashing through me.

The last fading rays of the day fell across the edge of the crowd. Just beyond the dancers, I saw a glint like the evening star—it was the sun catching on the tip of a crossbow bolt. Staring into the shadows, I realized that there was a ring of soldiers, beyond the dancers, crossbows drawn. Of course; Teleso knew this was coming as well as Giovanni did. From where I stood, though, I could see who the crossbows were pointed at. *Enemies of Ravenna will be dealt with.* This was why Lucia's name was circled on Teleso's list. As soon as the riot broke out, they were going to kill Lucia. For a moment my own anger roared in my ears, drowning out the anger of the crowd, and I realized what I could do. *Bastards won't shoot unless there's trouble.*

The dance was ending; I couldn't just stop playing, because people would take that as the signal for the riot to start. Gritting my teeth, I decreased the tempo of the music. I wasn't sure if this would make the dancers slow down, but it did. I slowed it more. The buzzing in my head became disjointed, confused, but this wasn't working well enough. I felt like a fragile dam trying to hold back a blinding white river of anger. I closed my eyes and concentrated. Opening myself to the tide, I poured the energy into the earth under my feet, like rainwater into a field. *Down.*

My E-string snapped. The dance ended. Instead of exploding into a riot, though, people stopped, heads bowed, and slowly shuffled off, back toward the tents. Lucia looked around, drained and confused. She didn't know what had happened, what had gone wrong. But Giovanni did. I could feel his glare burning against me like magefire; if he could have killed me right then, he would have. "Damn you," he hissed, and I met his eyes for a long moment across the dark sea. "Traitor."

Something jerked me backward, and I realized that Teleso had come up the steps to the scaffold and grabbed my arm. "Let's go," he said, and yanked me back down the steps. "You made the wrong choice."

"My violin case," I protested as Teleso dragged me into the keep.

"Shut up!" he shouted, and backhanded me across the face. I didn't see it coming; the impact knocked me back against the wall. Teleso jerked me toward him again, then shoved me toward one of the soldiers. "Lock her up." The soldier stared at Teleso. "You heard me! Lock her up."

The soldier took my arm, leading me down a narrow staircase. "It's all right," he whispered. "One of us will get the case for you."

"There was supposed to be a riot this evening," I said.

"Yes," the soldier said. "I don't know what it was you did, but thank you." He stopped where he was and released me to look into my eyes, wincing at the bruise forming across my cheek. "My orders were to shoot Signora Lucia. I didn't want to."

"What's your name?" I asked. "You speak with a Verdiano accent. Does your family live near here?"

"No, thank the Lady. I am Verdiano, but my family lives well north of the wasteland. My name is Tomas."

My cheek was beginning to ache and I pressed my hand against it, hoping that the cold from my hand would ease the swelling. "So you were supposed to reduce the number of mouths to feed, and take out Lucia."

"Yes." Tomas looked angry. "But we're soldiers, not murderers. We won't kill unarmed people in cold blood." He met my eyes hesitantly. "That's what Mario says."

Mario. Why was I not surprised?

"Isn't it just as bad to deliberately provoke a riot, just to have an excuse to kill people?"

Tomas's gaze faltered. "Probably," he said. He was young, much younger than Mario, and he suddenly looked tragically sad.

"Never mind, Tomas," I said. "It isn't your fault. You'd better take me wherever it is you're supposed to be taking me. Are you pulling a double shift already?"

"Yeah," he said with a tired smile. "This way."

We made our way down a hallway, then down another staircase that led to a row of cells. Tomas hesitated, looking embarrassed to be locking me up. "I heard you play, the other night," he said. "You're really good."

"Thank you," I said. I considered offering to play for him right there, but I was too tired. It was chilly, deep under the keep, and I shivered. "Can I have a blanket? It's cold down here."

"Oh!" he said, and looked around. "Here, you can have my cloak." He shrugged off his black-and-red cloak and wrapped it around my shoulders.

"Is this allowed?" I asked.

Tomas shrugged. "I don't think I'll get into too much trouble." He shuffled his feet. "Is there anything else I can do for you?"

I loosened the strings of my violin and laid it carefully on the stone slabs of the floor, wondering how I was going to get a new E-string. "One thing," I said. "Am I a dangerous enough prisoner to rate a guard? I'd rather Teleso not visit me unescorted."

Tomas blushed. "I understand, Signora Eliana. I'll talk to Mario—he'll arrange something." He closed the door to the cell.

Even with the cloak, I was chilled. Without Tomas's candle, the dungeon was darker than anywhere I'd ever been. I couldn't even see my hand in front of my face. I wrapped the cloak around me and curled up on the floor of the cell. I could hear my heart beating, and an echo of something else—I imagined I could hear a heart beating in the ground under my ear, or the echoes of the stamping feet earlier. The sound lulled me and comforted me, and I drifted off to sleep.

• • •

I closed my eyes, knowing that in an instant I would feel my flesh burn, and there was nothing I could do about it. As I heard the screams of my friends, though, I felt no pain. Unbelieving, I opened my eyes, and realized that as the magefire burned the air around me, it didn't touch me.

I turned toward the hill. Five mages—that was all it took. I couldn't see their faces, but suddenly I knew with utter certainty who one of them was, and that she was protecting me. Even as she killed everyone else.

• • •

I woke with a start in utter darkness. I was jumpy and imagining things that I couldn't see, and without really thinking about it, I cupped my hand to summon witchlight.

To my shock, a dim glow leapt to life and stayed there. In the feeble but steady white light, I could see Mario sleeping in the guard's chair, on the other side of my bars. I stared at the light and, after a moment or two, let it go out and lay back down.

Our magefire drained the Verdiani borderlands of every drop of energy and life they had.

Witchlight doesn't work here. No magery does.

I thought about the surge of energy I'd poured into the earth. Could this be done, for all of the wastelands? Or would you need the kind of anger that could start a riot? Or was I dreaming? I drifted back to sleep.

I woke later to find Mario shaking me gently. "Teleso wants you outside," he said. I sat up and rubbed my eyes.

"Tomas's cloak," I said.

"I'll get it back to him," he said, so I took it off and laid it across Mario's arm.

"My violin," I said.

"We have the case," he said. "Will you trust me to take care of your violin? I'll return it to you later."

I didn't want to let him take it, but I wasn't sure I had a choice, so I nodded and gave him the violin and bow. He took the violin gingerly, like he was afraid the thin wood would break, and I laughed and showed him how to hold it. "Don't go swinging it around like a club," I said, "and don't drop it, but it's not going to break in your hands or anything."

He tucked it under his arm. "Ready?" he asked.

"For what?" I said, but he avoided my eyes.

I followed Mario up the stairs; we were joined by a larger group of soldiers and Mario passed my violin off to Tomas. They marched me out the side entrance. "There she is!" someone shouted, and I saw Lucia and Giovanni and a few others. I could tell Giovanni was still furious, even from here, but Lucia just looked worried. The soldiers led me up onto the scaffold to stand next to Teleso. For a split second I was terrified that he was about to have me hanged, but there weren't any nooses.

Instead of making a speech to the onlookers, Teleso turned to me. He was as angry as he had been the previous evening, maybe even angrier. "I treated you with courtesy and hospitality," he said. "I offered you comfort and safety. And you spit on the hand I extended. Do you have anything to say for yourself?"

I raised my voice slightly. "I averted a riot. Is that why you're angry? Why does the commander of Ravenna *want* a riot?"

"Shut up!" he shouted, then lowered his voice again. "You could still apologize, Eliana. If you apologize sincerely enough, you might be able to persuade me to reopen the offer I made yesterday."

I felt my face flush and I drew myself up to my full height, pitching my voice to be heard by everyone watching. "My body is not for sale, Teleso."

His face slammed shut and he nodded once. Then he turned to the soldiers. "Tie her."

Mario and the others took hold of my arms, Mario still avoiding my eyes. They bound my hands to the cross beam of the scaffold. Someone untied my sash, then pulled my tunic over my head, and I realized they were going to whip me.

I could feel Teleso's eyes burning into my naked back and my face became scarlet. "For insolence," Teleso shouted to the crowd. "For attempting to instigate a riot. For insubordination. Thirty lashes."

I couldn't see the conversation behind me, but I could hear it. "Mario can do it," I heard Teleso say. Then Mario's voice: "This is goatshit, Teleso, and you know it!"

"Fine," Teleso's voice, gloating. "Wouldn't want to make you do anything you thought was *wrong*. Niccolo can do it." I heard a choking gasp from Mario, and someone else coming up onto the scaffold, then everyone moving out of the way. Then Teleso's voice again: "And I'll deal with you later, Mario."

I clenched my hands into fists and tried to brace myself. There were a few moments of silence; Niccolo was letting me get scared, and I wished I could turn around to spit in his face. Then the lash hissed through the air and came down, and I felt my back tear like rent cloth.

I bit down on the edge of my tunic and managed to keep from crying out. There were tears in my eyes, but no one could see them. If I couldn't spit in their faces, I could deny Niccolo and Teleso the pleasure of hearing me cry out. My blood pounded in my ears; I tried to focus on *not* crying out, like that would distract me from the lashing. I tried to count, but I kept losing track. I could smell my blood, and my stomach lurched; I gagged on my saliva. I clenched my fists, screwing my eyes shut, and waited for it to be over.

"That's *thirty*," I heard Mario's outraged shout, but the whip came down once more.

"Oops," I heard another voice say smoothly, and knew

that must be Niccolo. Someone cut the rope around my wrists and I fell to the floor of the scaffold. I lay for a moment, my eyes closed, trying to get my legs to obey me. There was a scuffle somewhere near me, and I heard Mario's voice speaking low and urgently. "Do yourself a favor, Teleso, and *leave her*." Mario picked me up and lowered me off the scaffold into Lucia's arms. "Take care of her," he muttered.

My legs still weren't holding me up; my head spun, and the edges of my vision were wavering. Lucia eased my tunic back over my head and I nearly cried out as the wool rubbed against my back.

"My violin," I said.

"I have it," Lucia said. "Mario gave it to me." She had slung my arm over her shoulders and was holding me up. Rafi ducked under my other arm. "Let's get you home."

My sight was clearing. "Let me sit down a minute," I said. "I think if I wait for a moment or two, I'll be able to stand by myself." As soon as we were past the edge of the piazza, they let me sit.

People were staring at me from their tents again, I realized. I could see them peering out. But it was a different kind of stare, now. "She didn't cry out," I heard someone say, "not once. Just about told Teleso to go screw the horses, too." Beyond Lucia, I could see a stranger touch his fist to his chest, then hold it out silently as he met my eyes.

"I think I can walk, if you'll help me," I said to Lucia, and she gave me her hand. I winced as I stood up, but I felt oddly buoyed. Rafi smiled at me kindly, and Lucia's eyes glowed with her own inner light. On the other side of Lucia, I caught Giovanni's eye. Pure malevolence met me, and I smiled back at him. Teleso had just made a serious mistake.

"Beneto was wrong," I said to Lucia, once again pitching my voice to be heard by the onlookers. "Our strength is not *just* in numbers. Our strength is in our hearts. Our will is stronger than Teleso's. When the time comes, we will fight him. And we will *win*."

PART FOUR

As Long As I Like
Where You're Leading

CHAPTER TWELVE

There is power in strangeness.
—*The Journey of Gèsu, chapter 7, verse 2.*

Isabella was at the door of Rafi's tent almost as soon as Lucia had gotten me settled. "She's resting," I heard Lucia say, but I interrupted her.

"I'm fine," I said. "Tell her to come in."

I was lying on my stomach, a wet cloth across my back; I propped myself up on my elbows when Isabella came in. "I've sent for Petro," Isabella said. "He's one of my closest friends, and the best healer in Ravenna."

"Would you like some tea?" Rafi asked Isabella. "Eliana got us some of the good kind a few nights ago."

"Yes, thank you," she said, settling against one of the rolled-up blankets. Giovanni glowered at her; she ignored him completely. Rafi brewed the tea and there were several heartbeats of strained silence.

"So what are you doing here?" Giovanni asked Isabella. "Come to tell us babes how we can't do anything right?"

"You'd be well served to listen to me more often," Isabella said mildly, taking the cup of tea Rafi handed to her. "As would Eliana here. That funeral was an excellent opportunity." She looked at me over the cup. "You have much to answer for, girl."

"I will lead a breakout," I said. "But I will do it on my own terms."

"What are your terms?" Isabella asked as Giovanni sputtered.

"We are peasants, not targets for crossbow bolts or fuel for magefire," I said. "Our strength is not just in numbers, it is in our arms and our hearts. When we break out, we'll know how to fight, and how to work together so that we can watch each other's backs instead of getting in each other's way. We'll wrest the crossbows from the hands of the soldiers who don't throw them down. We'll break out when Teleso is *not* fully prepared for a riot. And Lucia will *not* be the first to fall, as she was supposed to be last night." I gave Giovanni a measured look, and he glowered back at me.

"*You* will lead a breakout!" he sputtered. "*You*. You? Her?"

"Where you lead, Generale," Isabella said, "I will follow, and so will those who follow me." She touched her fist to her chest and held it out in a salute.

This was too much for Giovanni. "Generale? Generale! With Beneto and Jesca gone, *I* am the Generale of the Third Army."

"You may be the Generale of the Third Army," I said, "but I am the Generale of the Army of Ravenna."

"I can't believe I'm hearing this," Giovanni said. "You're all traitors! All of you!" He leapt to his feet and stormed out.

Rafi shrugged. "Eliana's right," he said to Lucia. "People will follow her now."

"She's still a stranger here," Lucia said.

" 'There is power in strangeness,' " Rafi said.

Isabella snorted. "That's just a nice way of saying that because she's new, no one hates her yet."

"People may hate me soon enough," I said, "but at least they won't hate me because I want to make them learn how to fight with swords they'll never have."

Isabella smiled slowly. "Don't take my support for granted, Generale-girl. You may lose us yet. But for now . . . we're with you." She set down her cup. "If you'll excuse me. Petro should be here soon." She ducked out.

"Petro better not be one of those healers that likes to use salves that sting," I said. Rafi laughed. Lucia was still staring after Isabella. "Lucia," I said, and she looked up. "How many people does Isabella lead?"

"More than Beneto did, honestly," Lucia said. "Although her influence doesn't extend beyond Ravenna."

"And she's—what did you say she does, exactly?"

"Isabella is an old-time dissenter," Lucia said. "She was making trouble for the Circle back when we were babies. Or at least complaining a lot." She shrugged. "Isabella never committed herself to Beneto. That's quite a coup you just made."

"Giovanni's going to be furious," I said.

"He's already furious," Rafi said. "As you knew he would be." He picked up Isabella's cup and finished off the last few drops of tea. "So, Generale Eliana: where do you intend to lead us?"

"Out of Ravenna," I said.

"And then?" Rafi wiped out the cup and put it away. "Beneto could never answer this question for me. What then? March on Cuore?"

I hesitated. "Yes," I said. "Eventually."

"Everyone here? Children and grannies?"

"No, we'll have to send them somewhere else."

"Where?"

"I don't know," I said. "But I'll think of something."

Rafi smiled. "And food? Supply lines? You won't have the Cuore bureaucracy shuttling food to you."

"No," I said. "I suppose not."

"How will you feed your army?"

"I'll figure something out for that, too," I said. "Before I lead the breakout."

Rafi suddenly smiled at me, a radiant grin that took over his entire face. "Answer those questions, signora, and I am yours to command." His smile faded to a wry hesitation. "Assuming I like the answers, of course."

"Of course," I said.

Lucia was smiling. "Giovanni's going to kill me."

"He'd better not," I said.

"—but I'm yours to command as well, so long as you're listening to good counsel. I am the Redentore priestess of Ravenna—I lead the Old Way followers, at least when they care to listen to me. We stand behind you, Generale."

I regarded the two of them. "Why?" I asked. "Just because I told off Teleso and got beaten for it?"

"The truth is," Rafi said, "we need a leader. Isabella knows it, and so do the other groups in Ravenna. Beneto had the wit and charisma to pull people together, at least some of the time. Giovanni does not."

"So people will follow me because I'm the alternative to Giovanni?"

"You understand your position pretty well," Rafi said.

Lucia tipped her head and narrowed her eyes as she regarded me. "You do realize that you will still need Giovanni. We may all accept you as our general, but Beneto's old commanders won't. As far as they're concerned, Giovanni is the only one qualified to lead. So long as you send Giovanni to deal with them, you should be all right. But you'll have to come to terms with him, sooner or later."

The healer arrived shortly after that. Petro was an old man who walked with a limp. He had a tiny store of herbs, which he could not replenish here in Ravenna and guarded jealously; Isabella had evidently ordered him to use some of them up to treat me. The salve didn't sting, although being touched hurt enough as it was. When Petro had left, Lucia said, "You can lead the uprising starting tomorrow. For the rest of today, you're going to rest." I'm not sure how she kept Giovanni from coming back to the tent, but I dozed peacefully for the rest of the day.

By the next morning, I had settled on my top priority: military training. Not only did we need to train people to fight as a cohesive force, we needed to train more than the handful that Giovanni could teach in his tiny training ground. The trouble was, I couldn't imagine Teleso sitting still for mass military exercises. I raised the issue over morning gruel.

"We're not stupid," Giovanni said. "Of course we'd like to train more people. There's just no way to hide more than a handful."

"Don't fool yourself," I said. "Teleso knows you're there. He probably just figures it's a harmless diversion, like the Old Way."

"Well, I think Teleso would see more than a handful as more than a diversion," Rafi said.

"We need a way to disguise military training *as* a diversion," I said.

"There's no way," Giovanni said. "You're being ridiculous. This is what happens when someone who doesn't know the *first* thing about the subject—"

"What exactly is it you want to train people to do?" Lucia asked, pressing her hands to her head as if to shut out Giovanni.

"Fight as a group. Watch each other's backs. Move

when the others move. Work together without getting in each other's way."

"An army is *not* an orchestra," Giovanni said, and stalked out.

I watched him go, then turned back to my breakfast, scraping the sides of the bowl with my fingers to get the last of the gruel. When Lucia had also finished eating, I eased on my tunic and we went down to Giovanni's practice ground.

Giovanni was bullying Michel again. He called a break as soon as we came in and snarled, "You're going against Beneto's *explicit* orders."

"You took orders from Beneto," I said. "I didn't. And Beneto's dead."

"You're not the one in charge here," he said. "I am!"

I glanced past Giovanni at the seven boys clustered against the wall. Michel's face had lit up when I walked in, and something caught my eye. He had discarded his worn belt and replaced it with a red sash similar to mine. So had the others.

I lowered my voice and spoke just to Giovanni. "Giovanni, look around you. Who do you think they're going to follow? You'll be less embarrassed if you back down now."

Giovanni's face went red, then white, and his lips tightened. He turned with mute appeal toward Lucia, but she stared him down.

"We'll see," he said, backing out of the training ground. "We'll *see*." He turned and ran out. I didn't watch him go.

Michel and the others edged away from the wall. On a signal from Michel, they formed a ragged line and saluted me in unison. "What are your orders, Generale?" Michel asked.

"You know how to fight," I said. "With a weapon or

your fists. That's not what you need to learn. What you need to learn is how to fight *together*." I looked them over. "Round up a few more. Then practice fighting as a group— three against three, four against four, five against five. And pull your punches. Am I clear?"

"Yes, Generale," Michel said; the others nodded.

I sat down to watch them train; Lucia sat down beside me. They quickly divided into a group of three and a group of four, and started to circle the training ground. Michel was tall and broad-shouldered like my brothers, but with a surprisingly light, quick step; he was by far the best fighter in the group. He didn't seem like the sort who'd be graceful; he seemed like he should be slow and awkward like my brothers, but he wasn't. "Are we just supposed to beat on each other?" Michel asked after a little while.

"No. You need a goal, I guess. Hmm. Pretend—uh, pretend those sticks are crossbows. Three of you can be soldiers—you have the crossbows. The other four are Ravenessi—you try to take the crossbows away."

After a few more false starts, we worked out the basic rules of the game. They switched to six on one, with the one playing the soldier. As long as the soldier had the "crossbow," he could "shoot" a Ravenesse every few seconds by stopping, pointing the stick, and calling out the person's name.

"It takes more time than that to cock a crossbow," Michel said.

"Stick with these rules for now," I said.

Watching them, I was suddenly reminded of games I'd played with my brothers, back when I was a child. Watching my army now was like watching a group of deadly serious grown-ups playing tag.

"That's it," I said aloud.

"What?" Lucia asked.

"This is how we're going to train the whole camp. Everyone who wants to fight. We'll make it a game." I turned to Lucia, and she shook her head, trying to understand my excitement. "Everyone can learn—everyone can play. Don't you see? Teleso doesn't care how we amuse ourselves. As long as it's a game, we can play it openly. We can train the whole camp that way."

Michel and the others had paused to watch my excitement. "Are there others in Ravenna who would learn to fight if there was a way?" I asked.

"Yes," Michel said. "Many. There isn't space."

"Listen," I said. "We don't need space. We're going to call this game *pastore e lupi*, shepherd-and-wolves, instead of soldiers-and-prisoners, but the rules—and the purpose—stay the same."

Michel and the others nodded, still a bit baffled.

"The wolves try to take away the shepherd's bow; the shepherd tries to take down the wolves. If all the wolves are dead before the shepherd loses his bow, the shepherd wins. If the wolves can take away the bow without losing more than half the wolves, they win. Play it in the open—the wolves can start from farther back, and the shepherd has to wait longer between shots. If it gets too easy, change the odds." I looked around the circle of boys, and saw them catching my excitement. "Practice for a day. Then I want *you* to start teaching others. People can play after they come back from work . . . it's almost midsummer, and the soldiers have been bringing them back well before dark. Don't you see? So far as Teleso will know, this is just a game. Keep it quiet, at first. I'm hoping the game will catch on fast enough that Teleso won't know where it started."

They were nodding more enthusiastically now. "Yes, Generale," Michel said, and they went back to the game.

When they stopped to rest, some time later, I took Michel aside.

"The seven of you already knew how to fight," I said. He nodded. "That won't be true for everyone with willing hands. I want you to find out how many people seem interested, but really don't know what they're doing, all right? I want them trained to fight—by you, or by someone else. This training ground may see some use yet."

"And Giovanni?"

"We need all the allies we can get," I said. "Even Giovanni." I grimaced so that he knew I understood. "Say, where'd you get that sash, anyway?"

Michel grinned broadly. "There was a lady with a red blanket. She traded for a brown one and some extra ration chits."

"Was it your idea?" I asked. He nodded. I slugged him affectionately on the shoulder. "I'm not sure I like the way you think, big brother. But it looks good on you."

On Lucia's suggestion, I made the rounds while people were lined up for evening gruel, as Beneto had. To show them who was in charge, and that I was back on my feet. People smiled at me warmly, clasped my hands. I didn't know how to work a crowd like Beneto, but the mystique of standing up to Teleso would carry me for a while yet—I hoped.

Later in the evening, Lucia and I got our own gruel. "Do you want to come to Mass later?" Lucia asked, as we waited in line.

"I . . . I think dancing would hurt my back," I said. "Playing, too; I'd have to rest the violin on my shoulder. I'll come another day."

"All right," she said. My cheeks burned as her eyes searched across my face, but I met her eyes without flinching. It was an excuse, but it was a reasonable one. Once we had our gruel, she excused herself briefly to go speak with Rafi, and I cupped my hands around my bowl, waiting near the shadow of the keep. I really was exhausted, I realized suddenly, and my raw back burned under my tunic.

"Hey, signora," a voice said softly behind my shoulder. I turned. It was the kind soldier, Mario, looking tired and ashamed.

"Mario," I said. "How are you doing?"

Mario shrugged. "How are *you* doing?" he asked, gesturing toward my shoulder.

"Better than it looks like you expected," I said. "I'm on my feet and the wounds aren't festering."

Mario lowered his eyes again. I stood uselessly, knowing that he blamed himself but not knowing what to say.

"I'm sorry," he said, a few moments later. "Way too much of that was my fault."

"Because you carried the message from Lucia? Because you helped to tie me? Because you told Teleso you wouldn't beat me, so he had Niccolo do it?" All of those; it was all of those things and more. "Mario, you're one of the few people in Ravenna who actually wants to do the right thing. Who even cares what the right thing *is*. Don't you think that's worth something?"

"I care," he said. "But not enough. Or I wouldn't have stood there and let them whip you." He lowered his head again.

"What do you think you should have done?"

"I don't know," he said.

I looked around; Lucia showed no sign of returning. "Let's go for a walk," I said.

Mario and I went out to the hills around Ravenna, walking along the edge of the fence.

"You lead the reformers now, don't you?" Mario said. "Not Giovanni."

I hesitated for a moment; was this really the sort of thing I should be admitting to one of Teleso's soldiers, even one I liked?

"It's all right," he said. "I don't blame you for not telling me. But everyone knows."

"Does Teleso have plans for me yet?" I asked.

"Not yet. But you know, Eliana—you're setting yourself up. That's why no one but Giovanni is challenging you for leadership. They're hoping that the next time Teleso decides someone should swing, it will be you and not them."

I was silent. Mario sat down on the dusty hillside, and I sat down beside him. "Thank you for keeping an eye on me, that night in the dungeon," I said.

"It was nothing."

"Is there anyone in this valley who *wants* to be here?"

"Teleso," Mario said. "But other than him, no." He chuckled dryly. "They promised us that when the war was over, we'd receive our pay and be released from our oath to the Emperor. But somehow they decided the war hadn't quite ended . . . so here we are guarding the lot of you. Even Niccolo resents it; he says the Circle should send down some bureaucrats to build the wall if they want one—hire architects and laborers like they would to build a monument in Cuore. But, well, the bureaucrats would have refused. And the Circle has to have its damn wall."

"Mario," I said. "Where do you stand? I need to know. Are you with me, in the end, or with Teleso?"

Mario was silent for a long time. "I know what's happening here is wrong. The Lady—" He glanced down at me and added, "I don't expect you to understand. You're

Redentore, like Lucia. I hope you don't hold it against me that I'm not."

I shook my head. "Of course not."

"The Lady has said that slavery is wrong. When she brought her Gift to Gaius, and told him the path we were to follow, that was one of the first things she said; we are all Her children and belong only to Her. And slavery is what's going on here, no matter what kind of word games Teleso and the Circle play with it."

I nodded.

"And is it truly what the Emperor wants?" Mario said. "I swore my oath to the Emperor, not to the Circle. But Teleso takes orders from the Circle. That's become blindingly clear to all of us."

I blinked. Bella and Mira had both said that the Emperor didn't really rule. I wondered if the rest of the army was as loyal to the Emperor as Mario.

"I helped to execute Beneto and Jesca. I stood by while Niccolo beat you," Mario said. He tilted his head to try to meet my eyes, then looked away again. "If I disobey a direct order, Teleso could have *me* executed. And he would. He hates me. I don't want to die, Eliana."

"Mario," I said, "I'm not asking you to throw your life away. Especially not when it wouldn't do any good. It wouldn't have done any good if you'd tried to protect me. But if there's something you can do that would *help*—"

"I don't know," he said. "I don't know if you can count on me."

"But you know what's right," I said.

"Yes," he said. "But I don't know if I have the courage to do it."

"Mario," I said, and took his hand. "Won't the Lady give you the courage you need?"

"What would you know about the Lady?" he said. "You're Redentore."

"I know what they told me when I was a child," I said. "That She would always take care of me; that She wants me to do what I know in my heart is right; and that She would give me the strength I needed to face anything, if I asked."

"But you don't believe that anymore," Mario said.

"It doesn't matter what I believe, Mario," I said. "What's right is right, and you know that."

For the first time that evening, Mario met my eyes full on. His eyes searched mine for a long moment. I'm not sure what he found there, but he squeezed my hand and said, "You're right. I will trust in Her strength."

"Trust Her," I said. "And trust me, Mario. You can do what you know you need to do."

"So what do you want from me?" he asked.

I held his hand tightly for a moment longer. "For now, I only needed to know that I will be able to trust you when I need you." I let go of his hand and he took a long breath.

"Eliana," he said. "Will you play for us again?"

"Of course," I said. "It's probably best if I don't go into the keep, but if the soldiers can meet me somewhere outside . . ."

"Of course," he said.

"Then I'll play as soon as my back is healed up enough that I can hold a violin without it hurting." His enthusiasm turned to distress again, and I said, "Don't *worry* about it. It wasn't your fault, and it's healing."

We walked back down to Rafi's tent. "I'll leave you here, then," Mario said. He folded my hand around something, then kissed my hand gently, before dropping it as if he was afraid I was going to slap him, and fleeing into the darkness. I opened my hand once he was gone, to see what he had given me: coiled tightly in my palm was a new E-string, to replace the one that broke during the funeral.

Rafi and Lucia were still at Mass. I thought about going to bed, but despite my exhaustion, my conversation with Mario had left me with a restless energy. I tucked my violin case under my arm and walked over to near where I knew they would be dancing. I circled the area and climbed a bit higher on the hill, sitting down in the shadow of the fence to watch them.

There were perhaps twenty Redentori, dancing in the moonlight. I recognized Lucia, Rafi, Michel, and several more. Michel was even more graceful dancing than he was fighting; he danced with a wild enthusiasm, an ecstatic abandon that made my heart quicken just watching.

They had no violin tonight, but Lucia and Michel sang, his baritone blending with her clear alto. They paused in the dance for a moment to sing. Lucia's face was shadowed, but I could fill in the details for myself. Her eyes were closed, her face sweet with delight in the ritual. I felt a stab of envy.

She will give you the strength you need to face anything. Lucia's God gave her the same strength—as much as she needed. I couldn't imagine having so much trust in something so powerful. Lucia *knew* we would succeed; I couldn't be sure. In fact, I wasn't even sure I'd wager tomorrow's rations on it. It struck me that I was staking my *life* on it, but I was in too deep to back out now. From the corner of my eye, I saw movement. Giovanni sat down a few paces away from me, resting his chin on his arms as he watched the dancers.

"Do you ever envy them?" I asked.

"Why would I?"

I looked over at Giovanni. "You never envy the strength your cousin draws from her faith?"

Giovanni paused. "Yes, I envy her sometimes," he admitted.

"Were Beneto and Jesca Redentori?" I asked.

"After a fashion. They preferred that the Redentori think them Redentori, while those that pray to the Lady also claim them as theirs." Giovanni shifted where he sat. "They had their own kind of faith. I think all Beneto needed to believe in was his cause and himself." His voice turned bitter. "Isn't that what *you* believe in?"

"I need more than just the cocky self-assurance of a naive schoolboy like Beneto," I said. Giovanni gasped and smothered a laugh, and I knew I'd spoken his opinion of Beneto as well. "I need support. I need counsel." I turned to Giovanni and saw him looking at me. "I need you on my side, Giovanni."

"Thank you so much for your confidence in me," he said. "You take away the one thing Beneto put me in charge of, and now you say you need me? Am I supposed to be impressed?"

"Beneto put you in charge of military training because he didn't think it was important," I said. "Was that what you *wanted* to be doing?"

"No," he said.

"What was it you wanted?"

"I wanted to be in charge. I wanted to be the one to make the important decisions." His voice became petulant. "I wanted to be Generale."

"If the title means that much to you, Giovanni, I'll call you whatever you want," I said. "Look, I know as well as you do that the organization that sent you here will never accept me as a leader. I'll do this with you or without you, but I would prefer to have you on my side." He turned to glare at me and I clenched my fists, resisting the urge to smack him. "Giovanni, I know that you would make a powerful ally. In any case, I think it's fair to say that as far as the reformers are concerned, you *are* in charge. As for important decisions, you've got one now: are you with me, or against me?" He was silent. "Giovanni, I need to know where you stand. Do we have a truce?"

There was another long silence. Then: "Generale Giovanni," he said.

"What?"

"Call me *Generale*, and I'm with you."

We stood up, slowly, in the darkness, and looked at each other. Even when he stood up straight, I was taller than he was. Slowly, grudgingly, he held out his right hand, and I clasped it briefly. "Then, *Generale*," I said, "as long as you understand that you take orders from me, I believe we have an understanding."

I could see in the moonlight that he was clenching his teeth; he could probably see that I was, too.

"Yes," he said. "We understand each other. Generale."

On the hill below us, Mass had finished; Lucia and the others had gone home. "Are you coming back to Rafi's tent?" I asked.

"Not yet," he said, so I headed back on my own.

Rafi's tent was on the other side of the piazza from where we were. I wound my way uncertainly through the maze of ragged tents, unsure of exactly where I was. The keep rose like a hulking shadow, my only landmark.

As I passed by the dark edge of a half-fallen wall, hands seized my arms and another clapped over my mouth. I bit down viciously on the hand that covered my mouth, and gagged at the taste of blood as I felt the hand tighten in pain. Something cold and sharp pressed against my throat.

"Shut up," a voice whispered, and the hands yanked me backward, behind the wall.

"Unlike your Redentore God," a soft voice said with malicious satisfaction, "the Lady has told us that She does not want human sacrifices. But in your case, we think She'll make an exception."

CHAPTER THIRTEEN

What need have you for friends? I am friend, lover,
teacher. I am father, mother, child. I am the earth
and the sky. I am the first and the last.
I am everywhere that you think of me.
—*The Journey of Gèsu, chapter 22, verse 23.*

The hands tightened, and the knife was pulled back
for an instant. I knew that it was being drawn back
for the final blow, and made a desperate attempt to wrench
free. Then something whistled past my ear, and I heard the
knife clatter to the ground as someone yelped. "Scatter!" a
voice hissed, and I was turned loose as my attackers fled
into the night. I stared around me, too stunned to move. As
the surge of fear faded, my back began to burn from the
fabric rubbing against the welts.

Giovanni stepped out of the shadows. "Some Generale
you are," he said, and pulled his knife. He wiped it clean
on a rag and then slipped it back into a sheath in his boot,
tucking his trousers around it to conceal it.

"Did you follow me?" I said.

"It occurred to me that something like this might happen," he said. "I thought it would be good to find out who
wanted you dead at this point."

"So you used me as bait."

"Better to be bait than prey, isn't it?" Giovanni said.

"Which was what you were turning *yourself* into." He picked up the knife my attackers had dropped. "Let's go before Teleso sends someone to arrest *us* for attempted murder or disturbing the peace."

"So who were they?" I asked.

"I didn't get a good look at most of them, but the one I wounded was a soldier named Rico."

"I didn't think they were in uniform."

"They weren't. Presumably, Teleso wants you assassinated rather than executed. Or maybe Rico and some friends decided to show some initiative." We were about to cross the piazza, and Giovanni ducked into a shadow. "Here, you can keep this. Tuck it inside your boot." He handed me the dropped knife.

"You're cracked. I'll cut myself."

"You really don't know the first thing about taking care of yourself, do you?" he said.

"Want me to break your arm to prove I do?"

"That won't be necessary." Giovanni tucked the knife into his own sleeve and wrapped a piece of cloth around his arm to bind it flat and secure. "Let's go."

I studied Giovanni as we crossed the piazza; he had a little bounce to his step. The smugness would have been obvious at twenty paces, and the self-satisfaction at forty. "So this proved . . . ?" I asked.

"You need a bodyguard."

"A *bodyguard*?" That really seemed ridiculous. "What, to follow me everywhere?"

"Yes," Giovanni said. "I'll talk to the men who've been training. Michel would make a good one, and the others can trade off with him. Also," he added, and turned to give me a patronizing smile. "I'll teach you some knife-fighting."

"Knife-fighting."

"You can have the knife the assassins dropped. We'll

make a sheath for it that will fit into your boot and keep it from cutting you. I'll start training you tomorrow."

Just what I need, I thought. We'd reached Rafi's tent, and went inside.

Lucia and Rafi were horrified by the assassination attempt; Giovanni told them he'd headed home right after I had, and "fortunately" came upon the assassins just before they were going to kill me.

"Knife lessons are a good idea," Lucia said. "This could happen again. And if Rico *was* motivated by faith, things could get even worse as we get closer to Dono alla Magia, at midsummer."

I'd almost forgotten how soon the festival would be. "Did anyone ever try to assassinate Beneto and Jesca?"

"Yes," Giovanni said. "Once. *But*—" he thumped his hand on the ground for emphasis, "Beneto and Jesca were never *alone.* Everywhere they went, they went together. That's why you need a bodyguard."

"Hmm," Lucia said. "That's a good idea."

"Lucia." I turned to her. "There was something my attackers said that I was wondering about. They said that the Lady didn't want human sacrifices, *unlike* the Redentore God. What were they talking about?"

Lucia flushed angrily. "That's just libel," she said. "We say that through blood the land will be redeemed, but we mean *sacramental* blood, the wine that becomes the blood of Gèsu in the Mass."

"Ah," I said, and waited.

After a moment she continued. "There are those," she admitted, "that would like to take that passage of scripture more literally."

"Whose blood would they like to shed?"

"Well, Teleso's, for starters. And the Circle's. And their enemies, and the enemies of Gèsu . . ."

"That seems like it could become a rather large group."

"Well—yes. It could. But they're *wrong*, anyway, and distorting scripture." Lucia shook her head. "The only sacrifice that was needed is complete."

This reminded me of something. "Hey, Lucia," I said. "I've been meaning to tell you about this. The night I was in the dungeon—well, watch." I closed my eyes for a minute to concentrate, cupped my hand, and summoned a tiny witchlight.

The whole tent fell silent. Giovanni reached out to hold his hand over it to test for heat, as if he thought I'd somehow secreted a candle in my hand. "That's impossible," he said, after confirming that it was witchlight.

I closed my hand over it and let it go out. "Guess not," I said. "Not anymore."

"How?" Lucia breathed.

"When I defused the riot," I said, "I poured the energy down into the ground. Maybe you're right, Lucia—Old Way rituals really *can* redeem the earth."

"Or blood," Giovanni said. Lucia turned to stare at him sharply, and he tilted his head to look at her. "Beneto and Jesca's blood."

"That's not right," Lucia said. "It couldn't have been their deaths."

"Well, in a way, it might have been," Rafi said. "The anger from their deaths fueled the dance as lamp oil fuels fire."

"Either way, it doesn't matter," I said. "Not right now. Right now, what we need is to get out of Ravenna. But later—maybe the land can be restored."

Giovanni was cupping his hand and staring at it, frustrated. "I can't get a light."

"It takes a lot of effort," I said. "It's probably just as well if you don't. We don't want to drain the earth again."

"Besides," Lucia said, batting his hand aside. "It's a sin to use magery."

"What?" I said. I hadn't heard this before.

"It's a sin," she said.

"Because of the drain on the land?" I asked.

"No," she said. "Because the Book of the Lady says that magery was a gift from the Lady. And since there is only one true God, we know it can't be right."

"That makes no sense, Lucia," I said. "The Book of the Lady also says that slavery is wrong. Does that mean slavery is right?"

"No, of course not." Lucia gave me a look of earnest frustration. "There are plenty of reasons that slavery is wrong. But magery came only from Gaius, the Lady's First Prophet—how can it be right?"

"What does it matter where it came from? I can make witchlight whether I believe in the Lady or not."

"It *matters,* Eliana," Lucia said.

I noticed from the corner of my eye that Giovanni was watching our conversation with avid interest; his eyes flicked back and forth between me and Lucia, a slight smirk playing on his lips. I wondered suddenly if he'd been through this same argument.

"I never heard this from my grandmother," I said, "and she used to bless herself like a Redentore. I never heard this from Bella or Giorgi, at the conservatory."

Rafi cleared his throat. "Maybe it would be easiest just to think about the harm magery brings to the land. It's wrong for that reason—can you accept that?"

I nodded, a little reluctantly.

"It is wrong to go against God's will," Rafi said, "for no other reason than it is wrong to stand against God. But—" he caught my wrist and gave me a look even more earnest than Lucia's. "But often to go against God's word will *also* cause harm to others—and so it is wrong *twice*."

"Exactly," Lucia said.

"So magery is wrong because it goes against God, and also because it hurts the land." Rafi took a breath to continue the explanation, then decided against it. "Don't worry about why it goes against God, Eliana. It's enough for now to know that it hurts the land."

I nodded again, still uncertain. I wasn't sure I liked where this line of reasoning was taking us. "So what else is against God's will?"

Rafi and Lucia both laughed. "Get some sleep, Eliana," Rafi said. "I'm too tired for deep theology tonight. We can continue this in the morning, can't we?"

"I guess," I said. I glanced at Giovanni; he looked a little disappointed that the argument was ending.

As we made our beds and lay down, Giovanni brushed my sleeve briefly and caught my eye; in the last of the lamplight before Rafi put out the light, Giovanni gave me a sardonic smile. "It really isn't any stupider than some of the rules the Lady made," he said. "Those just seem less stupid because you grew up with them."

"Giovanni!" Lucia said. Her voice was shocked.

"Sorry," he said. "Good night."

• • •

"This is the hilt," Giovanni said. "This is the blade." He had carved two rough knives out of a piece of wood. We stood in the little training ground he'd been using to train Michel and the others—two mostly undamaged walls and a canvas sheet pulled across the gap. Teleso probably had his soldiers keeping a watch on it, but it was the closest thing to privacy we were going to get in Ravenna. "For obvious reasons, I don't want you waving a real knife at me while we're practicing." He handed me the knife.

He was going to enjoy this, I could already tell. "Do we assume that I get attacked with my knife already in my hand?"

"No," he said, and took the wooden knife back. "We're going to start with footwork."

"With what?"

Giovanni had me clasp my hands behind my back, then reconsidered when I winced and had me put my hands on my hips instead. "The most important thing in knife fighting isn't the knife, it's how you move your body."

"How about getting away from someone who grabs you?" I asked.

"We'll get to that." He had me follow him as he bounced oddly around on his feet, lunging forward, then back.

"What's the point of this?" I asked after about a half an hour. "This is useless."

"It's only useless because *you* don't know what you're doing," Giovanni said.

"Isn't that what you're supposed to be teaching me?" I asked. The morning was already growing hot; my face was damp, and my hair was sticking to my neck.

Giovanni turned around to face me. Far from snarling at me, he was half smiling; he really was enjoying seeing me run around in circles after him. "If you needed to teach me to play a violin, would you hand me your violin and a sheaf of sheet music?"

"No, of course not," I said. "You can't even read music."

"Actually, I can," he said. "I was taught at the university. But that's beside the point. You'd teach me how to stand correctly, wouldn't you? How to hold the violin and bow? You'd teach me to move the bow on the strings to make a noise that didn't sound like a dying cat, right?"

I nodded.

"Well, I'm teaching you how to move with a knife. Trust me."

He had me prancing in circles for another hour, then called a rest. "You're not bad," he said magnanimously.

"Thank you," I said, clenching my teeth.

"We'd better rest for a while; Rafi will have my head if I work you too hard. He's afraid you'll get sick from your injuries."

"I won't," I said.

Giovanni sat down on part of the fallen wall, tipping his head up to look at me. "You sound pretty sure of that," he said with a derisive half-smirk. "I'd still better not take any chances. Besides, you're out of breath. Have a seat." He gestured toward another fallen stone. I sat down. I *was* out of breath, and hot and thirsty besides. Giovanni had brought along a wineskin to his training ground, and he tossed it to me. "Cooled tea," he said. "It's what you drink when you're sparring at the university. Wine when you're sparring will just give you a headache."

I took a swig.

"I suppose if I'm training you I ought to tell you some principles, as well," he said. "The code of honor, and all that. You're a peasant, after all; I couldn't really expect you to know."

I looked at him over the wineskin and waited.

"Never strike from behind," he said. "Or rather, never strike without warning. It's dishonorable."

"So, waiting behind a wall for someone, and then jumping out and killing them, that's bad?"

"Exactly," he said.

"Why should I follow this rule if my enemies aren't going to?"

"You're better than they are," he said.

"What?" I said. "I've barely started to learn how to use a knife, and I'm up against trained soldiers. What do you mean I'm *better* than they are?"

"I mean morally better."

"A lot of good it's going to do me to be moral, honorable, and dead," I said. "Striking from behind without warning sounds like a good way to keep myself alive."

Giovanni was glaring at me. This really was my week; gain alliances with every leader in Ravenna, and then get every one of them angry at me over some article of faith. "Look," I said. "What if I'm leading the uprising to break out of Ravenna, and I've got a crossbow, and I come upon somebody who's got his back to me? What am I supposed to do then?"

"Warn him," Giovanni said. "Then fire."

"*Warn* him?" I said. "I should say, 'Hey you, I'm going to shoot you now'?"

Giovanni rolled his eyes. "It's more traditional to yell an insult, or order him to surrender."

"What if it's Teleso?"

"Wouldn't you want Teleso to *know* that it was *you* killing him?" Giovanni asked.

"As long as when we're done, *he's* dead and *I'm* not, I really don't care," I said.

Giovanni's eyes narrowed as he stared at me. "Well, you're a peasant," he said. "I suppose it isn't really fair to expect you to understand a gentleman's code of honor."

"And after all, you're a gentleman," I said. "I suppose it isn't really fair to expect you to understand a commoner's desire for survival."

Giovanni stood up. "Let's keep working." He picked up the wooden knives and handed me one. "I think it's time to try some attacks." He set down his own knife. "We'll assume that you're starting the fight, and I'm unarmed. Attack me." He put his hands on his hips and smiled at me.

Shrugging, I walked up and raised the knife. Giovanni caught my hand neatly and gave it a jerk to send me flying forward, off balance. A kick sent the knife spinning into the corner. "Grab it. Keep going," he urged.

My back was too raw to roll, so I stalked to the corner and picked the knife back up. "Maybe you should teach me *those* moves," I said.

He shrugged. "Later. Attack me again."

I ran at him, impatient now. "Are you going to show me the right way to do this," I demanded when he disarmed me again, "or are you going to keep me running around uselessly all day?"

"First you complain when I have you do exercises," Giovanni said, "and now you're complaining because I've got you holding a knife and *you* don't know what to do with it." He arched an eyebrow snidely. "Make up your mind. What do you want?"

I stepped close to Giovanni so that he had to look up to meet my eyes. "Teach me how to break the hold the assassins put me in. Teach me how to hurt somebody if I have to. I want you to show me what I need to know to *survive*, Giovanni."

He stepped back and set his knife down, looking thoughtful. "Show me what they did."

"They grabbed me," I said. "Here." I set down my knife and moved behind him. "One of them pinned my arms, and put his hand over my mouth." I started to cover Giovanni's mouth with my hand, then pulled my hand away. "I bit him. The other one had a knife to my throat, *here.*" I picked up the knife again and showed him. "When they were going to kill me, they pulled it back, like this, to stab."

"Huh," Giovanni said. "Rico must not know much about knife fighting; he should've just cut your throat. I mean—not that I wish he had. But—uh. I'll show you how to get out of the hold."

Giovanni led me through a series of moves designed to break most common holds. I felt more in my element now; this was like what my brother Donato had taught me when I was a child. "Keep going," Giovanni urged me as I broke free. "Pretend I attacked you. What are you going to do now?"

I kicked out, hooking Giovanni's ankle with my foot and jerking it out from under him. He squawked in surprise and fell in a heap; I jumped on top of him, one knee in his stomach, hand raised. "Never mind!" Giovanni yelped. "Let me up."

I climbed off Giovanni and he got up, brushing himself off. "I guess you know how to fight without a knife," he said. "Hold out your hand." I held out my hand as if I were going to clasp Giovanni's. He put the knife in my hand, point down, blade out. I closed my hand around the knife, tentatively raising the knife to stab. "Wrong," Giovanni said, and turned my fist so that the knife pointed out away from my body. "The easiest way to do some damage in a knife-fight is to hold the knife like this. Don't stab. Just punch, then drag the blade." He took his own knife and demonstrated a slashing sideways blow. "You probably won't kill anybody this way, but it shows you're serious, and dangerous. Anyone expecting easy prey will probably run."

" 'Probably'?"

He shook his head. "I'll teach you more tomorrow."

• • •

It was late spring, and the days were getting longer. The soldiers began refusing to keep their laborers out from dawn till dusk, since that meant working from dawn to dusk themselves. In the low-slanting daylight, the Ravenessi had found a new diversion: a game called *Lupi,* wolves. Even the people who weren't playing it watched, cheering and placing bets on their favorite players.

My back was healing, but I wasn't up for playing Lupi yet, so I spent most of my time talking to people, learning names and faces and home villages and family connections. Michel had taken to his new job of "bodyguard" with great enthusiasm, following me everywhere. When I turned and glared at him, he would at least fall back a pace or two.

A week or two later, I was talking with an old woman who had lined up for morning gruel when I saw a familiar face out of the corner of my eye. I whirled—I had seen familiar faces several times, but they had always belonged to strangers, rather than my mother or Donato or whomever I thought it was at first glance. This wasn't a family member— but it wasn't a stranger, either. She didn't see me; she was staring off into space, looking hungry and lost. "Giula?"

She looked up. "Eliana!" Her face lit up, and she left her place in line to run over and give me a hug. I winced as her arms rubbed against my back. "Love of the Lady, it's been how long?"

I calculated. "Six weeks."

Giula shook her head. "It seems so much longer."

I nodded. It seemed like months since I had seen Giula. "How long have you been in Ravenna?"

"Just a day. My mother and father are here, too, and some of my brothers and sisters. I'm *so* glad to find you here."

I followed Giula back to the line where her family still waited, Michel trailing me. "This is Eliana, one of my friends from the conservatory," Giula said. Her father took my hand gravely and bowed. Her mother was a sweet-faced woman with a wary, helpless smile. "These are my parents, Lina and Elmo." I smiled in greeting. "Are your parents here?" Giula asked.

I lowered my eyes. "They're dead. My family—they're all dead."

"Oh!" Giula covered her mouth. "Oh, I'm so sorry. I shouldn't have asked—"

"How were you to know?" It had been long enough, now, that I could say it without choking back tears. "Once you've gotten some food, I'll introduce you to some of my friends here."

Giula glanced past my shoulder. "Who's he? Is he your sweetheart?"

I followed her glance to Michel. "Oh—no. Michel is my bodyguard."

Giula's eyes went wide. "Your *what*?"

"It's a long story," I said.

Giula's family was much too large to add to Rafi's tent, but they had some blankets and canvas of their own and Michel and I helped them set up a tent on the perimeter near where Rafi lived. "Magery doesn't work here," I said. "Not even witchlight." Not entirely true, but if Giovanni couldn't get a witchlight, I was confident Giula wouldn't be able to.

"Really?" Lina asked, astonished. "Did you hear that, Elmo? Want me to show you how to use a flint?" She smiled, oddly pleased. I remembered that Giula had told me that her mother couldn't use magery.

"I'll just have you light the fire for us," Elmo said, putting one arm around her shoulders in a hug. Watching them, I felt the tears I hadn't shed earlier rising in my throat, and blinked them away.

"Eliana," Giula said. "What happened to your family?"

"The Circle burned my village," I said. "Refugees trying to go north had gone there, and wouldn't turn back."

Giula's eyes filled with tears. "Why do they hate us so much?"

"They're afraid," I said. "They don't want all those hungry, angry people in Cuore." Lina and Elmo were arranging their tent, so I pulled gently at Giula's sleeve. "Let's go," I said. "I want to introduce you to Rafi and Lucia."

Giula blushed shyly as I introduced her to Rafi, then looked up carefully to examine Lucia. "This is Giula," I said. "She's a friend of mine from the conservatory."

Lucia scrutinized Giula. "It's nice to meet you," she said blandly, squeezing Giula's arm. Next to Lucia, Giula's dimpled prettiness seemed dull and sallow; her sweetness seemed weak. Giula could never have survived Lucia's trip from her seminary down to Verdia, even if God had appeared to personally tell her that she should go.

Under Lucia's stare, Giula gulped anxiously and turned back toward me. "Is Lucia a musician?" she asked, flinching a little from my own appraising look.

"No," I said. "She's a dancer, though, and knows a lot of Old Way music." Lucia nodded, trying to catch Giula's eye again. "She's taught me some new songs."

"Oh!" Giula said, and glanced nervously at Rafi.

"Don't worry," I said. "The Fedeli don't come here."

Giula smiled again, but didn't look entirely convinced. I started wondering if I should have given her a few days to get her bearings before introducing her to my new friends.

Then Giovanni ducked into the tent, and Giula froze, her hand closing on my wrist. "What's *he* doing here?" she said, shrinking back against me.

"He won't hurt you," I said. "Don't worry, Giula." The inn in Pluma where Giovanni had slapped Giula seemed like a lifetime ago, but I could understand why Giula was upset. I stroked her shoulder, trying to reassure her.

"Is *he* one of your friends?" she asked.

"No, not exactly."

"I think I'd better go," she whimpered and stood up. I followed her out of the tent. She walked rapidly back across Ravenna. I ran after her, squinting in the bright sunlight. Out of the corner of my eye, I could see Michel, but he was keeping his distance.

"Giula—" I said.

"I understand you wanted me to meet your friends," she said, turning back toward me. "But I really don't understand why you have anything to do with him!"

"He's Lucia's cousin," I said. "No one really likes him, Giula, honest!"

Giula shook her head. "Maybe I'll like your friends more later," she said, and went in to her family's tent.

At a loss for what to say, I went back to Rafi's tent. "Fragile flower," Giovanni whispered as I came in, just loudly enough for me to hear.

"Giula seems nice," Lucia said, but looked troubled.

"What?" I asked.

"She's not one of *us,* is she?" Lucia meant that Giula was not Redentore.

"She played the music," I said defensively. "I don't think she's been sealed, but it was only by chance that I was."

"Nothing happens by chance," Lucia said, then bit her lip. "It's just—well, never mind. We'll see once she's settled in."

I shook my head. "I guess."

That night, listening to Lucia's even breathing in the

darkness of Rafi's tent, I found my thoughts drifting from Giula to Mira. If we had left the conservatory together that spring afternoon when she suggested it, we would still have found my village devastated when we arrived. We might have come to Ravenna together just as I came to Ravenna alone. What would Lucia have thought of Mira, I wondered? *She certainly wasn't anyone's fragile flower.* I rolled over, trying not to disturb anyone with my restlessness. It hurt too much to think about Mira.

I saw Giula only in passing the following day; she chatted with me, but made a hasty excuse to leave when Lucia joined me a moment later. Mario caught up with me that afternoon, and I agreed to meet some soldiers on the hillside to play that evening. I made one request: that at least for this first time, Mario bring soldiers like himself—men who hated what they were doing here; who knew, when they admitted it to themselves, that it was wrong.

My impromptu concerts had generally had a fairly good turnout, but that evening the Ravenessi avoided that corner of the valley, giving the gathering of soldiers a wide berth. Mario set up some torches so that the soldiers would be able to see me play, and the soldiers sat down on the hillside.

I played them some folk songs, then a solo piece I'd learned at the conservatory. "I need to rest for a minute," I said after that. "Tell me your names, and where you're from. I want to know who I'm playing for."

Mario passed a lantern around the circle, so that I could see the faces. I already knew a few soldiers here—Mario and Tomas—and I did my best to remember each name and each face. Many of the soldiers were from Verdia, although most of them were from parts that were well north of the wasteland. I asked them if they were worried about their families, and they nodded. Even the messenger service didn't like coming down to Ravenna; letters arrived four times a year, with the grain shipments. A few other soldiers were from Marino, and the rest from the more northerly provinces, near Cuore or Varena.

"Any requests?" I asked when the conversation paused.

"Something old," one of the soldiers said.

I nodded. I'd only practiced this one briefly, but the tune was simple and I really liked it. "The Dance That Turned the Storm," Lucia had called it. I sang the lyrics softly as I played. *Rachamin, Arka. Rachamin, Gèsu. Rachamin, Arka,* step-turn-*step. Rachamin, Gèsu,* step-turn-*step.* The soldiers didn't dance, but many closed their eyes, and I could see them whispering the words as I played.

"Lucia calls that the Dance That Turned the Storm," I said when I had finished. I lowered my violin. It was time to start talking; this was why I'd agreed to play, after all. I walked toward the soldiers, trying to make eye contact with as many as I could.

"I know that all of you are soldiers who serve justice," I said. "I know that each of you is a man with a conscience, and that you all have stronger, clearer souls than some of the others here. You don't glory in violence; you don't offer to deal pain. You are *men.* Not Maledori." I looked slowly around the dark circle, struggling to make out faces. They were nodding; some of them looked stricken, others relieved.

"None of you chose to be here, did you? And it's easy to start feeling alone. You're *not* alone. I just played the Dance That Turned the Storm. If you join together, you can turn any storm that comes against you." Everyone was nodding, now. "I want you to promise yourselves *not to be afraid* to do what's right. You know in your heart what the right thing is. And it doesn't matter whether you worship Gèsu or the Lady. They both say the same thing about slavery." I wasn't sure what Gèsu had to say about slavery, come to think of it, but as far as I could tell, the Redentori other than Lucia didn't know that much about what Gèsu said about anything.

"I want to teach you the dance I just played for you. Stand up and form a circle. It's not hard; Lucia taught it to me and even I could do it."

They were awkward and self-conscious for a minute or two, but as I picked up the pace I could see them smiling. The energy of the dance hummed in my ears like the strings of my violin, lighting the landscape around me like moonlight. I found myself dancing along with them, facing them as I skipped around the circle while I played. I ended the song, finally, and pulled the energy around me gently, down into the earth under my feet. The hum quieted. I was tired, but oddly warmed. The soldiers sat back down for a few more songs, and then I pleaded exhaustion. Mario passed a hat for me again; the haul was less impressive this time, but it would help feed the Lupi players who practiced instead of working on the wall. I went back to Rafi's tent and was asleep before I'd pulled my cloak over me.

• • •

"So have you figured out yet how you're going to feed your army?" Rafi asked. It was a warm day, but with a stiff breeze, and we sat outside Rafi's tent, watching a group of children playing Lupi. "I hope you're not planning to send those youngsters up against the soldiers."

"No," I said. "I've thought of what to do with the children." Rafi looked up with interest. "My village was not in the wasteland—it came through the war with Vesuvia unscathed. The Circle destroyed Doratura." I sighed into the breeze, closing my eyes for a moment. "The thing is, based on what the woman in the next village told me, the

Doraturiani must have finished some of the spring planting before the village was destroyed. And the plants wouldn't have come up yet when the fields were burned—in other words, there are fields of food that are probably still there."

"But if no one has been tending them—"

"There won't be a lot. But there's not a lot *here,* either."

"It's in ruins, though?"

"Yes. We would have to rebuild."

"Weren't there a few survivors from your village? What will they think of Ravenessi coming to live with them?"

"I doubt any of them went back," I said, thinking of my night in the rubble of my parents' house. "If they did . . . well, I don't think they'll mind living neighbors displacing the ghosts."

Rafi digested this for a few minutes. "The neighboring village," he said. "Won't they have taken over the fields by now?"

I shook my head. "I doubt it," I said. "They were ashamed, of what they had done—and the bodies lay in the open. I don't think they could face the consequences of their own cowardice yet."

"And if you're wrong?"

I looked down to see that my hands had clenched into fists over the ends of my sash. "Then we take it from them. They stood by while my family died. They turned me away from their door." My voice shook, and I looked up to see my anger reflected in Rafi's eyes. "But, once we break out—the children, the elderly, anyone who doesn't want to fight, they can go to Doratura. Plant what they can and harvest as much as possible."

Rafi nodded.

"As for provisioning the army," I said. "I saw a paper of calculations on Teleso's desk, back when he was keeping me in his guest room. I *think* that additional grain should be arriving soon. If we break out right after provisions arrive, we can take those provisions with us. Without the soldiers, the noncombatants, and those who will die in the fighting, those food stores will last a long time."

Rafi nodded. "So is that what you're waiting for?"

"Yes."

"Sounds like you've thought of everything."

The children who were playing nearby were finishing their game. The "shepherd" had just won and they were picking teams for the next game. "Not even close," I said softly.

I excused myself sometime later, to go to the latrine. Trenches had been dug along the base of the south hill; a rough wall of half-rotted boards had been staked up to provide at least a token of privacy, although the soldiers on guard duty could easily stare down at anyone relieving themselves. The more modest relieved themselves only at night, but I didn't care enough to worry about it. Michel, as my bodyguard, escorted me to the area, but let me duck behind the wall to relieve myself without his company.

The smell near the trench was terrible, especially in the heat of the day; the people who lived near it were the weakest and most destitute in Ravenna. The slum within a slum; most lacked even a makeshift tent, sleeping in the open and marking off territory by carving lines in the dust. I was stepping out to head back to Rafi's tent when I caught a glimpse of Lucia, kneeling in the dust by a small bundle. She glanced up briefly, and I quickly ducked back behind the latrine wall. She looked back down.

"Rachamin, Arka," she chanted. "Rachamin, Gèsu."

There was another woman kneeling beside her, staring down anxiously. I realized that what I had taken for a bundle of rags was a child, wrapped in blankets. A man stood nearby, staring at Lucia angrily.

"Good day, Lucia," another woman said as she approached.

"Good day, Margherita," Lucia said, and I peered around the wall again, shocked. Margherita was the closest approximation to Ravenna's High Priestess of the Lady. "I'll be done soon," Lucia added, and Margherita sat down on the other side of the child. The woman who knelt beside Lucia gave Margherita a hostile glare.

Lucia took out a small vial from under her dress, dabbed the contents onto her finger and traced a cross on the child's head. "Vinni, son of Ottone and Elettra," she said, and then continued in the Old Tongue, alternating between spoken and chanted words. When she had finished, she clasped the hand of the woman beside her—Elettra, presumably—and they briefly bowed their heads in silent prayer, eyes closed.

"Your turn," Lucia said, and backed off as Margherita pulled out her small pouch of dried crushed flowers. The man who had been glaring at Lucia knelt eagerly now, and assisted the priestess with the church healing rite. I was struck by the similarities of the rituals. Someone somewhere had done a lot of rather obvious borrowing. Lucia looked on, patting Elettra's hand and whispering to her.

Margherita and Ottone prayed silently for a minute, just as Lucia and Elettra had. When Margherita was done, she and Lucia both stood up to go, promising to speak to one of the local healers. Margherita headed back toward the main camp, but Lucia paused by the edge of the latrine curtain.

"You can come out now, Eliana," she said.

I stepped out. "Sorry."

"No need to apologize," she said, but her face showed hurt. I didn't know what to say—I'm sorry, Lucia, I just don't believe? I still don't understand what the rules are for this faith of yours? Maybe somebody drew a cross on my head with water, but they didn't draw it on my heart?—so I jerked my shoulder in a shamed shrug, and lowered my eyes.

Lucia turned her head to look at me and gave me one of her quirky smiles. "It's probably just as well you stayed in hiding. If you'd come out to help pray, poor Ottone's heart would probably have burst with fury."

"So the child who was ill—"

"Has a Redentore mother and a Della Chiesa father."

"Della Chiesa." Of the church. I hadn't heard the expression before.

"And Elettra just about had a fit at the thought of Margherita praying to the Lady over the boy. Fortunately," she shrugged, "Margherita and I are both sensible enough to recognize that a useless prayer to a nonexistent deity won't do any harm. I humor her, and she humors me." Lucia sighed and brushed off her dress where she'd knelt in the dust, then tucked the tiny vial back into her dress. "Let's go back to Rafi's tent."

"What about the healer?"

"Petro won't go to them on my instructions. I have to ask Rafi, and he has to ask Isabella, and she has to send Petro. Nothing's ever simple."

"Do you think Petro would go on my instructions?" I asked.

She grinned. "No. But you could go straight to Isabella." Her smile faded. "I doubt there's much that Petro will be able to do for the boy."

Isabella agreed, on my request, to send Petro. She seemed pleased that I had asked; I could almost see a balance sheet of favors being tallied in her head. Afterward, Lucia suggested that we go to one of the hills to sit. "I'm tired," she said. "I want to go somewhere quiet."

Nowhere in Ravenna was exactly quiet, but the hills

near the guard posts were less crowded. We picked an area patrolled by someone friendly and sat down. Michel was going to sit down beside us, but Lucia gave him a threatening stare, and he moved off along the hill to a spot where he could see us but couldn't overhear our conversation.

"Do you know about Tomas, Eliana?" Lucia asked after a while.

"You mean the soldier?"

"No, not the soldier. Tomas the Doubter." I looked at her blankly and she sighed. "Your education has been sadly lacking. Do you at least know of the Sacrifice and Resurrection? Oh, good God." It was a prayer, eyes rolled heavenward for strength. "You know of Gèsu, at least." I nodded vigorously and she sighed and began her story. "This is not the first terrible famine . . ."

• • •

Centuries ago, the land was shattered and wasted, and it seemed that perhaps all of humanity would die. Our only hope lay in God's mercy, but She turned Her back on us in anger. The world was Her child, but we had caused Her too much pain, and She had shut away the love She had once felt for us.

Aral Refuah, the Archangel Rafael, pleaded with Her to heal the world. *Aral Din,* the Archangel Michel, urged Her to give us one more chance—to devise a test for humanity, and if we passed the test, to spare us. Only *Aral Mot,* the Archangel Lucio, urged Her to let us die; we had brought this destruction upon ourselves, he pointed out, and deserved no mercy.

God listened to Her advisors, but then turned away from them, and spoke: *I will turn no more toward the world.*

There is one more archangel, *Aral Chedvah,* the Archangel Gabriele. Gabriele also believed that humanity should be saved, but he knew that God would not save us unless She could be moved to love us again. Gabriele stole a fragment of God's holy Light, and placed it in the womb of a pure young woman. And so she conceived a child, a son, and she named him Gèsu.

Gèsu was human, like us, but he carried the Light of God in his soul, and it would not let him rest—and so he began his journey. He became a teacher and a prophet, and many began to follow him, because they sensed the Light within his soul, and even when they did not understand his words, they longed for the Light of God. Because Gèsu was human, he loved his friends; because he had not God's bitter anger, he loved the world and all humanity. And his Light grew ever brighter.

But there was one, called Giudas, who came to fear the Light; and so he betrayed Gèsu, going to the soldiers of the Empire and saying that Gèsu was going to lead an uprising against them. Soldiers came to arrest Gèsu, but two of his friends—Tomas and Mara—stood by him and spirited him away to a hidden cave. The soldiers knew that they would never find him by looking, so they took Giudas prisoner, and said that if Gèsu did not turn himself in, they would kill Giudas.

Despite Giudas's betrayal, Gèsu loved him; when he heard this, he could not leave Giudas to die in his place. Tomas and Mara begged him not to go, but he kissed them and said, "I will be ever with you."

The Empire crucified Gèsu, spilling his blood onto the broken earth, and buried his body in the sand.

When Gèsu died, the Light in his soul returned to God, and suddenly She felt the love he had felt for the world, a love so complete that he had willingly died for a traitor. God wept, and spoke to Her Angels, saying *The world is My child; I will not let humanity die.*

So God resurrected Gèsu and said, *Through your blood shall the world be redeemed.* Where his blood had fallen, flowers bloomed, and the wood of the cross burst into leaf.

And so Gèsu returned, and clasped hands with his followers to dance with them. Then he poured them wine. "This is my blood," he said. "Share it among you, and redeem the earth." He broke bread with them and said, "This is my body, which was broken for you and for all the world. Eat, and live forever." Then he danced with them again and said, "Thus does God pour out Her Light upon us. So long as the children of Her Light sing and dance on the earth, God will never turn from us again."

• • •

Lucia was silent for a long time after she finished the story. Finally I asked, "Why is Tomas called the Doubter?"

Lucia sat up again and laughed. "I almost forgot why I was telling you the story. When God returned Gèsu to the earth, he went first to Mara, and sent her to tell his other followers. But Tomas didn't believe her. 'Not until I touch his foot and feel the warmth of life, and touch his hand and feel it clasp mine, will I believe.' When Gèsu came to them all the next day, he said to Tomas, 'Reach out your hand and touch my foot. Let me clasp your hand. Now, will you believe?' " Lucia fell silent again for a bit. "I've touched His feet," she said. "I've reached out and felt His hand grasp mine. But I don't know how to make someone else trust in something they can't see. Not even you, Eliana."

That night, I waited until Michel fell asleep and then went for a walk alone along the hillside. The moon was nearly full and I could pick my way easily. I could admit it; I had never trusted in things I couldn't see. Lucia, on the other hand . . . I found myself envious of her belief, even as

I feared it. She was *Fedele,* faithful, in her own way. I could see her eyes, as I stared into the darkness, steady with her absolute conviction, lit with her inner light.

"There are some things that are never meaningless," she had said. *"God's love is one."* Nights were cold in the wasteland; I clasped my arms around myself as I walked, trying to keep warm. There was something that I felt when I played the music that I could not explain. But I had had no grand visions like Lucia's, and the bread Lucia put into my mouth during Mass just tasted like bread. What was I supposed to see? What was I supposed to feel? Church had always left me cold, but you weren't expected to love the Lady with Lucia's brand of fervent love—just to pray to her and obey her.

Sweet and gentle Lady—the words of the prayer my mother taught me when I was just learning to speak fell from my lips before I thought about it.

Sweet and gentle Lady
Hear my little prayer
Hold me in your arms tonight
I know that you are there.

I had said that prayer before bed each night until my fourth year at the conservatory, but the arms I had ached for—then as now—were my mother's.

You keep us from the Maledori
You guard the way to wrong
Sweet and gentle Lady
I'll love you my whole life long.

The prayer didn't quite scan, I noticed suddenly, and wondered what sorts of prayers Lucia would teach her children to say before going to bed. Something in the Old Tongue, probably. *B'shem Arka, v'barah, v'nehora kadosha.* That sort of thing.

"All right, God," I said aloud. "I'll make the same bargain with you that Rafi and Isabella and Giovanni and Lucia made with me. I'll follow you as long as you're leading somewhere I want to be going." I knelt to touch the ground, then crossed myself. Looking up at the stars, I took out Bella's cross, and kissed it. "I'm one of Yours now."

I told myself that I believed. But perhaps it was just that I saw the Light in the light of Lucia's eyes.

CHAPTER FOURTEEN

*Michel the Archangel is coming from heaven to earth,
with his sword and his shield, with the fire and the
glory. Ready yourself for the battle. Arm yourself for
the battle. God stands beside us in glory.*

—*The Journey of Gèsu, chapter 7, verse 8.*

*B*ack at the conservatory, we always played a concert for the village during the Dono alla Magia
festival. Aside from the hours and weeks of rehearsals,
though, I participated little in the preparations. One day it
would be late spring, and then the next day the conservatory would be decked with lights and the conductors would
be shouting at the strings to pick up the pace, there was
only a week left.

Festival preparations at Ravenna were subtle, but visible. People couldn't really dress up, but they washed their
clothes. Some even washed their tents; Ravenna was suddenly more colorful. Tallow became an extremely valuable
commodity, and lamp oil even more so. "I didn't even
know there were this many Delle Chiese in Ravenna. I
thought most of Ravenna followed the Old Way," I said to
Lucia, as we watched an old woman named Betira making
candles.

Lucia sighed. "Many," she said, "but not most. There
were Delle Chiese that attended the funeral . . . just as

there are Redentori who will attend the Dono alla Magia festivities."

"Does that bother you?"

"Maybe. But it's pointless to fight against it." She shrugged. "They'll repent next week." We were silent for a bit. "Are you playing for the soldiers again tonight?"

"Yes."

"How much longer do you think you'll be able to keep it up, before Teleso starts getting antsy?"

"I don't know," I said. Discreetly, I eased my collar away from my throat. "Mario will warn me. I hope."

My concerts for the soldiers had become a twice-weekly event, once for the night shift and once for the day shift. More and more soldiers attended each time. That night I played for the day shift; Mario and Tomas were there, studying me from the darkness.

"You're not alone," I repeated. "It's *Teleso* who is alone. We have each other. *You* have each other. Together, you can turn any storm that Teleso can raise. *We* can turn the storm."

The regulars were already starting to form a circle, clasping the hands of the newcomers. Some of the newcomers looked nervous—others, relieved.

"You have the strength to do what you know in your heart is right," I said. "You have all the strength you need."

As they stood in the circle, I played the first notes of the dance, and they started, the regulars leading the newcomers through the steps. As always, I felt the energy building, tonight like a light that jumped from hand to hand through the circle. When the dance finished, I pulled the energy down into the earth. Later, as the soldiers dispersed, Mario approached me. "Arianna—Teleso's maid—says she wishes she could hear you again," he said.

"Does she ever get to leave the keep?" I asked.

"No," Mario said.

"If she can tell me the next time Teleso gets drunk," I said, "I can stand under one of the windows to play."

Mario liked that idea. "That should be soon," he said. "Teleso gets drunk pretty often."

"So let me know next time, and I'll come play."

He hesitated a moment longer. "The girl Giula. The other violinist. Is she a friend of yours?"

"Yes," I said. "We went to the same conservatory. Why?"

"You should know, then," he said. "She's been keeping company with Teleso."

"Keeping company," I said. "What do you mean, 'keeping company'?"

Mario opened his mouth, then closed it and shook his head. "Look for her in the piazza tomorrow," he said. "You'll see what I mean."

The next morning, I took a walk in the piazza when I had finished my gruel. I didn't see Giula anywhere, and for a moment I thought that perhaps Mario had her confused with someone else. Then the front door of the keep opened— the door only Teleso used.

Giula was clean, and she had ribbons in her hair. She clasped her hands around Teleso's arm, tucking herself into his side as they walked. She saw me from across the piazza; her eyes narrowed briefly in a malicious glare, then she turned away, tugging Teleso gently in the other direction.

Michel edged up toward me. "I still don't think this is such a good idea, Eliana," he said.

"Shh," I said. "Back off."

Teleso glanced idly toward us; his face brightened slightly when he spotted me. He bent his head to whisper in Giula's ear, then drew her across the piazza toward me.

Michel started edging up again and I stepped away from him, toward Giula and Teleso.

"Good afternoon, Eliana," Teleso said. His smile was broad; he nudged Giula forward, like a peddler displaying his best wares. "Giula tells me you're old friends."

"Yes," I said, looking at Giula. She met my eyes with a look of challenge that baffled me. "Hello, Giula."

"Hello," Giula said. "What are you bothering with me for? Where are your *new* friends?"

"I wanted to see you," I said. "It's been too long."

"It has," she said. "So why now, then? Are you jealous?" Again she shot me a look of challenge, then softened into a dimpled smile to look up at Teleso. Teleso gave her a perfunctory smile, then looked back at me.

"Jealous?" *Jealous?* "Why on earth would I be jealous?" *Just as long as it's not me.* I met Teleso's eyes evenly. "I'm delighted that you're happy, Giula. I'm sure Teleso is taking good care of you."

Giula glanced from me to Teleso, then huddled close to him again. "He told me what you did," she said. Her lip was trembling.

"What's that supposed to mean?" I said. "It wasn't what I did, it was what I refused to—"

"He said you tried to start a riot," she said. "At Beneto and Jesca's funeral."

My head snapped up, and Teleso met my eyes with a smirk. I bit back the urge to call him a liar right then and there—that seemed unnecessarily risky. "That's an interesting way of describing what happened," I said. "You might try asking a few other people for their version." Out of the corner of my eye, I could see Michel edging toward me again.

"Why should I?" she said. "Are you saying Teleso would lie to me?"

"Giula!" I said. Again, I glanced at Teleso, wondering if
there were some way I might get her alone, but he had a
tight grip on her. "We've known each other for five years.
Do you think I'd start a riot?"

"Well," she said, tossing her ribbons and curls back
over her shoulder. "I *used* to know you. But that was *before* your best friend was a boy who beats up girls he's
never met before."

"He's not my best friend!" I said. "I can't stand
Giovanni. Everyone else in Ravenna knows that, I can't
understand how *you* managed to miss it—"

"Right," she said mockingly. "Sweet little stupid Giula.
Don't worry about telling her; if she's too much of a fool
to figure it out, who cares?"

I backed up a step, stunned by her fury, and nearly
stepped on Michel's foot. "Why are you angry at me?" I
said. I realized that I was close to tears. "Giula, we're
friends."

"We *were* friends," she said. Her eyes narrowed, and
her lips pressed together into a painted pout. Then she
turned back to Teleso, all simpering dimples again. "Did
you have anything else to say to Eliana, darling?" she
asked him.

Teleso was still staring at me, looking disappointed.
Giula tugged on his sleeve and he looked down at her. "No,
sweetness," he said. "Let's go back in. I've had enough sun
for today."

Giula gave me a final nod, and then turned away to
sweep back across the piazza and into the keep.

· · ·

I didn't want to go back to Rafi's tent, after that—I wanted
to be alone, which was impossible in Ravenna, but if I
walked along the edge of the valley, maybe no one would

bother me. Maybe I could persuade Michel to keep his distance. Maybe.

"Generale."

"I really need to be alone, please," I said.

"Generale!" The voice was insistent, and I turned; it was Amedeo.

"Leave me alone, crazy man," I said.

"Leave *her* alone," Amedeo said. "She's already got one foot in the fire and she put it there herself."

"Giula?" I asked.

Amedeo spat onto the ground. "She's as good as dead," he said. "Let her go. You've got more important people to worry about. Shake her dust from your feet."

I started to turn away, but he grabbed my wrist with his bony hand.

"Besides," he said. "We've still got each other!" He kissed my hand and leered at me.

I snatched my hand away. "Leave me alone!" Michel started toward us, then backed off.

"Oh," Amedeo said, disappointed. "Scorned again! You prefer Mario, is that it? Or is it Lucia?" He smirked at me. "Bad luck there. Something the Redentori are going to have in common with the Lady—they won't like that sort of thing. Two girls, two boys, you know. Like witchlight." He held out his hand and a glow sprang into it. "It's a sin." He stared at the light in his hand as if it were a snake, screeched once, and put it out, shaking his hand as if he had touched something nasty.

I stared at him. "Do you have anything sensible to say to me, old man? Or are you just raving again?"

"God bless you," Amedeo said, and went off back down into the valley, humming to himself.

Prefer Lucia? I sat down on the hill, staring down into Ravenna. Two girls? I wasn't sure what Amedeo meant, what the Redentori were forbidding. I clasped my arms around my knees. Ten paces away, Michel stood idly, glancing around every few seconds to make sure nobody was getting into position to take a shot at me. I closed my eyes, trying to block out Michel, Ravenna, everything.

I've reached out and felt His hand grasp mine, I could hear Lucia's voice saying. What was it that made Lucia seem to exude light? *There are some things that are never meaningless.* I thought of her face, brown from the sun and the wind, her hair bleached to straw. I wanted to dance with her, I realized. I wanted to do more than dance with her.

I opened my eyes and stood up, starting to walk again, remembering the feeling of Lucia's hand in mine. I wanted to touch her face; I wanted to feel her skin, softer than the velvet dress. I wanted to touch her hair, windblown and tangled, to run my hands through it.

My hands were shaking, and I wrenched my thoughts back to Ravenna, the reform movement, Michel's patient step behind me. I stopped walking and closed my eyes again, trying desperately to focus. But instead of Ravenna, the image that flashed through my mind was Mira—Mira, by the conservatory wall, clasping my hand and looking into my eyes, giving me the smile that warmed me to the soles of my feet. Only this time her smile was knowing, and she took my hand tight enough to make me wince.

I opened my eyes again. Was that supposed to be against God's will, like witchlight? I didn't want to know. Walking quickly, like I could leave behind whatever part of myself Amedeo had seen, I headed back to Rafi's tent.

I saw Giula the next day, from a distance. I was crossing the piazza when she came out for a walk, simpering on Teleso's arm. They were inspecting the preparations for Dono alla Magia. I recognized the dress she wore; it was the wine-red velvet dress Teleso had tried to persuade me to put on. As I watched her, she looked over her shoulder and our eyes met. I could see her eyes flicking over me, looking me up and down, taking in my shabby clothes and dirty face. She had a little smirk on her face, and I knew what she was thinking. *Look at her. I am so fortunate, and she is so foolish, to turn her back on all that I have gained.* With a toss of her smooth-brushed hair, she turned back toward Teleso, who smiled down at her with pride in his most attractive possession.

I was going to be sick if I watched this much longer, so I strode off toward Isabella's tent and didn't look back.

A few nights later, Mario sent word for me to meet him on the hillside, a few hours after his shift ended. "The grain arrived," he said. "Late last night."

"I can move soon, then," I said.

"You can move *now,* and you should. You're going to be in serious trouble soon, Eliana."

"I'm going to wait until after Dono alla Magia," I said. "That's only another three days."

Mario shook his head impatiently. "There is exactly one thing that has kept Teleso from stringing you up like Jesca, and that's your old buddy, Giula. She's kept him distracted. She's done more for you than anyone else here—remember that when she's cringing at your feet."

"What do you mean?"

"When you've led the uprising. When you've led the breakout." Mario's face was stormy and I avoided his eyes. "That is what you're planning, isn't it?" he asked. I hesitated for a moment, and his voice grew impatient. "It's a bit late to decide you don't trust me. Those soldiers you've been lecturing on morality—are you going to lead us against our fellows? Against Teleso?"

"I'd sort of planned to play it by ear," I said. I'd mainly

been hoping the soldiers would stay out of the way when the uprising came—just stand back and not try to kill us—and that no one would try to kill them. "Leading you against your commander—" I shook my head.

"You could, you know." Mario gripped my arm. "We'd follow you."

" 'We'? Who are you speaking for, Mario? Not all the men who come to my concerts."

"No," he said. "But many of them."

"You hate Teleso that much? And the Circle?"

"We've been abandoned here," Mario said. "Just as you have. All I ask—" He paused. "All I ask is that you invite my men to join you when you lead your insurrection. *Ask* us to join you. Don't just turn your people against us."

"I don't turn away allies," I said.

"We can be of use to you. I can get you into the keep, once you've started your uprising."

"How?" I asked.

"A soldier named Bassio." I recognized the name; Bassio had recently started coming to my concerts. He was a tall, quiet man, and the other soldiers had been surprised to see him. I hoped Teleso would be similarly surprised. "Tell me when you're ready, and he'll get into position," Mario said. "He'll open the door to the keep."

"That's good to know," I said.

Mario nodded, and turned away to go, then turned back. "Remember what I said about Giula," he said, and strode quickly away.

• • •

Dono alla Magia preparations continued, and Margherita led nightly prayer services. I knew that there were nightly prayer services in the barracks, but Mario came each night to pray with the Della Chiese prisoners, taking off his sword and kneeling in the dust. Teleso, too, saw Mario at prayer, and I could see his eyes glint with anger and a hint of satisfaction. He strolled the piazza with Giula regularly; I could see his eyes sweeping the crowd looking for me, so I stayed out of his sight as well as I could.

The popularity of the game, Lupi, continued to rise. Permanent teams had formed, and the people who weren't playing the game were betting on the outcomes. Even Mario didn't seem to suspect; it had worked perfectly.

There was another strange thing I'd noticed recently. Red sashes had become the fashion among Lupi players. I had no idea where all the red blankets were coming from, but there seemed to be plenty of red sashes to go around.

•   •   •

"We shouldn't go," Lucia said.

"You don't have to," I said. "I can go by myself."

"I don't understand why you won't just stay here."

"I want to see how they do the Dono alla Magia ritual," I said. "Without magery."

Giovanni sat beside Lucia, in Rafi's tent, his eyes flicking from Lucia's face to mine. "I want to go, too," he said. *Great,* I thought, *just what I need. Giovanni as company all evening.* "I'm curious, too. I've been curious about all the Della Chiese rituals, but you never let me go to any." This last comment became a whine, directed at Lucia.

"Fine," she said. "We'll all go."

The ritual was to take place in the piazza. The tents along the edge had been taken down again, making the space larger. Unlit torches on high stakes ringed the periphery of the piazza, and dried horse dung had been heaped in the center for a fire. It was still daylight, and would be daylight for a while yet. Margherita was nowhere in sight, but the piazza was beginning to fill with the faithful and the onlookers. Some of the old women had brought drums to beat, and younger people were dancing. Not the careful ritual dance of the Old Way, though; they danced with their own internal partners, flinging their bodies in wild gyrations. Michel was dancing in the piazza; he was as graceful dancing for the Lady as he was with the Redentori. He had asked me several days earlier if Lucia and Giovanni could protect me for the day, and I had assured him that I would be fine.

"Harlots," Lucia said, her eyes locked onto the dancers.

Giovanni rolled his eyes. "I don't see any harm in dancing steps that God didn't write out for you," he said. "I always liked dancing before the Dono alla Magia service." Lucia glared at him, and he stayed where he was.

We spread out our cloaks and sat down on the ground on a slight rise at the edge of the expanded piazza. "You should see Dono alla Magia in Cuore," Giovanni said to me. "I thought there were a lot of lights in Varena, but it's nothing compared to Cuore. The Circle participates, of course. The whole city is lit up."

"I can imagine."

"I doubt it," Giovanni said.

Petro, passing by, offered us a swig from his clay jug. Lucia shook her head primly, but Giovanni took the jug. "You should have some, Lucia," he urged with a smirk, but she shook her head again and he returned the jug to Petro with a nod of thanks. "Best wine I've had in months," Giovanni said when he'd gone. "Should've figured Petro would have a stash."

"I'm surprised he's sharing it," I said, and Giovanni laughed. Lucia glared at both of us.

More of the old women arrived, joining the drummers. Some of them brought drums, but most just had pots or tin cups to bang together. The noise increased and sharpened. I wrinkled my nose. "We had drums at the conservatory," I said. "*Just* drums."

"You drive away the Maledori with noise," Giovanni pointed out. "Any noise. We had all sorts of noisemakers in Varena and Cuore."

"There's nothing that says it has to be an unpleasant noise," I said. Most of the old women had gotten onto the beat together, but a few were a hair behind, creating a clattering cacophony that sounded like a drunk cat in a room full of cymbals.

Twilight fell, and the faithful began to leave the piazza. The old women stayed, of course, still banging on their pots. Someone—Petro, maybe—was starting to light the torches. Giovanni fell silent. "I've never watched this before," I said. "I was always one of the Blind, at the conservatory."

"Figures," Giovanni said.

"Give me a break, Giovanni. I suppose you were an honorary drummer."

"Don't be ridiculous," he said. "Of course I was one of the Blind, too."

"Yes, you were," Lucia said softly. She was smiling a little bit when I glanced back.

On a signal from someone I hadn't seen, the drumming became more insistent, and more regular. They were almost all on the beat now. I remembered this moment, from the conservatory, standing blindfolded in the vestry of the church, my hand on Bella's shoulder and Giula's hand on my shoulder. Straining for the sound of the beat, for the signal that we could stop standing around and could wind our way into the church.

Here they came, finally. I'd never realized quite how simultaneously frightening and silly we must have looked. At the conservatory, we all had matching white blindfolds, but here people made do with what they could find. I saw more than a few red sashes used that way. The line was led by the priestess, Margherita, whose eyes were covered only with a thin veil that she could easily see through. Behind her was Giula, who had claimed the place of honor by virtue of her position as Teleso's lady, and behind her, one of the women who lived by the latrines. To be next to Giula was no honor. Each person was blindfolded, led by the person in front. The faithful wound through Ravenna like an endless blind centipede. When they reached the piazza, Margherita began to spiral the line, so that it wound tight, packing people in. She signaled, and the drumming stopped. Silence was the cue: everyone dropped hands and sat down in the piazza, feeling carefully underneath them first. Margherita pulled off her blindfold and spoke to the crowd.

"Tonight is the Night of the Gift of the Lady."

Crash. I jumped at the echoing cymbals.

"Centuries ago, our land was dark with war, ignorance, and superstition. The Empire that had kept the peace for a thousand years was crumbling, and barbarians invaded from the north. The Maledori nipped at our heels and leered at us from the shadows. Our people cried to their god in fear, but there was only *silence.*"

Crash.

"Then on this night, those centuries ago, the Lady came to a man called Gaius, shining in the darkness like a star come to earth. 'Behold,' She said. 'I bring the greatest of gifts.' "

" 'Behold,' " Lucia muttered beside me, " 'I am a stranger among you, yet I bring the greatest of gifts.' The Journey of Gèsu, chapter 1, verse 1."

"So the Lady borrowed," Giovanni said. "She steals only from the best."

Margherita continued from the center of the piazza. "Gaius said, 'What have you brought us?' And the Lady said, 'Open your eyes, Gaius. Open your eyes, and *see*!'"

Crash.

That was the cue for everyone to pull off their blindfold, to see the ring of light that surrounded them.

"In Cuore," Giovanni said, "the Circle created lights in the sky—not magefire, it wasn't dangerous. Just pretty. All colors, too."

At the conservatory, we were ringed by teachers, each of whom held a globe of witchlight. No one held witchlight here in Ravenna, of course. Instead, torches flickered brightly in the summer night.

"The Lady's Gift to Gaius was magery," Margherita said. "Gaius also learned the other things the Lady wanted for Her children—peace, prosperity, fertility, abundance, freedom. To provide these things, Gaius taught as many people magery as he could, and gathered in those with the strongest talent to serve the Emperor and protect the land."

Giovanni snorted softly behind me. "To take over from the Emperor," he said under his breath. "And divide power with the Fedeli, as poachers might divide the spoils from their hunt."

"Mario is loyal to the Emperor," I said.

Giovanni shrugged. "What good is the army without the Circle?"

"The Circle united the land, and magery spread," Margherita said.

"Actually," Giovanni said, "the Empire fell apart anyway. Magery spread all right, and now there are thousands of little Circles out there. Tough to control an empire with a handful of mages who don't want to leave their comfortable enclave . . ."

"Our people abandoned superstition. The Lady does

not ask us to believe in things we can only imagine, but gives us light we can *see* by and faith we can touch," Margherita said. "We can hold the Lady's Gift in our hands."

"Not here!" someone shouted. I realized with a lurch that it was Rafi. I looked at Lucia, but her eyes were as wide and horrified as mine.

Margherita never missed a beat. "The Lady promised Gaius that She would *never* turn away from us; Her love is perfect, true, and complete. And so, Her blessings were passed from Gaius to our grandparents to us. Please join with me—" and everyone joined in with her in a long hymn.

Lucia shook her head, not quite able to hide her smile. "You never expect *Rafi* to be the one who makes trouble, you know?"

Giovanni shrugged. "So what did you think?" he asked me.

"It's strange, with fire instead of witchlight. It looks like we're saying that until the Lady came, we didn't have fire," I said.

In the piazza, Margherita lit the bonfire and people tossed in handfuls of incense. A wave of rose-scented smoke washed over us.

"I'm going to be ill," Lucia warned us. "I can't stand that smell."

"I've seen what I came to see," I said. "We can go."

"I'm staying," Giovanni said. "Next is more dancing. I always liked dancing."

"Harlot," Lucia said to him.

"I'll repent tomorrow," he said with a mocking bow. "Or the day after. Tomorrow night is Midsummer's Eve, isn't it? And you *know* what they say about Midsummer's Eve."

"You're hopeless," she said, and turned her back on him. I followed her toward the hills.

"What do they say about Midsummer's Eve?" I asked when we'd gotten a ways away.

"Oh, you know," Lucia said. "Didn't they say this in your village? Anything that happens that night doesn't 'count.' "

I grinned. "That does sound familiar. People said that sort of thing at the conservatory, but you know, if we were caught with a boy it would count no matter what night it was."

"Well, the priests and priestesses at the seminary always said it was heresy, but it's a very popular heresy all over, I think."

We sat down on the hillside. From here, the torches looked like a ring of dancing jewels against the darkness. I sighed.

"You can go dance, too, if you like," Lucia said. "I won't hold it against you."

"That's all right. I've never been a very good dancer."

Lucia leaned against my shoulder. "Lying's a sin too, you know. You're a fine dancer."

"How would you know?" I said. "I play, I don't dance."

"I *know*," Lucia said. She turned her head to look up at me, and give me a wry smile. My gaze nearly faltered, but I managed to smile back at her.

Lucia pulled away from me briefly and spread out her cloak; we lay down on her cloak and covered ourselves with mine, leaning against each other to stay warm in the wasteland's chill night breeze. "Do you ever think about your parents, Lucia?" I asked.

"Not very often," she said. "I haven't seen them for a long time."

"Are they alive?"

"As far as I know." Lucia sighed. "I tried to write to them once, last year. Before I came to Ravenna. Apparently, they refused to open my letter. So I might just as well be dead, as far as they're concerned."

"And Giovanni?"

"I don't know what his parents think. He was their only son and they always let him get away with a lot. Joining a reform movement is probably just another little boy's game, as far as they're concerned."

"I don't know what my parents would have thought," I said.

"Would you be here, if they were still alive?" Lucia asked.

"No."

Under the cloak, Lucia's hand found mine. "Your hands are cold," she said.

"Sorry," I said, and my voice trembled slightly.

Lucia turned her face toward mine in the moonlight; she smiled. I pulled one hand free of the cloak, and reached to touch her cheek. It was as soft as velvet; she closed her eyes briefly at their cold touch.

"Lucia," I said, and my voice shook. "The last time I saw Amedeo, he said something—about women who feel toward women as Giula feels toward men." I wanted to stop, but I had gone too far not to finish asking now. "He said that—that it's one of the things that goes against God. Is it?"

Lucia's hand tightened gently over mine. "Amedeo is a foolish old man. Gèsu never said anything one way or the other."

We lay in silence for a moment, and Lucia brushed my cheek gently. "I am not as you are, Eliana. But I don't believe that God thinks any less of you."

I was comforted, though I felt an odd wrench at her

words, *I am not as you are.* But at least this didn't fall into the strange category of things that the Redentori forbid. As Lucia's hand fell away from my cheek, though, I remembered that Amedeo hadn't said that the Redentori *had* this prejudice in common with the followers of the Lady; he had said that they *would have* this in common. *Amedeo is a crazy old man,* I told myself, my hand tightening on Lucia's. *I've heard him say nothing that makes sense.*

We stared up at the stars for a long time. Then—"Look!" Lucia gasped, and I turned my head to see the shooting star.

"Do Redentori wish on shooting stars?" I asked.

"I've never heard anyone say we can't," she said. "There was an old woman in one of the villages I visited before the war—she said that a shooting star was the Archangel Michel coming to earth from heaven."

"Why?"

"I don't know. So he can lead a battle on God's side. Michel is *Aral Din,* the Angel of Justice. The patron of those who fight and die for God."

"Like Beneto," I said.

"Yes," she said. "Or like you."

I didn't sleep that night.

•   •   •

As the sky lightened to gray, I got up quietly to go to the latrines, covering Lucia carefully so as not to wake her. I wished before long that I could have brought my cloak; I could see the puffs of my breath as steam in the air. I didn't think I was likely to sleep, but by the time I was finished at the latrine, I had decided that I was going to go back and lie down next to Lucia again, just to get warm.

"Eliana."

I turned to see Mario, his cloak pulled around his face.

"You're in danger," he hissed. "Come on. We need to get you somewhere hidden."

"Isabella's," I said.

"No. They'll look there. Come on." He had brought an extra cloak, and flung it around my shoulders; I pulled the hood over my face. The cloak was so long it trailed on the ground, and he hustled me along toward the keep. I pulled the wool around me, shivering. I still wanted to be sleeping next to Lucia.

"Teleso has ordered your arrest," he said.

"Lucia—"

"Is *not* in danger," he said. "It's you he wants."

Mario led me through the back door into the stables. The two young men on guard duty there were Tomas and Plautio; they saluted me gravely as Mario led me in.

"Do you have a plan, then?" Mario asked. "Or will we need to smuggle you out?"

"I'm not leaving," I said.

"You have a plan, then?"

"Yes." I closed my eyes for a minute, tipping my head back to rest it against the wall of the stable. "I was almost ready to lead the breakout. I wanted a few more days— people tend to get drunk during Dono alla Magia, if there's any wine at all to be had. But I could do it now. I just need a crowd."

"There's a crowd—"

"Not in the piazza. That's Teleso's territory and he knows it. North hill. I need a crowd on the north hill at dawn." I opened my eyes again and looked Mario in the face. "Tell Michel. He'll get people there."

"What then?"

"Then I start the uprising," I said, and tried to smile.

Tomas and Plautio hid me in the stables as Michel and Mario were sent out to gather the Ravenessi to the north hill. All I could do at that point was to stay out of sight, so I huddled in a corner behind barrels of grain. The grain used for horse feed, I noticed, was better than what was fed to the Ravenessi. I wished I had Lucia with me, to keep me from worrying. Over and over, in my head, I rehearsed the words I was going to say. At one point, one of the horses snorted and stamped its foot, and I started with such force that I almost knocked over the barrels I was hidden behind. My heart pounded like a drum, and my head throbbed with each knock. My hands were shaking.

It's just one of the horses, I thought, pressing my cold hands against my forehead and trying to rub away the pain. *Nothing worth getting scared over.* I realized a moment later that I had thought—for an instant—that the noise was someone like Niccolo coming into the stable. *You're going to be leaving the stable in a little while,* I thought. *Facing Teleso and Niccolo and all the other soldiers who won't surrender. It's a bit late to be getting scared now.*

I tried to focus again on what I would say, but the ache in my head and the sickness in my stomach were getting worse. *I'm sick,* I thought. *Lady's tits, I'm getting a fever.* I pressed my palm against my forehead, but of course to my icy hands, anything would feel hot. *I can't get sick now. I'd let down Lucia, Mario, Michel . . . and Giovanni would gloat.* That thought made me angry, and for a moment, I no longer felt afraid. *And Teleso would be so pleased that I'd failed.* I thought of Teleso laughing, his cold eyes brightening, his arm curling around Giula's waist—

"Eliana." Mario had come back so quietly that I hadn't heard him. "Everything's ready."

I stood up. "Let's go," I said.

A handful of the soldiers closed in around me to conceal

me as I left the stable; when we reached the edge of the crowd at the north hill, I slipped out. The crowd parted to make way for me as I strode toward the north hill. Some lowered their eyes as I passed; others held out their fists in salute. I climbed to the top of the hill, painfully aware of what an easy target I made; the crowd fell silent as I turned to them.

"I have no music for you today," I said. "The dancing that was needed has been done."

Deep in the crowd, I could see Lucia and Giovanni. Lucia's eyes burned with her own light, but Giovanni's face was lit too—and I realized with shock that his eyes burned with faith in *me*. Suddenly, I was no longer afraid. I could face down Teleso. Nothing was going to stop me.

"We have the strength we need," I said. "We have the will that we need."

Mario moved along the edge of the crowd, speaking urgently to each soldier.

"The Circle killed my family," I said. "They burned my farm and herded me here like a dog. Why? Because they are afraid of us. They are afraid of thousands of hungry, angry people, standing outside their gates in Cuore and shouting, 'Why? Why did you fight this war? The Vesuviano army could have done nothing worse to us than you have done!'

"They have left us to starve. They *want* us to die—they want our skeletons to lie bleached in the sun like those of our families that they have killed. They want us to die quietly. They have treated us like dogs that they can shut away or kill at will. But we are not dogs any longer. We are *wolves*."

The crowd cried out. "Yes!" I heard someone shout.

"We are the wolves," I said. "We have learned to hunt as a pack. We have learned to bring down the shepherd that would pick us off one by one with his crossbow. The sheep *Teleso* is now our easy prey. And we can *turn* on those who would leave us to starve!"

There was another cry from the crowd.

"Not all the soldiers are our enemies," I said, and gestured so that people turned to face the soldiers that now ringed the edge of the crowd. "We are not the only ones who have been abandoned to die. They are prisoners as much as we are. Join us!" I shouted to the soldiers. "Cast aside Teleso and join us against our enemy. Against your enemy! Once we are dead Teleso will have no use for you, either. You are men, not monsters! You are not Teleso's sheep—you are wolves, like us!"

Mario stepped forward, very deliberately. He held up a red sash, like the Lupi wore, for all to see, then tied it around his waist. Around him, other soldiers brought out red sashes and tied them on.

A cheer broke forth from the crowd.

"To the *keep*," I shouted. "We will tear down the walls with our anger! We will break into the storehouse of food! We will water the hills of Ravenna with the *blood of our enemies*."

I raised my fist, and the battle cry of the Ravenessi army echoed across the valley like a pack of a thousand wolves hunting under the full moon.

CHAPTER FIFTEEN

Who can stand against the tide?
—*The Journey of Gèsu, chapter 22, verse 23.*

As I stood on the hillside, I heard a *zip* near my ear and heard Giovanni shout, "Look out!" Realizing that I was being fired on, I scrambled down the slope and into the mass of Ravenessi, and we started to run.

I could see very little from the middle of the crowd; once we were moving, I realized that I had no way of communicating with my army, no way to direct our actions. *To the keep* ran through the crowd like spilled water; I pushed my way toward the front of the refugee army, trying desperately to lead it.

There were so many of us! I could see soldiers scattering like leaves in wind. Many of the soldiers had followed Mario's lead and joined us, their insignias ripped from their sleeves, and others threw their crossbows to the ground, getting as far out of our way as they could. I saw Isabella hit a soldier on the head with a short club, then rip the crossbow from his arms and turn it against his fellows.

I heard screams of pain around me as we reached the

keep and realized that we had been met with a torrent of crossbow bolts. I scanned the side of the keep, noticing the tiny narrow windows that provided just enough space for the bowmen to pick us off. Some of my men were trying to batter down the door. Where was Mario's friend Bassio? I scanned the keep and with a sickening lurch of my stomach realized that his body swung from a rope out of one of the upper-story windows of the keep. "Oh no," I whispered.

Another curtain of bolts fell on us and people scattered. Someone jerked on my arm—Giovanni. "Cover!" he shouted. "You idiot! We need to get under cover—don't you realize they're aiming for you?"

I let Giovanni drag me toward one of the residual walls at the edge of the piazza. "What now?" he asked.

"The soldier swinging by his neck was going to let us in," I said.

Giovanni looked over the wall and quickly ducked back down. "Do you have a backup plan?" he asked.

"Got any suggestions?"

"Well, now is just a *grand* time to ask, Generale. You sure let us *think* you had everything under control."

"Well, if you don't, then—"

"We could leave," he said. "Retreat now. The soldiers are in the keep; they'll have to come out to follow us. We could get a head start—"

"We need the grain," I said. "We *need* it. Or this is all for nothing—we'll just starve even faster. Unless *you* had some ideas about how to feed our army."

"You never asked," he said.

"Well, do you?"

"No. Maybe if you'd asked earlier I'd have thought of something."

Most of our army had found some cover by now, and we stared across the piazza. "Stalemate," Giovanni said.

"Generale!"

I looked behind me as Mario ran up. "I can get us inside," he said breathlessly.

"Bassio is dead," I said.

Mario's jaw tightened. "I know," he said. "But I have another way. Through the south door. Get some people together to give us cover; the soldiers in the keep will fire as soon as we're out in the open."

I looked around, at a loss. The Lupi weren't going to want to leave cover. Maybe if I left it first . . . I leapt up onto the wall I'd been hiding behind. "Follow me!" I shouted, and a new cheer went up from our army.

"What the hell," Giovanni sputtered, but fortunately the crowd surged around me again and we ran through the rain of bolts.

The south door Mario had referred to was near the back of the keep, the smallest and grimiest entrance. We pushed and the door opened easily.

"How?" I asked as Mario passed me.

"Arianna," he said. "She said she'd leave it open for us if she could."

"I owe you," I said.

"No," he said. "You owe *her*."

Our army surged into the keep. This was better; Teleso's men would lose some of the advantages of their crossbows, firing along the twisting hallways of the keep. But it would be harder for us to use our numbers against them. "Spread out," I said as my army surged in. "Open all the doors, set guards over anything of value. Find Teleso. Kill the ones who don't surrender. *Tonight, Ravenna will be ours.*"

The wolves were on the hunt; the keep had become a trap. We could smell our prey, fleeing helplessly into the farthest corners. I found myself with Mario, Giovanni, Michel, and about a dozen more Lupi. Giovanni had a sword and a crossbow that he'd taken from a surrendering soldier; I realized, looking at him, that all I had to defend myself with was my knife.

"Upstairs," Mario said, so we followed him up the narrow spiral. As we emerged into the corridor, there was a snap of a bolt hitting the wall, and we saw a soldier retreating into a room, trying frantically to reload his crossbow. It was Tullo, one of the boys who'd come to my concerts. As we advanced on him, he dropped the bow and drew his sword. "Traitors," he said in a shaky voice. "We should have hanged you with Jesca and Beneto."

"Wrong way to say you surrender," Michel said, and the Lupi surged forward. Tullo got in one good swing, wounding someone across the arm, and then they ripped the sword out of his hands like the shepherd's "bow" and threw it aside.

"Bastardo," Michel said, and threw Tullo against the wall. "*Bastardo.*" I heard a coughing choke and saw a gush of red; one of the Lupi had stabbed Tullo in the chest. They backed off as Tullo fell onto his face, his hands grasping at the rug under him.

"I surrender," Tullo choked, and died.

"Come on," I said, willing my voice not to tremble. "We are wolves. This is war. Come on."

The hallway outside the room was empty. There was a row of doors; several were open, the rooms empty. Then we came to a barred door. "Leave us alone," a voice shouted from behind the door. "Teleso isn't in here."

"Break it down," I said, and Mario and Michel slammed into it, knocking it off its hinges. I started to follow them into the room, but they pulled up short. I saw two men backing up against the far wall—Vincente and Ilario, not soldiers I liked. I shouldered Michel out of the way so that I could see the rest of the room.

"One step more," Vincente said, "and she dies."

I felt myself blanch and my hands started shaking. They had Arianna, Teleso's maidservant. Vincente gripped her firmly by the arms, and Ilario held a sword to her throat.

"Stay back," I said over my shoulder.

"What is it?" Giovanni asked.

"How are you planning to get out of Ravenna?" Michel asked. "Even if we let you walk out of this room."

"Let her go," Mario said. He was clenching his teeth so tightly I could see the veins in his neck. "*Damn* you. Let her go."

"Oh yeah," Vincente said. "Teleso's maid is your little cunt, isn't she, Mario?" Vincente glanced at Ilario, who raised an eyebrow, then nodded. "We'll give you an even trade," Vincente continued. "You for her. You'll make just as good a hostage."

"Mario—" I whispered.

"You for her!" Vincente shouted, jerking Arianna's arms behind her so that she grimaced in pain. "You have five seconds to make the trade."

"I'll do it!" Mario said. "Don't hurt her. I'll do it."

"Drop your weapons," Vincente said.

"Don't do it," Arianna said.

Ilario slapped her on the face with the flat of the sword. "He didn't ask *you*."

"Don't touch her!" Mario said. "Leave her *alone*." He handed me his sword and his bow. "Me for her. Swear on your honor as a soldier to honor that."

"Swear on the same honor you swore your loyalty on?" Ilario said.

"Mario, don't," I said. "He's going to kill both of you."

"They need a hostage to get out of here," Mario whispered. "I'll have a better chance of breaking free than Arianna." He started slowly across the room. As he approached, Ilario lowered the sword from Arianna's throat, and Vincente relaxed his hold on her arms. Finally, they shoved her away; Vincente grabbed Mario's arms and twisted them behind him.

"I never liked traitors," Ilario said, and drew back his sword.

"*Mario,*" Arianna screamed, as Ilario stabbed Mario in the gut.

Vincente dropped Mario onto the floor and looked up with a smile of vicious satisfaction. "You're right; we'll never get out of Ravenna. Might as well take the opportunity to kill the traitor."

"You can join him!" Michel shouted, running across the room, Giovanni on his heels.

Arianna had thrown herself to her knees next to Mario. "Help him," she begged me, and I knelt beside them.

"I don't know anything about healing—" I whispered, tearing his shirt open. I gagged at the smell of blood and rent bowels. If I could stop the bleeding . . . I used my knife to cut loose the edge of Mario's tunic, to try to hold it over the wound. "Mario, Mario, hold on. I'll find Petro—"

Mario shook his head, his face contorted in pain. "Waste of time," he muttered. "Go on, both of you. We are wolves, and this is war."

Arianna clasped Mario's hand and raised her anguished eyes to meet mine. "Teleso was here," she said. "There's a secret door behind that tapestry." She pointed. "It opens to a staircase that leads down to his study. Maybe you can stop him—"

I looked down at Mario; he had closed his eyes, pressing

Arianna's hand to his lips. Then I stood up. "Giovanni!" I said. The Lupi were tearing apart the two soldiers; I pushed aside the tapestry. "This leads to Teleso's study. Six of you—with me. The rest—meet us there."

I spared a last glance toward Mario; he was whispering something to Arianna, pressing a knife into her hand. Then I turned and tore down the stairs. The darkness closed around us as we ran. I still clutched Mario's sword and bow, although now that I was running down the stairs it occurred to me that I didn't have a clue how to use the sword, and the bow would be useless on a spiral staircase. Oh well; it was too late to back off now. We emerged, breathless but unchallenged, in Teleso's study. Giovanni burst in a moment later. "No one," I said.

"We need to organize," Giovanni said. "What do we still need to secure? Teleso's soldiers have scattered, but it's a safe bet that they'll try to cause us as much trouble as possible."

"The horses," I said. "Teleso won't get far on foot, and we need the horses. Also the wagons. And this study; there might be information here we can use. And—Oh, hell. The grain." I stood, my arms still full of useless weaponry. "I didn't send anybody to guard the grain. What if Teleso—"

Giovanni glanced past me to the Lupi. "You—stables. You—wagons. You guard the study." He looked back at me. "Come on. No, wait." He pulled the sword out of my hand. "You're holding this wrong."

"Giovanni, who *cares*? Let's *go*."

"You don't know how to use a sword. The middle of a battle is not the time to take up new weapons. Stick with your knife and the bow—you're less likely to kill yourself with your own weapons. Just don't shoot yourself in the foot." He handed off the sword to one of the soldiers, then grabbed my arm to run for the granary.

It was down near the kitchens; the small northwest tower was used entirely for food storage. The keep swarmed with refugees. We went down some more stairs and then down a narrow hallway to a door that was already open. I felt panic beginning to rise in my throat, *I'm such a fool, Teleso knows how badly we need this grain. He knows.* Through the door. Into the tower—

Giovanni pulled up short, putting out one arm to hold me back. "Shh," he said.

From beyond the door into the granary, we could hear someone talking. "Can't you think of anything more original than carving my guts out?" a calm woman's voice demanded. The voice was pitched to carry as far as possible. "Niccolo, I'd have expected something more interesting from you."

It was Lucia's voice. I looked at Giovanni and saw my own horrified expression in his face. Gesturing for silence, he pulled me closer to the door and we peered in.

Niccolo stood with his back to the door, his sword in one hand, a torch in the other. Lucia sat in front of him. Her knife was a few feet away. He'd apparently disarmed her and then paused to gloat.

"I could burn you alive along with the grain," Niccolo said. "Would that satisfy your desire for a novel form of martyrdom?"

"Well," Lucia said, her voice still calm and cheerful. "It is the sort of thing I'd expect from a lackey of the Fedeli—"

Giovanni raised his crossbow and peered carefully down the sights. For a moment I thought he was going to do the sensible thing and shoot Niccolo in the back. Then—"Niccolo!" he shouted.

Niccolo whirled just as Giovanni fired the bow. The bolt missed him by inches. I raised my own bow, fired, missed.

"What kind of idiot stands with his back to the door?" Giovanni demanded, drawing his sword.

"What kind of idiot messes up a perfectly good shot by warning the target?" I said.

Niccolo didn't answer. He glanced from me to Giovanni with a leer of satisfaction. He opened his mouth to speak, then cried out in pain, twisted around to look behind him in astonishment, and collapsed onto his face on the floor. The torch fell from his hand.

Lucia stood behind him, a bloody knife in her hand. "Sorry to mess up your duel, Giovanni," she said. She stamped out the torch, then wiped the knife off on Niccolo's tunic. "Teleso's last orders, apparently—burn the grain."

"Why didn't he?" I asked. I still had my own knife in my hand. I slipped it back into the hidden sheath in my boot.

"You know Niccolo," Lucia said. "I think I could have kept him talking for another hour. He wants to see you scared, or it's just no fun." She looked down at Niccolo's body. "I think I'm going to be ill," she said, and threw up.

Back upstairs, we headed outside to take stock of the situation. Nobody seemed to be firing; the clash of swords had been replaced by the cries of the injured and dying. The dusty ground of the piazza was stained a dark mud brown from blood, and there were bodies everywhere. Fallen Lupi mixed with loyalist soldiers and mutineers; many had clothing so bloody I couldn't have said which side they'd died for. I saw Rafi moving from fallen body to fallen body, comforting the living and drawing a cross over each of the dead.

"Did we win?" I said.

"Yeah," Giovanni said, looking surprised that I'd asked. "We won."

The Ravenessi began to swarm through the keep, touching the rugs and the curtains and the eggshell-thin glasses, breaking and stealing and dirtying. People were carrying off an amazing variety of items. Michel dragged a wine barrel toward the piazza with one of his friends. Isabella had carved up a haunch of meat from the pantry and was cooking it in the gruel pot. I thought I saw the glint of a gilt-edged mirror, and several people had carried off rugs and tapestries and furniture to decorate their makeshift tents.

I heard a piercing screech from the door of the keep. "Behold," Severo cried. "Teleso's whore."

"No," Giula shrieked, trying to tear her hand away from him. "Leave me alone, leave me alone."

"You know where he is," Severo said. "You know where he's gone! Tell us!" He smacked her hard across the face.

"*I don't know.* He left me alone. He said he'd come back but he never came, leave me *alone*." Giula still wore the dark red velvet dress, but it was crumpled and blood-stained. "Help me, please, *somebody. Please.* Please leave me alone."

I watched for a moment in silence.

"Tell us what you know," Severo said.

"I don't know *anything.* I swear. I'll swear by anything you want. I don't *know*." Giula was nearly hysterical.

"Well, we have *you,* in any case," Severo said gently, touching her cheek, then backhanding her again. "*You,* Teleso's whore."

The one other person who would have defended Giula was Mario. So I strode over to where Severo was beating her. "Leave her alone," I said.

Severo turned toward me, an ugly expression on his face. "What do you mean?"

"I mean what I said. Leave her alone. It's because of her

I didn't follow Jesca and Beneto to the gallows. She kept Teleso distracted. So *leave her alone*." He released her slowly, letting her fall to the ground. "Have your fun with someone else," I said.

"Niccolo's already dead. I was hoping to kill him myself."

I snorted. "If you'd thought to go guard the grain, you'd have had your opportunity. Go help guard the horses. If Teleso tries for a horse to escape, you'll have a shot at him."

Severo shuffled off, and I helped Giula to her feet. "Go change into a different dress," I said. "Something less conspicuous."

"I don't know what Teleso did with my old clothes," she said.

"Take some clothes off one of the bodies," I said, but she burst into tears again, so I stripped a soldier and gave Giula the uniform.

"Those are boy's clothes," she said.

I rolled my eyes. "You're going to have to live with it," I said. "You'll just get into trouble again walking around in the velvet." Still pouting, she took the clothing and vanished into a tent to change.

Tomas approached. He'd torn the insignia off his uniform and wore a red sash. He saluted me. "The stables, granary, and armory are secured," Tomas said. "Teleso's study is under guard."

I blinked at Tomas for a moment. "Does anyone know what's happened to Teleso?" I asked.

"No, Generale," Tomas said. "We've checked all the hiding spots that the soldier-Lupi knew of."

"Are any of the horses missing?" Giovanni asked.

"No," Tomas said. "If he got away, he fled on foot. We've sent out a search party."

"Keep looking," I said.

Tomas saluted and headed back toward the stables.

"Your orders will be needed," Lucia said, "on the question of the soldiers who surrendered."

"Lock the ones who surrendered in the dungeon," I said. "We'll let them out before we leave—without weapons or food, the ones with any sense will head north. The ones who mutinied, let them go free. They're ours now."

"What next?" Giovanni asked.

I stared at the bloodstained piazza. "We bury our dead."

Giovanni and Lucia were both silent for a moment. Then Giovanni asked, "Did Teleso keep papers somewhere?"

I blinked at him.

"That's something I can take care of this afternoon and tonight," Giovanni said. "We should sort through them systematically. See if there's any information of use to us."

"Oh," I said. "Of course. He kept papers in his study, I believe. That's why I wanted a guard placed over it—as much to keep out the Ravenessi as the soldiers."

Giovanni grinned—the friendliest look he'd given me yet. "I'll take care of that tonight, then."

Lucia slipped her arm around my waist. "Was there anything else you wanted to save, here? Or take for your own?"

"No," I said. "I think everything important is under guard."

"Then you've won," Lucia said. "Celebrate your victory."

Rafi had formed uninjured volunteers into two groups, moving the injured inside out of the sun, and carrying the bodies down to the gravel pit near the wall. "Right," I said. "Celebrate." I walked out to the piazza and picked up one of the bodies. "We won."

I couldn't believe the number of dead, as I carried bodies. If I'd been asked, I wouldn't have thought there were so many people in all of Ravenna. The bodies were still warm from the sunshine, and were only beginning to become stiff. Some of the bodies, I could carry alone—the Ravenessi were thin and light from deprivation. The soldiers I carried with one other. We stripped the soldiers' bodies before placing them in the gravel pit to be buried, because we would need what they had to survive; the Ravenessi had nothing worth taking.

I did this.

The bodies were my fault. I hadn't struck a single fatal blow—personally—in the entire battle; the only attempt I'd made was my wasted shot at Niccolo. Nonetheless, every body here, every soldier or Ravenessi dead was my fault. *Lady forgive me,* I thought, *when I started this I didn't realize so many would die because of me.*

In the midafternoon sun, I called over someone to help me with the body of a soldier. Michel had come to help carry bodies—I think he was trying to keep an eye on me, uncertain if his job as "bodyguard" was still required now that we'd won—and he came over to help me carry this one. It wasn't until we were halfway to the gravel pit that I looked at the face of the man we carried. "Oh—" I gasped, and stumbled, nearly falling. "Lady's tits. Mario."

"Are you all right?" Michel asked. He lowered Mario's feet and came to support me. I knelt slowly, cradling Mario's body. I'd known he was dying—no one could survive a wound like that—but I'd managed to push it out of my mind, telling myself I'd overestimated the severity of the injury. "Mario," I said again.

"Do you want me to get someone else to carry him?" Michel asked.

"No!" I said. "No, I'll do it—" I looked toward the gravel pit, only a short distance away. "Michel, go get a shovel. They'll have some in the stables."

"Yes, Generale," he said, scrambling back to his feet. "I'll be right back. Don't go anywhere, all right? Don't try to carry him by yourself."

Mario's hands were warm from the sun, and his eyes were closed, his face peaceful. The red sash he'd put on to start the mutiny was stained a darker brown and black from his blood. I closed my eyes for a moment, squeezing his warm, light hand.

"Generale," Michel's voice said, and I opened my eyes again. He'd brought a shovel, and Giovanni. *Just* who I wanted to see.

Giovanni's face was sober as he lifted Mario's feet. Michel carried the shovel. "Where did you want to take him?" Giovanni asked me.

"Out of the camp," I said. "The other side of the hill."

Giovanni nodded, and we carried Mario's body out of the camp. We set Mario down and I took the shovel from Michel. "I didn't want to bury him in the mass grave," I said. My throat was tight. I waited for Giovanni's sarcastic response, but he only nodded.

"Do you want to get your violin?" Giovanni asked. "To play him a funeral Mass?"

I shook my head. "Mario worshipped the Lady. We can't give him a Redentore funeral."

We took turns digging the grave. Finally it was deep enough; we lowered the body in.

"Should we get Margherita?" Michel asked.

I shook my head. "The Book of the Lady says that a soldier should be buried by his fellows," I said. My voice caught again. "Mario was one of us. It's right that we do it. Just—" I looked at Michel and Giovanni. "Don't tell Lucia."

"Don't worry," Giovanni said. "This will be between the three of us."

We joined hands around the open grave. "From earth we come, to earth we return," I said. My voice was shaking. "From dust we come, to dust we return. From our mothers' wombs we come, to the Lady's womb we return."

"So shall it be," Michel and Giovanni said.

We clapped our hands three times, to drive off the Maledori. "Those who walk with the Lord and the Lady in life will walk with Them in the life to come. Those who look to the Lord in life will regard Him in truth in the life to come. Those who cling to the Lady in life will be held in Her arms in the life to come."

"So shall it be," Michel and Giovanni said.

We clapped our hands three times again.

"Lord and Lady," I said, and fell silent for a moment. Tradition required each of us to speak briefly, out loud to the Lord and the Lady, to tell Them why Mario's soul deserved to be guided quickly to the life to come. My throat closed, and I bowed my head, fighting back tears.

Giovanni touched my arm gently, then raised his hands to the sky. "Lord and Lady," he said. "Mario was Your faithful servant when anyone else would have turned away from You. I have seen many in my life who claimed to have faith, of one kind or another. I've met Your Fedeli, I've prayed in Your cathedrals. I've met only a few who truly believed. And Mario put them all to shame." Giovanni paused and started to lower his arms, then changed his mind and raised them again. "Guide his soul to the life to come," he said, "or You're a couple of petty small-minded deities with no respect for the best kind of man." Giovanni lowered his arms.

"So may it be," I said. I felt my lips twitch into a smile. I wasn't sure what Mario would have thought of that eulogy. I hoped he'd approve.

Michel raised his hands to the sky. "Lord and Lady," he said. "Mario was the bravest man I ever met. I'd been afraid of the battle I knew was coming—even though I was training to fight in it, and training other people to fight in it, I was afraid that when it came right down to the actual battle I'd panic and run away. But Mario stood up and put on a sash like ours, and I knew I could fight. I could fight because *he* could fight, and he was turning away from everything he'd ever known. I was fighting for survival, but he was fighting because he believed in us— how could I not live up to that?" Michel paused. "So You'd better take his soul." He looked as if he was going to continue, but thought the better of it and lowered his arms.

"So may it be," Giovanni and I said.

It was my turn. I raised my arms again. "Lord and Lady," I said. "Mario was the truest man I ever met. He joined our cause because he believed in us—and because he believed in *You*. His faith in You drove him to stand against slavery; his faith in You made him turn against his commander. You were dearer to him than his life. But I'm not going to ask You to take his soul." My voice broke. "You can give him back to us. We wouldn't refuse."

"So may it be," Giovanni and Michel said.

We were silent for several minutes. Then I said, "Mario, return to the womb of the Lady." We shoveled the dirt over his body, filling in the grave.

That was all there was to the funeral service. "Are you ready to go back?" Giovanni asked.

"I have another prayer to say," I said, so Giovanni and Michel both bowed their heads and waited.

I knelt and drew a cross in the mound of dirt. "God," I said. "Mario was not a Redentore. He believed in and loved the Lord and the Lady as Lucia believes in You. But Mario gave his life for Arianna because he loved her. He died like Gèsu to save someone else. There's a line from The Journey that I've heard a few times: 'There is no greater love than that of the one who gives his life for his friend.'" I took a deep breath. "I've heard people say that You turn Your back on those who lack God's seal. Well, if You turn Your back on Mario, You're a small-minded deity with no respect for the best kind of man." I took out Bella's cross and kissed it. "I have faith that You see beyond the form of worship to the faith and love below. Grant Your Light and Your peace to Mario. B'shem Arka, v'barah, v'nehora kadosha."

"Amen," Mario and Giovanni said.

"If you don't mind," I said, "I think I'd like to be alone for a little while."

* * *

Mario died because of me. He gave his life to save Arianna, but he died *because of me*. I wept by his grave for a long time. There would be more fighting from here—I knew that. People would look to me to lead it. But all I could think of was all the people who had *died*. I didn't want any more deaths on my soul.

I stared at Mario's grave. I remembered him saying, "I don't want to die," his face sad and frightened like a child's. Well, he had died anyway. What now? I stared down, remembering the last grave I'd dug, when I'd worked alone to bury my family. Could I bear to dig any more graves? What if I just walked away?

What would Mario say, if he were here? I closed my eyes, imagining Mario's gentle face. *Honor my memory,* he would say, *that was easy enough. Honor my sacrifice by not wasting it. Honor my life by showing the courage I showed, by doing* what's right *even when it's terrifying. Honor my memory by leading this struggle, if it's truly the right thing to do. Bear this burden by being the best leader you can, and knowing that many more would lie dead today, had anyone else led this battle.*

I stood up. "Good-bye, Mario," I said, and brushed the dirt to erase the cross I'd drawn. "Thank you."

When I returned to Ravenna, all the bodies had been buried, all the injured moved indoors. The keep's contents had been largely emptied. I wasn't sure what the Ravenessi were planning to do with the furniture; as far as I knew, no one was taking up permanent residence here, and the beds didn't look portable.

I decided to visit my troops, and made a tour of the stables, the granary, and the armory. The Lupi responded enthusiastically when they saw me; I shook everyone's hand, told them they'd done a fine job, assured them there'd be more fighting if they were interested, and moved on.

As evening fell, Margherita lit a bonfire in the piazza. It was Midsummer's Eve; I'd forgotten. Only a few families had decamped; most seemed inclined to stay with the festivities for a while yet. Margherita started to lead an almost Redentore-style dance in the piazza, and I realized suddenly that I had left my violin lying on the hill next to Lucia, where we had slept last night. In a panic, I ran to find it—of course, it was gone. *Lady's tits, Lady's tits,* I thought as I ran to Rafi's tent—not there either. *How could I be so stupid? What am I going to do? Where am I going to get another one?* Maybe Lucia had taken it with her, left it somewhere. I went looking for Lucia.

Rafi's hospital was in the keep; he'd taken over most of the first floor. Lucia knelt next to a woman with a wound so severe I was stunned that she was still alive. I waited for a moment, and Lucia looked up.

"My violin," I whispered.

Lucia smiled. "Took you this long to go looking, did it?" She patted the hand of the woman she'd been sitting with, and rose to come over near me. Lucia walked stiffly, like she'd been kneeling for a long time. "It's fine. I left it with Rafi, and he put it in Teleso's study, with the Lupi guarding there. It's probably still sitting on the chair in the corner by the desk."

"Thank you," I said. I lowered my eyes and glanced toward the woman Lucia had been sitting with. She had taken a bad wound from one of the bolts, and would not live much longer. I realized with a shock that it was Elettra—the Redentore woman with the sick child Lucia had prayed for. "It's odd, Lucia—I feel very useless just now."

"Come pray with me," she said. "Just for a minute. It would comfort Elettra."

I allowed Lucia to draw me to the woman's side and knelt down. Lucia pulled a loop of ribbon from around her neck; it held a tiny vial. "Holy oil," she said. "You know how to pray for healing?"

"Not really," I said. Was she going to try to get me to do the full ritual? "I saw you do it once, that's all."

"Improvise, then," she said. "Go on. Elettra knows you're here."

Elettra moaned softly, and I tentatively took her hand. It was cold and damp, and I held it for a moment, trying to warm it with my own. "Elettra, daughter of . . ." I didn't know her parents' names. "Elettra, daughter of God." I dabbed some of the oil onto my finger from the bottle

Lucia had given me, and drew an X on Elettra's forehead, then kissed it; it was hot under my lips, like the dust of Ravenna at midday. I drew an X on her hands, her feet, and over her heart, then clasped her hands and closed my eyes. "Refuya, Arka," I sang. "Refuya, Gèsu." A tiny thread of the energy I felt as I played the Dance That Turned the Storm came through me, and instead of sending it into the earth under my feet, I tried to send it through my hands, into Elettra's body. I imagined her wounds closing, color returning to her cheeks, hope returning to her eyes. For just a moment, with my eyes closed, I could almost believe it was true.

Elettra moaned again, as the last notes of the song died away, and I opened my eyes to see her wound unchanged. I told myself that I wasn't really disappointed; what did I expect? I shook my head and squeezed her hands gently, then detached myself. "I think I should go."

Lucia caught my sleeve briefly. "I've been in here, Eliana, so I haven't heard what's going on—do you know if Mario—"

"Mario is dead," I said.

Lucia nodded, her face grieved but serene. "What's next?" she said. "Do we take on the Circle?"

I sat back on my heels. "Lady's tits, I hope not," I said. "We can defeat a demoralized pack of soldiers with eight-to-one odds when half of them mutiny and the other half run like hell. Do *you* think we're ready to take on the Circle?"

"What, then?"

"I don't know," I said. "I'll think of something." Elettra moaned again, and Lucia glanced back toward her. "I think I'll go down to Teleso's study," I said. "I should get my violin."

• • •

Giovanni was alone in the study. He'd barred the door; I had to bang on it to get him to let me in. "Is working alone a good idea?" I asked.

Giovanni gave me a defensive look. "The Lupi wanted to go join the party. I didn't see any harm in that. I barricaded the secret door, too," he said, and pointed at the chair he'd shoved in front of it.

"You're assuming that's the only secret door."

"What kind of idiot would build all his secret passages leading to the same room?"

"Teleso vanished without a trace," I said. "And we still don't know how. Have you found anything of interest?"

"Teleso's hit list," he said, waving a piece of paper at me. I took it and looked at it. I'd seen the list before. Beneto and Jesca's names, circled and then checked off. Lucia's name, circled. My name had been added to the bottom, and circled. I snorted.

"I've also found demonstrable evidence that Teleso was embezzling," Giovanni said. "Pocketing part of the money that was supposed to feed the Ravenessi and his men. He was doing a clumsy job of it, too. My father taught me some bookkeeping. I never took to it, but even I could spot Teleso's number-juggling."

"Is that all?"

"I'm afraid so. There's plenty of paper left to go through, though." Giovanni waved his hand at one of the piles. "Feel free to make yourself useful."

No sarcastic comments came immediately to mind, so I sat down and started reading. I made slower progress than Giovanni. "Anything in particular that you're looking for?" I asked.

He shrugged. "Stuff that's interesting. Stuff we didn't already know. You know. *Useful* information."

I found a roster of soldiers' names, with a small mark

next to each. I took a close look. "I think this is a list of who Teleso thought was on his side," I said.

"That's useful," Giovanni said. "Tell us which mutineers to keep an eye on."

I leafed through a sheaf of folded papers tied with a blue ribbon. "Letters from his sister," I said.

Giovanni snorted. "Those are useless."

I read through one anyway and concluded he was right. I tossed the rest aside.

"Hey," Giovanni said. "Intelligence on the situation in Cuore. We can read these over later."

The next stack was supply inventories. The next pile had a diagram of the wall, and how it should look when construction was complete. Under that was a rough sketch—a curving line with seven slashes along it. One was labeled "Ravenna." "Hey, Giovanni," I said. "What is this?"

He took the piece of paper and then spread it out on the desk, his interest growing rapidly. "You've found something," he said. "Eliana, you have *definitely* found something."

"What?" I asked. "I don't have that oh-so-useful university background, you know."

"Oh, give it up," he said. "It's a map. See, this is Ravenna. This is the wall, or where the wall will be when it's all done. These other marks—they're other camps like Ravenna. Probably also working on part of the wall."

"Seven camps?" I asked.

"Six, now," Giovanni said.

"Do they have the same numbers of soldiers and slaves?" I asked.

"It doesn't say. They're probably smaller. Up in Cuore, the reformers had only heard about Ravenna . . . but, well, that probably doesn't mean much. And who knows, these might be new. I've been out of touch for a while." He pushed back a lock of glossy black hair. "So what do you think?"

"I think those are excellent targets," I said. "I didn't want to take the Circle on starting tomorrow—we're still too new at this, and new in ways that playing Lupi isn't going to solve."

Giovanni nodded, his eyes glinting with excitement. "We need real battles," he said. "We can become a real army once we've had a chance to fight."

"It looks like we've got six chances," I said. "More recruits, too. And even the ones who don't join up—"

"They can stir up trouble," he said. "Serve as distractions. Make our enemies divide their strength."

Our eyes met, across the desk. Giovanni's eyes were almost as bright as Lucia's. "This could work," I said.

"This could *really* work," he said.

Our eyes held for a moment. Then he cupped the back of my neck with his hand, and drew my face toward his, pressing his lips against mine. I could feel the heat from his cheeks, and the roughness of his stubble; his hand was sweaty and damp on my neck.

I jerked away. "What are you doing?" I demanded.

His face flared red. "Um. Nothing."

"Good," I said. I felt a flush rising to my own cheeks.

Giovanni's wounded pride was fueling irritation, then anger. "I think I'm going to go out for a walk," he said. "Let me know if you find anything else interesting." He slammed the door behind him.

I turned back to the pile of papers, trying to shrug off Giovanni. It was Midsummer's Eve, I realized suddenly, and thought with a half-laugh that if I had slept with Giovanni, it wouldn't *count*. Somehow, that didn't make the idea any more attractive. I suddenly wondered if he was just outside in the corridor—I could imagine him out

there, face flushed, heart pounding. I got up to check,
ready with a wisecrack if he was out there, but the hall
was empty. Disappointed, I closed the door and sat back
down. As I sorted through the papers, I heard a very, very
faint *creak*. My head snapped up and I turned to look—
and saw Teleso, emerging from behind a set of cabinets.
He didn't see me right away, but started toward the desk.
If he had heard our voices, then heard the door open and
close twice—he'd have thought the study was empty.

I sucked in my breath to shout for help and Teleso
turned. Our eyes met; he was just as stunned to see me as I
was to see him. Giovanni's crossbow lay across the desk; I
snatched it up and fired at Teleso. He howled in pain, and
for an instant I thought I'd mortally wounded him, but I'd
only caught him in his left thigh.

Teleso drew his sword. "Why, Eliana," he said. "You
just don't like *any* men, do you?"

Lady's tits, Lady's tits, I thought, and threw down the
crossbow, pulling my knife from the sheath hidden in my
boot. "Not if you and Giovanni are a representative sam-
ple," I said. This was going to be a very uneven fight, I
thought, and a short one. Teleso was a soldier, trained for
years in swordplay, and I stood here waving a knife, after
a couple of lessons from Giovanni, that master of swords-
manship and tutelage. "Help!" I shouted. "Michel! Tomas!"
I'd settle for Giovanni, but I'd be damned if I was going to
shout for him.

Teleso lunged toward me, and I threw my chair into
his path. He stumbled and I realized I'd injured his leg fairly
badly with that crossbow bolt. Giovanni would probably
know exactly how to use that to his advantage. Attack
from the left side, I supposed, but I wasn't really sure that
was how it worked. Teleso circled the room warily. I mir-

rored him, trying to look convincingly dangerous. As Teleso passed with his back to the study door, I looked straight past his shoulder and slapped a smile of relief onto my face. "Michel! Thank the Lady!" I exclaimed.

Teleso whirled to look, and I threw the knife at him. It embedded itself nicely in his right shoulder blade and he screeched again. Unfortunately, he still wasn't dead, and I no longer had the knife. I grabbed the fireplace poker as Teleso wrenched his other arm around to pull out the knife, and hurled that at him as well.

"Bitch," he shouted, and dodged aside. It missed his head, but bounced off his arm. He wasn't dead, but he was holding the sword with his left hand now, and limping badly. His clothes, previously unsullied, were turning red with his blood.

"Help!" I shouted again. Where the hell was everybody?

"Enough with this," Teleso said. Clenching his teeth, he lunged toward me again. I threw another chair in his path, but he saw it coming this time, and vaulted over it, throwing me against the wall and pinning me there with his sword's blade. He smiled at me as I felt the blood drain from my face.

Talk fast, I thought. "You know, you're really not a very good judge of people, Teleso," I said.

"Why do you say that?" Teleso asked.

"Giovanni and I found that list of soldiers—who you thought were on your side." Teleso was silent, the sword still at my throat. I closed my eyes for one heartbeat, then opened them again and looked him straight in the eye. "Assuming we interpreted your list correctly, you thought Niccolo was yours. You know how you sent him to burn the grain? He jumped, Teleso—he betrayed you."

Teleso went rigid with shock, and I threw myself to the side. The sword grazed my throat, stinging. I shoved a chair between us, then ran behind the desk. I thought I remembered a weapon here earlier, and sure enough, stacked in Giovanni's "useful" pile was an ornate dagger that had probably come out of Teleso's desk. I grabbed it up, armed again.

"Not Niccolo," Teleso said. "He wouldn't betray me. He was the only one on my side!" His sword half sagged, he was still so stunned, and I grabbed up the poker in my left hand and advanced on him.

"Niccolo betrayed you," I said. "And Giula was working for *me*. Day after tomorrow, she was going to poison your wine. Unfortunately, you moved before our plans were fully in place. But that's all right—we beat you anyway."

Teleso threw himself at me; I slammed the sword aside with the poker, almost knocking it out of his hand. "I'll see you dead," he shouted.

"Keep dreaming, *bastardo*," I said. His sword was coming back up, and I decided to try for one more lie. "You know, it's too bad you want me dead now," I said. "If it weren't for your garlic breath, I'd have found you *very* attractive."

Teleso blanched, his sword sagging completely in total stunned shock. I lunged toward him, slamming my knife into his gut like the soldiers had stabbed Mario. He screamed in agony and fell to the floor, his sword slipping out of his hand. I kicked it out of his reach. Blood was pouring from the wound, drenching the rug, my hands, my tunic. The room smelled of blood and bowels, and I backed up, gagging.

The room was silent for a moment, except for Teleso's gasping sobs.

"You had me beaten because I wouldn't sleep with you!" I shouted. "You turned my friend against me! You ran a slave-labor camp while mouthing loyalty to the Lady!" I bent to pick up his sword. His eyes were closed. "But you know, Niccolo didn't betray you. Giula wasn't working for me. I never found you attractive, and you never had garlic breath. I hated you for what you *were*."

I wasn't sure if he heard me, but his face was in agony. Raising the sword, I brought it down as hard as I could. I didn't fully sever his head, but his breathing stopped and his face went slack. I half expected to throw up, as Lucia had, but I was so relieved to have survived the fight that I couldn't even smell the blood. "I am a wolf," I said aloud, trying to catch my breath.

The door opened and Giovanni stared in. "*Lady's tits!*" he shouted, and ran into the room. My hands were slick with blood, and the sword slipped out of my grasp and clanged to the floor. Giovanni grabbed my shoulders, looking me up and down. "Is any of this blood yours?"

"No," I said. The gush of Teleso's blood had been warm, but the blood was starting to cool, to solidify. I was suddenly overwhelmed with the disgusting feeling of it on me. "I need to go wash my hands."

"Did you kill him?" Giovanni asked. "By yourself?"

"Yes," I said.

"See?" Giovanni said. "Those knife lessons did come in handy. Come on. I'll find Lucia and we can get you cleaned up."

"Teleso came out to look for something," I said. "Something in the desk—and he was listening, so he must have assumed that we hadn't already found it."

Giovanni's eyes lit up. "I'll find it," he said. "I'll take the desk apart if I have to."

When I came back to the study, damp but clean, Giovanni held out a small box. "There was a hidden compartment in the back of the top drawer. This was inside."

I sat down by the desk and opened the box. Inside was a single lock of black hair.

"His daughter's," Giovanni said. "I'd heard a rumor that he once had a wife, but I hadn't quite believed it."

I touched the soft curl gently. "What are we going to do with this?" I asked.

Giovanni shrugged. "Up to you."

"What was done with Teleso's body?" I asked.

"It was taken outside. Someone will toss it in with the rest of the bodies in the grave in the morning."

Teleso's body lay just outside the keep, with a few others who had died from their wounds tonight. The person who had carried out the body had set it down carefully, aligning the head with the rest of him. His body had stiffened, and I shuddered at the touch of his cold flesh, but this wouldn't take long. I tucked the box with its lock of hair into Teleso's torn shirt, beside his heart. Even Teleso deserved that much.

• • •

In the gray dawn, I stood by the ashes of the bonfire that had been kindled with the chairs from Teleso's dining room. My hungover army was assembled before me, Teleso's body wrapped in a shroud behind me.

"You have a choice now," I said. "We know of villages that are not in the wasteland but were destroyed by the Circle. Those who don't want to fight—especially the children and the elderly—can resettle those villages. The land is good; the spring crops were planted and may even be growing. Hopefully, the rest of us will be making enough trouble soon to keep the Circle busy and well away from you." I paused and looked at the faces of the people in my army. They looked back—sleepy in some cases, breathless in others. When my eyes met Michel's, he saluted me, and I found myself smiling.

"For the rest of us," I said, "yesterday is only the beginning of the fight. There are six more camps like Ravenna, with thousands more people like us, enslaved and starved and brutalized by the Circle. Six more camps." I started to pace, energized by the anticipation of the crowd. No one looked sleepy anymore. "We're going to march in like the tide—no one will stop us. We're going to sweep in like fire—nothing will be left in our path. We're going to run in like *wolves*—we hunt in a pack. We are going to free every one of our people, and give them a chance to join us. And then we will sweep into Cuore itself and burn the Circle with God's fire—the fire of justice, and freedom, and righteous *anger*." The crowd shifted and I knew they were coming. I had my army. "Are you with me?" I demanded.

"Yes!" The force of the cry nearly knocked me down.

"Are you *with* me?"

"*Yes!*"

"Then gather up what you need and meet me on the north hill in two hours. We march at midday."

Giovanni waited for me at the door to the keep. "Good speech. No one is going to go to Doratura."

"None of the children will march with the army," I said. "I won't allow it."

"Wise policy," he said. "There weren't any other papers of interest. I burned what was left."

"Good."

"Noon," he said, and shook his head. "We'll be out of here in midafternoon, at the earliest. Tomorrow would have been a bit more practical. Are the horses and wagons ready?"

"Maybe," I said.

Giovanni shook his head in studied disbelief. "Meaning that you haven't actually sent anyone to take care of it? What the hell kind of Generale are you, anyway?"

"The one who's in charge here," I said.

Giovanni sighed. "You need to learn how to delegate," he said. "It's the only way you're going to be able to make this work. Generali don't do everything themselves; even Beneto had a second."

"Are you asking for the position?"

"Are you kidding? You should be *my* second." He paused for a moment. "Also, you need to learn to ride a horse."

"Why?"

"Because generali do not *walk* to battles. Besides, when you're on a horse, it's easy to get people's attention. You're up high where they can see you."

"And shoot at me," I said.

"Well, that's why you also need a bodyguard, on another horse."

"That would *not* be you," I said.

"No, of course not. I don't want to take a crossbow bolt for you. I'll teach Michel to ride as well."

"Great," I muttered.

"The knife-fighting came in handy, didn't it? Trust me on this." He was enjoying himself, I could tell; he was going to enjoy the riding lessons even more.

Still, on Giovanni's suggestion, I divided up my red-sashed soldiers into smaller companies, then put someone I knew and trusted in charge of each group. I could demote my officers later if they caused too much trouble. I sent the obvious children off to the village. My army was a strange mix—two dozen of the mutineer soldiers mixed in with the Ravenessi. I hoped not too many of those were spies.

As I was checking over the soldiers, I found myself face-to-face with Arianna. She met my eyes challengingly, daring me to send her off to Doratura with the children.

"Do you really want to be here?" I asked.

She lifted her chin. "I won't let you leave me behind. If you don't let me join you, I'll follow you. If you tie me up, I'll—"

I touched her shoulder. "Fine," I said. "You've convinced me." She'd found a red sash somewhere. Looking at it for a moment, I realized it was a strip torn from the skirt of that red velvet dress.

Arianna noticed my look and smiled cautiously. "Giula wasn't wearing it at the time," she said. She carried Mario's knife at her side.

"Well." I looked around the army. There were hundreds of people, spreading out across the ruins of the camp, and the plains around me. "Let's go hunting."

ABOUT THE AUTHOR

Naomi Kritzer grew up in Madison, Wisconsin, a small lunar colony populated mostly by Ph.D.s. She moved to Minnesota to attend college; after graduating with a BA in religion, she became a technical writer. She now lives in Minneapolis with her family. FIRES OF THE FAITHFUL is her first novel.

Be sure not to miss

Naomi Kritzer's

Turning the Storm

The riveting conclusion to Eliana's tale
Coming in January 2003
Here's a special excerpt:

"Eliana? Eliana!" Giovanni stared down at me, flushed in the late summer heat. I squinted up at him and he sat back, looking relieved. "That was one hell of a fall."

I groaned and lay still for a moment. Two months of leading an army—two more successful battles, even—and I still couldn't stay on my horse and reload a crossbow at the same time. I pushed myself up with my elbows. "Nothing hurts," I said. That was blatantly false, but nothing *especially* hurt. "I must have just had the wind knocked out of me." I turned to glare at Forza, my horse. She had skidded to a stop shortly after throwing me, and was staring at me with wary sheepishness from farther down the hill.

"It's getting late anyway," he said. "Let's just make a quick circuit of the hill and head in."

"Where'd the bow land?"

"Got it," Giovanni said. I stood up and Giovanni handed it back to me. "Let's go." He whistled for Stivali, the horse he'd claimed from the Ravenessi stables, and we remounted, turning to head back to the army encampment.

"Hold on," I said, reining in Forza. "Who the hell is that?"

Giovanni turned to look north and squinted at the figure walking toward us. "I don't know." He unslung his own crossbow and cocked it. "But whoever it is, he's alone."

The man headed straight toward us. He seemed to be carrying weapons but had not drawn. I loaded my crossbow— easy enough now that Forza was standing still—and checked behind us in case the man was supposed to be a distraction. I saw nobody but stayed on my guard. We had an outer ring of sentries, but this man, at least, had gotten past them unchallenged.

"Hello there!" the man said, saluting us as he approached. "I come in peace, to meet with your leaders. I assume you are soldiers of the Lupi?"

Giovanni's eyes narrowed and he squinted down the sights of his crossbow. "Maybe."

I decided to let Giovanni go ahead and intimidate the stranger. He wouldn't fire without cause, and I found the stranger's breezy manner irritating. "What do you want with the Lupi?" I demanded.

The stranger bowed low, showing off a freshly sunburned

neck. "My name is Felice. I have come from Cuore as the delegate of the reformers."

Giovanni lowered his crossbow just a hair. "Fire falls from the sky," he said challengingly.

"And the land weeps," Felice said.

Giovanni lowered his bow completely. "I guess you are who you say you are. We're—"

"—pleased to make your acquaintance," I said, cutting Giovanni off. "We'll take you back to the camp." I swung down from my horse and confiscated Felice's visible weapons—a decorative sword and an ornately carved crossbow. I was not so impressed by a two-year-old password that I was going to tell this man that he'd just met the generali of the Lupi army, alone. For all we knew, he was a spy on a suicide mission to kill us both. "You can ride double with me."

Felice mounted Forza effortlessly and I climbed up awkwardly behind him. I regretted not making him ride with Giovanni but said nothing, not wanting to look foolish. We rode back toward camp.

Felice even smelled like an aristocrat: clean, despite his long walk, with a very faint whiff of perfume. His tunic was made out of a delicate fabric that caught the light oddly, and was covered with a well-tooled padded leather vest. His hands carried the light calluses of a gentleman-fencer, like Giovanni—except Giovanni did some real work these days.

Back in camp, I dismounted and passed the horses off to Vitale, the youngest of the Lupi. He'd joined us when we'd liberated that first slave camp after Ravenna. I'd tried to send him off to Doratura or one of the other resettled towns, but he'd stubbornly followed us across the wasteland until I shrugged and said that anyone so determined was clearly old enough to make himself useful. "Take Forza and Stivali," I said to Vitale. "And tell Michel we need him right away."

Vitale vanished into the camp, and Giovanni and I stood awkwardly, facing Felice. I wanted a private moment with Giovanni, to ask him the significance of the pass-phrase and how secret it really was, but I needed Michel to take custody of Felice first. Fortunately, Michel arrived almost immediately, still tying his sash. He was rumpled, and I suspected he'd been napping. "Michel," I said. "This is Felice, allegedly one of the reformers from Cuore. Take him to the generali's tent; they'll be with him shortly."

Michel picked up his cue and saluted without addressing either of us as "Generale." "Please follow me," he said, and led Felice off toward my tent.

I turned to Giovanni. "What was it he said to you?"

"It's a pass-phrase—"

"I guessed that. How secure is it? Couldn't he have found it out some other way?"

"We can trust him," Giovanni said confidently. "He's been sent by Beneto's commanders. I'm just surprised it took them this long. We ought to have a contact with the main University Reform organization."

"Really." I stared off past Giovanni's shoulder. An argument was brewing between two of my men over whose turn it was to dig latrine trenches. "Hey!" I shouted, and they both jumped to give me a guilty stare. "It's both your turns. Fight over it and you'll be filling them in, too." I turned back to Giovanni. "Well, let's go see what he wants, then." I caught Vitale as he passed by. "Send Lucia to my tent when you get a chance. I don't want Isabella, not yet. Try to get Lucia alone."

Giovanni beamed as we entered the tent. My tent was larger than Rafi's tent in Ravenna had been but not a whole lot higher; we didn't have much in the way of real tent poles. Felice sat cross-legged on a cushion, looking around dubiously at the rough accommodations.

"Welcome to the Lupi encampment," Giovanni said. "I am Generale Giovanni, and this is Generale Eliana."

I nodded to Felice, returning his aghast look with a predatory smile. "Charmed," I said.

Felice closed his mouth with a snap, but his eyes were still wide. "Really? I'd pictured you"—he studied me, his lips parted—"differently."

"Were you expecting me to be taller?" I asked. I glanced toward the tent flap, wondering how long it would take Lucia to arrive. "Male?"

"No, no, no. Of course we knew your, ah, basic description. Older, I'd say. I guess I'd assumed you'd be older."

"Hmm." I decided to let him stop flailing. "I suppose you're expecting us to bring you up-to-date."

"That would be helpful, yes."

Lucia came in and sat next to me. "This is Felice," I said. "He claims to be a reformer from Cuore."

"Do you know him, Giovanni?" Lucia asked.

"No," Giovanni said.

"I joined the Cause after you departed for Ravenna," Felice said. "I am originally from Parma."

Lucia gave Felice a long, careful stare. I looked at her; she shrugged.

"Well," I said, "you probably know that we led the uprising at Ravenna." Felice nodded. "That was about a month and a half ago. We've liberated three more slave labor camps since our escape, adding former slaves to our army when possible." Our army had doubled in size from the original group, but then the other camps had been smaller than Ravenna.

"At the last camp, reinforcements had been sent down," Giovanni said. "Fortunately, they had not been well integrated. The new troops and the old did not trust each other and fought together poorly. Still, we can't count on that being true everywhere."

"What sort of training have you done with your men?" Felice asked.

"Tactics," I said. "Some sword training, and bow."

"Three victories," Felice said. "That's quite something."

"Minimal losses," I said. "That's something we hope to keep up."

"Any problems?" Felice asked.

"Well, you know, we're fighting a war," I said. "People get injured sometimes, or die. *That's* a problem."

"But other than that?" Felice asked.

There were the constant petty squabbles, the rivalries between the original Lupi and the mutineer soldiers from Ravenna, the constant shortage of supplies, and the fact that half of the people I'd impulsively made leaders couldn't lead their way out of a stable if you drew them a map, but I wasn't about to share those problems with Felice. "That's pretty much it."

"Well," Felice said, his face lighting up. "Sounds like you're in good shape, then." I nodded. "So, anyway, I'm here to take over."

I froze, not entirely sure I'd heard right. Lucia's jaw dropped, then she closed her mouth and sat back quietly, her eyes flickering from me to Giovanni and back. The slight quirk of her lips made it clear she was waiting for the show.

"You're here to *what*?" Giovanni demanded, just barely restraining himself from attacking Felice. "I am doing just fine myself, thank you very much."

"Oh, er, yes, of course," Felice said, glancing from Giovanni's face to mine. "Of course you're doing fine. We really appreciate what an excellent job you've done since Beneto's execution. The reformer leaders in Cuore have voted to give both of you a commendation, in fact. But you have to understand, a position like this requires someone with experience—"

I cut him off with a raised hand. "So how many armies have *you* led into battle?"

"Oh, I'm very good at strategy," Felice said confidently. "I won nineteen out of twenty-five mock battles with my tutor—"

I laughed. "You're not taking my army away from me."

"Excuse me?"

"You heard me. Signore Felice, you can *try* to command here if you enjoy being laughed at, but this is *my* army. If you think we're putting our men into your manicured hands, think again. You don't command here; I do."

Felice was putting on a patient expression, and that did it. "Michel!" I said.

Michel was waiting outside the tent and poked his head in. "Yes, Generale?"

"Take this man to the stockade and place him under guard. He is not to be left alone at any time."

Michel took Felice's arm. "If you'll come with me, signore," he said.

"But—but—wait—" Felice said as Michel started to haul him off.

"Oh, one more thing, Michel," I said. "He's a guest. Treat him with courtesy."

"He won't have anything to complain about, Generale."

The tent was quiet for a moment after Felice had gone.

"I don't know if that was quite appropriate—" Giovanni started.

"If he's going to stay here," I said, "I want him to be absolutely clear on who's in charge. Besides," and I relaxed slightly, "what an ass."

Lucia laughed. "I agree. Let him cool his heels in the stockade for an hour or two at least. . . ."

Giovanni was opening his mouth to say something else when Isabella came into the tent. At least Michel was gone by the time she arrived. "Who's the fop?" she demanded.

"An old friend of Giovanni's," Lucia said. "The reformers sent him to take over."

Isabella looked at me with a single raised eyebrow.

"I declined his generous offer," I said.

"Just what is it you hope to accomplish by locking him up?" Giovanni demanded. "Fine, you get to gloat, but is there really any point to this, or is it just to humiliate him?"

I leaned forward. "I've seen no reason that I should trust him. There's nowhere else in this encampment designed to keep people under guard. So until I'm convinced that he's not a threat, he stays in the stockade."

Giovanni snorted. "A threat? That pretty-boy probably had a servant to reload his crossbow back in Cuore. You're actually afraid of him?"

"I've got enough things to worry about without Felice," I said. "I promise I'll have Michel let him out soon. Do you want to go see about the scout reports?"

Giovanni left, still grumbling, leaving Lucia and Isabella in the tent with me. Unfortunately, Isabella showed no inclination to leave. She pulled up a cushion to sit on and poured herself a cup of tea. "Generale," she said, "I wonder if I could have a word with you."

I suppressed a groan; when Isabella called me Generale, it usually meant that she wanted something. She was going to have her word with me sooner or later, so I poured my own cup of tea and sat back to listen, gesturing for her to go ahead.

"Yesterday you ordered one of my people to scrub pots for insubordination."

"Which?" I asked, trying to remember who'd gotten in trouble recently.

"Gemino."

"Ah, right." Gemino was a short, stocky boy who'd come with us from Ravenna. Isabella led a unit within my army, but it was made up mostly of "her people," the old-time malcontents who'd followed her in Ravenna. "Isabella, you aren't going to have me reduce his punishment, are you? It's not like scrubbing pots is that dreadful a task, and someone has to—"

"It's not this instance so much as it is a general pattern. The problem was not Gemino, it was Michel. You should realize that by now."

"I thought I told Gemino he didn't have to take weaponry lessons from Michel anymore."

"You did. This wasn't a weaponry lesson. Michel was trying to give my people orders, and Gemino refused—"

Now I remembered. "Isabella, Michel was trying to tell Gemino he needed to move the horses. It was a perfectly reasonable request—"

"—and coming from anyone else, it might have sounded reasonable. Michel can make the most reasonable request sound like an insult."

"So what do you want me to do?"

"Michel needs to be taken down a peg." Isabella's large eyes glared at me from behind a stray lock of gray hair. "He's unsuited to a position of authority."

This was true. Michel *was* unsuited to a position of authority. But so was Isabella and most of my unit commanders. "I need him where he is," I said.

"But Gemino—"

"I'll tell Michel again to stay away from your soldiers." We'd be fine if I could find enough other things for Michel to do. Or if I could somehow keep him and Isabella permanently separated. The trouble was, I really did need him where he was. I needed his loyalty, his skills as a bodyguard, and his ability to get things done for me. He wasn't a bad soldier, but the power had gone to his head. I just wished I knew what to do about it. Isabella's suggestion had merit, except that if I hurt his pride, I might lose his loyalty—or he might simply leave. And I needed him too badly. Besides, if I disciplined Michel, I'd have to do something about all the lousy unit commanders, including Isabella. I *had* removed the really atrocious ones—the lecher, and the coward, and the one who turned out to be dumb as a donkey—but if I set about trying to ensure that only the best were in positions of authority, we'd be left with me, the woman who led the scouts, and Giovanni on his good days.

"Well, thank you, Generale," Isabella said stiffly, and took her leave.

Alone with Lucia, I sighed. "Are you sure you don't want to command a unit, Lucia?"

"And have Isabella on *my* back, as well as yours and Michel's?" Lucia raised an eyebrow. "Positive."

"So." I wiped out my teacup and put it away. "What's on my list?"

Lucia considered for a moment. "The scouts are due back this evening but probably won't get in until late tonight. If they're not back by morning, we'll have to assume that they were captured. That's the most significant news."

I nodded.

"Other than that . . . We're in pretty good shape for grain, but we're low on horse feed. If we absolutely have to, we can feed some of our wheat to the horses, but for obvious reasons that's not the best option. In any case, it's critical that we capture food at the next camp. And if they have horses, we should send them north with the refugees, rather than keeping them ourselves. Cavalry is nice, but we just don't have the food stocks."

I nodded; she was right, although this would only increase resentment among the people who didn't have horses but thought they should. Never mind that most of these people could barely ride, let alone fight from horseback; a horse was a symbol of status, so everyone wanted one.

"Other than that . . . Nerio and Viola split and have made quite a fuss about it."

"Move them into separate units. I don't care if they reconcile and miss each other; we're keeping them separate from now on. This is, what, the fourth time?"

"Fifth. Let's see. Ulpio and Bruttio were fighting."

"Latrine duty."

"Paulo and Severo are rumored to be spoiling for a fight."

"Paulo and Severo?" They were two more of the men I'd put in charge of units—and now regretted putting in charge. "What's their problem?"

"Paulo's convinced you're favoring Severo's men. He wants a horse, and he thinks you're sending his men to dig latrines and scrub pots a bit too often. He blames Severo for turning you against him."

I sighed. "Remind me to ease up on Paulo's men. He's wrong, but it's not worth losing his loyalty over. Maybe I *should* give him a horse." I looked up; Lucia gazed at me levelly, a glint of humor in her eyes. I sighed again. "Once we're out of the wasteland, the horses can graze—"

"According to Giovanni's calculations, that won't be until the end of the summer."

I shook my head. "No horse for Paulo, then. Maybe I'll arrange to outfit all his men with swords and crossbows."

"Think you can get Giovanni to train them?" Lucia asked. "If you give them the swords without training, they'll only trip over them in battle."

"I could try making Felice do it," I said.

"Think he'll be any better than Michel? Or Giovanni?"

"Could he be any worse?" I said. "Don't answer that. I suppose I should go spring him from the stockade. What else do I still need to take care of?"

Lucia considered. "Five more people who want you to mediate disputes."

"Oh, for— Can't you do it?"

She shook her head. "They specifically requested you. Look, at least they aren't fighting."

"Right, I know. Fine. Later, before the scouts get back. Was that it?"

"That's all," Lucia said.

"In that case . . ." I stretched. "I'm going to visit Felice."

The stockade was really just a fenced area with two guards standing over it. The fence was a flimsy, makeshift affair; any determined prisoner could escape by uprooting a fence stake and running. Most of the time, when I tossed someone in the stockade it was more for the symbolic humiliation than actual confinement.

I expected Felice to greet me with a glare, but he merely looked sad and hurt. "I had no idea you'd take it like this," he said when I arrived.

"Then you were poorly briefed."

"Is this really necessary?" He gestured at the fence and the guards. "I promise not to try to take away your army."

"I don't think you'd be able to," I said. "I had you locked up because you're a stranger and you might be here to cause trouble. Why should I trust you? I was never one of the Official reformers of Cuore; I don't know the pass-phrases and countersigns that so thoroughly impressed Giovanni." I stepped close to the fence, noticing that Felice was sweating. "Why should I trust you?"

Felice placed his hands flat against the fence posts. "Signora Generale," he said, "I may be soft and I may be weak compared to you and your men. The orders I was sent with may betray a terrible arrogance on the part of my leaders. But the fire that burns in my heart springs from the same flame as the fire in yours. My brothers were among those murdered by the Circle to keep secret the devastation caused by magefire. And I will do whatever it takes to bring them down." He met my eyes with urgent sincerity. "Let me fight with you, Generale. You won't regret it."

"Well," I said. I uprooted a fence post and gestured that he could step out of the prison. "Welcome to my army." I fitted the post back into the ground and started to walk away.

"Wait," Felice said. I turned back. "What do I do now?"

"That's for you to figure out, isn't it? His look was so pitiful, I relented. "Fine. Report to—oh, you can be in Paulo's unit." I flagged down Vitale. "Escort Felice here to Paulo. Do you know how to use a sword for anything other than jewelry, Felice?"

"Of course," he said.

"Tell Paulo that Felice will be helping him with arms training." With any luck, Felice would be better at it than Michel. Vitale saluted and marched Felice off.

● ● ●

"Martido won't return my bracelet."

I stared at Fiora, baffled. "Why does he have it?"

"I gave it to him when we were—you know. And now we're not. But he won't give it back to me."

I glanced at Lucia, who sat beside me. She gave me her faintest wicked grin, and my spirits lifted slightly. I didn't understand why I was the one who had to mediate these stupid arguments. Lucia would have been better at it.

"Where did you get the bracelet?"

"From Teleso's keep." Fiora glared at me stubbornly now. "It's mine. I want it back."

"You only had it because I said you could have it, you stupid cow," Martido said, speaking up for the first time since they'd come in. He sat as far away from Fiora as he could and still be in the tent. "I saw it first."

"Why do you want it?"

They answered in unison: "Because it's mine."

How did I get involved in this sort of thing? And this was only the first dispute of the five Lucia had mentioned. "Give it here," I said to Martido, and he reluctantly handed it over. I studied the bracelet. Teleso must have kept it to adorn his mistresses, or else it had belonged to his sister. It was a woman's jeweled bracelet, ornate and fairly delicate. It would look silly on Martido's wrist.

"Generale!" The voice came from outside the tent, and then Vitale poked his head in through the door. "Generale, the scouts have returned."

I slipped the bracelet onto my own wrist. "We'll finish this later," I said to Martido and Fiora. "I'll hold the bracelet for now." Martido started to protest, then thought the better of it and followed Fiora out of the tent.

Vitale held the tent flap open for the scouts as they came in—six haggard and exhausted men and women. "Vitale," I said, "get Giovanni, then fetch food and wine for the scouts. Then tell all unit commanders I want them here in an hour." He saluted and slipped back out. "Report, Camilla," I said to the scout leader.

Camilla was a farm girl who had entertained herself as a child by testing how close she could get to wild birds before they saw her and flew away. Now she used her noiseless step and her ability to disappear into the dusty ground of the wasteland to scout out the slave camps before we attacked.

She was slightly built, with tiny hands and feet and a dark cap of short-cropped hair.

She pulled up a cushion and sat down, tucking her feet neatly under her. "Chira is about the same size as Ravenna," she said, "but more heavily guarded. They've received reinforcements, and Demetrio—their commander—has taken the trouble to train them." She sketched the camp's layout in the dust. "Like the other camps, Chira is set into a valley. They've done a better job with the perimeter, though; they built the camp up against a section of the wall they're building, and used that for some of the defenses."

"The wall could work to our advantage," I said. "If we could get some of our people onto it, to fire down—the valley location makes it easier to keep your prisoners contained, but it's hard to defend."

Camilla looked up. "In addition to the keep, they have five other buildings, also solidly built. And they must know that we start with a cavalry charge, but they haven't set up lances to impale the horses; I think they want to draw us in, then use those subsidiary watchtowers to shoot us down."

"Sounds plausible," Lucia said as Giovanni joined us. I briefly repeated what Camilla had told me, then gestured for Camilla to continue.

"The thing that worries me the most," Camilla said, "is that Demetrio runs drills. I saw them practicing, and it looked like they were rehearsing exactly what to do if there was an uprising, or if we attacked."

"You saw the drill?" Then we knew his strategy. One of them, at least.

"Yes." Camilla described the procedures the soldiers ran through. "He even had a soldier whose job was to go torch the grain. They're onto us."

"That's what they think anyway," I said. "Which building holds the grain?" Camilla pointed to one of the scuffs she'd drawn in the dust. "Then we know what to protect. What are the people like?"

"Scared. Beaten down. Demetrio keeps a tight grip; we saw two executions during the time we were watching. Both were escape attempts who got caught."

"The soldiers?"

"Brutal. And loyal to Demetrio."

Vitale arrived then with food and wine for the scouts, and they paused to have something to eat and drink. We finished the briefing before the rest of the commanders arrived, but I already had a pretty good idea of what I was going to do. Camilla's seeing those drills had been a stroke of luck.

It was very late when we finished; I sent the scouts off to sleep and slipped out of my tent. Michel trailed me as I headed past the edge of the camp and into the wasteland, keeping a respectful distance.

The hills of the wasteland were silvery in the moonlight. Even on the darkest nights you could tell that the land here was dead. I sat down at the crest of one hill and opened my violin case. Learning to fight with a sword had callused my right hand, despite the gloves I always wore. It felt a little strange now to take my bow in hand and tuck my violin under my chin, but I could still make my violin sing. I tuned up and played for an hour, just for myself. I played the songs I'd learned with Mira and the violin part of some of the ensemble pieces from the conservatory. Finally I played the Mass. I glanced at Michel, standing watch a short distance away. I always wondered if he wanted to dance when I played the Mass, but tonight he probably just wished I'd stop playing and go to bed so that he could get some sleep as well. I had to admit that I was tired. I put my violin away and headed back for the camp. As I reached my tent, I turned to Michel. He was still trailing me sleepily.

"Martido and Fiora," I said. "Whose unit are they in, anyway?"

"Severo's," he said.

I nodded. "Good." I took the bracelet off my wrist and handed it to Michel. "Take this to Severo and tell him that *he* can deal with it. I have an army to lead." Michel blinked at me, puzzled, as I went inside to bed.